The Temptation
of
Father Lorenzo

The Temptation
of
Father Lorenzo

Ten Stories of 1970s Tuscany

Cover photo by the author: Storefront in Florence

PAUL SALSINI

iUniverse, Inc.
Bloomington

The Temptation of Father Lorenzo
Ten Stories of 1970s Tuscany

iUniverse books may be ordered through booksellers or by contacting:

iUniverse
1663 Liberty Drive
Bloomington, IN 47403
www.iuniverse.com
1-800-Authors (1-800-288-4677)

ISBN: 978-1-4697-9076-3 (sc)
ISBN: 978-1-4697-9077-0 (e)

Library of Congress Control Number: 2012904509

Printed in the United States of America

iUniverse rev. date: 3/12/2012

For Barbara
Jim, Laura and Jack

Also by Paul Salsini

Stefano and the Christmas Crib

Dino's Story: A Novel of 1960s Tuscany

Sparrow's Revenge: A Novel of Postwar Tuscany

The Cielo: A Novel of Wartime Tuscany

Second Start

Author's Note

In 2006, I published *The Cielo: A Novel of Wartime Tuscany*. It was inspired in part by the experiences of my cousin Fosca, who, with others from her village, was trapped in a farmhouse in the Tuscan hills for three months during World War II. Afterwards, I thought there must be a sequel, and so I wrote *Sparrow's Revenge: A Novel of Postwar Tuscany* set in the 1950s. With the characters still in my head, I thought "A Tuscan Trilogy" had a nice ring to it, and so I wrote *Dino's Story: A Novel of 1960s Tuscany* set in the 1960s.

But the characters had taken hold, and since I couldn't write a fourth book in a trilogy, I am continuing their narratives in this collection of stories, which takes them through the 1970s. Some of the people stretch back to the first book, others to the second and still others to the third. Through blood or friendship, they are all linked.

Again, I have many people to thank for their encouragement and support, chiefly my wife, Barbara, our daughter, Laura, and our sons, Jim and Jack. Also to Dulcie Shoener, who read every line and made helpful suggestions. And again in Italy, to my still indefatigable driver/ interpreter Marcello Grandini and my relatives there, especially my cousin Fosca, who started this all with her stories.

Will the characters demand further stories? I am waiting to hear their voices.

The Main Characters

Florence

Father Lorenzo, a Franciscan priest who runs a soup kitchen, *cucina popolare*, at the Basilica of Santa Croce.

Tomasso Nozzoli, a former soccer player who owns a ceramics shop.

Dino Sporenza, who came from Sant'Antonio to study art in Florence.

Sofia, Dino's longtime girlfriend from Calabria.

Francesca, Dino's high school girlfriend, now living in Florence.

Roberto, Dino's uncle, who works for an agency helping the poor find housing.

Adolfo, Roberto's brother, who works with him.

Mila, Adolfo's wife.

Anna, Dino's aunt, the sister of Roberto and Adolfo, a former nun.

Sant'Antonio

Father Sangretto, the parish priest.

Ezio Maffini, a former partisan who now owns the Cielo, a farmhouse in the hills.

Donna Fazzini, his wife.

Lucia Sporenza, Dino's mother, the sister of Roberto, Adolfo and Anna.

Paolo Ricci, her husband.

Rosa Tomaselli, a neighbor.

Antonio Maffini, Rosa's husband and Ezio's father.

Annabella Sabbatini, Rosa's friend.

Contents

Florence

The Temptation of Father Lorenzo

Chapter One

Since she couldn't see out of her right eye and had only limited vision in her left, Caterina Rossi had to lean down to little Pietro when the soup kitchen suddenly became very quiet.

"What's going on, Pietro? What happened? Why has everyone stopped talking?"

The boy tugged at his mother's arm. "Father Lorenzo just came in," he whispered. "He looks really mad."

"Why?"

"I dunno. He just looks mad. His face is all red. People look scared."

"Maybe he's sick. Maybe he doesn't feel…"

"Can we keep the line moving, please!" Father Lorenzo suddenly called out. "There are other people waiting to eat. You can talk at your tables."

No one said anything as they went through the line, but they did as he commanded. Normally, the *cucina popolare* off Piazza Santa Croce in Florence was a boisterous place, with more than two hundred people lining up each night for hot Tuscan bean soup and bread, for many their only meal of the day. Until recently, Father Lorenzo often told loud jokes and sang Beatles songs, badly, as he supervised the volunteers.

But in the last weeks everyone noticed that his mood had drastically changed. They worried.

Standing next to Father Lorenzo in the serving line, a volunteer asked, "Everything all right, Father?"

"Yes, Gregorio, everything is all right. Everything is perfectly all right. You've been volunteering here long enough, so you don't have to ask me if everything is all right."

"OK. Sorry, Father."

"And you don't have to be sorry, dammit! Just serve the soup. And

I wish you'd get here on time. Can't you see the line is backing up?"

"Yes, Father."

Pietro had guided his mother to the line. Caterina's hands shook as she reached out to take a bowl. "Father..."

Father Lorenzo's face paled. Of all the people who came to the *cucina popolare*, he cared for no one more than Caterina Rossi. Her hair may have been tangled, her clothing threadbare and her shoes frayed, but she always had a smile on her haggard face. Although she was only thirty, she looked at least ten years older.

But those eyes. Unseeing, they were still pools of liquid blue. Father Lorenzo was caught up in them.

His voice softened. "Oh, Caterina. I'm sorry if I was too loud a minute ago. How are you today?"

"I'm fine, but how are you, Father? Pietro says you look angry. Has something happened?"

Father Lorenzo sighed. "No, nothing, Caterina. Don't worry. I'll be all right."

"We wouldn't want something to happen to you, Father."

"Nothing's going to happen, Caterina."

"And you're not leaving us, are you, Father? We'd miss you so much!"

"No, Caterina, I'm not going anywhere."

"Thank God!"

"Now, please, have some soup, OK?"

"Thank you, Father." She took the bowl of bean soup that he placed in her hands. Pietro took his own, picked up a couple of pieces of bread and guided his mother to a table near the front.

Few people saw the priest flee to the tiny storeroom at the end of the hall. It was dark there, and quiet. He leaned against the wall, one hand rubbing his aching head.

"What is the matter with me? What is happening? This isn't me. I don't act like this. Not even during the flood I didn't act like this. Lord, please help me! Please!"

He slid down the wall and sat hunched with his face in his knees. "Have to settle down, have to settle down."

When he returned, still sweating, to the line fifteen minutes later, Father Lorenzo found that his place had been taken by Brother Andrea, who always found it necessary to lecture each of the diners before filling their bowls. Now he was telling a woman with two little girls that she should have gone to Mass today.

"It will help you lead a better life, a more holy life, and help you bring up your little girls here. Now after you have your soup why don't you go into the church and say a rosary. The Blessed Mother will help you lead a virtuous life. Will you promise me that?"

"Excuse me, Brother," Father Lorenzo said. "I'll take care of this." He pushed the younger man out of the line and told the woman she should pay no attention to what she had just heard.

The woman smiled, and Father Lorenzo glared at Brother Andrea. "There's no need to lecture our guests, Andrea. They've got enough to worry about."

"I was just looking after their souls, Father."

"Well, think of their stomachs before their souls. What the hell do you think we're here for?"

Brother Andrea suddenly found the need to go to Santa Croce and say the rosary.

But then the priest began muttering to two volunteers. "You're slowing down again, Veronica. Move a little faster, Benedetta."

"Working as fast as I can, Father," Veronica said.

"Then why is the line backed up to the door?"

"It's moving pretty fast, Father," Benedetta said.

"No, it's not!" The priest was no longer whispering, and the room fell silent again. "Jesus Christ, can't you serve the soup faster? Do I have to do everything around here?"

Throughout the hall, spoons fell on tables as everyone stopped eating. They had never seen Father Lorenzo so angry before, had never heard him raise his voice before, had never heard him take the Lord's name in vain before.

Slowly, and with Pietro's help, Caterina got up and approached the serving table. Pietro helped her stand in front of the priest.

"Father," she began.

"What is it, Caterina?"

"Father, I know this isn't my place to talk to you like this."

"Say whatever you want, Caterina. It's all right."

"Well, I just can't stand to know you're upset like this."

"Caterina, I'm not upset."

She ignored him. "Father, you've helped me so many times, and

I'm grateful for all you've done."

"I just tried to help, Caterina."

"You found me a place to live after the flood. You helped when Pietro was born and you got us some clothes. You saw to it that that bastard Victorio left for good."

"He was beating you up."

"Yes. Every day. And now for the first time in years I feel safe. And Pietro, too. And I'm so grateful. And that's why I am concerned about you. You've never acted like this before. You've always been so happy, singing and joking all the time. After the flood, you were the one who held everything in Santa Croce together. This *cucina popolare* was known all over Florence. You even made us rooms upstairs when we didn't have homes. You were the only one. You were a saint, Father. Everyone said you were a saint!"

"Well, I'm not a saint, Caterina! I'm not a fucking saint!"

Chapter Two

Father Lorenzo knew who it was as soon as the phone rang an hour later.

"*Ciao*, Father Alphonsus. Yes…no…yes…No, that's all right, I'll be right over."

Although Father Alphonsus was the Father Superior of all of the Franciscans in the Basilica of Santa Croce, his office across the courtyard was only slightly larger than anyone else's. And since he needed so many files and books, there was little room for his desk and two small chairs.

"Ah, Father Lorenzo. Come in." He greeted the younger priest with a palsied hand. "Sit down. Brandy?"

"Yes, please. Make it a double."

A discarded and desanctified tabernacle that once graced a side chapel in the basilica now stood on a small table behind the desk. With shaking fingers, Father Alphonsus took a key from a drawer and opened the ornate gold-plated door, revealing an abundant supply of wine and liquor. He poured two hefty drinks.

"This is one of my few indulgences, but I think it's why I've lived to be eighty-three," he said as he handed Father Lorenzo a glass.

"Thanks. I need this."

"Today, I do, too. Well, Lorenzo, I imagine you know why I asked you to come over."

"Yes, and I know who ratted on me, too."

Father Alphonsus leaned back in his chair but didn't answer.

"The little prick."

"Now, now, Lorenzo, Brother Andrea means well."

"Means well? Means well? Father, do you know what he was doing the other day? He asked all the people to wait to begin eating so that everyone could pray together first! Pray together! These people were hungry! And their soup was getting cold!"

"You're shouting, Lorenzo."

"Sorry. But that little jerk gets me so riled up. You'd think Vatican II never happened. He thinks only Catholics are going to be saved. He hates the altars being turned around. He doesn't like people shaking hands during Mass. And don't get him started on birth control. I think he's memorized every word of *Humanae Vitae*."

"You're shouting again, Lorenzo."

"Sorry. Think you can get someone else to help me?"

Father Alphonsus sighed and took another drink. "I wish I could, Lorenzo, but there's no one else. Certainly there aren't any priests, the way they're dropping out."

"I know Father Damien left."

Father Alphonsus took another drink. "Yes, and with the clerk from the gift shop. And Father Gerardo, with a teacher from the school. And, oh, yes, Father Xavier, with a nun from Santa Maria Novella. Santa Maria Novella! At least he could have picked one from Santa Croce."

"That's a joke, right?"

"Only a little. I don't know what's happening. So many good priests are leaving and that just leaves more work for the rest of us. But that isn't what I wanted to talk to you about, you know."

"Yes, I know. I was trying to avoid the subject as long as possible."

"I'm told you used some interesting words tonight, Lorenzo."

"Father, I don't know how they came out of my mouth. I never talk like that. Never!"

"Well, you probably heard them around the soup kitchen."

"Maybe once or twice."

Father Alphonsus put his glass down and took out a cigar from a leather box on his desk. "My other vice, my *Tuscano* cigars." The match in his shaking hand almost set his brown robes on fire. "One brandy and one cigar a day. That's my advice. Would you like one? They're very good."

"Thanks, but no."

"Lorenzo, how many hours do you put in at the *cucina popolare* every day?"

"I get there about 7 o'clock, after my morning Mass, and I'm usually there until about 8 at night. Not too bad."

"Every day?"

"We're open every day, Father."

"Any vacations lately?"

"As they say, Father, the poor don't take vacations. Oh, I did miss two-and-a-half days last year when I had the flu. I didn't want to spread my germs."

"The only days off were when you had the flu?"

"Yes."

"Last year?"

"Yes."

Father Alphonsus sighed and looked at the younger priest over his glasses. "Lorenzo, how often do you read books, go to the cinema—in other words, have a life apart from the soup kitchen?"

"I love doing what I'm doing, Father."

"Lorenzo, do you have any friends? Priest friends or volunteers or people from the *cucina popolare?*"

"I know a lot of people, Father. The volunteers, the people who come in for soup."

"Would you call them your friends? People you can talk to?"

"I don't make friends easily, Father."

"So you're pretty much alone?"

"I guess so. Hadn't thought about it."

"At night, when you go back to your room, what do you do?"

"Say my evening prayers, take care of some paperwork, then go to bed. I'm usually exhausted."

Father Alphonsus drew a long intake from his cigar and gazed at the Della Robbia above the pile of books on the shelf across the room. How peaceful the Madonna looked.

"Lorenzo, I don't know if I've ever thanked you enough for what you did after the flood. That was such a terrible time. All those people dying, all the poor people left without homes, without food, without clothes."

"Well, I had to. Everyone seemed so upset about the artworks that were damaged and the books that were destroyed. Tell you the truth, Father, I don't give a damn about Cimabue's Crucifix. I mean, I'm sorry it was destroyed, but the poor people around here are more important than a damn crucifix, or the other paintings and books."

"Now, now, Lorenzo."

"Well, it's just how I feel."

"You were truly remarkable," Father Alphonsus said. "Feeding all those people. Where did you find the food?"

"Don't ask, Father."

"OK, I won't. But then you made rooms upstairs for the homeless. You delivered food baskets. You really kept the community around here together."

"It had to be done, and somebody had to do it."

"You're far too modest. You did everything for those poor people. You were a saint, Lorenzo."

"Father! Please! Don't call me that. That's what Caterina said tonight. And then I yelled at her! That was terrible! I apologized later, but that's the worst thing I did. And I yelled at my volunteers, Gregorio, Veronica, Benedetta. I feel so bad. I didn't mean to yell at them, Father, I didn't. I don't know what came over me. I am so ashamed."

He took out a handkerchief and blew his nose.

"Lorenzo, helping all those people during the flood. That must have given you a great deal of satisfaction."

"Yes."

"Lorenzo, it's natural to feel a bit down after all that. You were doing wonderful things in helping those people. Everyone was grateful. And now that time is over. That was 1966 and now it's 1974. And you're tired. But you have to realize that you don't have to do this all by yourself."

Father Lorenzo took another drink and put his glass down. "Then who would, Father? Brother Andrea, for God's sake?"

Father Alphonsus shook ashes from his cigar into a plastic tray. "We'll let that pass. Lorenzo, what do you think caused the outburst tonight?"

"I don't know. Maybe because what we experienced after the flood isn't over yet, Father. More people seem to be coming, we're not getting some supplies, there are fewer volunteers. I've been so frustrated. I guess what happened tonight just built up."

Father Alphonsus leaned forward. "Lorenzo, it doesn't take a psychologist to know that you're burned out. You need to get away from this for a while."

"I can't do that, Father."

"Why not?"

"Because…because…"

"Good answer, Lorenzo."

"What do you want me to do? Go off on a retreat? Father, I really don't want to go off and pray for two weeks."

"No, not a retreat. A vacation. A real vacation. Get away from Florence. Go skiing in the mountains."

"I don't ski, Father."

"Then go to the seaside. Lie in the sun. Read a book. A novel, not too trashy. Go to movies. Meet some nice people. See what the rest of the world is like. It's only May, so there shouldn't be too many tourists. It will get your energy back."

"Let me think about it."

"Lorenzo, I could order you to go, you know."

"I know, I know. But Father, I do have to go to my mother's in Siena next weekend."

"A weekend with your mother? From what you've told me about your mother, that isn't the kind of vacation I was thinking about. I don't think it would be very relaxing."

"Probably not. But she'd kill me if I wasn't there for this big award she's getting."

"Lorenzo, Lorenzo. How old are you?"

"Forty-three."

Father Alphonsus laughed. "Forty-three. Just another nice Italian boy doing what his mother wants him to do. You really are a saint."

Father Lorenzo winced. "Tell you what. I'll go to my mother's, and if I need a vacation after that, I'll take it."

"Promise?"

"Promise."

Chapter Three

Father Lorenzo knew he couldn't go to Siena, even overnight, without lining up Dino Sporenza to be in charge of the soup kitchen and giving him very specific instructions. So after all of the diners had left and only a few volunteers remained to mop the floor, the priest met with the young man in the kitchen to wash the last dishes. But Dino already knew what to do.

"Father, I've been volunteering here for nine years. I think I know when to open the doors, how to make the soup, how to clean up."

"I know, I know," the priest said. "I just want to make sure."

"We'll be fine, Father. Don't worry about us."

Father Lorenzo wiped a huge steel pot and hung it on the wall. "OK, but make sure that there are enough gallons of water and enough vegetables in the bins, especially the beans."

"Yes, Father."

"And see that Caterina finishes her soup and eats her bread. She always gives hers to Pietro and she looks far too thin lately."

"Yes, Father."

"And watch Guido. He comes in with a bottle of booze in his pocket every once in a while. He knows we don't allow liquor in here."

"Yes, Father."

"And keep Francesco and Mateo at separate tables. They start to fight."

"Yes, Father."

"And give Angelo and Salvatore some extra soup and bread. I was really nasty to them the other day and I'm so sorry about that."

"I'm sure they understand."

"And make sure Emilio eats well. That poor guy, he can hardly see anymore."

"Lucky he has Fico to guide him around."

"That dog is amazing," Father Lorenzo said. "I'm trying to think if there's anything else. Oh, yes. Dino, you know what to do if Brother Andrea starts lecturing our guests?"

"Yes, yes, of course. I'll just stuff a towel into his mouth. Don't worry, Father, he's not going to be a problem. I promise." Dino illustrated this by wrapping a towel around his face.

"He'd better not, the little prick."

"You don't have to worry about us, Father. We'll be fine."

"I know, but…"

"Just go enjoy your weekend and don't even think about us."

"Yeah, well, I'll try."

The priest patted Dino on the back. Dino was the soup kitchen's most faithful volunteer, ever since the disastrous flood of the Arno eight years ago. Under the priest's guidance, he had helped to salvage the lives, the homes and the hopes of the flood-stricken poor.

"Father, I can't believe you're really taking off for a weekend."

"Well, it's not my choice. My mother is getting this big award for her work on the divorce law, and she wanted her two sons there. No, make that, she ordered her two sons to be there."

"Isn't it a little ironic, Father," Dino said as he hosed down the soap in the sink, "that your mother worked for the divorce law when her son is a priest and the church was campaigning against it?"

"I can't control what my mother does, Dino. And no matter how much she wants to, she can't control what I do."

Dino asked a question he had long wanted to ask. "Father, what did your mother think when you told her you were going to be a priest? You've said in the past that your mother didn't take much interest in you. What did she say? Most mothers would be thrilled, wouldn't they?"

Father Lorenzo laughed. "Thrilled? My mother? Well, if she was, she certainly expressed it in an unusual way. Like throwing a lamp across the room. And breaking into tears whenever I mentioned it. Oh yes, she was very, very thrilled."

"But you still went ahead?"

"The guilt trip didn't work. I was twenty-four years old when I entered the seminary. There wasn't anything she could do about it. I didn't need her money, and you know that she has a lot, and I didn't need her permission."

"I guess not."

"I think the thing that upset her most was that I joined the Franciscans. 'Those ugly brown robes,' she kept saying. If I was going to become a priest, she wanted me to become a parish priest so that I could become a bishop and wear all those silks and brocades. And she didn't like it that I'd get a tonsure. 'You're going to lose all that beautiful hair,' she said. My God, it's only a little circle in the back of my head. My mother is very big on appearances."

"Did she come to your ordination?"

"Oh yes. With her boyfriend. She had one then. The bishop wasn't too pleased about that."

"Your father had already died?"

"Yes. Killed in the war. And she was devoting her life to investing his money and taking up feminist causes. I dread going this weekend and I won't be able to come back soon enough."

"Well, don't think about the *cucina popolare*. Everything will be just fine."

"OK. But I'll give you the phone number in case you need to reach me."

"Father, you're just going for two days. Don't worry about us so much."

Chapter Four

Although Florence was less than two hours away, Father Lorenzo rarely returned to Siena and had gone there only once in the last five years, for his grandmother's funeral. He was one of a dozen priests at the Mass in the cathedral, his mother having declared that the cardinal should be the celebrant. Since it was his father's mother in the coffin, Father Lorenzo didn't see why his mother should even care, but his mother asked, "What would people think if the cardinal didn't do this?"

Instead of taking the express bus to Siena, which would get him there faster, he chose to take the one that stopped at a couple of towns along the way. As he settled in, he noticed a woman across the aisle who reminded him of Caterina. She had bright blue eyes. "Wonder how Dino is doing," he thought.

Minutes out of Florence, the bus was in Chianti country, where vineyards alternated with olive groves, where little villages perched dangerously on hilltops, and where medieval castles looked down on stone farmhouses and rows of stately cypresses. No postcards, calendars or picture books could adequately capture the beauty of this countryside, Father Lorenzo thought, and he knew that he missed it terribly.

The bus went past San Casciano, a village still being rebuilt from the destruction of the last war, with only remnants of the walls around the castle remaining. Then the bus rumbled past Tavarnelle, almost destroyed when it was caught in the battles between Florence and Siena in the Middle Ages. And Barberino, where only parts of its medieval walls remained. Then a stop at Poggibonsi.

Father Lorenzo leaned back in his seat and closed his eyes, trying to dismiss the fact that the woman across the aisle reminded him of Caterina. Poggibonsi. He remembered the class trip he took here when he was sixteen years old. How could he ever forget?

On the school bus from Siena, he sat next to Maria-Teresa, a cute blond-haired girl he had long noticed across the room. He didn't think she noticed him, because he was the quietest boy in the class. But they whispered to each other as their teacher droned on about the wars between the Ghibellines and the Guelphs in the twelfth century and how the Florentines destroyed the town in the thirteenth century and how it was rebuilt in the fourteenth century. Instead of that boring history stuff, they learned that they shared a mutual love for music.

"My mother thinks all the new songs are dirty," Maria-Teresa said, "but I have a little radio in my room and I listen there."

"Sometimes in my room I pretend I have a guitar and I play it to the music on the radio," Lorenzo said.

He couldn't believe a pretty girl was talking to him.

Perhaps not so oddly, they found themselves walking away from the rest of the class and to the Basilica of Saint Lucchese, the patron saint of the town. They didn't go inside, having no desire to look at his tomb, but they found themselves on the far side of the church, where their teacher and classmates couldn't see them.

"For two kids who had just met, we certainly got to know each other pretty fast," he thought. The woman across the aisle must have wondered why Father Lorenzo was chuckling.

That encounter led to others in Siena in the following weeks. Lorenzo and Maria-Teresa couldn't go to her home, which was on the second floor of a building near the *campo*, but he knew of a long-forgotten bedroom in the palazzo where he lived off Via delle Terme. By entering from the courtyard, they could climb to the third floor without being seen by the servants, or, more to the point, his mother.

It was there that the sixteen-year-old Lorenzo and the fifteen-year-old Maria-Teresa discovered the mysteries of their bodies and, once discovered, how the mysteries could be solved. This took a lot of experimentation and practice over many months, but they were young and eager to learn.

Father Lorenzo opened his eyes. Outside the bus window, a line of men and women dressed in shabby clothes snaked to a church. "They would be heating the soup at the *cucina popolare* now," he thought.

The bus stopped at Colle, and Father Lorenzo had other memories. He was nineteen and, after some tempestuous fights, Maria-Teresa had been replaced by Patrizia, who was eight years older than he was and worked as a clerk in a candy store. Lorenzo had gained more confidence by now and owned his first Vespa. On moonlit nights or warm Sunday afternoons, they went riding to the bubbling River Elsa with a bottle of wine, some crusty bread and cheese. One night they took off all their clothes and swam in the frigid waters, then hurried back home to the third-floor bedroom to dry off and warm up.

"Ah, Patrizia," Father Lorenzo thought as the bus rounded a corner and moved on to Siena. "I wonder what she's doing now." He thought briefly about stopping in the candy store, but abandoned the idea.

As the bus entered the outskirts of Siena, the priest had the usual mixed feelings he always experienced returning to his hometown. He loved the distinctive red-brown colors, the stately medieval public buildings and palazzos, the dramatically hilly streets, the shops, the bustling *campo* and the overwhelming pride the Sienese had in their city. On the other hand, his memories of family life were anything but happy, what with a mother who pursued her own interests and paid little attention to her sons. He had spent many lonely nights in his room.

But he knew there was another reason he hesitated to return to Siena. It was the scene of the hedonistic life he lived before he entered the seminary, and he had abandoned that. Maria-Teresa and Patrizia were followed by Francesca and Daniella and Leila and many others who lasted one or two nights. It was safer that way. He didn't have to get too close to any of them.

And, since he had no reason to hold a job after getting his degree from the University of Bologna, many nights involved drinking with young men from the neighborhood in one *osteria* after another. Sometimes, they shared more than drinks. Nothing hard like heroin or cocaine, but two of his friends could be counted on for fresh supplies of pot. He never got close to any of these men, either.

But that was then. It was a past he didn't want to remember, but the memories kept returning whenever he was back in Siena and passed a familiar *osteria*. No matter how hard he tried to forget, he sometimes felt wistful for a life that had no cares, no poor people who needed so much.

After leaving the bus in Piazza Gramsci, he wanted to avoid going to the family palazzo for as long as possible. Lugging his small suitcase, he walked to Piazza Matteotti, then down the steep Via Banchi di Sopra to the Piazza del Campo. In late afternoon, crowds of tourists mingled with Sienese shopping at the gift stores around the vast piazza. The restaurants weren't open yet, and waiters spread white tablecloths and straightened chairs under the awnings outside. Father Lorenzo bought a chocolate gelato at the shop in the corner and settled down on the hard stones across from the ancient tower to watch the pigeons.

Since this was May, the *campo* was not getting ready yet for the Palio. Father Lorenzo had gone to the horse race every year when he was a boy but he could never understand the rivalry of the different neighborhoods as they watched the horses careen around the piazza in the middle of the city. But he did attend the celebrations, even when his own neighborhood, or *contrada*, didn't win, because he always went home with a different woman.

A few yards away, a young woman eased herself onto the stones, took off her sunglasses and rummaged in her purse. She seemed smart and self-assured. He liked that. The priest watched as she took out a compact and gently applied powder and then lipstick. She lifted her cotton skirt above her knees and unfastened the top button of her white blouse. She leaned back on her elbows to absorb the late afternoon sun. Father Lorenzo couldn't take his eyes off her.

Aware that he was staring, the woman smiled. "*Buongiorno*," she said.

He hardly heard her with all the kids shouting as they chased the pigeons. "*Buongiorno*," he said.

Father Lorenzo suddenly felt stirrings and emotions he had long suppressed, and he realized that he was not wearing his brown robes but an ordinary shirt and pants.

He wondered what to do next. Should he talk to her? That might be dangerous. Then a little boy ran by, waving a stick at a frightened pigeon. The boy reminded him of Caterina's Pietro. Father Lorenzo made a determined effort to watch the boy, not the woman.

Chapter Five

Palazzo Murano had been in Father Lorenzo's family for more than two hundred years, but actually was built in the sixteenth century in the row of palaces erected near Palazzo Tolomei. Unlike that delicate palace, Murano always seemed like a fortress when Lorenzo was growing up, but he was thankful for the courtyard and rear stairwell that allowed access to the third-story bedroom.

Father Lorenzo's father could trace his ancestry back to the House of Savoy, something his mother would never let anybody forget. Although his father died when Lorenzo was a boy, Signora Renata Salvetti proudly kept up the face of the family, even though the upper floors of the palazzo were now used as offices.

A new servant girl greeted the priest when he rang the buzzer on the golden door. She wondered who he was.

"I'm Father Lorenzo. The other son."

In the salon, the reception before the awards banquet was well under way, and dozens of people clustered around tables laden with *antipasti* and the bar at the end of the room. Father Lorenzo quickly realized he was not properly dressed. His brother noticed that, too.

"Padre!" Giorgio slapped Father Lorenzo on the back and steered him towards the door. "Well, how nice of you to leave your poor people for a night and hang out with the filthy rich."

"I wouldn't be here, Giorgio, if our mother hadn't ordered me to come."

"Well, since I live here, I didn't have an excuse," his brother whispered. "I think she's getting worse. Wants to know everything I do."

"Maybe she has reasons to suspect something?"

"I'll never confess."

Everyone in the family knew that Giorgio had ties to unsavory banking interests and that he was deeply involved with a woman in

Rome while living with his wife on the second floor of the palazzo. But everyone in the family kept the secrets.

"Well, dear brother," Giorgio said. "I'll see you at the dinner. It's at Palazzo Franconi. You'd better change, though, before our mother sees you. But not into your brown robe. Didn't you bring a suit?"

"I don't own a suit. There aren't many chances to wear a suit in the soup kitchen."

"Lucky we're both about the same size. Look in my closet. You'll find something that fits. There are shirts in the drawers. Oops. Here comes our mother."

Signora Renata Salvetti glided past the other guests and was soon at Father Lorenzo's side. His mother, as always, was dressed simply but impeccably, the better to show off her well-endowed figure. Her dark blue evening dress, topped with a silver shawl, was accented only by an heirloom brooch. No necklace, no earrings. Not a hair was out of place.

"Lorenzo, Lorenzo, you've come at last." She allowed him to kiss her cheeks. "So pale, so tired looking. You have to get out of that terrible Florence, my dear. It's not good for your health."

"I love Florence, Mama."

"Oh, it's all right, but it can't compare with Siena, now can it? That muddy river running through it and all those foreigners traipsing around with their loud music and their drugs. How can you stand it?"

"I'm used to it, Mama."

"Ah well. You were always obstinate." She straightened his collar. "Lorenzo, you really should think about changing careers, you know. I'm sure Giorgio can find you a very nice position in a bank. And if you want to do good, like you always say, think of all the good you could do there. You could spread a lot of money around."

"Changing careers? Mama, I'm a priest."

"Oh, priests are leaving all the time, haven't you heard? I'm sure we can arrange something if you want."

"I don't want, Mama." He glared at her. "Look, I've got to change for the dinner."

"I'm so glad you didn't wear that awful brown robe, Lorenzo. You never looked good in brown. Please go to Giorgio's room and find a nice suit."

As usual after he had even the briefest conversation with his mother, Father Lorenzo was furious. "Change careers, change careers," he muttered as he ran up the stairs to Giorgio's rooms. "What the hell..."

Father Lorenzo could choose from a dozen black, blue or brown suits in his brother's closets and selected a dark brown Brioni with thin stripes. He found a white dress shirt in a drawer and a red-and-white striped Canali tie on a hanger. He even exchanged his work boots for Canali shoes. When he looked into a mirror, all he could think of was, "Who is this guy?" Certainly not the humble Franciscan friar from Florence. Did he like what he saw? He didn't know.

By the time he had changed, everyone had gone off to Palazzo Franconi, leaving him to walk the streets alone. Siena was magical all the time, but he always felt it was especially enchanting at sunset when the brick buildings seemed even more red. Still needing time to cool off, he walked deliberately around the *campo* instead of through it.

Dinner, he found as he entered the long banquet room in the cold and forbidding Palazzo Franconi, was to be by candlelight, and most guests were seated at tables of six. He saw his mother at the head table with a row of elegantly dressed men and women. She was smiling and nodding, obviously pleased by the attention she was getting.

Father Lorenzo's table was near the front. At his left, a middle-aged couple was deep in conversation with the elderly couple next to them. It seemed as though they were somehow related. No one acknowledged the priest when he sat down.

"I imagine I'd get a little attention if I had worn my robes," he thought.

The place on his right was vacant. "They must have thought I'd bring a guest. Why would I want to bring someone to this thing?"

Served by an army of tuxedo-clad waiters, the dinner began with calamari marinated with mint, garlic and pecorino, followed by wide-ribbon pasta with a duck ragu in red-wine sauce, followed by a slab of wood-roasted fillet of beef with vegetables, followed by a mixed green salad. It went on forever, with the other couples in heated conversation and Father Lorenzo eating in silence and staring at the other tables. "We could serve two dozen people at the soup kitchen with what's on this table," he thought.

It was not until the dessert, a thin slice of *panforte* served on a gleaming white china plate, that the last dinner guest arrived at his table.

"So sorry! You wouldn't believe the traffic from Rimini."

For someone who had just driven from the eastern seacoast and then had to run in high heels from a parking lot outside Siena's gates, the woman seemed only a little flustered.

"Hello," she said, reaching out a hand to Father Lorenzo, who had gotten up to greet her. "I'm Victoria Stonehill. I worked with Signora Salvetti on the last campaign."

If her upturned nose didn't give her away as not being Italian, her American accent did.

"And I'm Lorenzo, the signora's younger son."

"Really? Signora Salvetti always talks about Giorgio, but I don't think she ever mentioned she had another son."

"Understandable," Father Lorenzo said. Both her smile and her perfume were intoxicating.

"By the way, I love your tie."

"Thanks."

He knew his mother had something to do with this, and as he resumed his place at the table, he wondered why he didn't tell Victoria Stonehill that he was a priest.

Chapter Six

Father Lorenzo took only two bites of his dessert. Living in one of the poorest sections of Florence, he had little contact with American tourists, and certainly not attractive American women. He was fascinated by her red hair, piled on top of her head, the faint freckles on her cheeks and nose, her tanned arms, the perfect teeth and the wide smile.

She also smiled a lot, wanting to know all about him as she dug into her dessert.

"Florence?" she said. "I love Florence. The Pitti Palace. The Uffizi. The Baptistry. Where do you live?"

"Near Santa Croce."

"Ah yes, where everyone is buried. Michelangelo, Galileo, Machiavelli, Rossini."

"Yes. It's a magnificent church." Why was he so tongue-tied?

"And what do you do in Florence?"

"Um, I...I...I work for a charitable agency." Why wasn't he telling her what he really did? "And you? You live in Rimini?"

"Yes. Rimini. What kind of charitable agency?"

"We...we...help the poor. But how long have you lived in Rimini?"

"For almost three years now. And what do you do to help the poor? Find them employment, homes, all those things?"

"Some of those things." He could feel sweat break out on his forehead. Why didn't he tell her he was a priest? "I haven't been in Rimini for a long time. I liked it." He was stuttering like a schoolboy.

"It's nice, but tourists take over in summer. It's terrible then. You can't breathe. But tell me more about your work, Lorenzo. I'm fascinated."

The priest was saved from more evasions when the first speaker got up at the front table. Then, speaker after speaker extolled Signora Renata Salvetti for her long and devoted work on behalf of women in Italy, and especially for organizing the campaigns that resulted in the establishment of the law legalizing divorce three years ago and the defeat of a referendum just this month that would have overturned the law.

"This fearless woman," one speaker said, "took on the mighty Christian Democrats, the Catholic Church and those Fascists in the Italian Social Movement to bring Italy out of the dark ages!"

Everyone in the room stood and applauded.

"Imagine!" another speaker said. "She was responsible for a vote that won by sixty percent to forty percent. This woman is indomitable!"

Everyone stood again.

Father Lorenzo applauded, but he knew that the speaker greatly exaggerated his mother's contributions and also that there was much confusion about the referendum. Those who voted "yes" wanted to outlaw divorce, those voting "no" wanted to retain the law granting the right to divorce.

"And so," the final speaker said, "we proudly present the Clara Maffei Award to Signora Renata Salvetti. She continues the great tradition of powerful women in Italian history."

A loud round of applause filled the room as the speaker held up a large silver medallion. Like the recipient, it was simple and tasteful.

"Your mother is quite a woman," Victoria said, putting her hand on Father Lorenzo's arm. "I mean, to take on the Catholic Church. That took a lot of courage."

"Yes. She's quite a woman." He kept staring at her hand. She didn't take it away. He also noticed that the only ring she wore was a pearl on the third finger.

Eventually, the applause died down. A line formed to congratulate Signora Salvetti, and Victoria Stonehill wondered why Lorenzo didn't want to join it.

"I can talk to her later," he said.

"I guess I can, too," she said. "Look, do you want to go out on the terrace? This room is stifling."

In the moonlight, Siena seemed even more magical than at sunset. The dome and bell tower of the cathedral glimmered in the distance.

"I love coming to Siena," Victoria said. "I should do it more often, but the shop keeps me busy and I go home to New York every few months. My mother isn't well."

"I'm sorry to hear that. What kind of shop?" He liked the way her eyes crinkled when she smiled.

"Jewelry. I have three designers that I work with. All their work is very simple and elegant." She pointed out the ruby pendant that rested between the curves of her breasts above her emerald green evening gown.

"It's…it's lovely." He was transfixed.

"Now, now, Lorenzo," she teased, "I was just asking you to notice my necklace."

His face redder than the ruby, he quickly looked away. She put her hand on his. "Don't be embarrassed. Many people tell me I have a very nice figure."

"Yes," he stammered, "you do." Just like a schoolboy again.

"The ruby is a symbol of passion, you know." She grinned. "But don't let that put you off."

"I…I won't."

"You know, Lorenzo, I like the way you're so shy. Are you married?"

"No! I mean, no, I'm not."

"I thought not. So why is a handsome man like you still available?" Her hand was still on his.

This should have been the time to tell her he was a priest. Instead: "Oh…oh, I don't know. I've been busy." That was true.

"Helping the poor."

"Yes."

"Somehow, Lorenzo, I don't think you're telling me everything. But I love a man of mystery."

He had to change the subject and get out of this. "Well, Victoria, you're sort of a mystery, too, you know. Are you…have you been…I mean now…I mean, are you married?"

Stutter, stutter, stutter.

She smiled at his confusion. "It's a long story. I met him at the beach at Rimini. I was just out of college—I won't tell you how many years ago—but I was on the beach with my girlfriend and this great looking guy, Bernardo, sat down next to us. He was older, but we started talking and, well, to make a long story very short, we started dating, we got married a year later in this big ceremony at the cathedral in Rimini and we moved into his palazzo in Verona.

"And to make a long story even shorter, it turned out that this handsome guy, though not as handsome as you, was keeping a mistress in Cecena and then he had one in Modena, and that one was followed by one in Ancona. I wondered why he traveled so much. But, thanks to the new divorce law, I am now going to set myself free. I've started the process. And that's why I worked on this referendum to keep the law. Maybe it's because I'm American, but I think people should be able to make their own decisions on whether they should be married or not."

"It doesn't sound like you're bitter."

"No, why should I be? Bernardo doesn't care. He's got another woman somewhere or other and he's already given me a very nice settlement, so now we can proceed with the divorce. We're both looking forward to being free at last, at least I am."

"No looking back?"

"No. The settlement let me move to Rimini and take over the jewelry shop on Corso d'Augusto that I liked so much. Even with the crowds in summer, I always wanted to live there because I just love the beach and I spend all my free time there. I don't go in the awful water, of course. I just lie in the sun. Yes, I gave up twelve years of my life to that guy, but it's over. Oops, I guess I gave away my age, sort of."

Lorenzo did some addition. If she was, say, twenty-two when she met Bernardo and she married when she was twenty-three, and there were twelve years in the marriage and then maybe three years since she separated from Bernardo, that would make her about thirty-eight. But why should he care?

"You're adding it up, right?"

Caught red-handed. "No! Well, yes, I was."

"It's all right," she said. "I'd guess that you are, what, forty?"

"Right." Good Lord, now he was even lying about his age.

"And never married."

"No." At least that was true.

She hugged herself against the cool night. "Look, it's getting late,

I should be leaving. I can visit your mother tomorrow."

"Yeah, it is late. Can I walk you to your hotel?"

"I'm staying at the Antica Torre, this wonderful sixteenth-century tower that's been turned into a hotel. It's on Via di Fieravecchia near the *campo*. I've stayed there before in the very top room with a terrific view. But first I have to get my things from the parking lot near Porta Romana. That's quite a hike. And you look tired."

"No, no. I'd love to walk with you. Let's go."

Chapter Seven

The next afternoon, after collapsing into a seat in the last row of the bus, Father Lorenzo seethed all the way from Siena to Florence.

He was angry at his mother for not paying much attention to him when he was a boy, for being so active in the divorce movement, for commanding him to come to Siena for the award ceremony. And now he was sure that his mother had deliberately placed Victoria next to him at the banquet. He had a whole list.

He was angry at Siena for reminding him of his libertine former life, bringing up memories he had long tried to forget.

He was angry at Victoria Stonehill for being so genuinely interested in him, for asking too many questions and, dammit, for being so terribly beautiful. If she had not been so attractive, or if she had been openly flirtatious or seductive, he could have dismissed her. But she wasn't. She was gorgeous and she was also very, very nice.

Mostly, he was angry with himself. For being so captivated with Victoria and acting like a schoolboy. And why the hell did he put on this pretense and evade her questions, even lying? Why didn't he tell her he was a priest? What kind of game was he playing?

There were no thoughts of Patrizia as the bus rode through Colle or of Maria-Teresa as it thundered through Poggibonsi. Instead, he replayed every minute of his long walk with Victoria to the parking lot and then to her hotel the night before. He remembered every word.

She had begun by telling him about growing up on what she called the upper east side of New York, with loving parents and a nanny. She attended a private school and then a college he thought was named something like "Brin Marr." Her father, whom she adored, died when she was a junior, and she missed him still.

"I suppose one reason I fell in love with Bernardo was that he

30

was older."

"And you were looking for a father figure."

"Yes. But I'm over that. I want to find someone my own age now."
He wasn't sure how far he should go, but asked, "Any luck so far?"

"There have been two possibilities." There was no hesitation.
"Amadeo. He owns a flower shop in Rimini, and Marco, an editor
at the local newspaper, but both of them seemed interested only in
themselves and their bloody work. I can't imagine either of them
working for a charitable agency. Or asking me questions about me."

That intoxicating smile again. Americans have such beautiful
teeth.

"Maybe questions are asked because you're a fascinating
woman."

"That's very kind of you to say." She waited before continuing.
"Well, Lorenzo, are you going to tell me anything about yourself?"

He knew he had to say something, so he told her about growing
up in Palazzo Murano, how he didn't get along with his brother, how
he did all right, but not spectacularly, in school. He told her about
Maria-Teresa and two or three other women, and even gave an edited
account of his carousing. That, of course, led Victoria to ask why he'd
decided to seek seemingly selfless work, like a charitable agency.

"I…I…guess there was something that attracted me to helping
people who couldn't afford to live in a palazzo."

"Or go to a school like Bryn Mawr. Lorenzo, you're quite a
guy."

"Don't believe everything you hear."

Dammit, he thought. Why can't I tell her?

By this time, they had reached the parking lot and found Victoria's
car. She retrieved her suitcase and he carried it the rest of the way.
As they walked to the hotel, Victoria caught a high heel on the brick
pavement, and he reached out to help her. She held his hand, and
from there to the hotel, they held hands on the quiet streets, saying
very little.

"I love Siena in the moonlight," she said.

"Me, too."

They went into the tiny hotel lobby together, and after Victoria
registered and received her key, there was an awkward silence. Should
he shake her hand? Should he kiss her? Should he ask to see her

again? He had to go back to Florence the next day. Victoria resolved the situation by flashing an enormous smile and kissing him quickly on the cheek.

"Lorenzo, if you're ever in Rimini, look me up, please. My shop is on Corso d'Augusto. Or you can find me on the beach. I'd love to talk with you some more."

The words still echoed through the roar of the bus the following afternoon. "I'd love to talk with you some more, I'd love to talk with you some more."

He had hardly slept, thinking of her soft voice with its quaint American accent, her sparkling eyes, her devastating smile and the ruby necklace on her breasts.

This is insane, Father Lorenzo thought, gazing out the window but not seeing the rolling hills and the stone farmhouses. Tomorrow, he would be back in his old routine at *cucina popolare* and have forgotten all about Victoria Stonehill. Clearly, there was no future with her, so why should he even think about her?

He still could not understand why he put on this phony act with her. At first, he blamed it on the suit, but that was hardly an excuse. It shouldn't have changed his personality. Then he thought it had something to do with being so exhausted and not thinking clearly. Or perhaps it had something to do with the feelings he always had when he returned to Siena.

In order to make sense of all this, he thought, he had to think back, back to the time when he decided to become a priest.

It had not been a sudden decision. He did not see a light from heaven like Saint Paul on the road to Damascus. Instead, it was more like the gradual reckoning of Saint Francis, a series of experiences spread over a year or more. He remembered looking in a mirror one morning after a particularly dissolute night in an *osteria*. He saw his craggy face and disheveled hair and thought, "Who is this guy?" He didn't recognize the figure anymore than he recognized himself in Giorgio's suit.

A month or so later, he woke up to find a naked woman's arms spread across his chest. He couldn't remember who she was or where they had met. She was just as anonymous as the woman he had slept with the week before and the week before that. "I've got to stop this," he thought.

But if he were to end that life, what life would he have? He was twenty-three years old. He needed something to live *for*.

He was never a devout Catholic, had never been an altar boy, had missed more Sunday Masses than he attended every month. But he thought perhaps a priest could give him some advice. Since he didn't like the priests at his family's parish church, San Martino, he tried a few other churches in Siena, but he wasn't impressed with the priests there, either.

One day, pondering his future as he sat on the stones of the *campo*, he saw a man nearby talking to a young woman with a boy and a girl. The woman needed better clothes, Lorenzo thought, and so did her kids. The woman suddenly began to cry, and the man, maybe in his late thirties, patted her on the shoulder and talked to her gently.

"It will be all right," Lorenzo heard the man say.

"I don't know how it could," the woman sobbed.

"Look, why don't you come to the rectory tonight and let me try to help you. We've got a little fund we can dip into. Please?"

The woman nodded and shook the man's hand, but before they left, he took her children to the gelato stand. The two kids went off with big grins on their faces and chocolate ice cream streaming down their shirts.

For the first time, Lorenzo noticed that the man's head was shaved in a small circle in the back, and, although he was wearing an ordinary work shirt and pants, that he had a wooden crucifix on a leather chain around his neck. He was wearing sandals on this cold March day.

"Excuse me," Lorenzo said. "I didn't mean to eavesdrop, but I heard you say rectory and I notice that you have a shaved head and you're wearing sandals, so I wonder..."

"If I'm a priest? Yes, a Franciscan. I work out of the Basilica of San Francesco. May I help you?"

"I don't know. I wonder if we could talk sometime."

And they did. For weeks, Lorenzo Salvetti sat down with Father Michele over an espresso in a *bar* or in his book-lined study or on a bench in a park. Father Michele's life had been similar to Lorenzo's, in some ways even more wanton, and he described it all in detail. He was ordained only six years ago.

For his part, Lorenzo said that his life had always seemed empty and that he wanted to do something where he would feel rewarded. He didn't know what that would be.

"Are you thinking of the priesthood?" Father Michele asked Lorenzo one day.

"I don't know. I think I am. I wouldn't want to be a parish priest. I couldn't handle all those responsibilities. But if I could somehow help poor people, that would be great."

"Serving the poor is what Franciscans do, of course."

Father Michele described the life of Saint Francis of Assisi, the founder of his order, and Lorenzo found so many similarities to his own: son of a wealthy father, educated, and a young man who enjoyed a life of revelry, though probably not as much as Lorenzo did.

"Learn Saint Francis' prayer, Lorenzo," the priest said, handing him a card. "It can guide you."

Lord, make me an instrument of your peace;
where there is hatred, let me sow love;
where there is injury, pardon;
where there is doubt, faith;
where there is despair, hope;
where there is darkness, light;
and where there is sadness, joy.

"Don't rush this, Lorenzo," Father Michele said. "Just think about it. And pray."

A year later, after many more talks with Father Michele and spending time in a monastery, Lorenzo Salvetti said good-bye to his tearful mother, left Palazzo Murano and entered the Franciscan seminary. Helping others, he reasoned, would take away the loneliness in his life and give it some purpose. Next month would be the tenth anniversary of his ordination.

As the bus neared the Florence bus station, Father Lorenzo knew that he had made the right decision. He would not think of Victoria Stonehill again. Or her red hair. Or her smile. Or her breasts. Ever.

Chapter Eight

At first they were a little hesitant, but then everyone cheered when Father Lorenzo walked into the soup kitchen the next night. *"Benvenuto a casa!"*

"I've only been gone two days!" he shouted back. "And I'm glad to be back."

Dino shook the priest's hand. "How was it? Everything go all right?"

"The ceremony was very impressive and my mother was very pleased."

Dino noticed that the priest didn't smile. "And you're pleased, too?"

"Of course. Why do you ask?"

"I don't know. You just look a little tired, or worried."

"Maybe a little tired. But not worried. I'm just fine, Dino."

"All right, all right," Dino said, but what he was thinking was, "I sure hope so. He doesn't look so good."

"And how did everything go here, Dino? Any problems?"

"No, smooth as silk."

"No problems with Guido?"

"No."

"Francesco or Mateo?"

"They were just fine."

"OK. And Caterina and Pietro?"

"She asked about you, said she hoped you'd feel better now."

For the rest of the evening, Dino noticed that Father Lorenzo seemed distracted at times and did not greet every diner with the enthusiasm he had before. At the end of the night, Dino made some small talk about getting together to play the guitar, something both of them enjoyed.

"Guitar? Oh. Oh, I don't know. I'll let you know, all right?"

35

"Sure."

On the following night, Father Lorenzo seemed even more distracted, gazing into the distance and pouring the soup perfunctorily.

On the third night, he did not even acknowledge Caterina and her son when they held out their bowls.

"*Ciao*, Father," Caterina said. "Pietro seemed worried about you last night."

"Why was he worrying?"

"Tell the priest, Pietro."

"Are you all right, Father?" the little boy asked. "You don't look so good."

"Yes, Pietro," the priest said, patting his head. "I'm quite all right. Don't worry about me."

"Are you sure?" Caterina asked.

"I'm sure. Don't worry."

But Caterina did worry about him.

In the weeks that followed, Father Lorenzo became more sullen or distracted or irritable, sometimes all three. He occasionally snapped at volunteers, rarely made little jokes and never sang. Diners and volunteers learned to stay out of his way and some regular patrons did not come every night.

In his lonely room, sleepless night followed sleepless night. "I've got to forget about her, I've got to forget about her."

There were dreams, sometimes involving a ruby necklace wedged between two lovely breasts. At other times, he was walking in the *campo* with a laughing red-haired woman who refused his offer to hold her hand.

He was often late for his morning Mass in the Rinuccini Chapel in Santa Croce and sometimes stopped reading from the missal, forcing the altar boy to prompt him to continue. He made a point of getting his tonsure shaved and he never wore anything but his brown Franciscan robes. "I'm a priest, I'm a priest," he kept repeating to himself. He tried to say the rosary at night but invariably forgot whether he should be thinking about the joyful, the sorrowful or the glorious mysteries.

A month after returning from Siena, Father Lorenzo returned from the kitchen to the serving line and found Brother Andrea taking a particularly long time explaining the importance of Mass to one diner.

"Look," Father Lorenzo yelled, pushing him aside. "I've had enough of this. These people come here to eat, not to listen to your pious sermons. Jesus Christ! Now just shut the fuck up and serve the food!"

In the silence that followed, Caterina put her hands over Pietro's ears and Brother Andrea rushed from the room. Father Lorenzo went to his own room, waiting Father Alphonsus' call.

The old priest, however, knew that this time it was better not to call right away. He had dealt with enough angry priests to know that a cooling-off period was needed. It was not until midafternoon the following day that Father Lorenzo found himself again in his superior's office.

"Brandy?" the old priest asked patiently.

"Yes, a double, triple, whatever."

"Lorenzo, Lorenzo. I gather the trip to Siena didn't help. Your mother?"

"My mother was as expected."

"Did something else happen?"

Trying to avoid the piles of papers on the floor, Father Lorenzo paced the room as well as he could. Should he tell his superior what had happened? How could he? There was no explanation.

"I'd like to tell you, Father, but I don't understand what happened myself. It was all very strange."

"Are you fine physically? You didn't have a heart attack or anything like that, did you?"

"No, no, nothing like that." Father Lorenzo sank into the chair opposite the desk.

"So it's up here?" Father Alphonsus pointed to his head.

"Yes."

"That can be more dangerous than what could happen to the rest of your body."

"Yes."

Father Alphonsus took a healthy drink from his glass and leaned back.

"Lorenzo, tell me this. Are you thinking about leaving the priesthood?"

"No! No, that's never occurred to me."

"Good. Then let's go through this. You still like being a priest, right?"

"I love being a priest. I really do."

"What do you like best?"

"Serving the poor at the soup kitchen. No question. That's the very best part."

"Why?"

"I guess I've always had this need to serve. And it always reminds me of Saint Francis."

"Mass? You like saying the Mass?"

"Yes. It's still a beautiful experience for me. But I still feel worthless during the consecration."

"Lorenzo, I've been saying Mass every day for almost sixty years. Do you think I feel worthy saying those words? 'The body of Christ, the blood of Christ.' Never. It doesn't get any easier."

"I thought it would."

"No, it doesn't. But there are some things that you don't like, right? That's natural. What parts of being a priest don't you particularly like?"

"Confession. All those people with their tiny little sins. Funerals. I get so sad when I have to bury someone I know. Marriage preparation. What the hell do I know about marriage?"

Father Alphonsus took out a cigar and struggled to light it. "None of us do. We just muddle along and try to do our best."

"I don't know, Father. There's just something that's been weighing so heavily on my mind. I can't stop thinking about it."

"Want to talk about it?"

"No."

"Can you talk about it to anyone else? A friend?"

"No. I don't have any friends."

"Right. Working all the time, you don't have time to make friends." Father Alphonsus leaned forward. "Lorenzo, I told you before that I could order you to take a vacation. I'm doing that now. You simply have to get away. We'll find someone else to run the soup kitchen, Lorenzo. And it won't be Brother Andrea."

"Promise?"

"Promise."

Father Lorenzo knew he was right.

"You look awfully pale. You've been in that soup kitchen far too long. Why don't you go to a beach? It's June now, so there will be a lot of people, but you can find a place. Maybe there will be someone there you can talk to. I don't know what's going on with you, but it's obviously something serious. Am I right?"

"Yes."

"I thought so. How about Positano? No, you don't have a yacht. Capri? Nah, you couldn't afford even a cappuccino there. I've never been to either place, but my banker friends talk about them."

"Father, what about Rimini?"

"Rimini?" Father Alphonsus said. "Rimini? Why on earth? It's overrun with tourists and rowdy young people. From what I hear, anyway. Why would you want to go there?"

"I've heard the sun is good there."

The older priest looked over the rims of his glasses. "Lorenzo, this wouldn't have anything to do with what happened in Siena, would it?"

Father Lorenzo's face reddened. "Father, you told me I needed sun!"

Father Alphonsus sighed. "All right, all right. Rimini. Go there. Tomorrow. And don't come back until you're feeling a hell of a lot better."

Father Lorenzo found himself whistling as he went back to his room. He never whistled. Well, what could he do? Father Alphonsus had virtually commanded him to go to Rimini to see Victoria Stonehill. And Father Alphonsus was his superior. He had to do what he commanded.

Chapter Nine

Father Lorenzo had told Victoria that he liked Rimini, but he had been there only twice before. Once was on a class trip even before Maria-Teresa and he was too shy to talk to girls and too bored to learn about Rimini's history and architecture. He wasn't impressed that the Tiberius Bridge was two thousand years old and still carried traffic, that the Arc d'Augusto was also built by the Romans and that the Malatesta fortress was used as a prison until a few years ago.

He remembered little about his other visit. He had gone to Rimini with a group from the *osteria* and a couple of girls. He thought he might have made love to one of the girls on the beach early in the morning, but almost twenty years later, he wasn't sure.

He was sure of one thing now, though. As he prepared for Mass in the Rinuccini Chapel, he knew exactly what he was doing.

"I'm going to go there and tell her it was all a mistake. I'm sorry if I misled her. I don't know why I did that. It was stupid. I'm a priest. I can't get involved with women. I've taken a vow of chastity. And I've got responsibilities in Florence. I've got to run the soup kitchen. She should know the truth. I'm forty-three years old. I'm not a seventeen-year-old kid. I'm a priest. Nothing is going to come of this. Even if she is so beautiful and nice."

He knew he would feel better after he told Victoria the truth. First, though, he would spend a few days at the beach, just to satisfy Father Alphonsus. He would wait until the last day to see Victoria. But he would be back within a week. He hadn't even left, but he already missed Dino and Francesco and Mateo and Caterina and Pietro and even Guido. But not Brother Andrea.

The altar boy that day wondered why Father Lorenzo roared through the Mass like a speeding train. It was over in twenty minutes and the priest rushed into the sacristy, out of his vestments and onto the street.

Since he hadn't gone to a beach since his seminary days, Father Lorenzo had to do some shopping. At the San Lorenzo market he bought a pair of sunglasses and plowed through the swimming trunks adorned with photos of the statue of David's genitals to find something more suitable for a priest. It was plain blue. He went to Feltrinelli's on Via de' Cerretani to find a book and finally selected Ignazio Silone's *Bread and Wine* because the jacket indicated it was anti-Fascist and pro-Socialist.

It turned out that he had to take a train to Bologna, and then another to Rimini, each taking almost an hour. So although he left Florence at 3:30 in the afternoon, he didn't get to Rimini until almost 6 o'clock. As he feared, the town was overrun by both tourists and Italians, most of them young and intoxicated, and the foul smells from the Adriatic mixed with the strong odors of suntan oils. Everyone was either going to or coming from the beach. Father Lorenzo could almost feel the eroticism in the air, and quickly elbowed his way through the half-naked bodies to his *pensione*.

With only a bed, a dresser and a chair, his room was not much more elaborate than his cell at Santa Croce. Instead of a cross on the wall, a garish painting of a buxom nude woman hung against bright floral wallpaper.

"I don't think I'll be distracted by her," Father Lorenzo thought as he unpacked three shirts, two pairs of pants, underwear and his swimming trunks. The closet lacked hangers, so he draped his shirts and pants on the chair. He didn't want to think why he hadn't brought his Franciscan robes.

He thought he might rest a little before getting something to eat, but the bed was lumpy and he didn't want to look at the buxom lady. He pulled the torn curtains aside and saw only garbage cans and cars in an alley. He opened *Bread and Wine* but couldn't get past the first page. Why was he so nervous? He needed something to eat.

In the *trattoria* next to the *pensione* he found the linguini stringy, the bread stale and the red wine bitter. He left no tip and went back to his room, attempted to say the rosary but gave up after the third decade. With all the revelry outside, it was not until early in the morning that he fell asleep, only to dream again about a ruby necklace on a lovely breast.

He awoke with the same thoughts he had when he went to sleep.

"I've got to stop thinking about her, I've got to tell her the truth."

The June sun streamed through the torn curtains, and after waiting for the lone lavatory down the hall to be free, he carefully selected a shirt, light blue, and pants, khaki, for the day. He liked what he saw in the mirror.

"Well, I just want to look nice."

The *bar* across the street was crowded, and Father Lorenzo took his place at the end of the line. Then he saw a *La Gazzetta dello Sport* on a table and sat down to read it, though he had almost no interest in soccer. The line had grown shorter by the time he finished the report on the Fiorentina team, but he took a long time trying to choose between the apple or the raspberry pastry in the display case. Finally, he ordered the apple and a cappuccino and stood in a corner. Funny, he thought, how long it takes for coffee to cool down.

Returning his cup to the counter, he told himself, "Well, maybe I'll just wander around town for a while. She said her shop was on Corso d'Augusto. Just want to make sure I can find it at the end of the week."

To get to Corso d'Augusto, he had to cross under the monumental Arc d'Augusto and he remembered his grade school teacher saying the arch was built in 27 BC. Father Lorenzo was not nearly as interested in history as he was in the scattering of beggars around the arch. Behind the glitz and glamour of Rimini, he realized, was the same kind of poverty he found in Florence.

"*Lire* for food?" The little boy was about four years old, with curly black hair, dark skin and piercing blue eyes. He looked very much like Pietro, and when Father Lorenzo put some loose coins in his grubby hands, the boy ran back to his mother, who was crouched on the ground near the arch. "*Grazie!*" she murmured, her pale blue eyes grateful. Father Lorenzo put his hand on the woman's shoulder. "God protect you," he said.

Beyond the arch, Corso d'Augusto was in a fancier part of Rimini than he expected and lined with boutiques and bookshops. And jewelry shop after jewelry shop. Father Lorenzo put on his sunglasses as he looked in awe over the displays of rings, bracelets, necklaces, earrings, brooches, pendants and cufflinks and then all the gold and silver vases, bookmarks, knives, pens, trays, boxes, picture frames, candlesticks, cups, bowls and tea sets.

"Caterina would love one of those necklaces," he thought. "She'd also like a decent meal."

This wasn't what he was looking for. Victoria said she had three designers and they made simple necklaces and rings. He almost walked past the door between a bookstore and a women's fashion boutique before he noticed the small white card in the window. "Victoria's."

At midmorning, no one seemed to be inside. He walked down the street and returned. Still no one. He walked the other way and returned. He walked across the street, back to the Arc d'Augusto and returned.

He was about to leave when the door opened.

"Lorenzo? I thought I saw you walking back and forth outside. Come in!"

Chapter Ten

Large posters of jewels and stones decorated the tiny office in the back of the jewelry shop. Victoria's round mahogany desk was bare except for a file folder and pen. She again wore green, a suit with a low-cut white blouse. The ruby necklace remained in place.

"Lorenzo! How lovely to see you again. I wondered if you'd ever come to Rimini. Are you here on vacation?" She stretched out a hand. He thought she seemed pleased, though of course she was surprised.

"Um, yes." He was stuttering.

"That's wonderful. Did you have a nice trip? The trains can be so crowded this time of year."

"It was fine."

"I can't believe you're here." She seemed nervous as she straightened the folder on her desk. "Oh my, we've got to catch up. Let me think. Can we have dinner tonight? I've got so much to do here this afternoon."

"You sure you're not busy?"

"No, no. I can easily change some plans. OK?"

"Um, yes."

"Super! I know a little place on Via Carlo Cattaneo. It's called Luigi's. You'll like it. 8 o'clock?"

"Sure."

"Great. I'll see you then."

She smiled. He needed to get out of there, fast.

So much for waiting until the end of the week. Maybe it was better this way. He'd get it out of the way tonight and then be free for the rest of the week. But maybe he'd better find the restaurant so he wouldn't get lost tonight. He asked directions from an elderly gentleman and walked over to Via Carlo Cattaneo. Luigi's was simple and elegant, the kind of *trattoria* Victoria would like.

44

He could have walked around Rimini, visiting the monuments that he wasn't interested in when he was in fifth grade and cared even less about now. He could have gone back to his room, changed into his swimming trunks and gone to the beach. But the sun was hot and he didn't feel like looking at half-naked bodies.

Instead, he returned to his room, reciting his speech all along the way. "I'm going to go there tonight and tell her it was all a mistake. I'm sorry if I led her on. I don't know why I did that. It was stupid. I'm a priest. I can't get involved with women. I've taken a vow of chastity. And I've got responsibilities in Florence. I've got to run the soup kitchen. I'm forty-three years old. And a priest. She should know the truth. Nothing is going to come of this."

He picked up *Bread and Wine* again, but couldn't get past the second page. He lay on the bed and counted the cracks on the ceiling. Maybe he could catch up on the sleep he missed last night. Sunlight made that impossible at first, but then he fell into a deep and dark slumber with only one dramatic dream in which he ran and ran and ran through the streets of Rimini, chased by a mother and a boy who looked like Pietro.

When he awoke, the sun was so faint that he had to switch on the light to see his watch.

"Damn!"

It was 7:55, and he was supposed to be on Via Carlo Cattaneo in five minutes.

He hurriedly changed into a fresh shirt, splashed water on his face, brushed his teeth and ran out the door. And ran like he had just run in his dream. All the way to the Arc d'Augusto, where he looked at his watch again and found that it was 8:30. "Damn!"

In front of the arch, the same little boy was begging for money again. "*Lire* for food? *Lire* for food?"

Not one person in the crowd responded and most of the people brushed past him. The boy was invisible. He ran back to his mother and buried his head in her skirts. She patted him on the head, then stood up and stalked into the street. "Look!" she cried. "My son and I haven't eaten a decent meal for three days. How can you refuse us? How can you refuse us?"

Her tears were more in anger than in bitterness, but her pleas brought no responses from the shoppers who ignored her.

Incensed, Father Lorenzo instinctively went over to help the poor woman. Then he stopped. What was he thinking? He was a half-hour late to give the most important speech of his life. What if Victoria had already left the restaurant?

He threw some coins at the woman, still reciting in his head, "It was all a mistake. I should have told her. I'm a priest. She has to know." Father Lorenzo rushed under the arch and found Via Carlo Cattaneo and Luigi's again. Victoria was seated at a table in the back, attempting to read a book under the table's dim candlelight. She wore a low-cut green print dress, the ruby necklace resting in the curvature of her breasts.

"Lorenzo! I thought for a minute you stood me up." She held on to his hand. "But I knew you wouldn't. Did you have trouble finding this place?"

"Yes. It took a while." One lie after another after another. When would he stop?

"Well, I'm just pleased that you're here. I didn't mind waiting. I carry this great novel around, *The Great Gatsby*. This is the third time I've read it. It's so sad. I just love Fitzgerald. Have you read it?"

"No. I haven't read many American novels. None, in fact." Her perfume was breathtaking, her smile even more so.

"That's a shame. But you have such wonderful writers in Italy. I'm still getting to know them."

"I haven't read many of them, either. Victoria, there's something I want..."

"*Buonasera*, Signorina Stonehill, Signor. Welcome to Luigi's."

Damn. Father Lorenzo hadn't noticed the waiter standing at his side.

Victoria smiled. "*Buonasera*, Marcello. It's good to see you again. This is my friend, Lorenzo."

"You have a lovely dinner companion, Signor."

Father Lorenzo looked down at the wine list. "Yes. Yes, I know."

"Now," the waiter said, "may I bring you a glass of our house wine?"

"No, no," Victoria said. "Tonight is special. The *Brunello di Montalcino*, please."

"Excellent."

When the waiter had left, Father Lorenzo tried again. "Victoria, there's something…"

But she reached over and put her hand on his. "Lorenzo, I can't believe you're here. This is so wonderful. I didn't think I'd ever see you again."

"Well, here I am."

"When I didn't see you the day after the reception, I thought you might be upset with me, something I said, or something."

"Upset? No, Victoria! I had to return to Florence. How could I be upset with you?"

"I'm so glad. That was a lovely dinner, wasn't it? Your mother was so pleased. When I told her the next day that I met you, she seemed so delighted. She said she hoped we would be friends." Victoria squeezed his hand. "I hope so, too."

Only two other tables, on the far side of the room, were occupied. Soft music—Scarlatti?—played through hidden loudspeakers. Ornate frames on the red velvet walls held elaborate landscapes of the Tuscan countryside.

"Victoria, there's something…"

"Because," she said, "when we talked that night, you seemed so interested in me. You asked so many questions. I've met so many Italian men who are so wrapped up in themselves that they aren't interested in anyone else. Not to mention the Italian men who are wrapped up in their mothers."

"Well, I'm not, as you can tell."

"Yes. And I love that." That dazzling smile again.

"Victoria…"

"I'm glad you're calling me Victoria. Some people think they can call me Vicki, and I hate it. Sounds like I'm twelve years old."

"Victoria…Victoria…" He looked around. "I think…I think this is a very nice *trattoria*."

Damn. Well, he might as well enjoy the dinner. *Brunello di Montalcino*. He hadn't had that in years. Then one fish dish after another: shrimp, salmon, sea snails served with Rimini's famous focaccia bread, *piadina romagnola*. Then homemade *tagliatelle* and the main course, a lobster, *langoustine*, roasted with onions and yellow bell pepper. Father Lorenzo hadn't had such a feast since he was a boy at Palazzo Murano.

Then he again thought of the soup kitchen, of Dino and Caterina and Pietro. He needed to get back there. But, mesmerized by the beauty, the laughter and the smiles of the woman across the table, he couldn't concentrate on anything. Then as they were sharing a slice of tiramisu layer cake, he put down his fork.

"Victoria…"

"Lorenzo, guess what?" Victoria said. "I'm taking tomorrow off. I've already told Annabella and Mia. They can take care of the shop. We'll go to the beach, OK?"

"Well…"

"It's supposed to be a lovely day, not so hot. We'll go to Maramare. That beach won't be so crowded."

"Are you sure you can take the day off?"

"Of course. I own the place, remember?"

"OK. All right." He would tell her tomorrow.

Unsteady either from the wine or her company, he helped her from her chair. Perhaps he shouldn't have had so much *Brunello di Montalcino.*

Her apartment was only a few streets away. Rowdy young people, now singing loudly and drinking openly, still jammed the area, and Father Lorenzo put his hand on Victoria's back to guide her through the crowds. When they reached her door, both were a little out of breath.

"Whew!" she said. "Sometimes it's not safe here."

"And they say Florence is rowdy."

"Thanks for walking me home." She took both of his hands in hers.

"Thank you for a great evening."

Another awkward moment, resolved when Victoria kissed him on the cheek. "I'll see you tomorrow. About 11 o'clock? At Maramare."

"Yes."

Chapter Eleven

On the way back to his *pensione*, Father Lorenzo counted the times Victoria had flashed her dazzling smile or crinkled her eyes or laughed out loud. Each time, he melted like a fourteen-year-old on a first date. He remembered each time she held his hand and, especially, the kiss on his cheek. What was he doing? Well, as soon as he told her he was a priest, it would all be resolved. And he would tell her tomorrow.

When he passed through the Arc d'Augusto, he was certain that the mother and son would have gone home by now. He was wrong. The mother slept fitfully on the grass next to a bench, with her son almost concealed by her skirts.

"Good God. They don't even have a place to go at night."

At the *pensione*, Father Lorenzo knelt briefly in prayer by his bed but decided he was too confused to concentrate. He threw his clothes on the floor and crawled into bed. The dreams this time were different, something about getting violently sick over the *langoustine* and having to be helped by a beautiful woman in a green print dress.

When he awoke, it was already 9 o'clock. Only two more hours. He should get ready for the beach. Donning his swim trunks, he looked in the mirror. "Who is this guy?" he thought again. The main impression was that he was awfully white. He had to admit, though, that he didn't look bad for a forty-three-year-old, even with flecks of white dotting his chest and with his belly starting to show signs of too much Tuscan soup. He pulled on a flowered shirt and his Franciscan sandals. "Nobody will ever know where I got these."

At the *bar* across the street he read more news about soccer in *La Gazzetta dello Sport* than he cared to know and took his time choosing a pastry. This time, the raspberry. After getting conflicting directions from three shopkeepers who should have known the way, he found the beach called Maramare.

"If this beach isn't crowded today, I'd hate to see it when it really is."

He started to make his way through the rows and rows of deck chairs, each occupied by a tanned or scorched person who should have been wearing more clothes. Boisterous children ran back and forth, throwing balls or chasing each other. How could he ever find her? After forty-five minutes, he was ready to go home. "I can call her tomorrow. I'll tell her then."

"Lorenzo! Over here!"

She was standing with a tall man near two empty deck chairs in the third row from the edge of the beach. Father Lorenzo blinked and headed her way. Like every other woman on the beach, many of whom should have known better, Victoria wore a bikini. A light green bikini that barely covered her breasts and lower regions. Since Father Lorenzo hadn't been to a beach in years, he had forgotten the feats of engineering involved in putting together these bits of cloth and strings.

With a daily visit to the beach, Victoria was uniformly tanned. She was also glowing.

"*Buongiorno*, Lorenzo. Isn't this beach great! Oh, sorry. This is Fabiano. He's in charge of the beach and a good friend."

"*Buongiorno*, Signor Lorenzo." Fabiano stretched out a hand. He was middle aged, bronzed and with dark hair. "You have a lovely day for the beach."

"Yes. Yes, I know." Why did Fabiano seem to be inspecting him?

"Thanks for saving the deck chairs, Fabiano," Victoria said. "See you later."

Father Lorenzo wondered if she kissed every man on the cheek.

As they settled into the two chairs, he was pleased that Victoria was wearing sunglasses. Maybe she wouldn't notice that he was staring.

"That's a lovely shirt, Lorenzo, but take it off and sit down."

Reluctantly, Father Lorenzo took off his shirt. "A lot of people here."

"Yes. Good heavens, you're white. You're going to get burned."

"I can put my shirt back on."

"Don't be silly. I've got some suntan oil right here." She rummaged in a big canvas bag and found the bottle. "Here. I'll do it."

Father Lorenzo's face turned as red as the arms of the pudgy woman on the next deck chair. "Wait. I can do it." He pulled the bottle away and made a few swipes across his chest.

"Then let me do your back at least. Turn around."

Her hands were cool but firm as she massaged the oil onto his shoulders and back. When her hands got too low, he pulled back. "That's fine. I can do the rest. Thanks."

"This is where I met Bernardo," Victoria said as she put the bottle back into her bag. "Right over there."

"Does that make you sad?"

"No, not sad. Maybe just a little wistful."

"For?"

"For the years that have gone by. I'm not getting any younger, and for a woman, it's pretty discouraging to be looking at forty in a couple of years and still be single."

"Forty's not bad."

"For a woman it is." She lay back on the chair.

He couldn't tell if she could see him absorbed in her breasts, the taut belly, the firm hips. He remembered one of his professors in the seminary telling him that whenever he saw a beautiful woman he should thank God for creating her.

But prayers to God weren't on his mind now. He had not felt this way since…since whoever that last woman was in Siena years ago. No, this was different. He'd had no feelings for any of those women in Siena. He looked at the woman lying next to him and tried to figure out what his feelings for her were. He knew he was in dangerous territory, but he also knew that she was certainly beautiful. He leaned back. Thank you, God.

"Lorenzo," she said, "I still can't believe you're here. Are you on vacation?"

"Vacation? Well, yes, sort of."

"Things are slow now at your…your whatever it is you do?"

"Um, yes." Lies, lies, lies.

"Lorenzo, you really are mysterious."

He had to change the subject. "But the jewelry shop? Isn't that busy now in summer with all these tourists?"

Victoria laughed, a deep throat-catching laugh that he had come to love. "Busy? This is our worst time of year. Those tourists are mostly twenty-year-olds who don't have any money but think they can come into the shop and handle the merchandise. We've learned to padlock all the cases, and Annabella and Mia stand guard."

"Has anyone taken anything?"

She laughed again. "A month ago, Annabella saw this kid swipe a bracelet out of a display case we thought was locked. Now Annabella is not a small woman, and she chased the kid out into the street, knocked him down and sat on him until the *carabinieri* came. The word must have spread because there haven't been any attempts after that."

"Think the kid may have been poor and needed the money for food?"

"Lorenzo, Lorenzo, always thinking about the poor. No, this was a rich kid from Bologna who needed the money for his habit."

For a long time, they lay there, engulfed by the rancid smells of the Adriatic and the cries of children as they ran between, around and sometimes on top of the sunbathers. He closed his eyes to the teenagers kissing and clutching in tight embraces wherever he looked. When he opened his eyes, he saw a little boy digging under his chair.

"Sorry, Signor. I lost my ball."

"That's OK."

The boy's mother suddenly appeared at his side. "Filippo! Don't bother the nice man. Come play with your sister."

"Yes, Mama."

As the boy ran away, Father Lorenzo thought of Pietro and the boy at the Arc d'Augusto.

Chapter Twelve

Throughout the afternoon Father Lorenzo studiously avoided making his speech as Victoria told stories about her life in Rimini, her friends and her trips. It was a life far different from his own, and he was fascinated.

When they finally left the beach they found a crowded and overpriced pizza place and he walked her home. She planted another brief kiss on his cheek before it started to rain.

"Victoria…"

"I've had a lovely day, Lorenzo. See you tomorrow? Same beach, same time?"

"Sure."

It was raining harder now, and he hurried back to the *pensione*, dismayed when he found the beggar woman and her son sleeping under the stone bench. He found some newspapers and covered them as best he could.

What am I doing? he thought. Why didn't I tell her when I had the chance? I need to get back to Florence, to Caterina and Pietro. Now.

Back in his room, he peeled off his wet shirt and this time vowed to make a better effort at praying. Although he said his required priestly prayers daily, he was never very good at praying. His mind would wander and he couldn't focus on the words, much less their meaning. Father Alphonsus kept telling him not to worry about it. "Just have a conversation with God." But that was difficult, too, because it was always a one-sided conversation.

He dug out his rosary again, wooden beads he received at his ordination, and knelt by the bed.

"I may look silly kneeling here in my swim trunks, God, but I'm sincere nevertheless."

I believe in God, the Father almighty, creator of heaven and earth....

I do believe. Where would I be if I didn't believe in Your almighty presence guiding our world? I don't understand so many things in my life, but I have to trust You.

Our Father, who art in Heaven, Hallowed be thy name.

Father, I'm a priest. I'm not supposed to have these feelings. What am I doing? I'm getting deeper and deeper. Help me. Please.

Thy Kingdom come, thy will be done, on earth as it is in heaven .

I need to go back to Florence, and I need to go back to the soup kitchen. *Thy will be done.* Pietro and Caterina. Angelo and Salvatore. Guido and Francesco and Mateo. The poor people need my help. And here I am in this degenerate place, filled with sex and orgies. And I'm attracted to this beautiful woman.

Give us this day our daily bread. And forgive us our trespasses, as we forgive those who trespass against us.

But you made Victoria. You made her beautiful. Is it a sin to be attracted to beauty? My head is spinning. I don't know what to do, but I know I've never felt about any woman the way I do about Victoria.

And lead us not into temptation, but deliver us from evil.

I'm being tempted, God. She's so beautiful. I want her. I need her. I need someone in my life. I'm not close to anyone. No one. I've been alone for so long.

Having completed the rosary, more or less, he dug out the worn prayer card of Saint Francis that he kept in his wallet. He had long known the words by heart, but he liked to look at the painting of the holy saint.

O Divine Master,
grant that I may not so much seek to be consoled as to console;
to be understood, as to understand;
to be loved, as to love;
for it is in giving that we receive,
it is in pardoning that we are pardoned,
and it is in dying that we are born to Eternal Life.

Father Lorenzo put the rosary back in his suitcase and the prayer card in his wallet. Although the room was still hot and sultry, his body shivered under the thin sheet. He stared at the buxom woman on the wall.

He had never had good relationships with women. Unlike most Italian men, he wasn't devoted to his mother and they grew further apart over the years. Maria-Teresa and Patrizia were juvenile infatuations, and the women in his life later held no long-lasting attraction. As intriguing as they were, he found women too complex and complicated for him to understand. He was often pleased that the priesthood gave him an excuse for not getting involved.

But he was still a man, in fact, a good-looking man with dark curly hair, brilliant blue eyes and a ready grin. In his first assignment, as an assistant at Santa Croce, he had been tempted by women who ignored his Franciscan robes—or thought there was something erotic by getting involved with a priest. He returned their smiles and jokes until his superiors realized what was happening and gave him the job in the soup kitchen. Pretty young girls, they reasoned correctly, would not volunteer to help poor people.

There was, however, one volunteer, Amelia, who boldly flirted with him and he often laughed and teased with her. When things got dangerous, he told her she should volunteer someplace else. Another volunteer, Natalia, kept finding excuses to stand next to him in the serving line until he realized she needed professional help and he found a psychologist for her. A young office worker, Fredericka, came to his morning Mass every day and afterwards found some reason to talk. She wore low-cut dresses and too much perfume. He couldn't tell her not to come to Mass, but found an excuse to run off without a conversation.

But Victoria? Victoria was different. He didn't want to think where this was going to lead. Or if.

Chapter Thirteen

The following morning, Father Lorenzo didn't even look at *La Gazzetta dello Sport* at the *bar* and he wolfed down his apple pastry. At the Arc d'Augusto, he threw the little boy some *lire* and rushed on. He found Victoria in the same place at the beach.

But sitting next to her was Fabiano. Father Lorenzo noticed that Fabiano's swimsuit was considerably smaller than his.

"Lorenzo!" Victoria cried. "Another beautiful day here. You remember Fabiano."

"Yes, of course."

Fabiano shook Father Lorenzo's hand and the priest again felt as if he was undergoing an inspection.

"Well, you two have a good day," Fabiano said. "See you soon, Victoria."

"Yes." She kissed him on the cheeks again.

Father Lorenzo wanted to ask Victoria about any possible relationship she had with this handsome beach manager, but he didn't want to know the answer.

"You look terrific," he said, as he slid into the chair next to her.

"Better put more suntan oil on, Lorenzo. Your face looks pretty red."

They sat close to each other on their deck chairs, and he resisted the temptation to reach over and hold her hand. Instead, he talked about the sun already beating down so early in the morning, the teenagers necking nearby, the kids kicking up sand. And the music playing from portable radios. It was so noisy that he knew this was not a place to tell Victoria anything important. It would have to wait.

For her part, Victoria talked about the books she'd read and the movies she'd seen—he could contribute nothing to this—and about her recent trip to Paris.

"My girlfriend and I just decided to go. I'd been there before, of course, but she hadn't, so we went to all the tourist things, the Louvre, the Musee d'Orsay, Notre Dame. We climbed to the top of the Eiffel Tower, we went to the opera, we walked along the Seine, we ate on the Left Bank. All this in three days! It was so much fun!"

Fun? Father Lorenzo couldn't remember the last time he had fun. During his decadent days, he and some other guys from the *osteria* had gone to Greece for five days, but it was only a distant memory.

"I loved being a kid in New York," she said. "My nanny would take me to Central Park and I'd run all over. My mother took me to museums and matinees of Broadway shows..."

Father Lorenzo had forgotten the last play he'd seen.

"...but this was during the war. We had a few air raids, but I never felt threatened."

"We had more than air raids, I'm afraid. It was just my mother and my brother and me holed up in Palazzo Murano. We ran out of food sometimes, but it wasn't bad. My father was off fighting for the Fascists. And then he was killed."

"Your father was killed in the war?"

"Yes."

"Oh, Lorenzo, I'm so sorry."

"I never really knew him. He was always away. My brother and I heard some rumors that he had various mistresses, but we didn't want to believe them. My mother went her own way."

They lay in silence for a long time.

"Siena didn't suffer much damage," Father Lorenzo said, "but the Nazis occupied Florence. They declared it an open city, but that didn't prevent them from carting a lot of artworks away and destroying the bridges."

"Poor, poor Florence."

"It recovered from the war, but the flood was devastating."

"But it's recovered from that, too, hasn't it? Every time I go there it seems like it has. It's been, what, eight years?"

He turned on his side so that he could talk to her, as well as see her better. "It might look good on the surface. The museums are open, and most of the churches. The tourists are back. But there's still a lot of restoration of artworks to be done, and they may never finish restoring all the books from the National Library."

Victoria sat up and poured more suntan oil on her arms. "I was in Verona then and I kept reading how awful it was, and I was watching it on television. I started to cry when I saw all those beautiful things damaged."

Father Lorenzo's voice turned harder. "Florence isn't just art, you know, Victoria. Sure, at Santa Croce, where I live, a lot of homes have been repaired and restored. But there are still many, many people without jobs and many who still need clothing, food, the basics. They're so poor, Victoria, they're so poor. I always say they're the other side of Florence, the one that tourists don't see."

She held his arm. "Don't get upset, Lorenzo. I'm sure you are helping them a lot."

"Not enough! There's so much to do." The people on the other deck chairs stared at him. "I do get upset. I get so frustrated sometimes."

"I'm so sorry."

"And nobody seems to care anymore! The tourists don't. They don't even know. They just visit the museums and the churches and walk right past all the poor people, the ones who are begging."

"Oh, Lorenzo."

"What the hell…"

He lay back down on the deck chair and the people on the other deck chairs went back to sleep.

Victoria started to say something, but then folded her hands over her stomach and closed her eyes. He was grateful for her silence. He didn't want to continue this conversation.

They lay still, letting the sun's rays penetrate their bodies. Victoria was becoming even more tan while Father Lorenzo's legs, arms and chest were turning bright pink.

Over dinner at another quiet *trattoria*, they told little jokes and Father Lorenzo realized he had not laughed for so long or so often in a long time. Once, instinctively, he reached for her hand across the table, but she pulled it away.

Over a loudspeaker, a classical guitarist was playing Monteverdi, and Father Lorenzo confessed that he liked to play the guitar and used to play the Beatles but wasn't very good.

"I don't really like the Beatles, but I bet you're wonderful, Lorenzo. Better than me, at least. I took piano lessons for three years and my parents finally gave up."

"When I sing, people run out of the soup kitchen."

"Soup kitchen? Is that one of your projects?"

"Sort of."

Lies, lies, lies. When would he stop?

"Lorenzo!" she suddenly cried. "Let's go dancing!"

"Dancing? Me?"

He hadn't danced for more years than he could remember and he was never good at it, adopting a one-two step for all purposes.

"Oh, come on. It'll be fun."

There were dozens, maybe hundreds, of discos to choose from along the coast, but swinging youngsters packed most of them. Victoria walked him to a club away from the beach where a small combo played more melodic tunes. Father Lorenzo attempted a tango. Too complicated. A fox trot. His feet got twisted. A rumba. His hips got sore. Finally a waltz. He didn't step on her feet too often, and she guided him smoothly around the floor.

"You're a great dancer," he said, trying to talk and count at the same time.

"I have to go out with my girlfriends because I can't find a guy to dance with me. What's with Italian guys and dancing? Are they afraid?"

"Maybe Italian guys just like to hold women, not move them around to music."

"Not good enough, Lorenzo. Anyway, you're not half bad."

"I think that's a compliment."

"It is."

He held her close and her breasts felt soft against his chest. He suddenly pulled away.

"Victoria?"

"Yes?"

"Victoria?"

"Yes?"

"You know something?" he stumbled. "You're quite amazing."

She looked up and smiled. "You are, too."

At her doorstep that night, she kissed him quickly on the cheek and flashed her dazzling smile again.

"Tomorrow?" she asked.

"Of course."

"Let's not go to the beach tomorrow. Let me show you Rimini. Meet me at the shop. I've got a few things to do and then I'll have the whole day free."

That night, Father Lorenzo said the prayer of Saint Francis but didn't take out his rosary. "I'm too tired," he said to himself. "No use trying to pray if I just botch it up."

He got into bed and soon began imagining lying in bed with Victoria, her hands across his chest. He threw off the thin sheet and raced to the lavatory down the hall. He splashed cold water on his face and studied himself in the mirror. His face, besides being sunburned, looked very, very tired.

"What am I doing? Where is this going to lead?"

Chapter Fourteen

The next morning, he was on the beach just as the sun rose. Except for flocks of seagulls and old men salvaging for coins, the beach was almost deserted at this hour. The sun barely rose from the horizon. He took off his sandals and plodded along in the sand.

"What am I doing? I'm a priest. I've taken a vow of chastity."

He knew what the Franciscan order said:

"In chastity a Franciscan not only renounces the goods of marriage, but also promises to avoid all familiarity with women, as well as every interior and exterior act which is against virginal purity. By this vow the Franciscan religious, while on earth, takes on the angelic life of purity which is the life of all the saints in Heaven."

He had already disobeyed part of the rule. *"Promises to avoid all familiarity with women."* It wouldn't be hard to violate the rest.

Then he thought of Caterina and Pietro and Angelo and Salvatore and Emilio and his dog Fico and all the others at the soup kitchen. The first volunteers would be getting things ready even though the meal was hours away. He missed the volunteers, but mostly he missed the people who came in every day for what for many was their only meal of the day.

All right. He would spend one more day with Victoria. Tonight he would tell her the truth, and tomorrow he would head back to Florence. Father Alphonsus might be surprised that he returned early, but he could explain.

But bringing her a few flowers would be OK. On the way to Victoria's, he stopped at a flower shop, hoping it wasn't the one owned by her former lover. He hadn't been in a flower shop in years and didn't remember ever bringing flowers to a woman. Fingering the *lire* in his wallet, he decided to take the chrysanthemums over the red roses.

At the Arc d'Augusto, he gave some coins to the boy and

spontaneously pulled out one of the chrysanthemums and handed it to his mother. The woman was so surprised she started weeping.

"*Grazie*," she said.

"God bless you."

Father Lorenzo hurried on, carrying the remaining flowers.

"They're beautiful," Victoria said, kissing him on the cheek when he entered her shop. "Thank you!"

"You're welcome."

"I'll just move these a little." She put them next to an enormous vase of red roses, obviously just received as well. Father Lorenzo couldn't help but think of Fabiano.

"So what would you like to do today? We could visit some churches, but they're all pretty ugly, if you ask me. Are you interested in churches?"

"No, not particularly," he said.

"I'm not either. Well, everything in Rimini starts at the Piazza Tre Martiri. Let's start there."

They walked down Via Giuseppe Garibaldi until they reached Corso d'Augusto. At this time of day the piazza was filled with tourists looking for bargains in the shops and perhaps delaying the sun-scorched beach for a few hours more.

"This is the site of the old Roman forum," Victoria said. "This is where Julius Caesar is supposed to have given his famous speech to his soldiers after crossing the Rubicon."

"Wish I could remember the speech," Father Lorenzo said. "Never was very good at Roman history."

"Italians have so much more history to learn than Americans," Victoria said.

"Why is this piazza dedicated to three martyrs?" he asked. "People like Saint Paul, Saint Peter, Saint Sebastian?"

Victoria laughed. "Lorenzo, you sound like someone who knows Catholic history at least."

"No, no. Hardly know it at all." More lies.

"Well," Victoria said, "these weren't Christian martyrs at all. From the stories I've heard, this happened in the summer of 1944. The Germans still occupied this territory, and partisans were attempting to sabotage them. They especially wanted to stop grain from being shipped to Germany.

"So three young partisans sabotaged a threshing machine just outside Rimini. The Germans caught them, put them in prison and then hanged them right over there."

She led him to a street called Via IV Novembre and pointed to a plaque. "See the three nooses? And right here, this marker? That's where the scaffolding was."

Father Lorenzo took her hand. When she closed her eyes, he said a silent prayer.

"Well," Victoria said, "let's find something a little more cheerful. We could go to the amphitheater. That's from the second century. Or the Palazzo dell'Arengo e del Podestà. That's from the thirteenth century. Or Tempio Malatestiano. Thirteenth century."

"You know," he said, "when I think of Rimini I think of Saint Anthony."

"Saint Anthony? Good heavens, why?"

"There's a legend that he came to Rimini and wanted to preach to a bunch of heretics but they wouldn't listen to him. So he went to the seashore and he started preaching to the fishes and they all came up with their heads out of the water and they formed perfect lines and they listened to him."

Victoria laughed. "Lorenzo! That's the funniest story I've ever heard! The little fishies listened to Saint Anthony?"

"Well, that's the legend. I guess it does sound kind of ridiculous." He was sorry he brought it up. "So what else is Rimini famous for?"

"Fellini!" she cried. "Are you a big fan? He was born here, you know. He went to school here, he saw his first movies here."

"I don't go to the cinema very often," Father Lorenzo said. "I guess I've been too busy."

"Right. The soup kitchen. Since I've been here, I've become obsessed with Fellini. I forget about his membership in a Fascist youth group when he was a kid. But you know, he started out wanting to draw cartoons, and he wrote his first humorous article for our local newspaper, *Domenica del Corriere*."

She was so excited that she started talking fast.

"Mostly, though, I'm fascinated that he used Rimini in so many of his films. There was a giant fish marooned on the beach here—no, not one of Saint Anthony's fishes—and that was the basis for the sea creature found on the beach at the end of *La Dolce Vita,* one of my all-time favorite movies."

"I saw that!" Father Lorenzo was pleased to make a contribution to the conversation. "I was in the sem…college…at the time and a few of us went." He didn't add that the rector of the seminary was quite displeased that his students would go to such a blasphemous film.

"And there's a scene in *Amarcord* that was shot right here in this piazza. There are some streets of Rimini in *I Vitelloni.* It's very exciting. Every time I see a Fellini film I walk to the area where it was shot, just to pay homage. I love Fellini!"

Father Lorenzo had heard of these films, but hadn't seen them. He kept that to himself.

"I guess I should get out more often." He was starting to feel uncomfortable. Victoria led a life far different than his own. He had more in common with the people at the soup kitchen than he did with Victoria.

"Think we can find a place to just sit?" he asked.

"Marecchia Park! It's huge. We can find a place that's quiet."

They walked up Via Marecchiese to Via Nuova Circonvallazione. Along the way, they stopped to pick up a loaf of crusty bread, a slab of cheese, a couple of apples and a bottle of red wine.

The tourists hadn't discovered the park, or perhaps they thought watching seagulls was too boring. On this sultry afternoon, a dozen mothers guarded small children and a few elderly men and women drowsed on benches.

"Look at that couple over there," Victoria said. The man, grizzled with a hat pulled down over his eyes, held the hand of a woman who was reading a newspaper aloud to him. "Isn't that sweet? Every time I come here, they're on the same bench and she's reading to him. I think he may be blind."

"Sometimes a man needs a good woman to help him," Father Lorenzo said. He wondered if he was talking about himself and didn't want to admit it.

"Yes," she said, smiling again.

She led him to a small lake where the only inhabitants were flocks and flocks of seagulls.

"Let's see if I can find him." Victoria crept to the edge of the water. Some seagulls fluttered and some flew off, but a couple of dozen stayed.

"He's here," she whispered. "Come see."

He crawled next to her. "What? Who?"

"That little white bird over there."

"Victoria, they're all white."

"No, the small one swimming by himself. See? He has a black mark on the back of his tail. His name is Nero."

"Really? He told you that?"

"No, silly. I named him. He's my friend. He's here all the time."

She dug into the brown sack and broke off a chunk of bread. "Now watch when I throw this at him. All those other guys are going to want some, too, but watch what he does."

The other birds swooped down on Nero, biting and scratching him. He fought right back, screeching and fighting and fending them off.

"Feisty little guy, isn't he?" Victoria said. "I love him."

"Seems like he can take care of himself."

"I look at him and I think how I take care of myself, too."

"I've always thought that I could, too," Father Lorenzo said.

"Doesn't that get kind of lonely?"

"Yes."

They sat on the grass and munched their food, then lay back and let the sun wash over them. An hour later, they were surprised that they had dozed off. As they left the park, a thin elderly man, on crutches and wearing a tattered coat, stopped them.

"*Lire?*" He had his hand out.

As Victoria watched, Father Lorenzo dug into his pocket for some coins and then whispered something in the man's ear. The man nodded. Father Lorenzo said something else and the man wiped away tears. Father Lorenzo put his arm around the man and the man's shoulders shook.

Victoria took Father Lorenzo's hand when he returned.

"Lorenzo, that was so kind. There are so many beggars now in Rimini and the city says we shouldn't give them money because that only encourages them. They're supposed to get jobs."

"And how the hell is this guy supposed to get a job when he's on crutches?"

"People say beggars just pretend they have disabilities."

"Yeah, they say that in Florence, too. Bastards."

She gripped his hand tighter. "I wish I had the courage to do what you just did. I'm afraid I don't."

"It doesn't take much courage to say a few kind words."

She smiled her gorgeous smile and hugged him. "Come on, let's get something to eat. I know a good place near here."

They walked silently back to the heart of Rimini. Father Lorenzo gradually cooled down, and over dinner, he realized that Victoria had not asked him any more questions about his life. Did she know what a fool and liar he was? He had to tell her.

"Victoria…"

"Lorenzo, let's go to a movie!"

Reluctantly, Father Lorenzo folded his napkin and helped Victoria get up from the table. They had only two choices. One theater was showing *The Way We Were*, starring Robert Redford.

"He's the sexiest man alive," Victoria said, squeezing Father Lorenzo's hand. "Present company excepted, of course."

Father Lorenzo ignored the compliment.

The other theater was having an Italian neorealist film festival, with *Umberto D* ready to begin.

"I've never seen that," he said, "but I've heard it's very sad."

"It is. But let's go anyway."

They sat silently through the film. Victoria suddenly became aware that tears were flowing down her companion's cheeks, and she reached over and held his hand. Father Lorenzo didn't withdraw his.

"Something wrong, Lorenzo?" she asked.

"No. It's nothing."

Afterwards, she couldn't help noticing that he seemed to be in a daze.

"Are you all right, Lorenzo?"

"What? I…it's just…it brought to mind…that old man in the movie…Victoria, we need to talk."

"Come up to my place. We can talk."

Chapter Fifteen

White. White walls, white ceiling, white furry rug on the floor. The only color, Botticelli's *Primavera* in a golden frame dominating one wall.

"Your apartment is…white," he said. Stupid comment.

"I like it. It's very peaceful. Grappa? Limoncello? Sambuca? Your choice." She draped her green scarf on the back of a white sofa.

"Maybe I'd better stick with coffee."

"Coffee it is." He lowered himself gingerly into a white chair, stared at the *Primavera* and folded and unfolded his hands while she worked in the kitchen.

"It's very quiet up here," he said when she returned with two white cups.

"Yes, that's why I chose the fourth floor."

"Have you lived here long?" God, what a dumb question.

"A few years. I lived closer to the shop before."

"This is a nice place."

"I like it."

All right. He could avoid it no longer. "Victoria?"

"Yes?"

"Victoria, there's something I've been trying to tell you all week."

"So tell me." She poured two spoons of sugar into her cup.

"Victoria…Victoria…I'm a priest. I'm a Franciscan priest."

She smiled, slowly, deliberately. "You know, Lorenzo, somehow I'm not surprised."

"Really? Why not?"

"I'm not sure. There were a few clues early. I saw that shaved spot on your head and I remembered that the priest who married Bernardo and me had one. But then I thought, well, maybe he's just getting bald."

"Not yet."

"And then when you talked about helping the poor, and when you got so upset talking about the flood, I thought, this isn't an ordinary guy, this is a pretty special guy. I wanted to get to know you more."

"Not very special since I haven't told you the truth until just now."

"And then, this afternoon, when you helped that old man in the park. And tonight, when you got upset at the movie. I guess I began to suspect something about you...."

"Why didn't you say something?"

"Well, I thought if you didn't want to tell me you are a priest there must be a reason. I like you too much, Lorenzo, to ask such a question."

"I've wanted to tell you, God knows. I don't know why I didn't that first night at my mother's reception. There was just something about you that didn't let me. You fascinated me so much. I had never met anyone like you. So I guess I wanted to pretend I was someone else. And then this pretense just kept growing and growing and I couldn't seem to stop it. After that night, when I didn't tell you anything on our walk to the parking lot or when we came back to your hotel, I knew I had to come here and explain."

"Lorenzo!" She seemed surprised. "Is that why you came to Rimini? Just to tell me that? You didn't have to, you know. You could have called on the telephone. Or written a letter. Or you could just have forgotten about me."

He could have said that Father Alphonsus had told him to come, but that was hardly the reason.

"Victoria, I couldn't forget about you. That was the problem. I just wanted to see you again, and I promised myself I would tell you everything. But once I got here, and we had that great dinner..."

"...with the *Brunello di Montalcino*."

"Yes. And the *langoustine*. And then I just couldn't say anything the next day at the beach or the next day or even today."

"Why not? We were alone together every day."

Father Lorenzo kept folding and unfolding his hands. "Victoria, I don't know. I wish I did. The truth is, I haven't been able to get you out of my mind. Before I met you, I was acting crazy at the soup kitchen in Florence. Yelling and cursing, mad at everyone. I guess it was because I was exhausted and overworked, like my superior said.

But since I met you I've also been acting crazy, but in a different way. I haven't been able to think straight.

"I've been planning to tell you all week, but today, when I saw that man at the park and then when we saw that movie with the old man and the dog, it reminded me so much of a man who comes to our soup kitchen, Emilio. He has a dog, too, just like Umberto in the movie. Victoria, I have to get back to the people who need me in Florence. I really want to, Victoria!"

"Lorenzo, you're amazing."

"Please. I'm not. I deceived you. That was cowardly and heartless of me."

"Lorenzo, you didn't deceive me. You just, well, you just didn't tell me everything. What I do know is this: You are the kindest, the most generous man I've ever met. Can you believe me?"

"I don't know, Victoria."

They sat in silence for a long time as their coffee got cold and the setting sun cast shadows on the white walls.

"Aren't you upset with me, Victoria?"

"Upset? Why should I be upset?"

"I lied to you!"

"Lorenzo, you've given me four days of wonderful companionship. I so enjoyed being with you. I don't know why you didn't tell me you're a priest. Only you can answer that. And I don't know why I didn't ask you specifically when I suspected it. I guess I didn't want to know. If you were a priest, I knew you would tell me eventually. Until then, I just wanted to be with you. To be your friend, to get to know more about you. That's all, really."

She leaned forward, and looked him in the eyes.

"Because you've taught me so much. Lorenzo, I wouldn't have known about the poor in Florence. My God, I don't even see the poor in Rimini. I wouldn't have even seen that man on crutches today if you hadn't helped him. I've been in my own little world, running the shop, going out with my friends and lying on the beach. I haven't seen what else is out there, who else is out there. You've opened my eyes, Lorenzo."

"You're quite a woman, Victoria."

She smiled. "Don't believe everything you hear."

He leaned forward and took her hands. "I'm sorry, Victoria."

"Don't be sorry, Lorenzo. You look so sad. Please, don't be. Be happy. OK?"

"I'll try." He could feel his eyes moisten and knew he had to get out of there. "Well, I'd better leave now."

"Back to Florence?"

"Yes. First thing tomorrow."

"And…"

"I don't know. I've got a lot of thinking to do."

"Lorenzo, may I say something? Remember Nero, the seagull at the park?"

"The little feisty one."

"Yes. He manages to take care of himself. I think you do, too."

"I always have. I guess I will from now on, too."

"Lorenzo, I'm sure you will. And those poor people at the soup kitchen will love you for it."

He turned to leave, then turned around. "Victoria, there's something I want to ask you."

"Go ahead."

"Fabiano. Is he…is he…?"

Victoria smiled. "Yes, we're dating. He's really wonderful, Lorenzo. I wish you could get to know him. He's kind and generous, not as much as you, but he tries. He sends me flowers most every day. But there's more than that. I've seen him with his workers on the beach and he's so kind to them. Too bad there's such a turnover, he's always looking for new people."

Lorenzo couldn't explain his feelings, which were very mixed, but he knew that envy was among them.

"Good-bye, Victoria."

"Thank you for a wonderful time, Lorenzo. I'll always remember it."

She stood up, took his hands, smiled her dazzling smile and kissed him. On both cheeks.

"Thank you, Victoria." He bent down and kissed the top of her red hair.

Lost in thought, his eyes moist, Father Lorenzo didn't see or hear the boisterous crowds as he walked through the streets of Rimini. When he arrived at Arc d'Augusto, he found the woman crouched on a bench, clutching the chrysanthemum and sobbing into her arms while her son tried to hug her.

Father Lorenzo moved closer. "Signora?"

No answer.

"Signora?"

She didn't look up, but whispered, "What do you want?"

"Can I help?"

"There's nothing you can do."

"Maybe if you tell me something, I might be able to help you."

Her voice was barely audible. "I have nothing, nothing. I don't have any money left. I don't have any food. I don't know how I'm going to feed Marcello here. We don't have a place to stay." She sobbed even harder.

Father Lorenzo knew he could give the woman some *lire*, but that would be only a temporary solution.

He sat down next to her. "Signora, may I ask how you came to these circumstances."

The woman wiped her nose on her sleeve. "I had a job in a laundry. And I was really, really good. I got the clothes so clean. Marcello helped me. I never missed a day. Not a single day. But then I got sick and I lost my job. And then I lost the rooms where Marcello and I lived. And now we've been here for weeks and nobody cares. You're the only one who has given us some *lire*, the only one. And this lovely flower." She tried to muffle her sobs.

"Your husband doesn't take care of you?"

"He left right after Marcello was born."

Father Lorenzo looked at the crowds rushing to the beach, ignoring the scene on the bench and all the other beggars. "Signora, would you be able to work again if you had a job?"

"Of course! I just don't know where to get one. I've tried. God, how I've tried."

"Would you wait here? Please?"

"Where else would I go?"

Bumping into people all along the way, Father Lorenzo raced back to Victoria's apartment and rang the bell.

"Lorenzo! What on earth?" She was already in her green print robe and her red hair hung down on her shoulders. She looked ravishing.

"Victoria," he said, "you said Fabiano needed people to work at the beach. If I send a woman I know over to him, would he talk to her?"

"Lorenzo! Of course he would. That's so kind of you! Thank you!"

Chapter Sixteen

The train deposited Father Lorenzo in Florence in midafternoon, and he went straight to Father Alphonsus' office. Holding a brandy glass in a shaking hand, the elderly priest was reading the latest copy of *L'Osservatore Romano*.

"Ah, Lorenzo, back already? Only four days? But thank you for saving me from more of the Vatican's latest diatribes." He folded the newspaper and dropped it into a wastebasket.

"Back, yes."

"Well, it looks like at least the sun agreed with you very much. It'll take weeks to get rid of that burn."

"It's starting to hurt."

"Well, I hope you've got rid of your other hurts. Brandy?"

"Of course."

They settled back in their chairs, warmed by the smooth liquor.

"You look exhausted, Lorenzo. Tell me about it."

"I think...well...can you put on your stole and can we do this as a confession?"

"That serious? Of course." He reached into a bottom drawer of his desk and pulled out a long purple cloth and draped it around his neck. "This stole will do. No need to go into the box in the church, unless you want to."

"This is fine."

They both made the sign of the cross and said, "In the name of the Father, and of the Son, and of the Holy Ghost."

"Go ahead, Lorenzo."

"Bless me, Father, for I have sinned."

There was a long silence. Father Alphonsus gently prodded him. "Go on, Lorenzo."

"Well, to begin with, I met this woman."

Silence.

"Go on."

And then, like a stream that gains power to become a mighty river, the story all came out, from the first awkward meeting at his mother's reception to the days at the beach and the park, to the dinners and the movie and the dancing...

"Dancing, Lorenzo? I'm impressed."

"Well, I don't know if I'd call what I did dancing."

Father Lorenzo sat back in his chair and closed his eyes. Father Alphonsus ran his finger around the rim of his brandy glass and stared at the Della Robbia on the wall.

"Quite a vacation, Lorenzo."

"Well, you told me to take one, Father."

"Yes, I did."

"But, Father, I've sinned."

"Really? When? Where? I've listened to your story, but I don't see much sinning there."

"Well, first, the lies. I never told her that I was a priest until yesterday. I had plenty of chances but I never told her. I don't know why. That's what I still can't figure out."

"Well, it seems pretty simple to me, Lorenzo. First, you were exhausted and frustrated here and you weren't yourself. You met a beautiful woman and you thought, subconsciously, I'm sure, that maybe you could be someone else for a while. Someone to stop you from worrying about the soup kitchen or the terrible demands of the poor. That's understandable."

"Sounds like a fourteen-year-old kid with fantasies, Father."

"We all have fantasies, Lorenzo. Life would be pretty dull without them."

"I'm really ashamed of making such a fool of myself."

"Did Victoria think you were a fool?"

"No, no. Quite the opposite. She seemed to understand completely."

"She sounds like quite a remarkable woman. No wonder you were attracted to her. But let's get beyond that. OK, you may not have told her the truth right away, but I don't think you were actually lying. You didn't pose as a rich banker from Siena, right?"

"No, that would be my brother."

"That would have been lying. So, if anything, it was a sin of omission, rather than commission, as they say. All right, what else?"

"Father, I took a vow of chastity. You know what the Franciscan vow is: 'to avoid all familiarity with women, as well as every interior and exterior act which is against virginal purity.' I know it by heart. Well, I certainly was familiar with Victoria."

"You had long talks."

"Yes."

"You went out to dinner and a movie."

"Yes."

"You went dancing."

"If you can call it that."

"Did you exchange passionate kisses, Lorenzo?"

"She gave me a kiss on the cheek every night."

Father Alphonsus tried not to smile. "Sounds pretty lascivious to me. And you? Did you kiss her, long and passionately?"

"I kissed the top of her head just before I left."

Now Father Alphonsus had to suppress the laughter that built in his stomach. "Lorenzo, you're a priest, but you're still a man. It sounds as though you acted like a man, maybe not a very mature man, but a man nevertheless."

"But Father, I wanted her. I wanted her sexually. I thought about her at night."

"And priests don't do that? Lorenzo, if I told you about the times I thought of a beautiful woman, well, I wouldn't have time to tell you about all of them. Look, let's just say that you did some sort of lying and you committed some form of lust. Nothing terribly serious, and I can't get too excited about these so-called sins, Lorenzo. Are they grievous? I don't know. Only God does. I've always hated the terms 'mortal' and 'venial' sin, as if we were choosing between a big black box and a little black box. There are probably a lot of middle-sized black boxes, and some huge boxes and little tiny boxes. But that's for God to decide. I think I need a cigar. You?"

"No, thanks."

Father Alphonsus opened the leather box on this desk and took out a *Toscano*.

"And Lorenzo, give yourself a little credit here," he said, lighting the cigar with a shaking hand. "You came back, right? That was a conscious decision. Why did you come back?"

"I wanted to come back to the *cusina populare*. I really did miss the people here. I realized it every day when I saw a woman and her boy begging. I couldn't help think of Caterina and Pietro. And when I saw an old man I thought of Emilio."

"Exactly. So at this moment at least, you chose the soup kitchen and all the poor people there, and priesthood, over Victoria Stonehill."

"Yes, and I'm sorry, I'm sorry for everything I did now."

"Ah, that's the key, Lorenzo. You're sorry."

Father Alphonsus put down the cigar, opened the tabernacle and removed the bottle of brandy. "Today, I'm going to have another. You?"

"Yes, I need it."

"Lorenzo, we also have to consider your state of mind. You know yourself that you haven't been the same person in the last months. You've been exhausted and frustrated and acting pretty crazy. Frankly, you've been a little off your rocker, if I may say that."

"You can say it."

"So it wasn't really Father Lorenzo the saint of the flood who was acting the way you did, it was some other Father Lorenzo that neither of us had ever met before. He was the one who went to Rimini and had long talks and lay on the beach and went dancing, right?"

"Right."

"Look, I believe in a loving God, a forgiving God, and I truly believe He knows what has been happening to you. And I know He forgives you."

Father Alphonsus adjusted his stole. "All right. Let's do it."

The elderly priest leaned forward and put his hand on Father Lorenzo's head. "Therefore, Lorenzo, through the ministry of the Church, may God give you pardon and peace, and I absolve you from your sins, in the name of the Father, and of the Son and of the Holy Ghost."

Father Lorenzo's eyes watered. Father Alphonsus put his hands on his shoulders. "It's all right, Lorenzo. We sin. We wouldn't be human if we did not. And we try to do better."

"So what happens now, Father?"

"I've been thinking about you, Lorenzo. And I think I know what's causing all this. I believe this all started long ago, when you were ordained. I call it the malady of the priesthood and it must be something in the oil they put on our heads."

"Malady?"

"You know as well as I do what this is, Lorenzo. The loneliness of the priesthood. God, every pop psychologist in the world has studied it. It doesn't happen all the time, and most of the time it's not serious. But in your case, it may have been more severe because from what you've said, you had a pretty lonely childhood to begin with."

"I know."

"So no matter that you were surrounded by hundreds of people, and you talked and laughed with them during the day, at night—8 o'clock, Lorenzo?—you went home to your empty room and went to bed and then the next day you got up and did it all over again. Not much of a life, is it?"

"I guess not."

"You know, as priests, we give up a close relationship with one person so that we can give ourselves to many. That's the nature of priesthood. But that doesn't prevent us from having friends, Lorenzo."

"Except that I don't have any."

"You've said that."

"And I don't know how to get friends. What do I do, go out in the piazza and yell out, 'Who wants to be my friend?'"

Father Alphonsus took a long sip of brandy. "It might not work quite that way. But while you were gone, I thought of a few things that you might try. There's a group, professional people, doctors, lawyers, low-level bureaucrats, who meet at a different home every month and make an excellent Tuscan meal. You like to cook, right?"

"I like to eat."

"That's enough of a qualification. Also, I've heard of a group that meets to watch documentaries about some of the smaller cities in Italy, and once a year they go to one of the places. They've been to Rivoli, Chioggia, Siena."

"Not Siena."

"Well, there are plenty of other places. And there's also a new group in the parish that somehow gets hold of old neorealist films from the 1950s, the classic ones, and they set up a projector and watch them and talk about them. Fellini, Rossellini, Visconti, De Sica."

"I don't think I could watch another De Sica film right now. Maybe not Fellini either."

"Well, I'll write out the names of these people and you can contact them. Will you?"

"Father, I don't know if I can take the time off."

"Lorenzo, Lorenzo. OK, I'll find someone to take over."

"Not Brother Andrea?"

Father Alphonsus sighed. "Ah, Brother Andrea. Well, Brother Andrea is no longer with us."

"He died?"

"No, no. But the rumors turned out to be true. He was caught fooling around with an altar boy in the back of the Pazzi Chapel. We packed him up and sent him to our nursing home for elderly priests in Urbino. I don't think he can do much harm with eighty-year-old priests."

"Oh. Poor Brother Andrea."

"Poor Brother Andrea? The little prick."

"Father Alphonsus!"

The old priest took one last puff from his cigar and put it out. "Lorenzo, not all stories have neat happy endings. It would be nice to say that you've solved all your problems. You know you haven't. But I think you've learned a lot about yourself in the last few days, with Victoria's help, and things aren't going to be the same, are they?"

"No, no, I don't think so."

"Good, now go back to your soup kitchen and help the poor and say Mass and celebrate the sacraments and be the good holy priest you've always been."

"That's it?"

"I think that's quite a lot, Lorenzo. Will you do it?"

"Yes. But Father, my penance?"

"Ah, yes, penance. Well, here's what you must do. You must go to the *cucina populare* every day, Monday through Friday."

"That's not a penance."

"But you will not go there on Saturday and Sunday. Instead, you will read books and go to movies and concerts and plays and you will meet new people and maybe join one of those groups I've mentioned. And you will be a better priest because of it."

Father Alphonsus made the sign of the cross on the younger

priest's head and embraced him.

Before he went to the soup kitchen, Father Lorenzo stopped in the Rinuccini Chapel in the basilica. He settled onto a bench and focused on Giovanni da Milano's fresco of Mary Magdalene washing Jesus' feet.

Lord, make me an instrument of your peace;
where there is hatred, let me sow love;
where there is injury, pardon;
where there is doubt, faith;
where there is despair, hope;
where there is darkness, light;
and where there is sadness, joy.

A few minutes later, when Father Lorenzo walked into the soup kitchen, everyone shouted *"Benvenuto a casa!"* Dino rushed to hug him, Angelo and Salvatore shook his hand, Fico barked and Emilio patted the dog's head. Little Pietro, holding on to Caterina's skirts, gave Father Lorenzo a flower.

Father Lorenzo greeted every one of the hundred or so guests, pausing to shake hands, hug shoulders and pat little heads. He got in the serving line and doled out big bowls of Tuscan soup and broke off huge chunks of bread. And when he started singing, badly, *"It's been a hard day's night/And I've been working like a dog,"* everyone groaned.

Caterina came up at the end, her eyes glistening. "I'm so glad you're back, Father."

He hugged her. "I am, too."

Pietro tugged at his pants leg. "I knew you'd be back," the boy said.

Father Lorenzo hoisted the boy onto his shoulders. "You knew more than I did."

A month later, he received a note card from Victoria. It had a photograph of a heart-shaped ruby on the cover, and on the back, a description:

"It is said that the power of Ruby is in its encouragement to follow your dreams and your bliss, helping you to change your world. Ruby will bring light to the dark places in one's life, bringing a spark of awareness to those places where you might still need work, and giving you the opportunity to clear that path. Ruby also heightens our love for life, giving us motivation and inspiration to choose wisely for ourselves and others."

He opened the card for the simple message: "Dear Lorenzo, Please help change the world. Thank you for all you do for the poor, and what you did for me. With much affection, Victoria."

"I'll never forget you, Victoria." The priest wiped his eyes and jammed the envelope in his pocket. He was late for the monthly session of the old-time movie group, and they were showing one of his favorite films, *La Dolce Vita*.

Forty-four Cats

Chapter One

Tomasso Nozzoli never had dreams, good or bad. At night, after the obligatory pasta with either chicken or veal downed with a glass of watered-down wine, he read a little, watched television a little and then crawled exhausted into bed. Managing the Nozzoli Ceramics Shop on a side street in Florence had become more and more tiring.

He let little Bella crawl under his armpit, and slept soundlessly until sunlight awakened him. He hardly moved, and when he did, an irritated Bella would stir and then settle back down.

When Tomasso's friends told him how hard it was for them to sleep, he told them, "I sleep like a baby."

When they described their mysterious dreams and even nightmares, he didn't know what they were talking about.

"I think the last dream I had was when I was five years old," he said.

So he couldn't understand why, on this cold November night, he had a baffling dream that left him confused and exhausted. Jolted, he sat upright in bed, his heart racing, his hands shaking and his face covered with perspiration. He looked at the clock on his bed table. It was only 3:15 a.m.

"What the hell…?"

He lay back down and pulled the sheet over his shivering body. Some of his friends had told him that when they had dreams they remembered only bits and pieces afterwards. But afterwards, Tomasso remembered every little detail.

He had been sleeping as usual when he heard a noise in the ceramics shop just outside his bedroom. He threw off his blankets and went into the store, finding it odd that it was pitch dark. Normally, a streetlamp illuminated the shop even during the night.

Then he saw a light flickering on the top shelf of a display of pots and vases. The light began to turn colors, from white to red to green to purple. It grew brighter, and he realized it glowed from inside the kitty teapot he had placed there for safekeeping.

The teapot was the most expensive, the most delicate and the oddest piece in the shop. Handmade by an artisan in Arezzo, it was shaped in the form of a cat, with a removable head so that water could be put into it, an outstretched paw for pouring water out of it and a curved tail to form a handle. It was painted in bright blues and yellows, and was, Tomasso thought, pretty in an odd sort of way. He kept it on a high shelf to prevent rambunctious kids from breaking it.

"What the…?" he muttered.

Bella had followed him from the bedroom, and she was both mesmerized and terrified. With her back arched and her black tail straight up, she circled around and around Tomasso's legs, alternately sniffing and hissing.

"Don't be afraid, Bella," Tomasso said. "A kitty teapot isn't going to hurt a real kitty."

Then Tomasso heard sounds, as if the teapot was humming. Yes, it was humming a song. He scratched his head. The song was familiar, but he couldn't quite place it. It sounded like a children's song. Over and over it hummed.

As Tomasso watched, the teapot rose from the shelf and glided slowly across the shop. Screeching, Bella fled to the bedroom. As if guided by invisible wires, the teapot swooped up and down, barely missing the ceiling and walls and performing a little dance right in front of Tomasso's face. Whenever it went by, the humming became louder, but Tomasso still didn't recognize the song.

The teapot did cartwheels in the air. It slid upside down. Its humming became louder.

"This is like a movie I took Massimo to," Tomasso thought.

Then the little teapot glided back and settled on its shelf. The humming gradually stopped. The lights flickered and went out. The room was again in total darkness.

It was then that Tomasso woke up. He ran into the shop and flipped on the light. The teapot was in its place. The door was locked. The streetlamp was still lit.

While Bella supervised, he took out a stepladder, climbed up to the top shelf and cradled the teapot in his arms.

"I hope nothing happens to this," he said aloud. "Massimo always loved this little kitty so much. Ah, Massimo."

But, of course, Massimo wasn't here anymore.

"All right, Bella," he said, "I don't know what that was all about, but come on, let's go back to bed."

Tomasso didn't get much sleep. Four times, he eased his big body out of bed because he thought he heard sounds in the shop. He not only turned on the light but he also took a flashlight and aimed the beam to the top shelf. Once, he even got the stepladder again to see that the teapot hadn't moved. But it appeared to be sleeping peacefully.

Others might have been frightened by this mysterious dream. Tomasso had mixed feelings. He couldn't understand why, after years of not having a dream, or at least remembering any, that he had such a vivid, baffling one. He hadn't eaten anything different the night before. He wasn't any more troubled than usual. Why now?

He had to admit he was amused by the teapot's antics, but hearing that children's song reminded him of Massimo, and that made him very sad.

"Ah, Massimo."

Chapter Two

When streams of sunlight woke Tomasso the next morning, he sat straight up in bed. Letting Bella fall to the floor, he grabbed his robe and rushed into the shop.

Everything was still quite peaceful. The kitty teapot was safe on its shelf. After a breakfast of coffee and hard bread, with milk and leftover bits of chicken for Bella, he got dressed. The shop would open late, for today was his monthly visit to the cemetery at San Miniato al Monte.

"See you later, Bella. I'm going to see the principessa."

He checked on the kitty teapot one last time and locked the door, making sure the key was in his pocket.

For the last ten years, on the fifth of every month, Tomasso made a pilgrimage to the cemetery that was so high above Florence that the entire city could be seen. As other shopkeepers along the way raised their metal awnings for the day, Tomasso made his way through Piazza Santa Croce and crossed the Arno at Ponte alle Grazie. Soon he went through Porta San Miniato, where there were notably fewer tourists and less traffic.

As always, he stopped at Giorgio the Florist and, as always, took part in the same monthly exchange.

"*Buongiorno*, Giorgio!"

"*Buongiorno*, Tomasso! Here is your red rose."

"How much do I owe you?"

"Nothing. Nothing. My best to the principessa."

"*Grazie.*"

Tomasso clutched the rose to his chest.

With trees shading the walks and birds singing, he climbed to Piazzale Michelangelo and suddenly more tourists were there taking photos, first of the copy of David that dominates the piazza and then of Palazzo Vecchio, the Campanile and the dome of the Duomo in the distance.

The hill along Viale Galilio Galilei to San Miniato was steeper, and, at seventy, Tomasso found that he had to stop more times now to catch his breath. But every time he came here, he had to laugh to himself at the story of the saint for whom the church and cemetery were named.

First, he couldn't understand why an Armenian prince would serve in the Roman army under Emperor Decius in the third century. Then why the prince would become a Christian and a hermit. More incredible was the story of how the emperor ordered Miniato thrown to beasts in the amphitheater, but how a panther refused to devour him. So Miniato was beheaded. Not letting a little thing like that bother him, the saint picked up his head, crossed the Arno and climbed up the hill to his hermitage. And that's where the shrine in his honor was erected.

Tomasso shook his head. "I mean, who made all this up?"

He avoided the exquisite Church of San Miniato and was now inside the cemetery, the Porte Sante. He walked past the grotesque statue of a naked man sprawled on a grave, the young couple on another and the weeping woman on a third. He knew that Carlo Collodi, who created the story of Pinocchio, was buried here somewhere, and some day he'd look for his tomb.

Instead, he went straight to the mausoleum where, almost ten years ago to the day, Tomasso had placed the body of Principessa Maria Elena Elizabetta Margerita di Savoia next to her husband, the prince. Removing an ornate key from his pocket, he unlocked the metal gate and went inside. The musty air was at least ten degrees cooler, and it was already cold on this November day.

He threw away the now-withered rose that lay on top of the principessa's marble tomb and replaced it with his new one. Then Tomasso drew up the wooden folding chair he brought years ago. He thought briefly about telling the principessa about his dream, but he knew it would sound foolish. So he took out his handkerchief and wept for the romantic days and nights he had spent with the woman he had loved so much.

Chapter Three

Exhausted as always when he returned from the cemetery at San Miniato, Tomasso needed to lie down for a half hour before opening the shop. "I'm not so young anymore, Bella. I have to rest." Bella nestled at his side and when she wanted to be fed again, he got up and unlocked the door.

There weren't many customers in early November. Florence endured rain on many days, and tourists had mostly disappeared. Things would pick up before Christmas.

But Tomasso kept busy. He met almost every day with Dino Sporenza, the amazing young man who, at age twenty-nine, was running Tomasso's company, *Gli Angeli della Casa*, the "angels of the home."

Financed with millions of *lire* left by the principessa "to do good," the company had rehabilitated more than seventy homes, mostly in the impoverished Santa Croce neighborhood that had suffered great damage when the Arno overflowed in 1966. Dino had shown extraordinary ability at organizing the work, almost always hiring the residents themselves to refurnish their homes. Dino had put his uncles, Roberto and Adolfo, in charge of the projects, so that left Dino time to volunteer regularly at a soup kitchen at Santa Croce.

Tomasso himself had no interest or ability to operate a business and preferred to keep running the ceramics shop he had owned for almost thirty years, ever since the war ended. At his age, that was enough to do. Dino came in mostly to get his approval for new projects.

Although they were the closest of friends, Tomasso didn't mention the dream about the kitty teapot when Dino came that day, and over the weeks he almost forgot about it himself. At first, he found himself glancing up at the shelf several times a day, but then less frequently. One day he neglected to look at all, and that night woke with a start and went into the shop. The teapot was still here, but Tomasso checked the door and window just to make sure no one had entered.

Tomasso also endured the visits of Teressa, the principessa's longtime maid. Although her mistress had provided an abundant inheritance, Teressa still lived in a sparse single room on a high floor of an old apartment building near the Arno. Always in black, with a lacy veil, she hobbled over to Tomasso's shop on her cane at least once a week and always asked the same questions.

"Oh, Signor Nozzoli, how will we ever manage without the principessa?" She collapsed in Tomasso's favorite chair, shoving Bella out of the way.

"It's been ten years, Teressa. We have to try."

"I miss her so much. Why did she have to die like that?"

"We don't know, Teressa."

"We weren't even in the room! If we had been in the room, we could have helped her. Do you think she didn't want us there?"

"The principessa was very strong-willed and very private, Teressa. I think that is the way she wanted to go."

"Do you think it had something to do with those dreadful pills she was taking? I hated those pills so much. The doctor said they were so strong. But you know, she never wanted me around when she took them. I would hand her the pills and the water and she always told me to leave the room. I don't think they were helping. She never seemed any different afterwards. What do you think, Signor Nozzoli?"

"I don't know, Teressa."

"If only," Teressa said, "it hadn't happened during the flood. We could have found a doctor. Why do you think she died during that terrible flood?"

"I don't know, Teressa. We'll never know."

"I don't think I can go on living without her, Signor Nozzoli. Do you think I can go on living?"

"I think you'll be fine, Teressa. Just make sure you eat well and get enough sleep, all right?"

"I'll try, Signor Nozzoli. *Grazie. Ciao.*"

Each visit from the old woman upset Tomasso, and he had to sit again in his big chair, with Bella in his lap, to calm down. So many memories.

Chapter Four

For the next month, Tomasso slept peacefully again, undisturbed by mysterious dreams or Bella's faint snoring. Then there was another dream, this time even longer. After awakening with a start, he remembered every vivid detail.

It was shortly after midnight, and he heard the bell on the door of the shop faintly ringing.

"What the...?"

Moving Bella to the other side of the bed, he got up, pulled on his robe and shuffled into the shop. The door was still locked and bolted, and the bell was silent. He looked outside on the moonlit street. No one. He checked the window. All safe. He looked at the high shelf. The kitty teapot was in place.

An hour later, after he had just gotten back to sleep, he heard the bell again, only this time it was louder.

"What the...?"

Again, he checked, and again, the bell was silent and the clapper hung straight down. This time, he opened the door and went out into the street. Perhaps there was a breeze, a gust of wind. But the leaves on the ground on this early December day lay quietly. He went back to bed only to be awakened again when the bell began ringing so incessantly that he thought it might wake the neighbors. Bella flew under the bed while Tomasso checked again.

"Stop that!" he yelled, as if expecting an answer. Now something even more astonishing happened. Although there was just a single bell, the sounds expanded so that it seemed that there were dozens—indeed, as if the entire bell chorus of the Basilica of Santa Croce was in the shop. It was playing a tune, a childhood tune, the same one that the teapot had hummed.

Tomasso tried hard to remember the song, but couldn't quite place it.

"All right, that's it." Tomasso went to his toolbox in the back room and

took out a screwdriver. He disconnected the bell from the door, and even though it was still ringing, carried it to his bedroom. He found an empty box, wrapped the bell tightly in old rags and stuffed it inside. Then he closed the box and carried it downstairs to the basement. There was no sound.

Ever since the flood ten years ago, Tomasso had left the basement empty. He had lost too many dishes and other ceramics, and he wasn't about to take a chance on the Arno overflowing again.

He put the box in a corner and went back upstairs, closed and locked the basement door and went back to bed.

That's when he woke up, shaking and perspiring. He ran into the shop, only to find the bell in its place, with no sign of recent movement. He went down to the basement. There was no box.

"Another one," he told Bella. "What the hell do these dreams mean? They've got to mean something. I've never had such dreams. I don't know what's happening to me. Bella, I think I'm going crazy."

He lay back on the bed.

"What a night. I always liked that little bell. I got it when Massimo was three and he used to have such fun just opening and closing the door so that it would ring and ring and ring. Poor Massimo."

Chapter Five

The following day was again the day of the month to visit the mausoleum. Tomasso crossed the Arno, received a free rose from Giorgio, and climbed the steep hill to San Miniato. Cold December winds made him stop more frequently, and he could see his breath ahead of him.

The mausoleum was even more frigid, and Tomasso worried that the principessa would be cold. He knew that it was only her body in the marble crypt, but he still worried.

He placed the new rose on top of the tomb and sat down. This time, he needed to tell the principessa.

"Oh, Principessa, I hope you don't mind, but you're the only one I can talk to about this. You know I never dream. I never dreamt when I was with you. But twice in the last two months I've had dreams that reminded me of Massimo. Nobody but you knows how much I miss my son. It's been so many years now.

"Principessa, I'm afraid I will never see him again. I know his mother won't let me. Why would she, after what I did to her? I was foolish. But you were so beautiful, Principessa. I couldn't resist you. We had such wonderful times together, didn't we? We made love in so many places. We were so happy. But now I'm paying for it. I wish you could help me, Principessa, but I know that's impossible. What could you do?

"Since the dreams, Principessa, I keep thinking about Massimo. And then I feel so sad. I don't know why I taught him how to play soccer. I don't know why I got him to play in the *Calcio Storico*. Just wanted to show him off, I guess. And look what happened. I'm so sorry. It's all my fault.

"Principessa, do you know why I'm having these dreams? Can you give me a sign?"

When he finished, Tomasso felt foolish. Talking to a tomb.

Describing his dreams. Maybe he really was getting senile.

When he returned home, Tomasso was trying to relax the muscles in his legs when the doorbell rang. Both furious and worried, he ran into the shop and found Dino standing there.

"Tomasso! It's only me. I just came in to check some bills with you. Why are you looking so strange?"

"Dino, Dino. It's a long story."

And, because he was now so confused and needed to talk to someone, he told Dino the story of his dreams about the flying kitty teapot that hummed and the maddening doorbell that sounded like a chorus.

"I tell you, Dino, I don't know what these dreams mean. I never dream! I think I'm losing my mind."

"No, no, Tomasso. Of course you're not losing your mind."

Dino did try to look into the older man's eyes for clues, but saw nothing unusual.

"Tomasso, what did you have to eat last night?"

"Eat? I had some pasta as usual, and some chicken. Dino, you know me. I don't cook very well. I make the same thing every night."

"And drink?"

"Just a glass of wine, as usual. And you know I put water in it. No, Dino, nothing I ate or drank."

"Did anything unusual happen during the day?"

Tomasso thought for a long while. No, nothing.

"Tell me what happened again, Tomasso."

So Tomasso repeated the stories. Dino took the teapot down from the shelf and inspected the bell, opening and closing the door three times to make it ring.

"Is there anything else you can remember about the dreams, Tomasso?"

Tomasso thought for a long while. "No, nothing....Well, there is one thing. The song. I can't remember the name. The teapot was humming it and the doorbell was playing it. That sounds silly, doesn't it?"

"Dreams always sound silly. The same song. Hmm. Do you know the name of it?"

"That's what's bothering me. I can't remember the name, just the tune. It was a kids' song."

"How strange."

Dino paced the floor of the shop while Tomasso settled back in his chair. Neither had an explanation. Then Dino asked, "Tomasso, do you remember the date of that first dream?"

"No…wait…it was the day I visited the principessa. November 5. I always go to see her on the fifth of the month. That's the day she died. November 5, 1966. The day after the flood, ten years ago."

"And today is the fifth, right?"

"Yes, but what's the difference?"

"I'm thinking," Dino said. "November 5, December 5. I wonder why the same date."

The old man and the young man were baffled. Dino said he couldn't think of anything else that could tie the two dreams to the dates, and they went over the bills he had brought.

"Well," Dino said as he was leaving. "Let's see if you have another dream on the fifth of January. Are you…are you worried, Tomasso?"

"Worried? Hell no. I just want to know what's going on."

Chapter Six

With Christmas only weeks away, Tomasso was too busy to be concerned about teapots and doorbells. A steady stream of customers found so much to buy that he had to order new supplies from his distributor. Teressa came even more frequently, since she missed the principessa and her parties particularly at Christmas.

Dino stopped in every day now. He always claimed that he had to write a check or had an order to complete, but Tomasso knew that the young man was worried about him.

"How are you today, Tomasso?" Dino invariably asked.

"I'm just fine. Don't worry about me, Dino."

Dino looked around the shop and then they settled down to the checks and order forms. Both men were pleased because by Christmas, *Gli Angeli della Casa* would complete the rehabilitation of its seventy-fifth home.

A week before Christmas, Tomasso dug the old *presepio* from a closet and arranged the little figures of Mary and Joseph and the Three Kings and the shepherds and the cows and sheep under the wooden stable in the window. He held the Baby Jesus for a long time.

"Massimo loved this little Baby Jesus." He wiped his eyes and put it in its straw cradle. "I wish Massimo was here now. I miss him so much."

On Christmas, Tomasso went to Mass in the Rinuccini Chapel at Santa Croce celebrated by his friend Father Lorenzo. Later in the day, he joined Dino and dozens of other extra volunteers to serve a mammoth turkey and ham dinner to hundreds of people at Father Lorenzo's soup kitchen. He brought some scraps home for Bella.

"That was a good Christmas, Bella." He settled into his chair and was soon snoring.

On the fourth of January, Dino came to visit as soon as the shop opened. Asked why, he told Tomasso that he "just wanted to hang around and see if you're all right."

Tomasso ordered him to go home when the shop closed.

"Dino, I'll be all right. If I have another dream tonight, I'll call you in the morning. Go home and get some sleep."

Tomasso himself did not go to sleep right away. After tossing for hours, he finally fell asleep, and promptly had another dream.

It was about 3 o'clock in the morning, and he was jolted awake when he found a sharp object under his side.

"What the…?"

Why was the little Baby Jesus suddenly in his bed?

Tomasso let it lie there and went to the shop window. Sure enough, the cradle was empty. He returned to his bed and tried to lift the little statue.

"What the…?"

It may have been only two inches long, but it was so heavy that Tomasso could not lift it. He tried moving it from side to side, he tried moving the entire sheet, he tried a pair of pliers. Nothing.

Then the Baby Jesus stood up, held his arms to the sky and, in a clear, childlike voice, began to sing:

Nella cantina di un palazzone
tutti i gattini senza padrone
organizzarono una riunione
per precisare la situazione.
Quarantaquattro gatti…

In the basement of a tower
The kittens without a master
Organized a meeting
To clarify the situation.
Forty-four cats…

The Baby Jesus smiled and slowly disappeared.

Tomasso woke up. "Forty-four Cats!" That was the song in the other dreams. He remembered it as sort of a nonsense song, *"Six to seven forty-two,/plus two forty-four!"*

And:

They asked for all children,
who are friends of all the kittens
one meal a day and on occasion,
to sleep on the chairs...

It made little sense, but it was Massimo's favorite song. He watched kids sing it on television and then he'd go around the shop laughing and singing.

Tomasso ran into the shop. The Baby Jesus slept peacefully in His crib.

"What the hell is going on? I'm losing my mind. Why is all this happening? What did I do to deserve this? I'm being punished. I got involved with the principessa. I ruined my marriage. I lost Massimo. God is punishing me. How I miss Massimo."

Dino arrived an hour before the shop even opened, knocking on the door to waken Tomasso, who was nodding in the chair. The old man told his young friend about the dream and pointed out the Baby Jesus in the *presepio*.

"I'm going crazy," Tomasso said. "I swear. Do you think I'm going crazy?"

The old man's eyes were moist and his hands were shaking.

"No, no, Tomasso. Look, I believe you, I really do. I just don't understand why you're having these dreams. Let's go through this again."

So Tomasso again recited the story about his dreams of the teapot and the doorbell and the Baby Jesus, and how the same children's song was in each of the dreams.

"*Quarantaquattro gatti*... Forty-four cats," Dino said. "Every child in Italy knows that song. I used to sing it myself all the time. I'd drive my mother crazy."

"Massimo sang it all the time," Tomasso said. "His mother got tired of it, but I kind of liked it. He was so cute."

"Tomasso, you said that all of the dreams happened on the fifth of the month. And you said that it was on the fifth of the month that the principessa died. Do you think, subconsciously, she's somehow related to this?"

"What would the principessa have to do with this? She's been dead for more than ten years."

"I don't know, Tomasso. I don't know."

Putting on his coat, Tomasso decided to ask the principessa herself.

"Wait for me here, Dino."

Panting, Tomasso got another rose from Giorgio the Florist and climbed the hill to San Miniato. It was even colder now in the mausoleum, and he was exhausted from the long walk.

"Principessa, I hate to ask this. I'm just a foolish old man. But I loved you so, and I want to know if you have been trying to tell me something the last months. I've been having these strange dreams. Not terrible, just strange. And they always happen on the fifth of the month, and you know you left me on the fifth of the month. Is it you, Principessa? Are you trying to tell me something? What message do you have for me?"

Tomasso waited a long time, but the mausoleum remained silent and the air did not get warmer. Restoring his woolen cap to his cold head, he returned home.

Chapter Seven

Dino was waiting in the shop when he got back. Together they went over the whole story again. If the principessa was somehow involved in these dreams, Tomasso and Dino reasoned, then this was a matter for the church to consider. Both of them vigorously denied believing in ghosts—"Of course not!"—but if the principessa's spirit had something to do with the dreams, then a higher authority needed to be consulted.

The next day, Tomasso stopped Father Lorenzo after Mass in the Rinuccini Chapel.

"Tomasso! Here on a weekday?"

"Father, there's something I need to talk to you about."

In the priest's tiny office, both men stood because Tomasso would have destroyed one of the rickety chairs. Fumbling, with his hands plunging in and out of his pockets and his eyes looking at the ceiling and then the floor, he told the priest about the dreams he had had in the last three months.

Seeing how upset Tomasso was, Father Lorenzo didn't laugh or dismiss the story. Like Dino, he asked Tomasso what he had to eat the day before each of the dreams, but, again, that didn't offer any clue.

"Tomasso, I'll be honest with you. I don't really know much about dreams. Nobody does. I have a psychiatrist friend in my film group who even says that. He says they probably have to do with the subconscious, and maybe your subconscious is trying to tell you something. The fact that they all occur on the fifth of the month might relate to the date of the principessa's death, and maybe your subconscious knows that.

"Is the principessa giving you signs? I don't think so. But you know, nobody really knows what happens after death. We believe that our souls go to Heaven, or someplace else, after we die, but perhaps that doesn't happen right away. Maybe sometimes it might take a while before our souls find their place. And maybe our spirits want to settle some things on earth before they go to their eternal resting place. So maybe the principessa won't quite rest until she does that. I know I've said a lot of 'maybes' but it's just because I don't know, Tomasso.

"The principessa loved you very much, Tomasso. I think she wants you to be happy and perhaps she's giving you some signs. Or maybe, you know, it's just your subconscious finding some meaning in the fifth of the month. So let's think about the items that were in your dreams. The teapot and the bell and the Baby Jesus. They all remind you of Massimo, right?"

"Oh yes! He just loved the teapot. Bella was just a tiny kitten then, so he pretended that the teapot was her mother. I had to watch him, because it could break so easily. But he was real gentle with it."

"And the bell?"

"He thought that was so much fun. He'd open and close the door for hours just to hear it ring. Well, maybe not hours, but for a long time."

"And Baby Jesus?"

"Probably every little kid likes the Baby Jesus in the *presepio*. I always let him put it in the cradle the night before Christmas, but then he'd take it out and pretend it was his own baby and then he'd put it back. I'll tell you, I used to get tears in my eyes just watching him. His mother, too."

Father Lorenzo leaned against the wall. "So, Tomasso, do you think your subconscious is somehow linking the principessa, because of the dates, and Massimo, because of the teapot and the bell and the Baby Jesus and the song?"

Tomasso scratched his bald head. "But the principessa never even knew Massimo."

"Did she know about him?"

Tomasso hesitated. "The principessa, well, she always felt guilty because after I took up with her, my wife left me. The principessa blamed herself, but she wasn't to blame, Father. It was me."

Everyone in Florence, or at least in the Santa Croce area, knew what had happened. How Tomasso and his wife, Rosaria, seemed to be happily married, and how they doted on their son. When he grew up, Massimo helped his father in the ceramics shop, arranging the items, sorting boxes, sometimes waiting on customers.

But besides running the shop, Tomasso was known as the hero of the *Calcio Storico*, the bloody event held every June in Piazza Santa Croce. Although it was called a soccer game, the event that started in the Middle Ages had deteriorated into not much more than a fistfight, with the players battering each other and tearing their clothes off. It had become a great tourist attraction.

Tomasso, though, proved to be a different kind of player, sometimes almost gentle as he lifted an opponent and deposited him on the ground. He developed an enthusiastic following, especially among the women. And one in particular took notice, Principessa Maria Elena Elizabetta Margerita di Savoia. Although she had buried four husbands and had had many lovers, she was still, in her sixties, a beautiful woman and famous for her elegant salons in her Palazzo Tuttini.

Invited to one of her parties, Tomasso was smitten, and a passionate affair soon began. Incensed, Rosaria fled to her parents in Sardinia. Massimo stayed with his father and began playing in the *Calcio Storico*, too. Everyone in Florence knew what happened next. In one match, Massimo got into a fight with another player and then, while the crowd booed, fled from the piazza. Tomasso could never get over the embarrassment, and the following year, he quit the game himself.

Rosaria returned from Sardinia and took Massimo back with her.

"So the principessa did know about Massimo?" Father Lorenzo asked.

"Oh, yes. And she felt so bad because she knew I missed him so much. I still do, Father. I think about him all the time. Do you think there's a connection, in my subconscious, I mean?"

"I don't know, Tomasso, but it's the only connection I can make."

"But, Father, the principessa has been dead for more than ten years. Why are these dreams happening now?"

"I don't know, Tomasso. Maybe it has something to do with the anniversary of the principessa's death. I bet even my psychiatrist friend wouldn't have an answer to that. How long has it been since you've had contact with Massimo?"

Tomasso's ruddy face became redder. "Not since his mother took him away to Sardinia."

"Maybe you should try again, Tomasso?"

"I don't know. I'm afraid, Father."

"Afraid of what?"

"Afraid that he won't want to talk to me again."

Chapter Eight

Tomasso could hardly sleep for weeks, and he was distracted at his job. For the first time in his life, he gave the wrong change to one customer and forgot to order a ceramic platter for another. He thought of calling Rosaria, but he didn't know the telephone number for her parents. He thought of writing, but he didn't know the address, only that it was near the village of Calangianus in Sardinia. Anyway, Rosaria would undoubtedly hang up the phone or tear up his letter.

And then he thought maybe he shouldn't contact Massimo at all.

There was one thing that he hadn't told Father Lorenzo, and no one else in Florence knew either. During Massimo's last game in the *Calcio Storico*, he had fallen in the fight with the other player and struck his head against the sharp stones of the piazza. Dizzy, he had still gotten up and played until that ill-fated moment when he staggered away.

The following day, he had a severe headache, but it seemed to get better that night. Then the headaches increased, and he started acting oddly. He was no longer a twenty-year-old man but more like a five-year-old child. He played with toys that had long been in a closet. He watched children's television shows and laughed and giggled. He sat in a corner and sang. The same song, over and over. *"Quarantaquattro gatti…"* Tomasso kept him in the shop for months so that no one would see him.

"Nobody but me knows the real reason why he walked away from the *Calcio Storico*," Tomasso thought. "He was hurt, he couldn't fight anymore. I couldn't let him out of my sight."

And then Rosaria arrived from Sardinia and there was an angry argument in which she blamed Tomasso for getting Massimo to play and therefore was responsible for his condition. She said Tomasso was not capable of caring for Massimo. That was when Rosaria whisked her son back to Sardinia.

Tomasso had told only the principessa about this, and she tried to comfort him against the soft pillows of her bed.

"Tomasso, Tomasso," she would say, "some day, I hope you will see Massimo again. If I could make it happen, I would."

Finally, Tomasso made up his mind. He knew that if he was ever to find peace, he had to go and find Massimo.

First, he climbed the hill to San Miniato. "Good-bye, Principessa. I'm going to see Massimo. If you have any connections up there, please help me."

When he tried to explain to Bella why he was leaving, she just glared at him.

"Oh, Bella, what if Rosaria doesn't want Massimo to see me? What if she shuts the door in my face? And what if Massimo doesn't want to see me? I don't know what condition he's in now. Maybe he's worse. Maybe he won't even know me. I don't think I could stand that."

Bella continued to glare as he finished packing. "Don't you worry, Bella. Dino will come by twice a day to feed you."

Except for the time when he was in Mussolini's army during World War II, and then afterwards when he deserted and joined the partisans after *Il Duce* fell, Tomasso had traveled little outside of Florence. He had never been to Livorno, much less to the island of Sardinia.

The trip would take a while. First, he had to take a bus to Livorno, which would take about two hours, and then a ferry to Olbia in Sardinia, which might take as long as ten hours depending on which boat he took. And then he had to go into the rugged mountains to try to find Rosaria's home.

The bus ride proved to be tedious, and, towering over the other passengers in a rear seat, he dozed off. What would it be like to see Rosaria again? He wondered if he missed her.

Tomasso was forty-one years old and resigned to a life of bachelorhood when a young girl, barely seventeen, came into the shop he had just opened in 1946. The oldest of a destitute family of thirteen children, she had found life unbearable in Sardinia and had fled to the mainland, and then to Florence. She quickly found work as a maid in a palazzo near the Duomo.

One day, her employer sent her to Tomasso's shop to buy a new pitcher for a dinner party planned for that evening. Tomasso helped her pick one out, and they got to talking. Normally extremely shy with strangers, Rosaria found the big older man charming and even rather handsome in a rugged sort of way.

For his part, Tomasso thought the girl, though hardly a beauty and far too thin, had a lovely complexion and a radiant smile. Soon, the girl found excuses to visit the shop, Tomasso took her to movies, and after only three months they were married. For Rosaria, marriage meant stability if not love. For Tomasso, it meant that he might finally have the son he had long wanted.

With an age difference of almost twenty-five years, the couple had to make many adjustments, Tomasso because he had developed his own habits and schedules, Rosaria because she didn't know what was expected of the young wife of a man old enough to be her father. Although not eagerly, she submitted to Tomasso's desires. And he was gentle.

After they had been married only a year, Massimo arrived and the child was everything they hoped for, bright, funny, precocious and obedient. Rosario took him to school and made him spaghetti almost every day. The kid loved spaghetti. Tomasso practically glowed as he walked the boy down the street, showing him off to his neighbors. It was quite a sight, the big man who was seven feet tall and the boy who had to walk on his tiptoes to hold his father's hand. Later, when Massimo was a teenager, he learned how to arrange the ceramics and do other chores in the shop, and Tomasso took him to Piazza Santa Croce and taught him how to play soccer.

"That was a mistake," Tomasso thought as the bus jarred him back to reality as it rounded a corner. "A big mistake. If I hadn't done that, he wouldn't have played in the *Calcio Storico*, and then this wouldn't have happened. Rosario never wanted him to, but, no, I insisted. Bloody fool. Dumb bloody fool. I'm to blame for all this. I bet I don't get to see either of them."

It was nightfall by the time the bus reached the dock at Livorno, and Tomasso had to run, panting, to catch the last ferry to Olbia. He found a bench in the rear, pulled his coat tighter and clutched his small leather suitcase to his chest. On the next bench, he thought the girl looked like Rosaria thirty years go. He remembered how he loved his wife then and wondered how deep his feelings for her were now. He wondered if he would even recognize her. Maybe she had grown fat.

The Mediterranean was angry throughout this cold February night, tossing the boat from side to side. More than a few passengers heaved into the tin buckets. Tomasso never closed his eyes.

"Wait," he thought as the boat finally landed early in the morning and the groggy passengers disembarked. "Today is February 5. This is the first time in ten years I won't be visiting the principessa on the anniversary."

He knew he should have felt bad about that, but he thought the principessa would understand.

Chapter Nine

Tomasso was one of the last passengers to go down the ramp and onto the grungy dock at Olbia when the boat docked at mid-morning. He kept an eye on the young woman from the boat and saw that she was greeted with a hug by a man about forty years old. Her husband or her father?

Leaden skies and fierce winds cast a gray pall on everything, and Tomasso rushed through the crowds to the three decrepit taxicabs waiting under a tin awning. He knocked on the grimy window of the first, interrupting the driver, who was reading *La Gazzetto dello Sport*.

"What you want?" the driver asked.

"I want to go to Calangianus." Tomasso knew the village was only about fifteen miles from Olbia.

"Too far." The driver rolled up the window and went back to the sports pages.

Tomasso tried the second taxi. Same response.

At the third, the short, swarthy driver seemed a little more interested. "Why do you want to go there?"

"Why?"

"Yeah, why?"

"Because I've got business there, that's why." Tomasso knew he could lift the guy out of the cab with one hand.

"We take care of our own business here."

"Not mine."

The driver looked at his watch. "Get in."

Tomasso could hardly understand the man. He remembered that even though Rosaria had been in Florence for a year before he met her, she still had had traces of the ancient Sardinian language.

As the taxi ascended into the mountains south of Olbia, Tomasso realized how little he knew about Sardinia. Some people thought the island wasn't really a part of Italy. For all of its beautiful beaches that had become the playgrounds of the wealthy, its mysterious mountainous interior was so wild and rugged it was sometimes impenetrable.

When Florentines talked about Sardinia, if they talked about it at all, it was in a condescending tone, as if it were entirely inhabited by peasants who spoke a different language, *Logudorese,* and always wore black-and-white costumes. Tomasso heard about the outlaws and bandits who roamed the mountains and stole livestock. He remembered news reports of a few years ago when bandits swooped down on unsuspecting travelers, robbed them of their money and clothes, and sent them naked into the wilderness. He'd also heard that almost every town had a resident witch.

In truth, the peasants were fiercely proud of their prehistoric beginnings and lived side by side with thousands of Neolithic stone forts called *muraghi.* If they vigorously enforced codes of conduct and carried on vendettas for crimes supposedly committed, it was because they fiercely guarded their customs and traditions.

After the first fifteen minutes, Tomasso could swear they were going around in circles, and he was convinced of it when he saw the same *muraghi* three times.

When they arrived at Calangianus' town square, Tomasso knew that the driver vastly overcharged him, but he reluctantly handed over hundreds of *lire.* His fingers frozen, he slammed the taxi's creaky door shut and took refuge from the winds in the nearest *bar.*

Sprawled in tiny metal chairs around the room, four men, each with a rifle at his feet, eyed Tomasso suspiciously as he ordered a coffee and asked directions from the bartender.

"Do you happen to know where Rosaria Contini lives?"

"Rosaria Contini?"

"Yes."

"Why do you want to know?"

"It's my business."

"Around here, we take care of business."

The bartender turned his back. This seemed to be the common reply, Tomasso thought. He also thought he might throttle the man, but knew he needed an answer.

"I'm her husband," he said loudly.

"Her husband!" The man turned around. "Like hell. Her husband's been dead for years. What the hell are you talking about?"

"I'm her husband, I'm telling you. I'm not dead. She came here to live."

"So she left you?"

"Yes."

The men laughed and pointed.

"Where are you from?"

"Florence."

Tomasso knew that was the wrong answer when the bartender and all the other men laughed even harder. The bartender turned his back and started washing cups and saucers.

Tomasso pounded his fist on the counter. "Hey, you! I need to go see my wife. I haven't seen her in years."

The four men grabbed their rifles and stood up.

"And my son!" Tomasso shouted. "I haven't seen him in years. I need to see him!"

"Your son?" the bartender said. "You're Massimo's father?"

"Yes. You know him?"

The bartender leaned closer, and the four men lowered their rifles. "Everyone around here knows Massimo. Poor boy."

Tomasso's voice was shaking. "I need to see him."

The bartender signaled to the four men. "Take him up there."

With two short men in front and two in back, Tomasso towered over his companions as they left the bar in the blustery winds and proceeded down the street. Past the market, past the church, past the statue of a warrior holding a sword. A shopkeeper stepped out on the street and shouted.

"Hey, Silvio, where are you taking this guy?"

"To see Massimo."

"Massimo? Poor Massimo."

Soon after they left the flatlands of the town they began climbing into the mountains, which quickly became steeper than the road to the cemetery at San Miniato. Along the way, small groups of hunters emerged from the forest bearing some sort of wild game.

Soon they were in a vast oak forest of gnarled trees and huge mushroom-shaped rock formations. Now and then, open fields revealed shepherds tending to scraggly mountain sheep. They passed only a few ramshackle dwellings and Tomasso saw one family living in a cave.

Still carrying his suitcase, Tomasso could feel the muscles in his legs tighten, his breathing getting faster, and sweat forming on his forehead. He didn't think he could take another step but straightened up and plunged on.

As they climbed higher, Tomasso unaccountably began to pray. Although he went regularly to Mass, he never really prayed, just recited the words from the booklets. Now, as sweat penetrated his eyes, he pleaded with God. "*Jesu*, please, let me see Massimo again. Please."

When they turned a sharp corner near the top of the mountain, the men suddenly stopped.

"Go!"

"Where? I don't see anything."

"Behind that big rock. Go!"

The men turned, leaving Tomasso to stare at a gigantic rock formation. There was no sign of life until, without warning, a huge animal, which may have been a dog but looked more like a wolf, sprang forward. It stopped only because it reached the end of its heavy chain.

"Bruno! What are you doing? Who's there?"

Tomasso recognized Rosaria's voice immediately. She slowly emerged from behind the rocks. Her hair, which she had always worn long, was matted around her head, her clothes were torn and dirty, and her lovely complexion had turned into a leathery mask. Far from being fat, she was even more frail than he remembered.

"Tomasso! What the hell are you doing here?"

Chapter Ten

Tomasso could feel cold tears flowing down his cheeks, but he was afraid to move. Rosaria stood about twenty feet in front of him, her hands on her hips.

"Tomasso! I asked you, what are you doing here?"

"I came to see you. And Massimo." He could hardly hear his own voice in the raging winds.

Rosaria laughed. A strange cackle, like that of an old woman, not the light laughter that Tomasso remembered.

"After all these years? Why, Tomasso, why?"

Tomasso took a step forward on the barren ground. "Rosaria, can I come inside? I can explain."

Rosaria did not move. "I don't know. Why should I?"

"Rosaria, please."

Slowly, she turned and walked behind the rock formation, and Tomasso followed, with Bruno growling and ready to attack. Her dwelling—he could not call it a home—appeared to be just a lean-to carved into a cave in the rocks. A rusty tin roof shielded a battered door. They went inside.

Tomasso was surprised by the sudden warmth and saw a blazing fireplace. The wooden planks on the floor were uneven but clean. A small makeshift table and two wooden chairs. A cupboard with a few dishes. Beyond, he could see another space with a man sitting in a chair, a board across his lap. With a candle nearby, he was piling little pieces of wood on top of each other, then taking them down. And he was humming. Tomasso knew the song.

Massimo was almost thirty years old. Tomasso couldn't bear to go in there.

Tomasso and Rosaria sat at the table, both staring down, unable to fill the chasm that had developed over so many years. Finally, he raised his head.

"This is…this is where you live, Rosaria?"

"Of course. Why shouldn't I?"

"I thought you lived with your parents."

"My father died seven years ago, my mother a year later. My fuckin' brothers and sisters took over the house and forced us out. Bastards. This is the only place I could find."

Tomasso wondered if Rosaria ever smiled. "Just you and Massimo here?"

"And Bruno. He protects me. So do the farmers and the shepherds in the hills. And some people in the village."

Tomasso looked out the lone window, just a hole in the stone wall. Bruno had fallen asleep with one eye open. Gusty winds rattled branches against the tin roof, but he could hear Massimo humming.

Rosaria leaned back in her chair. "Tomasso, this is my life. I take care of Massimo. He can dress himself and take care of his needs, but he just sits most of the day, playing with those little pieces of wood and humming that same song over and over. I've learned to tune it out. Sometimes I get him to play card games with me. I read to him. I make him spaghetti almost every day."

"I remember how he loved spaghetti," Tomasso said.

"I wash clothes in the creek out back. I bring water from there to wash the dishes. I have vegetables in the back. The farmers bring me milk and eggs and chickens. The shepherds bring me wood for the fire." She looked away. "Sometimes, they want favors in return."

"Oh, Rosaria."

"Don't feel sorry for me, Tomasso. As I said, this is my life. You chose your own with that…that…"

"I'm sorry, Rosaria."

Her eyes flared. "Sorry? Sure, you can say that now. Now that she's dead. Yes, I heard that she died in the flood. But you weren't sorry when I was there, were you? You weren't sorry when you'd go off…"

Her voice broke and she went to the door. For a moment, he thought he might go to her, put his arms around her. He knew she would reject him.

"I'm sorry, Rosaria," he said softly.

"Yeah. Sorry."

"I am."

She turned around. "I ask you again. Why are you here?"

Tomasso didn't know where to begin. He could not tell her about the flying teapot, the clanging doorbell or the Baby Jesus. Who could believe such dreams? He knew that he missed Massimo very much and, now that he saw Rosaria, that he missed her, too.

"Rosaria, I'm an old man. I still run the shop, but it's getting harder. I know I've done wrong. Terrible wrong. But I want to mend things before it's too late. I miss Massimo so much."

Rosaria laughed. "Massimo? Massimo? What about me, Tomasso? What about me? I'm getting old, too. It's hard work here. I survive, but barely. And only because I give favors."

She began to cry.

"Rosaria…"

"What do you want me to say, Tomasso? That I forgive you? No! No! I will never do that."

"I'm not asking forgiveness, Rosaria."

"Then what are you asking? Why the hell did you come here?"

At home, Rosaria had been the quietest, the gentlest person he had ever known. She was no longer that person. He looked down at his hands, worn and beaten with age. "Rosaria, I wish I knew. I've been so lonely…I thought maybe if I saw Massimo again…"

"What then?"

"I don't know. I'd just like to say I'm sorry to him, too."

His shoulders shaking, Tomasso began to sob. He put his head on his arms on the table and let years of pent-up guilt and shame and sorrow wave over him. Rosaria sat quietly, her hands in her lap, but didn't offer to comfort him. Finally, he pulled out a red handkerchief from his pocket and blew his nose.

"Not much of an answer, is it?" he said.

"No."

"Rosaria, do you think I could talk to Massimo? Would he know me?"

"When I first brought him here, he kept asking for 'Papa, Papa' all the time. Now, he doesn't do that anymore. I think he's forgotten you. As he should have."

"Could I see him?"

"He's your son."

Tomasso hesitated, then got up and entered the other dark interior. He stood behind Massimo, who was humming his song over the pile of wooden chips. Tomasso went to his side and put his hand on his son's shoulders.

"Massimo?"

The man-boy looked up. Despite the long scar that ran from the top of his head to his right eyebrow, he looked like the boy Tomasso remembered.

"Massimo? Do you remember me?"

Massimo's eyes narrowed and his lips quivered. "Papa?"

"Yes, Massimo, it's Papa."

He pulled Massimo to his feet and held him by the shoulders. Then Massimo, with the mind of a child but the body of a man, fell into his father's arms. "Papa, Papa, Papa."

Chapter Eleven

A half-hour later, Rosaria was writing on a sheet of paper at the table when Tomasso and Massimo, tears in their eyes and their arms around each other, came back into the kitchen.

"Rosaria...," Tomasso said.

"Don't talk, Tomasso. I know what you're going to say. And this is my answer. Yes, Massimo and I will return with you to Florence. I hate this place, I hate it! And it's no place for Massimo. He needs help, a doctor's care. I want him to have that. It's too much for me. But we'll go back only under these conditions."

She picked up the paper. Tomasso braced for the worst.

"First, you will never—never!—mention the name of that bitch in my presence again."

"No, of course not."

"That's in the past, right?"

"Right."

"It's over."

"Yes."

"Second, I will do the cooking and the cleaning, but you will spend most of your time with Massimo. The boy may be thirty years old but he needs a father. And a friend."

Tomasso smiled and Massimo realized this must be good news. He took his father's hand.

"Third, you will set up a trust fund so that after you're gone, there will be money for me and Massimo for the rest of our lives."

"Yes, of course." He might have to sell the shop, but he was ready to retire anyway.

"Fourth, I want an apartment with three bedrooms. I may be coming back, Tomasso, but we will not be man and wife."

"Yes." Tomasso was grateful that she and Massimo were even coming back.

115

It took less than an hour to pack Rosaria's few clothes and Massimo's bits of wood and card games. Rosaria doused the fire, unleashed Bruno and took him up to a shepherd. With Massimo running ahead like a little boy, they made their way down the mountain to Calangianus, where Rosaria wanted to stop at the same *bar* that Tomasso had visited only hours before. The four men were still sprawled inside.

"Benedetto," Rosaria called to the bartender. "I'm leaving. With Massimo. We won't be back. *Grazie.*"

"You're taking Massimo?" one of the men asked. "Oh, Massimo, we're going to miss you!"

Each of the burly men hugged their friend, who began to cry.

"Come!" Rosaria said as she pushed her husband and son out the door. "We're going to be late."

"Buona fortuna!" all the men shouted.

And with that, she led Tomasso and Massimo to a taxi, which brought them to the ferry to Livorno just in time. On the boat, after Rosaria went below deck, Tomasso and Massimo sat on a bench near a railing. Watching the waves and the now much calmer Mediterranean, they did not speak for a long time.

"Massimo?" Tomasso put his arm around his son's shoulders.

"Hi, Papa." Massimo grinned.

"Remember when you were little and I used to take you for walks?"

Massimo thought for a while. "I remember."

"Remember how we used to stop for gelato, and you always wanted chocolate?"

"Yeah. Chocolate."

"And how we walked along the Arno and watched the boats?"

Massimo rubbed his hands together. "Boats. Water."

"Massimo, remember how you helped me in the shop?"

"Pretty dishes."

"Anything else?"

Massimo smiled. "Kitty teapot!"

"Oh, Massimo, you remember!"

"Pretty teapot."

"And that song you always sang?"

Massimo began to sing.

Nella cantina di un palazzone
tutti i gattini senza padrone
organizzarono una riunione
per precisare la situazione.
Quarantaquattro gatti...

"And remember how we used to play soccer? You know, kick the ball?"

Suddenly, Massimo began to shake. Tomasso hugged him tighter. "That's all right. We won't talk about that anymore. Massimo, listen. Remember how your mother made spaghetti all the time?"

Massimo grinned again. "Spaghetti. Red sauce. Salad. Gelato."

"That's right! That's what we had so many nights. You remember, Massimo! I'm so proud of you." Tomasso kissed the top of his son's head.

Massimo looked up at his father. "Papa!"

Chapter Twelve

After the bumpy bus ride to Florence, Tomasso made a phone call.

"Dino! We're just back from Sardinia….Yes, we. I'll explain later. We need an apartment right away. Do you have one? We need three bedrooms….Yes, three. I'll explain later….But away from Piazza Santa Croce, OK?…A nice one…You do? Where?"

Excited, Tomasso explained to Rosaria and Massimo that a family had just moved out of an apartment on Via Ghibellina. Dino would get furniture from the warehouse right away and would meet them there.

After years of living in a cave, Rosaria and Massimo walked around the new apartment with their arms outstretched, savoring the space. Tomasso inspected the walls and floors and rearranged some of the furniture. Then, while Rosaria went to the market down the street to stock up on groceries, he took Massimo to the ceramics shop.

When they arrived, Massimo excitedly opened and closed the door, opened and closed the door, opened and closed the door.

"Bell, Papa, bell!"

"Yes, Massimo, but look what else is here."

Bella came running to the door, upset that her master had left her, but, more to the point, that she hadn't been fed since morning when Dino came by. Tomasso found some bits of chicken in the refrigerator.

"*Gatto!*" Massimo cried. "*Gatto!*"

"Yes, Massimo, You remember Bella. She's grown, hasn't she? She can come live with us. Maybe she'll even sleep with you."

Then Tomasso got out the stepladder and climbed up to the shelf where the kitty teapot still sat. He took it down.

"Remember this, Massimo?"

Massimo's grin almost broke his face. "*Gatto!*" He ran his hands gently over its shiny surface, careful as he always was not to harm it.

"Yes, Massimo, your favorite kitty. But now you have a real one, too." Bella rubbed against Massimo's legs, and he knelt down to tickle her under her chin.

"One more thing," Tomasso said. He went into the bedroom and dug out the box with the *presepio* from the closet. "Look, Massimo!"

"Baby *Jesu*! Baby *Jesu*!" He kissed the little statue as he cradled it in his arms.

His knees cracking, Tomasso eased himself down on the floor and, with tears in his eyes, watched his son play with Bella and the tiny figure of a baby.

"I don't know how life is going to be now, Massimo. But it's going to be better for me. I hope it's better for you. I don't know how things are going to work out with me and your mother. I hope we get along. I'm going to try. And I'm going to try to make things up to you, Massimo. Oh, Massimo."

Tomasso knew there would be no more monthly visits to the cemetery at San Miniato, that his affair with the principessa was finally over. "Good-bye, Principessa," he said.

But he knew that each night he would sit and talk with the son he had missed so much. And they would sing together.

Sant'Antonio

The Miracle of the *Presepio*

Chapter One

Father Sangretto's emergency meeting of the parish board that Saturday started off badly and disintegrated quickly as the afternoon wore on. When Augustino Arca, the treasurer for twenty-three years, reported that he had deposited last Sunday's collection in the bank at Lucca, Franco Fortunato rose to complain for the twenty-third time.

"I ask again. Why are we putting our money in the bank at Lucca when we can get a better interest rate at any bank in Florence?"

Augustino tried to explain. "Because, as I've told you so many times, Franco, it costs a lot of money to drive from Sant'Antonio to Florence and I don't like to drive there anyway. The traffic is terrible and there's too many one-way streets!"

"And you get lost, right?" Franco said.

"Never mind that. I'm still going to use the bank in Lucca."

"Sure," Franco said, "and of course it has nothing to do with the fact that your brother is a vice president there."

Augustino rose, his face red. "Are you implying something, you *imbecille*?"

"I'm not implying anything, *stupido*. Just observing."

Augustino's wife, seated in the first row, burst into tears.

"Please," Father Sangretto said. "Can we move on? Augustino, tell us how much money we have in our account in the bank in Lucca."

Augustino looked down at his report. "Sixteen thousand *lire*."

A murmur went through the meeting room in the basement of the church where subfreezing temperatures forced the villagers to keep their winter coats on. "Sixteen thousand *lire*!" someone said. "That's not enough to heat this place for a month!"

Franco rose again. "Well, if we'd put our money in a bank in Florence, we'd…"

"Franco, please sit down," Father Sangretto said. "This is how much money we have. We have to live with it. Now, please, the report of the Building and Maintenance Committee. Marcello, tell us about the boiler."

"It's broken," Marcello Palazzo said.

Father Sangretto sighed. "Can you be a little more specific?"

"Well, the guy from Farina Plumbing and Heating in Lucca came and looked at it and just shook his head. He said there are lots of things that need replacing and we're spending too much on oil and we'd be lucky if it lasted the winter. We need a new one."

"But this is only December!" someone shouted.

Father Sangretto raised his hand. "You see, we have a very bad situation. The boiler needs to be replaced. We have only sixteen thousand *lire*, and that's hardly enough. We have to raise more money. So we're here this afternoon to see how we can do that. Any ideas?"

He looked over the now-silent group and sighed. Only fifteen people out of the seventy-eight adults who were members of the parish had turned out for the meeting.

"Any ideas?" he repeated.

Flora Lenci raised a tentative hand. "Well, we could have a bake sale."

Seated behind her, Sabina Melfi whispered loudly to her neighbor. "Flora wants to have a bake sale? Whoever would buy her soggy biscotti?"

Flora turned around and stared at Sabina, who suddenly found the need to search in her purse for something.

"How about a raffle?" someone in the back shouted.

"What would we raffle?"

"Maybe a broken boiler?" This was met by guffaws and titters.

"Maybe we could have a concert? A rock concert?" This was from Fabio Mortelli, who at twenty-eight was still a member of a band called the Fortunate Dead in Lucca.

Groans from his elders put that idea to rest.

There were other suggestions.

"A car wash?"

"Not many cars in Sant'Antonio."

"A Christmas pageant?"

"We should charge people to hear those kids try to sing?"

Finally, Mario Leoni raised his hand. Although he was only twenty-six, Mario had gained the respect of many villagers since he had taken over the *bottega* founded by his grandfather Nino. Mario's father Bernardo didn't want anything to do with the shop, but Mario, a recent graduate of the University of Pisa, couldn't find work as a history major and eagerly took over the shop.

Of course, villagers were also closely watching the handsome Mario's budding romance with the pretty Anita Manconi, who was now working in her grandfather's butcher shop next door.

"How about forming a committee to come up with some ideas, Father?" Mario said. We'll meet and we'll report back to you in, say, a month."

The priest looked relieved. "Thank you, Mario. You're a blessing. That's the best idea I've heard all afternoon. You get three or four people and get back to me. OK? Thanks again."

Chapter Two

When he first arrived to take over the little church just beyond the village in Tuscany, Father Sangretto was at best tolerated. The saintly Father Luigi, the villagers declared, simply could not be replaced. An accomplice in the Italian Resistance, Father Luigi was killed by the Germans during the war, as much a martyr as any saint who had been canonized.

Twenty-five years later, Father Sangretto's relationships with his parishioners had only worsened. With his blustery sermons, his rejection of many of the changes in the Catholic Church and his constant appeals for money, he was usually ignored as irrelevant.

He couldn't find any volunteers to help clean the church and so he washed the floors and cleaned the windows himself. Boys refused to become servers at Mass and he reluctantly relied on two girls, whose attendance was mostly sporadic. He was forced to prepare First Communicants alone, and since the organist quit last year he led the hymns himself.

Returning to the rectory after the meeting, Father Sangretto knew he should make an effort to be friendlier to the villagers, but that didn't seem to be in his nature. Chubby and shy as a boy, he had never learned to express his emotions very well. Sometimes he got upset when people didn't listen to him or take his advice, like urging boys to enter the priesthood. But he was only trying to be a good priest.

He had to keep up an image, the image of all the priests he had ever known. They were leaders. They made decisions. They were like fathers who had to be obeyed. They didn't have to be friends with their parishioners. And priests knew right from wrong, or at least they did until Vatican II made everything more complicated.

It didn't help that so many of the villagers didn't get along very well with one another. That was clear at the meeting. Twenty-five years after the war, when they had united to fight a common enemy, cracks had now developed in what was once such a strong little community. Neighbors weren't talking to each other, grudges lasted for years and little disputes erupted into noisy arguments.

Maybe that's why they didn't take any particular pride in their village. Other villages in Tuscany sat on hilltops and were photographed in books and magazines. Sant'Antonio was only a string of houses alongside a highway. It wasn't in any book.

Every night Father Sangretto lay in bed and stared at the ceiling. When the money finally ran out, and it would soon, what would he do? And how could they ever afford a new boiler?

Each June, the parish's *Festa di Sant'Antonio* was supposed to provide about half the year's annual income, what with the admission fees, raffles and the sales of beer, wine and pizza. But the *festa* last June was not a success.

When he counted the money after the last beer stand had closed, he couldn't believe it. "No, no, no, no!" he shouted, and his mother rushed into the room.

"Peppe! Peppe! What's the matter?"

"Look at this, Mama. This little pile of *lire*, this little pile of coins. This isn't going to last us three months! What are we going to do?"

"Oh, Peppe, I'm sorry. You worked so hard on the *festa*."

"Maybe I should have worked harder." He started counting the *lire* again.

"Peppe! You couldn't have worked any harder than you did!" She went behind his chair and kissed the top of his bald head.

"Well, not enough. And please stop calling me Peppe, Mama. How many times have I told you that? My name is Giuseppe. You know that."

His ruddy face flushed even more.

"I'm sorry, Pep...Giuseppe. I know you're upset."

"Leave me alone, Mama."

Now, on this December night, he pulled on a sweater and sank into the worn stuffed chair before the fireplace. The boiler wasn't working again.

"Might as well see what awful things are happening in the world today," he thought as he picked up the day's *La Nazione*. He didn't get any further than the front page.

Chapter Three

"Oh, Good Lord! Mama, did you see this?"

Wiping soapsuds from her hands, Signora Sangretto came running from the kitchen. "What, Peppe, what? Sorry. Giuseppe. What did you see?"

"Look at this!"

It was hard to miss. A large photograph on the front page showed in great detail the *presepio* at a church in San Giovanni Evangelista, a village in southern Umbria. The nativity scene was obviously modeled after the fabulous ones popular in Naples, with not only the traditional figures of the Baby Jesus, Mary, Joseph, angels, shepherds and wise men, but also with many scenes of life supposedly in a Neapolitan village. Dozens of houses filled a huge landscape that was populated by people working in shops, cooking and baking in their homes, plowing in the fields outside, praying in a church. A royal palace featured women dancing in ornate dresses. Cypress trees lined roads leading to miniature farmhouses in the hills. And at the center was the tiny figure of the Baby Jesus in a crib.

"What a magnificent *presepio!*" Signora Sangretto said. "Look at all those people, look at all those houses! I've never seen a nativity scene like that."

"No, no, Mama, not the *presepio*," her son said. "Look who's standing there. It's him!"

"Who?"

Standing in front of the *presepio*, a robust priest grinned broadly and pointed a stubby finger at the figure of the Baby Jesus. In large type above the photo were the words: "*Miraculo di presepio!*"

"A miracle? I can't believe this," Signora Sangretto said. "Read the article to me, Peppe."

Father Sangretto adjusted his glasses. "From the tiny village of San Giovanni Evangelista in the region of Umbria comes the most exciting and incredible news. A miracle has occurred. On the eighth day of December, the Feast of the Immaculate Conception, the church of San Giovanni Evangelista set up its amazing *presepio* as always. People have come from miles around for many years to see this beautiful depiction of the birth of the Christ.

"Now on this day, many people lined up to see the figures of the Baby Jesus, Mary, Joseph and all the others in this wondrous scene. Some knelt to pray. Some took photographs. Many lit candles. Then a woman who had been crippled since childhood, whose right foot was withered and useless, made her way to the railing in front of the *presepio*. She knelt for a while gazing reverently at this scene, overwhelmed by the power of what she was seeing. Then she slowly reached out and touched the tiny figure of the Baby Jesus lying in the straw in the manger."

Father Sangretto paused.

"What happened? What happened?" his mother cried.

"It was then that the miracle occurred," he continued. "The woman suddenly felt her foot grow stronger and stronger. She stood up! She threw away her crutches! She walked away! She was cured!

"We were told this in an exclusive interview with the saintly priest who is the pastor of San Giovanni Evangelista's humble church. His name is Father Romolo Monterastelli and he is indeed a very holy man."

"Father Romolo Monterastelli!" Signora Sangretto cried. "No!"

"I can't believe it!" Father Sangretto said.

"Is there more? What more do they say about the miracle?"

His hands shaking, Father Sangretto picked up the newspaper again.

"It was clear when the holy Father Romolo Monterastelli telephoned us late last night that he is a very gentle man, a shy man, and at first he didn't seem to want to talk and he stammered a bit. But then he told us what had happened and he began to cry. To cry! God, he said, has worked a wonderful miracle. And this is just before Christmas, too.

"We asked the holy Father Romolo Monterastelli if we could have an exclusive interview, only a brief interview, of course, with the woman whose foot had been miraculously cured by the Baby Jesus. Father Romolo Monterastelli told us that the gentle lady was in seclusion and would avoid all interviews. We can certainly understand that.

"Before we ended our telephone conversation, though, the holy Father Romolo Monterastelli told us exclusively that his church would remain open at all hours and that visitors were most welcome to come and see the place where this miracle occurred. And the *presepio* will remain in place until the feast of the Epiphany, on January 6. He also disclosed that because of the cost of heating the church and other things, a small fee would be asked for those who wished to enter the church."

Chapter Four

Father Sangretto threw the newspaper on the floor. "I can't believe it!"

"You never did like him, did you?" His mother picked up the paper and began to read the article again.

"In the seminary he was always pulling something or other. He had so many excuses for not coming to class or being late. He didn't turn in his papers on time. There was talk that he had a drinking problem. But his father was a good friend of the rector so of course they gave him a pass."

"I didn't know he had a parish in Umbria," she said. "Who would want a parish in Umbria? At least you have a parish in Tuscany."

"I don't know how he got to Umbria, but something must have happened if he's still in a little parish after all these years."

Signora Sangretto looked at her son. "Peppe, some good priests are in small parishes. You know that."

"The last time I saw him," Father Sangretto said, "was at that conference in Pisa. He wouldn't talk to me, of course. He still holds it against me that I got better grades than he did in the seminary. But I heard him talking at length with two other priests. He had been drinking rather heavily and kept saying, 'I've got to get out of that parish. I've got to get out of Umbria. I should be in Rome, not in Umbria.' And you should have heard the way he said 'Umbria.' Made it sound like it was deeper than hell."

Father Sangretto wiped his forehead.

"I wish," his mother said, "they could have interviewed the woman. It would be nice to know how she felt when she was cured."

"There's something fishy about this, Mama. Why wouldn't that woman want to be interviewed? You'd think she would want to tell the world about this miracle."

He got up, poked the wood in the fireplace, sat down and wiped his forehead again.

"Peppe, Peppe. You're getting all excited. It's not good for your heart. You're sixty-eight years old now, you know. And with your weight the way it is, you have to be careful."

"I know, I know." He settled back in his chair.

"Good. Relax. I'll turn on the television. Maybe there will be a good game show on and you can forget all about this miracle and that priest."

When the snow had cleared from the television screen and pictures finally emerged, the figure of a young woman behind a desk could be seen.

"Oh," Father Sangretto said, "it's that stupid news program and they've got that bimbo reading the news again. Why can't that station get some men to read the news?"

"Peppe, she seems like a very nice young lady. Shhh. Let's hear what she has to say."

What she had to say was not what they wanted to hear.

"And tonight," the announcer said, "all the region of Umbria, indeed all of Italy, is astounded by the news from the little village of San Giovanni Evangelista. There, a woman whose entire left side had been paralyzed since birth has been miraculously cured by the Baby Jesus lying in the *presepio* in the parish church."

"Her entire left side?" Father Sangretto shouted. "I thought it was her right foot."

"And now," the announcer continued, "we have an exclusive interview with the pastor of the parish church in San Giovanni Evangelista, the holy Father Romolo Monterastelli."

Father Sangretto looked through his fingers as television footage showed a hulking priest attempting to hold back crowds of people who were trying to enter the church. "Just wait, just wait," he was saying. "There's room for everyone. Just deposit your *lire* in this box over here."

Then a television reporter was at the priest's side, shoving a microphone into his face. "Father," the man said, "we have never seen anything like this."

"Yes, it's a miracle."

"What do you attribute the miracle to, kind Father?"

"I believe it is because we at San Giovanni Evangelista have been true to the Holy Roman Catholic Church for all these years and now the Baby Jesus has recognized us."

"Yes, yes. And do you think there will be other miracles?"

The holy Father Romolo Monterastelli smiled. "That is up for God to decide."

"It is such an honor for this little village to be graced with such a miracle. Can you tell us something about the woman who was cured?"

"The woman? Oh, yes. Well, the woman was…was a woman, of course."

"Her age?"

"Oh, fifty, sixty."

"A devout Catholic?"

"Oh, yes, very devout. Mass every day."

"Earlier, there had been some reports that it was her right foot that was cured."

"Her right foot? No, no. It was her left side. Yes, her left side. Well, I'd better go now. You see the crowds…"

"Of course. But may we ask, Father, if you have heard from the bishop? Has the bishop approved of all these people coming here and making, um, donations?"

The smile on the face of the holy Father Romolo Monterastelli seemed nervous. "I am a good friend of the bishop."

"Thank you, Father."

In Sant'Antonio, Signora Sangretto wiped her eyes. "Imagine! A miracle! And in front of a priest we know."

"Mama! You don't believe that, do you? There was no woman! There was no miracle! The statue of the Baby Jesus didn't cure anyone. This holy Father Romolo Monterastelli has made the whole story up. First it's her right foot and then it's her whole left side. He can't even get his story straight. And he can't produce the woman. Don't you see? He wants to get out of that village. He'll do anything. I never did trust him. Now he'll be famous and they'll transfer him to a big parish. Maybe even Rome. And he's going to make a fortune by charging people to come to his church!"

Father Sangretto slumped in his chair and pulled a blanket around him. "Turn off the television, Mama! Turn off the damn television!"

Chapter Five

Christmas had been a bleak affair for Father Sangretto for the last half dozen years and this year it was particularly grim. Because of low attendance at Mass, he scheduled only one, at midnight. Even then, the church was less than half filled, and it was dominated by the cries of sleepless babies.

As he was greeting the few participants as they left the church on this December night, he heard a conversation between two women.

"Did you hear what happened in San Giovanni Evangelista in Umbria?" one said.

"Isn't it exciting? Imagine, a miracle! Wouldn't you like to go there? The *presepio* sounds so nice. And such a holy priest. We could take a bus tomorrow."

"Tomorrow? Yes, maybe. My arm has been bothering me so much lately. I've seen the doctor I don't know how many times and yet he never..."

Father Sangretto didn't hear the rest. His own *presepio* consisted of a chipped Mary, a Joseph with a broken nose, an angel who lost a wing and one shepherd and three wise men in various stages of disrepair. Only Baby Jesus had remained intact, still smiling many years after it was made in some factory in Rome.

Afterwards, Signora Sangretto gave her son his present, a dark blue sweater. It was hardly a surprise as he had seen her making it since last August. He gave her a framed photograph of himself, one taken at his ordination. Their meal the next day consisted of veal cutlets with mushrooms and cream and a side dish of mashed potatoes. They barely talked.

Then they went to their drafty rooms. Signora Sangretto began knitting another sweater. Father Sangretto put some Vivaldi on his record player and sat in the chair to look out the window.

It was a dreary day, looking like it would start to rain any minute.

Clouds covered the hills nearby and dirty remnants of the last snowfall littered the street leading to the village. No one was around.

"Everyone is with their families," he thought. "They deserve it. I know they have a lot of expenses, but I wish they could give a little more to the church. Got to do something. I've got to do something."

He paced the room, sat down, got up, lay on his bed, got up, picked up his daily prayer book, got through two prayers and collapsed in his chair again.

"Got to do something."

He thought maybe he ought to pray for inspiration so, after putting on another sweater and his winter coat because the church was unheated, he went across the archway that connected the parish house to the church and descended into the sacristy.

"Oh, God. Please help me. Help me to come up with some plan. Can you help me?"

Not hearing a reply, he got up from the kneeler and roamed through the church, counting the panes of stained glass that had to be replaced, the watermarks on the walls, the broken floorboards.

In front of the forlorn *presepio,* he gently rearranged the figures so that the Baby Jesus was more prominent. He stared at the tiny figure.

"The Baby Jesus!" he cried. "Thank you, God!" He ran back to his room.

Chapter Six

Father Sangretto had to wait for the phone to ring five times before a breathless Rosa Tomaselli answered. *"Pronto!"*

"Rosa, it's Father Sangretto. May I…"

"Father Sangretto! Why are you calling? Who died?"

"Nobody died, Rosa. May I…"

"Oh, thank goodness. I thought somebody died. I came running down from upstairs when I heard the telephone. Why are you calling on Christmas Day then? Is it about the committee for the boiler? Mario has called a meeting for next week and we're going to come up with good ideas. We'll let you know, all right, Father?"

"It's not about the boiler committee, Rosa. May I speak to Antonio?"

"Antonio? You want to speak to Antonio?"

"Yes, Rosa."

"Antonio. Why do you want to speak to Antonio? I know he didn't go to Mass last night but he…he didn't feel well. I hope you understand."

"I understand, Rosa. Now may I speak to him?"

Rosa didn't cover the mouthpiece well enough with her hand, so Father Sangretto heard a muffled conversation. "Wants to speak to you…Why?…I don't know why…I don't want to speak to him… Antonio, he called, he wants to talk to you…Why?…I told you I don't know why…here…talk to him."

"Hello?"

"Hello, Antonio," Father Sangretto said. "How are you?"

"I'm…I'm fine."

"Good, good. Antonio, I'd like to talk to you about something."

"Me?"

"Yes, Antonio. A project I'd like you to do if you're willing."

"A project?"

"Yes. Could you come over here?"

"Over there? Well, I guess so. When?"

"Now?"

"Now?"

"Now."

Because Antonio had put the receiver firmly back on the phone, Father Sangretto did not hear the conversation between Rosa and Antonio.

Rosa: "What did Father Sangretto want?"

Antonio: "He wants me to come over to the priest's house."

Rosa: "On Christmas Day? *Santa Maria!* Why, for heaven's sake?"

Antonio: "He wants me to work on some kind of project."

Rosa: "A project? What kind of a project?"

Antonio: "I don't know. He didn't say."

Rosa: "I can't imagine. On Christmas Day! *Santa Maria!* But there's so much work to be done in that church. And he knows you're a carpenter."

Antonio: "Yes."

Rosa: "Well, don't let him get away with anything. I know he won't pay you, he doesn't have any money. But don't do it if you don't want to, Antonio. You're always doing something for other people. Like the time you fixed Fausta's door. Or when you put new legs on Annabella's dining room table. You're a good man, Antonio, but…"

By this time Antonio had put on his heavy boots, his warm winter jacket and his fuzzy cap, a Christmas present from Rosa. "I'll be back soon," he said.

Rosa stood on her toes to kiss Antonio on the cheeks. They had been married only seven years, but still held hands when they were alone and kissed whenever they felt like it. Rosa was now eighty-two-years-old and still robust despite growing arthritis in her knees. Antonio was eighty-four now, but looked, felt and behaved at least ten years younger.

Rosa watched from the door as her husband strode down the street leading to the church. "Such a good man," she thought. "I hope Father Sangretto doesn't take advantage of him."

Chapter Seven

Signora Sangretto opened the door for Antonio as soon as he rang the bell. Like her son, she was also making a good effort to be friendly to the villagers and rarely brought up the fact that she and her son had come from a much larger parish in Prato.

"Antonio! Father Sangretto said you'd be coming. How good to see you again. How's Rosa? Such a lovely woman. I do enjoy talking to her when we meet at Leoni's or someplace. Here, let me take your coat. No need to take off your boots, the floor is already muddy and I'll have to wash it tomorrow."

Antonio soon found himself in a red leather chair in the study, amazed at the paintings of agonized saints on the red damask walls. He had never been in such an opulent, if ostentatious, room.

"Ah, Antonio," Father Sangretto said as he entered. "Thank you for coming."

Antonio got up and was surprised when the priest shook his ruddy hand. "Well, you asked me…"

"Yes, yes. Thank you again. Now, I want to show you something."

He opened a desk drawer and pulled out a newspaper clipping and was about to show it to Antonio when his mother swept into the room.

"Coffee, Antonio? I just made it. And a few cookies?"

Antonio was never one to refuse cookies.

Signora Sangretto left the room but kept the door open and stood just outside. This was a conversation she keenly wanted to hear since her son had told her nothing about the purpose of Antonio's visit.

She could see her son and Antonio looking at a newspaper clipping. She couldn't make out what it was. What were they saying? She could hear only a few words. It sounded like Father Sangretto wanted Antonio to build something for the church. That would make sense. Antonio was known far and near as the best carpenter and woodworker in the region. He made the platform for the statue of Saint Anthony for the *festa,* and there was hardly a home in the village that didn't have one of his birdhouses in its backyard or a bookcase in the living room.

"So you'll do it?" she heard her son say. "It's going to take a long time, and I won't be able to pay you for a while."

"I know," Antonio replied.

"Good. And you can keep a secret? You won't tell anyone what you're doing?"

"Father," Antonio said, "I fought in the war as a partisan. I know how to keep my mouth shut."

Seeing them shaking hands, Signora Sangretto fled back to the kitchen. But as soon as Antonio left, she accosted her son in the hall.

"Peppe!"

"Giuseppe, Mama."

"Giuseppe, what was that about? What is Antonio going to do? Why did you ask him to come here?"

"You'll find out, Mama."

"Giuseppe, you're not going to tell me?"

"No, Mama."

"Giuseppe, you haven't kept a secret from me in all your sixty-eight years."

"Well, there's always a first time, Mama."

Chapter Eight

On January 6, the television news carried another story about the man the media now routinely called the holy Father Romolo Monterastelli and his *presepio*. His photo was shown in the background, and the good father appeared to have gotten larger in less than a month.

"Oh," Father Sangretto shouted at the television set, "putting on a little weight, are you, holy father? Maybe you've gotten so much *lire* you can afford to have some good meals?"

"Listen to what they have to say, Giuseppe," his mother said. She took up her knitting.

The young woman began reading from her script. "Today from the region of Umbria we have important and exclusive news from the village of San Giovanni Evangelista. You will recall that on December 8, a wonderful miracle occurred there. A woman who was dying—dying!—was brought to the church and when she touched the face of the Baby Jesus in the *presepio* she was miraculously cured and walked away completely healed."

"Now she was dying!" Father Sangretto laughed. "Next time she'll be like Lazarus and be raised up from the dead."

"Shhhh," his mother said. "I want to hear."

The video now showed crowds of people attempting to get into the church but held back by lines of *carabinieri*. A reporter struggled to hold up a microphone to the priest. "And here is the holy Father Romolo Monterastelli. What news do you have today, holy father?"

"I am happy to announce," the priest responded, "that instead of taking the *presepio* down as we usually do on the Feast of the Epiphany, we are going to leave it up as long as people want to come. Twenty-four hours a day. Every day."

"Well, that's wonderful news," the reporter said. "And can you tell us, good father, have there been any other miracles?"

"Not that we know of," the priest said, "but who knows what

miracles take place in peoples' hearts?"

"Yes, yes, of course. But we would really like to talk to the woman with the bad foot...side...the woman who was dying. No one has ever seen her."

"Yes, um, yes. Well, she prefers to remain in seclusion. We will let you know when she is available. And now I must go into the church and pray."

"And pray!" Father Sangretto laughed. "Yes, holy Father Romolo Monterastelli, you'd better do that. For your own soul."

"Why are you laughing, Giuseppe?" his mother said. "You don't sound bitter. I thought you didn't like him."

Father Sangretto just smiled.

"This has something to do with Antonio, doesn't it? I don't know why you won't tell me, Giuseppe."

"Just wait, Mama."

"He's down in that storage room every day and I can hear him using the saw and pounding. What's he making? Tell me, Giuseppe!"

"Just wait, Mama."

At home, Antonio was as secretive as the priest.

"Antonio," Rosa said every morning, "why are you going to the church every day?"

Antonio grinned. "Maybe I like to pray?"

"Oh, of course. You never went to church before and now you go every day? Tell me, Antonio."

"Just wait, Rosa."

"I'm going to get mad at you, Antonio."

"You know you won't."

"I know." She kissed him. "Now don't be late for supper. I've made ravioli."

Chapter Nine

In a village as small as Sant'Antonio, the secret between Father Sangretto and Antonio quickly became the major topic of conversation. Women buzzed about it as they bought chickens and rabbits at Guido Manconi's butcher shop. Next door, men put down their *briscola* cards in the back room at Mario Leoni's *bottega* to wonder what was going on. Everyone had a theory.

"Antonio's building a new platform for Saint Anthony," one said.

"Why would he do that? He just built one a few years ago."

"He's making a new altar."

"We don't need a new altar."

"Pews for the church?"

"We have too many now. Nobody goes to church."

"Well, one thing's for sure. Antonio won't get paid for whatever he's doing. Father Sangretto doesn't have any money."

And so the women went muttering down the street from Manconi's and the men picked up their cards again at Leoni's.

In March, *La Nazione* carried a column by a leftist writer that was picked up by newspapers throughout Italy.

"*Dove e donna?*" the headline said. Indeed, where was the woman?

"It has now been more than three months," the columnist wrote, "since this so-called miracle allegedly occurred at the church in the village of San Giovanni Evangelista in the region of Umbria. At first, it was reported that a woman with a bad right foot had been cured because she touched the figure of the Baby Jesus in the *presepio* in the church.

"Then it was reported that her left side was cured. And lately, it is said that she was dying. We demand to know the truth!

"For weeks, highly respected journalists have attempted to locate the woman who is the heart of this most suspicious event. She has not been found. The pastor of the church, Father Romolo Monterastelli, keeps making excuses. 'She is in seclusion,' he says. 'She wants her privacy. She is praying.'

"Well, we think it is about time this invisible woman stops praying and comes forth to tell her story. Who is she? What was her alleged ailment? Where has she been hiding?

"And what does the Roman Catholic Church have to say about this? In the past, the church has been skeptical of such happenings, but we have heard nothing from the bishop or the Vatican or anyone else to date. Is anyone investigating?

"And finally, a big question. Everyone who enters the church at San Giovanni Evangelista is asked to put some *lire* in a collection basket. What happens to this money? Is the church being repaired? Is there a new altar, a new organ?

"Or is the 'holy' Father Romolo Monterastelli enjoying life more since this alleged miracle? We have been reliably informed that the holy priest has been seen in some of the finest restaurants in Orvieto.

"We demand to know the answers to these questions! And there is only one person who can answer them. Come forth, 'holy' Father Romolo Monterastelli! Tell us what you know!"

Smiling, Father Sangretto clipped out the article and put it in his desk drawer.

Chapter Ten

A week after the column appeared, newspapers all over Italy carried the same headline: *"Miraculo secondo!"*

Underneath, the articles all read about the same:

"From the little village of San Giovanni Evangelista in the region of Umbria we have news that has come to us exclusively! Another miracle has occurred!

"Four nights ago, in the darkness of the church, a little boy of eight years of age hobbled up to the beautiful *presepio* which has been on display since last December 8. You will recall that on that day a woman who was dying—dying!—was miraculously cured when she touched the statue of the Baby Jesus in the manger.

"Now this little boy had been unable to see in his right eye for three years, ever since he was struck by a pellet from a rifle carried by one of his youthful friends. Four nights ago, his mother guided him to the *presepio* and gently put his hand on the face of the Baby Jesus. Suddenly the boy cried out, "I can see! Mama, I can see!" His mother fell on her knees weeping and she guided the boy out the door.

"We learned all this in an exclusive telephone call from the holy Father Romolo Monterastelli, the pastor of the church. Understandably, the priest was very nervous when he spoke to us, and sometimes his words were not clear. As we said, this was late at night and so he was probably very tired.

"We asked him if we could talk to the boy or his mother, but the good priest said they were so overwhelmed by what had happened that they could not talk to the press. We asked if we could talk to any witnesses, but the priest said everyone who had seen the miracle had left the church and they were not available.

"We would like to quote the holy Father Romolo Monterastelli, as follows:

"'I would like to thank the good people of Umbria and indeed from all over Italy who have come to our humble church to pray before our miraculous *presepio*. We know that God hears their prayers.

"'We would also like to warn people about those who would doubt that miracles have taken place here. We know that the Devil is still abroad in this land, and that he often uses Communist journalists to do his work. Do not believe what these people say. Come to my church and pray.'"

The articles continued, "We would like to add that Father Romolo Monterastelli reminded visitors to his church that a donation is usual in such circumstances."

All of the newspapers carried photographs of what had become a media circus. Television trucks and cameras, dozens of *carabinieri*, even helicopters. Father Romolo Monterastelli beamed as he directed the worshippers.

Putting down his copy of *La Nazione,* Father Sangretto smiled. "With all those people touching him, the Baby Jesus' face must be worn down by now." And then he went down to the storage room to see how Antonio was doing.

"It's looking good, Antonio."

"Thanks, Father. I'm enjoying this."

"Do you have an idea yet when you'll be finished?"

"I'm sure I will be finished by Christmas."

At home, Rosa continued to question her husband.

"Antonio," she said one night as they enjoyed their evening walk, their *passeggiata,* around the village, "if you don't tell me what you're doing I'm not going to hug you anymore."

"Oh, really?" Antonio hugged his wife and kissed her on the top of her head.

"Oh, all right," she said. "Maybe once in a while."

Chapter Eleven

The boiler committee still had not come up with a way to raise money, but the boiler had somehow gotten through the winter and even the cold spring. In June, attendance at *Festa di Sant'Antonio* was again down, but surprisingly, Father Sangretto did not seem too concerned.

"Aren't you worried?" his mother asked. "Last year you were so upset after you counted the money."

"I don't know, Mama. I think things are going to get better for our church."

"Why in heaven's name would you think that?"

"I just think so."

"It's because of whatever Antonio is doing down in the storage room, isn't it?"

"Just wait, Mama."

"Oh, Peppe."

Throughout the summer, newspapers and television programs reported on the long lines of people that were entering the church at San Giovanni Evangelista. The place had become a Mecca. Buses came from all over Italy, leaving the pilgrims off at the base of the hill where the church was located. Many pilgrims climbed the hill on their knees. Even more *carabinieri* were called in to direct traffic. Enterprising shopkeepers increased prices on their supplies, and stalls throughout the village sold replicas of the Baby Jesus along with rosaries, medals and holy cards. "The Miraculous Baby Jesus of San Giovanni Evangelista."

Most days, Father Romolo Monterastelli stood at the church door to greet the faithful. What had been one small box for donations had now grown to three large containers that had to be emptied at least twice a day.

Predictably, the report of a second miracle resulted in another column by the leftist writer in *La Nazione*.

"It is now reported," he wrote, "that God has again interceded in the church at San Giovanni Evangelista in the region of Umbria. At first it was said that a boy of eight who was blind in one eye because of a gun accident suddenly regained his sight when he touched the figure of the Baby Jesus in the *presepio* at the church. Later reports have described the boy variously as six, seven and ten years of age and that he had been blind in both eyes since birth.

"We wonder if the pastor, Father Romolo Monterastelli, can ever get his stories straight.

"But that's not all. Father Monterastelli still has not produced the boy or his mother or the woman who was supposedly cured of...well, we don't know what her problem was. They remain in seclusion, he says. Since he has not produced any witnesses, he is the only one who claims these so-called miracles happened.

"We would also point out that the hundreds of pilgrims to the church have left sizable donations and that Father Monterastelli is solely accountable for this largesse. Last month, the priest said he was exhausted and was going to make a weeklong retreat to pray. We think otherwise. This writer has sources in Capri and can reliably report that the good priest was sunning himself on the beach when he was supposedly praying.

"Again, we ask the good father to answer the questions that everyone is asking."

Also predictably, the column resulted in the report of another miracle at the church three days later.

"Miraculo terzo!" the headlines read.

"Again, we have exceptional news from the humble village of San Giovanni Evangelista in the region of Umbria. Two nights ago, an elderly woman of seventy-two years of age came to the church from her village in Calabria. For five years—five!—she had been suffering a palsied right hand and was unable to make the pasta for which she had so long been famous.

"That night, she approached the *presepio* in the church, and like others before her, touched the face of the Baby Jesus lying in the manger. Immediately, her hand stopped shaking, the skin smoothed over and she felt it grow stronger and stronger. In tears, she rushed back to the home of the relatives where she was staying and proceeded to roll out linguini.

"Once more we are thankful to the pastor of the church, Father Romolo Monterastelli, for telephoning us with the news. Since it was late at night, his words were sometimes garbled and he had to repeat himself several times. We asked if we could talk to this saintly woman, but he said she had returned to her home in Calabria, which, unfortunately, does not have telephone service."

In Sant'Antonio, Father Sangretto read the account and laughed.

"You don't believe this one either?" his mother said.

"Mama, isn't it strange that the people who have been cured are never available for comment, that the holy Father Romolo Monterastelli is the only one who has witnessed these so-called miracles, and that they always happen after questions have been raised about their legitimacy?"

"So you think he's making this up to make money?"

"Sounds like a good idea, doesn't it, Mama?"

"Peppe! What are you talking about?"

Father Sangretto smiled. "When people need money, Mama, they can do almost anything, right?"

"I just don't understand what's going on." She picked up her knitting and went to her room.

The next day, as he did every day, Father Sangretto visited Antonio in the storage room.

"Amazing, Antonio! It's beautiful!"

"Thanks, Father."

"You're sure it will be ready by Christmas?"

"I'm sure."

Chapter Twelve

If Antonio hadn't dropped the little figure when he was shopping at Leoni's in early November, villagers would not have had a clue about what he was doing in the storage room of the church. Although Antonio quickly returned the sheep to his pocket, two elderly men who had arrived to play cards in the back room were quick to decide what was happening.

"Antonio is making a new *presepio!* I bet it's going to be a Neapolitan village," Marco said.

"Why? What's wrong with the little one we have? We've had it for a hundred years!" Bruno said.

"Don't you follow the news? There have been miracles at San Giovanni Evangelista in Umbria when people touch the Baby Jesus in the *presepio* that's like a Neapolitan village," Marco said. "The people are cured."

"So?"

"Don't you see? If Father Sangretto has a new *presepio* here, maybe there will be miracles and people will come from all over and they'll put a lot of money in the collection box."

"Yeah, but how can he count on miracles happening?" Bruno wondered.

"*Stupido?*" Marco shouted. "Don't you read the news? The only witness to the miracles in San Giovanni Evangelista was the priest."

"So?" Bruno wondered again.

"*Imbecille!* Father Sangretto could say there was a miracle and people would believe it and they'd still put a lot of money in the collection box."

"Why would they believe it?" Bruno said.

"Because a priest said it happened, *asino*, and priests don't lie."

"Even if the miracles didn't happen?" Bruno said.

"Bruno, you are brilliant!"

Bruno thought about this for a while. "But what about those people who said they were cured?"

"*Stupido! Imbecille!* There aren't any people who were cured! The priest made them up!"

"A priest wouldn't make stuff up."

"Bruno, you are so *stupido!*"

It took a while for Bruno to get all this through his skull, battered as it was from shell shocks during the war.

"Oh."

Rosa did not take the news nearly as calmly.

"Antonio!" she cried when he returned home that night. "You're making a *presepio* for Father Sangretto, right?"

"Rosa..."

"Antonio! Are you making a Neapolitan village like the one at San Giovanni Evangelista so that Father Sangretto can claim that people can touch the Baby Jesus and they are cured and he can collect a lot of money?"

"Rosa, Rosa..."

"Even if there aren't any miracles? Oh, Antonio."

"Rosa, Rosa..."

"I don't want to talk about it."

It was the first fight they'd had in seven years of marriage, and indeed she never did talk about it again. She made the meals as always, she washed and ironed Antonio's clothes, she sat next to him when they watched television, but when they walked around the village each evening, she didn't hold his hand.

And when they went to bed, after a perfunctory kiss, she lay on the far side. Antonio didn't know what to do, but he had made a promise to Father Sangretto and he had to keep it.

Chapter Thirteen

Briefly, Father Sangretto thought he might put up posters at Leoni's and Manconi's to announce what would happen on Christmas Day, but then he ran into Rosa and it wasn't necessary.

"Mass will be at 10 o'clock in the morning," he told her.

"Not midnight?"

"No. People might want to talk afterwards and I don't want them staying up late, especially with all the old people in the parish."

"And the people who are sick or on crutches will be able to get close to...whatever it is you're planning?"

"Of course. That would be nice."

Rosa went off in a huff, stopping at Leoni's to spread the news.

"Yes, it's true. Father Sangretto had Antonio build a *presepio* like the one in San Giovanni Evangelista and he as much as told me that sick people could come. I wonder how big the collection basket will be. And how long it will take for him to claim there is a miracle."

Mario Leoni handed over her daily loaf of crusty bread. "One thing's sure. There will be a lot of people in church on Christmas."

Within two hours, everyone in the village knew of the plan. While some people were shocked by what seemed to be the priest's blatant attempt to copy what happened in Umbria, others had a more practical view. Since Sant'Antonio had only old Fernando as its one-man police force, the cousins Bruno and Marco thought they might get jobs controlling traffic. Holding hands while walking along the little stream that the village called a river, Anita Manconi and Mario Leoni thought that with this sudden influx of visitors, they might expand their shops. Anita said her grandfather thought the meat market needed new freezers and Mario wondered about installing an outdoor café, perhaps with green-and-white umbrellas and small white tables and...

"Maybe," he said as he kissed her on the forehead, "we would be

153

able to make enough money to, well, you know…"

"I know," Anita said. She kissed him back.

A light snow had fallen during the night but Christmas Day was brisk and sunny. Father Sangretto, flanked by the two girls who would be altar servers, greeted parishioners at the door. Everyone in Sant'Antonio had turned out, and the church was packed. People not only stood along the sides but also in the center aisle.

The only light was one shining down on the altar. Otherwise, tall candles stood in wreaths on every windowsill. Signora Sangretto had spent the last month learning how to play a few hymns on the organ, and before Mass began the little church shook to earth-shattering rumbles of "Silent Night," "Joy to the World" and "We, Three Kings."

People weren't listening to the organ, however. They buzzed about what was against the wall on the right side of the church. A white curtain, actually two sheets donated by Signora Sangretto, concealed what looked like a very large structure.

"I knew it!" one woman said.

"Why is he trying to hide it?" another said.

All the buzzing stopped when Father Sangretto entered the sacristy. For someone known far beyond Sant'Antonio for his short Masses, he seemed to be taking a long time this morning. He bent his head in prayer before the first reading, then sat down in silence until he read the second.

He began his sermon talking about the Baby Jesus' love for everyone present, and this seemed to confirm what people were thinking. Why talk about Baby Jesus? Is the statue going to perform miracles?

Then he talked about the need for everyone to love one another, too, and there was some squirming. Sabina avoided Flora's stare and Franco and Augustino looked straight ahead, perhaps thinking about their feud on where to deposit church funds.

Father Sangretto concluded by saying what a lovely village Sant'Antonio was and how grateful he was to be serving as its pastor.

"I hope," he said, "that this Christmas day will be long remembered in Sant'Antonio."

"Well, of course, it will," most everyone whispered.

Normally, Father Sangretto whipped through the consecration of the bread and wine. Today, he lifted the host and cup very reverently, and those in front saw tears forming in his eyes. The tears were also present as he gave little hosts to the long line of communicants.

By the end of Mass, most people were confused. They had come to see their claims of a fraud validated. Instead, they were moved by the words and solemnity of the service.

"And now," the priest said after the final blessing, "I want you to see something that I hope will bring you much joy and happiness."

"And lots of money for Father Sangretto," a scruffy-looking man who never came to church muttered in the back.

Chapter Fourteen

Father Sangretto led Antonio to the white curtain and everyone else followed. They crowded around as one of the altar girls held the censer and the priest blessed the curtain with incense. Then he told Antonio to open the curtain.

Stunned silence.

There was indeed a *presepio* against the wall, stretching almost ten feet. But it was not an elaborate scene of a Neapolitan village. Instead, Antonio had created an intricate, and exact, miniature replica of the village of Sant'Antonio down to the very last house and building.

First it was a whisper, and then it grew into a shout. "Oh, my God! It's our village!"

"Look! There's my house!"

"And mine!"

"And mine!"

There were only fifty-two houses in the village, most of them lining the highway that led to Lucca, with a few scattered just beyond.

"Look at how Antonio did the street, with the curve just in front of my house."

"There are the flowers behind Fausta's house."

"That yellow is the exact same color as my house."

But there weren't only buildings. The scene was animated by the presence of tiny clay figures.

"Look, you can see Rosa making ravioli in her kitchen!"

"And little Franco is on his way to catch the school bus."

"And Victoria is hanging out the wash."

"Look. That's us!" Mario and Anita cried together as they looked down at two little figures. "They're holding hands just like we always do."

"And, Augustino," Franco said, "here's your Fiat in your driveway.

It's a very nice car."

"Thanks, Franco."

Franco put his arm around the shoulders of the church treasurer.

Sabina tugged at Flora's arm. "Look, Flora, you're making biscotti. You make such good biscotti."

Flora smiled.

The nearly dry Maggia River, which was really only a stream, appeared as a ribbon of light blue against miniature stones.

"And look!" Rosa cried, "there's the Cielo!"

Not quite in scale, a hill rose to the right with the farmhouse at the very tip. Tiny figures of Ezio and Donna relaxed on the patio.

But this was more than a depiction of a village. It was a *presepio*, and so the traditional figures of a nativity scene were integrated into the landscape. Two shepherds cared for their sheep in front of the Minicotti house. A cow and a goat grazed on the grass outside old Benito Grazati's barn. From the east, the three wise men made their way along the highway, one of them atop a camel. Angels perched on the roofs of the Ferrara, Rinella and Cardinelli homes. And in the middle of it all, Mary and Joseph knelt before the manger holding the Baby Jesus right in the middle of the little piazza in front of Manconi's and Leoni's. An angel looked down from the rooftop of the Cielo.

Eventually, everyone formed a line, which was surprisingly orderly since little kids were jumping up and down pointing themselves out to their parents. Many of the villagers wiped away tears, and many held hands.

Rosa and Antonio also held hands.

"I'm sorry, Antonio," she said. "I had no idea."

"Father Sangretto told me not to tell anyone."

"You've never told a lie in all your life. How could you tell one now?"

Only Rosa saw Father Sangretto move quietly to the side of the *presepio* and take away a large basket. Then he returned, and the villagers lined up to shake his hand. *"Grazie, grazie."* "Thank you, Father," they said. "Antonio did such a wonderful job." "Our village looks so lovely."

It was well past 1 o'clock when the last person had inspected the tableaux, thanked the priest and left the church. Father Sangretto went to the sacristy to take off his vestments, but was soon joined by Rosa and Antonio.

"Father," Rosa said, "would you and your mother like to come to our house for dinner? It's just us, and I made ravioli."

"Really?" The priest had never been invited to a home for a meal before. "Mama was going to make veal cutlets, but she could bring them there, if you want."

"Of course," Rosa said. "Come! Come! We'll have a *festa!*"

Chapter Fifteen

Belying the well-known fact that two Italian women should not be in the same kitchen at the same time, Rosa and Signora Sangretto happily prepared their separate contributions to the Christmas dinner, chatting about the *presepio* and all kinds of other things. Antonio and Father Sangretto sat in the living room, discovering that they had mutual acquaintances in Florence.

When it was time for dinner, Father Sangretto said the grace, thanking God for the opportunity to serve the people of Sant'Antonio, for the well-being of everyone in the village and especially for those gathered around the simply decorated table.

Signora Sangretto couldn't get over how delicious Rosa's ravioli were and wanted to know the recipe. Rosa blushed and said it was a secret but maybe she would divulge it "the next time you come for dinner." Rosa herself marveled at the veal cutlets her guest had brought.

"Look, Antonio, I can cut this with my fork. With my fork!"

Afterwards, while the women cleaned up, Antonio and Father Sangretto enjoyed the last of the priest's Cuban cigars, imports he had saved just for Christmas. Then they thought they might watch a little television.

"Maybe they'll have something about the Mass at the Vatican last night," Signora Sangretto said.

Instead, the first thing they saw were the words *"FRODE!"* and *"SCHERZO!"*

"A fraud and a hoax?" Father Sangretto asked. "Who did that?"

The comely announcer answered his question.

"Tonight we have important and sorrowful news from the little village of San Giovanni Evangelista in the region of Umbria," she breathlessly reported. "You will recall that miracles were reported at the church in the village when three weak and suffering people touched the face of the little Baby Jesus in the church's *presepio*.

"You will also recall that there were no witnesses to these so-called miracles, and that the only person who said they occurred was the pastor of the church, Father Romolo Monterastelli. As respected journalists, we never did believe his stories, and we attempted to investigate these miracles ourselves, but Monterastelli always put up roadblocks and would not let us talk to these people who supposedly had been cured. Today, Christmas Day, the real story has come out."

The program switched to video clips of *carabinieri* pushing Father Romolo Monterastelli into a police car. He was trying to hide his face from dozens of cameras.

"We regret to inform you that this has all been a fraud," the announcer continued. "There has not been a dying woman or a boy who was blind or a woman from Calabria with a palsied hand. Monterastelli made all these stories up. Nothing like this happened. He was the one who reported these so-called miracles to the media. He was the one who insisted that they occurred even though many people began to doubt.

"Investigators from the bishop's office have now exposed the whole story as a fraud and a hoax, and he is also under investigation by civil authorities who want to know what he did with maybe millions of *lire* that were donated by unsuspecting pilgrims to his church.

"Why did he do this? Authorities say he gave a brief statement after his arrest. He said he desperately wanted to leave the little village of San Giovanni Evangelista. He thought that the church's hierarchy would notice him and move him to a church in Rome.

"Such is the sad case of Father Romolo Monterastelli."

Rosa and Antonio, Father Sangretto and his mother sat in silence.

"I knew it all along," Rosa said.

"Rosa, you did not," Antonio said.

"Yes, I did. I just didn't tell you."

"Well," Signora Sangretto said, "Peppe here, Giuseppe, really did know it. Right from the start."

"It's very sad," her son said. "I knew Father Monterastelli in the seminary. He had problems then, and I think his problems just got worse. Only God can judge him now."

"And the Vatican," his mother said.

"And the civil authorities," Antonio said.

"But Father," Rosa said, "you had Antonio build a *presepio*, too. I mean...people were saying...that is...they thought that you might be thinking of doing the same thing."

"Rosa!" Signora Sangretto said. "My son would never do anything like that. I know him well enough that he would never commit such a fraud and a hoax."

Father Sangretto held up his hand. "Wait, Mama."

"What? You mean you did? I don't believe it. Oh, Peppe."

Father Sangretto took a long sip of grappa. "Well, here's the story.

"When I saw what my old classmate Father Monterastelli, was doing in San Giovanni Evangelista I'll admit I got upset. I was jealous. Here he was getting all that publicity but, also, making all that money.

"I knew his miracles were a fake. My God, he couldn't produce any of the people who were cured, and you notice he always called the newspapers and television stations late at night and the reports even said his voice was slurred. Well, you can only imagine what kind of state he was in.

"But still he was making all that money. And you know the problems we've had here. Right now, we've got to get a new boiler. But people aren't coming to church and they're not giving money."

He paused. "And I know I'm to blame for that."

"No, no, Giuseppe, you're not to blame," his mother said.

"No, Father," Rosa said. "It's not you. Well, maybe it's partly you, but you know people here in Sant'Antonio, they're stubborn, they want to do things their own way."

"That's nice of you to say, Rosa," Father Sangretto said, "but I know it's mostly my fault. I haven't reached out to the people enough. Anyway, with the church needing so much work, especially with the boiler problem, I thought of an idea."

"Which was?" Rosa asked.

"I would have a *presepio* built, but it wouldn't be like the ones in Naples or the one in San Giovanni Evangelista in Umbria. No, it would be of our village. We have such a beautiful village, and I wanted people to be proud of it. And that's why I contacted Antonio here. You know, God works in mysterious ways. Who would have known that we had such a master artisan right in our midst who could make such a great thing?"

While Antonio suddenly examined his shoes, Rosa beamed.

"I was never going to claim that there were miracles," the priest continued. "I could never do that. But I thought, well, maybe our people would be so proud of their village when they saw what Antonio had built that they would invite relatives and friends from other towns and villages to come to see this magnificent *presepio*. Maybe it would become a tourist attraction, maybe even put Sant'Antonio on the map. That was my plan. And I'd put out a big collection basket so they could make their offerings. And that's what I did."

"But Father," Rosa said, "I saw you take a collection basket away from the *presepio* this morning. Why didn't you leave it there?"

"Rosa, when I saw the people there enjoying the *presepio* so much, how they were so proud of their village, how they loved seeing their homes there, and in fact seeing themselves there, well, I knew I just couldn't ask people to give money to see it. That would not be right."

"So you're going to have his replica of our village, but it will all be free?"

"Of course."

"And how long will you keep it up?"

"As long as people want to see it," the priest said.

Antonio raised his hand. "Father, I just thought of something. What if somebody came from another village and they liked the *presepio* so much that they just, well, they just happened to leave a few *lire* next to the Baby Jesus?"

Father Sangretto laughed. "Well, I hadn't thought of that. If it happens, it happens. If this brings people to church, fine. If people come from other places to see it, fine. It's such a splendid thing, Antonio, how can I ever thank you? And if they donate money, fine. But I don't want to set this up to make money. We'll be all right. We'll get along."

He leaned forward.

"But this is the most important thing. Did you see what people were doing when they saw the *presepio*? They were smiling and talking to each other. My God, Franco and Augustino. Flora and

Sabina. And all the others. But you know the best thing I saw? Signora Contini and Signora Nardini holding hands and chatting and laughing. They haven't spoken to each other in twenty-eight years even though they live next to each other. Just seeing that made this all worthwhile. All these people in our village were suddenly getting along! I tell you, I started to cry."

The women, and even Antonio, had tears in their eyes, now, too. Signora Sangretto put her hand on her son's arm. Rosa got up to get more cookies from the kitchen. On the way back, she happened to look out the window.

"*Santa Maria,*" she said. "Look at all the cars going by. We've never had so much traffic on this street."

Antonio got up to look. "They're going up the street to the church. They must have heard about the *presepio.*"

"Father," Rosa said, "maybe there has been a miracle in Sant'Antonio today after all."

"Yes, Rosa. I think there has. More than one."

Butterfly

July 10, 1974

The first time Rosa Tomaselli thought something was strange was when Annabella Sabbatini showed up at church without lipstick.

"I mean, she could just as well have come in naked! I was shocked!" Rosa told her neighbor, Lucia Sporenza.

"Because she didn't wear lipstick?" Lucia was rolling out dough for ravioli. Rosa was again trying to teach her, but these lessons had been going on for months without much success.

"Lucia, Annabella would never go out of the house without lipstick. Why would she do that?"

"Maybe she forgot?" Lucia tried getting the dough into the same thickness, but it wouldn't cooperate.

"How could she forget? A woman doesn't forget to put on lipstick."

"Rosa! You don't wear lipstick!"

"Yes, I do. Well, I have. When I married Marco. At his funeral. When I married Antonio."

"So three times?"

"I'm sure there were more times than that. Anyway, Annabella wouldn't forget to wear lipstick. She always wears lipstick. She's been wearing that same coral lipstick since we were in school. That's what, seventy years ago? I know. We went to Lucca and I helped her pick it out."

"You remember that?" Lucia wiped her forehead with a towel. The July heat was getting more oppressive. "My God, I can't remember what I did last week."

"*Allora*," Rosa said. "All I know is that Annabella didn't wear lipstick to church today. You know how Annabella is. Every hair in place, always a nice dress on, a pretty scarf. I don't care so much for looks."

"Rosa, do you really think anyone besides you even noticed?"

Rosa took over rolling out the dough. "Lucia, how could anyone not notice? I mean, Annabella always wears that coral lipstick."

They were silent for a time, Rosa rolling out dough, Lucia mixing ricotta and spices into the finely ground spinach. Then Rosa started up again.

"I know for a fact that Annabella has driven to Lucca just to get the coral lipstick. She can only get it at Giacometti's. Imagine, driving to Lucca to buy lipstick."

Lucia stretched her aching arms. "Rosa, Lucca's only twenty minutes away. And she's got her new Fiat."

Rosa wiped flour from the rolling pin. "I don't know why she had to buy a new Fiat. The other one was only three years old. We've had ours for eight years. Antonio says it's still running fine so we don't need a new one."

Lucia began placing the filling in small dabs on the dough and carving out the ravioli with a glass. Rosa thought she was making them too small, but she bit her tongue.

"Paolo won't buy a new one either," Lucia said. "Now with business at the *pasticceria* being so slow I guess we'll never get one. Annabella will be the only one in Sant'Antonio with a new car."

In forty-five minutes, they were finished. "Ninety-eight," Rosa said, disapprovingly.

"Next time I'll make them bigger," Lucia said.

Rosa took off her flour-covered apron. "I still can't believe that Annabella came to church without lipstick."

I wonder why Rosa looked at me that way in church today. You'd think I didn't have any clothes on. How strange. Maybe she's getting old. Well, we're all getting old. Rosa is the same age as me, so I should know. We've known each other forever. She's such a lovely woman. I know people say she's kind of nosy sometimes, but it doesn't bother me. She's just interested in other people. I'm glad she's my friend. I'm glad I have so many friends here in Sant'Antonio. Maybe someday I'll need them more. Not now. I'm fine just now. I have everything, nice house, nice car, good friends. I wish I could find my cake pans. How can I make my chocolate cake for Saturday night if I can't find my cake pans? Not in the cupboards. Not on the counter. Not in the oven. That's strange. Oh! How did they get in the refrigerator?

September 14, 1974

Having made her daily telephone call to her son, Dino, in Florence, and making sure that he was still perfectly all right, Lucia thought of something else to be concerned about. She had a list.

"Paolo, do you think I should be worried about Annabella?" Lucia and Paolo were having leftover ravioli for the third straight night. For months she had been trying to make them right.

"Annabella?"

"Yes, Annabella."

"Annabella Sabbatini?"

"Yes, Annabella Sabbatini. What other Annabella is there in Sant'Antonio?" Sometimes Lucia feared that her husband was losing his hearing. Or maybe he just didn't listen to her.

"What's wrong with Annabella?"

Lucia noticed that there were still three ravioli on his plate. "Well, at the cemetery this morning, she started acting so peculiar again, the same as she did yesterday and the day before that."

"How peculiar?"

"Every day, we all go and put flowers on the graves, say a prayer and leave. She always goes to Francesco's grave. Nobody stays around too long."

"I don't know why you women do that anyway."

"Well, we do. We all do. We have to. Anyway, for the last three days Annabella has knelt at Francesco's grave for a long time, and then today she started sobbing, and then she began kissing his picture on the tombstone. And she was sobbing more. Isn't that strange?"

"I guess she misses him."

"I guess so. But he was killed in the war thirty years ago and she's never done that before."

"I think it's kind of nice. After thirty years will you be bringing flowers to my grave and kissing my picture?"

"Paolo, I'm the one who will go first. You're so stubborn, you're never going to die. Anyway, it's not like Annabella and Francesco had a great marriage. Everyone in Sant'Antonio knows they didn't."

"All right, Lucia, let's not start talking about that, OK? What they did was their business. It's none of ours."

"Well, there's something else, too. You know how Annabella always looked so smart and dignified. Oh my, when I was young I thought she must be a queen."

Paolo moved the three ravioli clockwise on his plate. "And you were the little servant girl?"

"Never mind. But now, Annabella sometimes looks like she just threw on anything that was handy. Sometimes her hair isn't even combed. And she doesn't wear makeup. Sometimes her lipstick isn't on right. Paolo, make me a promise."

"Anything."

"If I start getting like that, don't let me out of the house, OK? I don't want anyone to see me. Don't let me get like that."

"You won't, Lucia."

"How do you know that?"

Paolo didn't know that, of course. Lucia picked up his plate. "The ravioli still aren't very good, are they? I don't know why I can't make them like Rosa." She threw the ravioli in the garbage can.

Paolo knew he had to be tactful. "Lucia, they're better than they were last time."

"I don't think that's a compliment. Well, anyway, I'm not going to worry about Annabella. Unless she keeps acting strange."

Where's my handkerchief? I had it right here a minute ago. Oh, Francesco, I miss you so much. I don't know why it's getting harder now. So long ago. I wish I could have told you that I really did love you. I'm sorry for the way I behaved. So obstinate. I know you were hurt. You hurt me, too, though. Remember? We didn't fight so much, but we didn't talk to each other. And I hated your violin playing. So long ago, so long ago. I don't care. I forgive you. I forgive you. I forgive you. I miss you. So tired. Where's my handkerchief?

November 20, 1974

Although Christmas was more than a month away, Mario Leoni had already arranged his grandfather's old *presepio* in the window of his *bottega*, careful because the Joseph had lost his staff and one of the sheep missed both of its ears. In the five years Mario had owned the shop he had come to look forward to the Christmas season, the busiest time of the year. He had stocked the shop's shelves with various boxes of candies and cookies, along with statues, toys, Christmas ornaments and gift wrap. Like his grandfather, Mario liked to say that his *bottega* was the best shop in Sant'Antonio. Of course, it was the only shop.

The first customers today were two neighbors, Flora Lenci and Sabina Melfi, who, to the relief and amusement of everyone else in the village, had finally settled their decades-old arguments and were the best of friends.

"*Buongiorno,* Signora Lenci, Signora Melfi! A beautiful day, right?"

"Well, if you like cold weather," Flora said. "*Buongiorno,* Mario."

"It's so cold my teeth are chattering," Sabina said.

"Look at my hands," Flora said. "They're blue!"

"I told you to wear gloves," Sabina told her friend. "Now you wear mine when we go out. I can put my hands in my pockets."

Mario thought he'd interrupt the complaints about the weather. "What can I help you with today, *signore?*"

"Flour!" they said in unison. "We both want flour."

"I'm going to make my crusty bread," Sabina said.

"And I'm going to make my famous biscotti."

They went to the shelf that normally contained at least a dozen bags of flour, the product of a mill just east of Lucca.

Except that the shelf was empty.

"Mario!" they both cried. "Where is the flour?"

Mario's face reddened. "*Signore*, I'm so sorry, but we will be getting some in on Wednesday. Maybe Thursday. Friday at the latest. I promise."

"Wednesday, Thursday, Friday! I want to make my bread today!" Sabina said. "My son and his wife are coming and they like my bread so much. I've always made my bread for them."

"And I need to make my biscotti today," Flora said. "I have to take them to the *briscola* group tonight. We always have them while we play cards. Everyone says how much they like them!"

"I'm sorry, *signore*. But I have ordered more flour and we should have it by the end of the week."

"You don't have any in the storage room?"

"No, I'm afraid not."

"Not in the basement."

"No, I wouldn't keep flour down there."

"But, Mario," Sabina said, "how could you run out so fast? Last week when I was here I'm sure you had the shelves filled."

"Yes, last week they were filled."

"And now they not. Why, Mario, why?"

Mario fiddled with the keys to the cash register, rearranged the cash receipts, cleared his throat and sighed. "Annabella bought it all. Just yesterday."

"Annabella? What on earth? All of that flour?"

"Yes."

"Why, for heaven's sake? Why does she need all that flour?"

"She said she wanted to make a chocolate cake."

"But you don't need a dozen bags of flour to make a chocolate cake!"

"I know, I know, but she wanted them, so she paid for them all and loaded up her car."

Sabina shook her head. "I can't believe it."

Flora put her hand on her friend's arm and lowered her voice. "You know, I think something very strange is happening to Annabella. Remember the last *briscola* game? She couldn't remember what cards she had. Not a one."

"And," Sabina whispered, "you know how she's always humming? Some little song, I guess. It drives Viola crazy, but she doesn't want to say anything."

"Poor Annabella," they said. "*Ciao,* Mario."

I wonder why Mario thought it was so strange. I needed the flour. Lots of flour. I need to make my chocolate cake. Poor Mario. He has so much work to do. I'm glad I have my flour. Now I can make a chocolate cake. Everyone loves my chocolate cakes. Now I'm going to make my chocolate cake. First I have to find my cake pans.

December 26, 1974

Putting on an extra sweater on this chilly morning, Father Sangretto went into the rectory dining room, the usual place to count money from the collection baskets. His mother, tightening a woolen scarf around her shoulders, sat down across from him.

"Well, let's see how little they could give and still feel good," she said.

After what everyone called the "miracle" of the *presepio* three years ago there had been a brief upswing in the Christmas collections, but a poor economy had left some men in the village without jobs this year, and Father Sangretto didn't expect the collection to be much more than on any Sunday.

His mother took one of the two cloth baskets and emptied the contents on the big oak table. There was a small pile of coins, some loose paper *lire*, and three envelopes.

"Have you noticed," she said, "that people don't use their envelopes much any more? I guess they don't want us to know how little they give. If they give at all."

"Who gave this year?"

Signora Sangretto looked at the number on the top of the first envelope and then at the ledger listing all parishioners by numbers.

"Let's see. Mancini. Poor Signora Mancini. She always gives a little."

She opened the envelope. 200 *lire*.

"Poor thing."

The next was from Fazio. "350 *lire*."

"That's nice," her son said. "Even with all those kids."

The third was from Andriano. "1,000 *lire!*" his mother exclaimed. "Oh, my. And he's been out of work for three months."

"You know, Mama, some of the people in Sant'Antonio are so good and generous. That's why I like being a priest here. I'm so grateful."

"You won't be so grateful when we won't be able to pay the heating bill again."

It didn't take long to count the rest from the first basket.

"8,745 *lire*. Well, that's about enough to buy two dozen candles," the priest said.

His mother dumped the contents of the other basket on the table. A little more this time, with a few coins, big bank notes for about 9,000 paper *lire* and a fat envelope held together with a rubber band.

"Who's the envelope from?" he asked.

"Hmmm. It's Annabella. Annabella Sabbatini."

"My goodness, she must have given a lot."

With palsied and trembling hands, Signora Sangretto opened the envelope. Out fell one 10,000 *lire* note after another.

"My God," she cried, "I can't believe this."

Together they counted. There were dozens of them, each adorned with the portrait of Michelangelo. Father Sangretto pulled out a calculator from a desk. "Oh my God! There's 2,300,000 *lire*!"

"Holy Mother of God!" his mother cried.

"Oh my. We have to give it back. She can't afford that."

"Peppe..."

"Giuseppe, Mama."

"Giuseppe, Annabella gave the money because she wanted to. It would be a sin to refuse it."

"Oh, Mama, don't talk to me about sin."

"Giuseppe, she can afford it. She has to be the wealthiest person in the village."

"I don't know about that, Mama. I don't look at people thinking how much money they have, how much they put in the collection basket. I'm sure God doesn't look at people that way."

Signora Sangretto ignored the insinuation. "Well, Rosa told me once that Francesco owned a *trattoria* in Reboli and after he was killed in the war she sold it. That's why she has money. Rosa says she gets some money every month from the bank. And she just bought a new car. So I'm sure she wanted to give some money to the church. She always gives 500 or 1,000 *lire* every Sunday."

"But she's never given money like this before, Mama."

"Well, maybe she just decided to do it this time."

"Mama, we all know that something is happening to Annabella. She comes to Mass late, her hair is all messed up, her dresses aren't buttoned. She spends too much time at Francesco's grave in the cemetery."

"I know, Giuseppe. Rosa tells me she's found her wandering around the village and doesn't seem to know where she is. Rosa has had to take her back to her house."

Father Sangretto started putting the coins and *lire* into a safety box. "No matter how much money she has, Mama, she shouldn't be doing this. And it just shows, no matter how much money somebody has, they can still get sick, they can still lose their minds. Poor Annabella. I'm going to bring this back to her."

"Are you sure, Giuseppe?" His mother got up, too. "I wish she had some relatives she could live with. But Rosa says there's no one. She never had any brothers or sisters, and of course she and Francesco never had any children. All these years, living alone in that big house."

The priest put Annabella's money back in the envelope. "I don't know what's going to happen to her. We have to pray very hard. I'm going to see her now."

Who's that man coming up the walk in a black dress? Oh, it's the priest. Father…Father…can't remember his name. Nice man. I don't want to see him. Don't open door. Bedroom. Safe in bed. Under covers. Safe.

February 2, 1975

If Ezio hadn't been late coming home from school in Reboli, he wouldn't have found her, and she would have spent the night in her car. He was still shaking when he finally got to the Cielo.

"Ezio!" Donna cried. "Where were you? I've been worried sick."

"Sorry, hon." He kissed her forehead. "What a night. I'm exhausted."

"Want something to eat? I tried out a new recipe of veal medallions and asparagus, but it's surely cold by now. I can warm it up."

"Thanks, but I'll wait." He sank into a chair. "Let me catch my breath. A little grappa would be nice, though."

After Donna had poured the drink and sat opposite him, he explained why he was three hours late.

He was driving up the hill from the village to the Cielo when he made the sharp turn.

"The one halfway up?" she asked.

"Yes, where we almost hit a deer last week."

Suddenly, he said, he saw a black Fiat in the ditch. It had smashed against a tree. He had to go farther up the hill to find a place to put his truck, then ran back to the Fiat.

"I didn't know what I'd find, but it didn't look serious. The car was just resting against the tree, it didn't seem damaged, but the motor wasn't running."

"And inside?"

"Donna, Annabella was in the car, just sitting there. She didn't seem hurt. I got the door open, and she smiled. It was like she was just on a drive out in the country."

"And she said?"

"She said something about how she was just out for a drive and thought she'd come to visit us. I think that's what she said. She's very hard to understand these days."

"Hmmm. She's been up here dozens of times, but she always calls first."

"And, Donna, it was cold! It must have been forty degrees in that car. And she didn't have a coat on, just her dress."

"Oh, my."

"So I got in, and I saw a blanket in the back and put that around her. That helped a little. So then she just started talking, but I wasn't sure what she was saying. Anyway, there's only a dented fender. I got the car started, and backed it out of the ditch and I drove her home. I took her in and she was still shivering. I saw she had some bean soup on the stove so I warmed that up for her. I tried talking to her, but I really didn't understand what she was saying. Something about Francesco, something about going to Lucca, I don't know. Then she said she was tired, I think that's what she said, and she went into the bedroom, didn't say thanks or good-bye or anything, so I left. Fausta's light was on next door so I went over there and told her what happened. Fausta said she'd go to see Annabella the first thing tomorrow morning."

"Dear Fausta. Who would have thought that cranky old woman would be so kind and sweet to Annabella? And then you walked all the way home?"

"Just to where I parked the truck. What a night."

"How long do you think she'd been sitting there?"

"I don't know. I got there about 8 o'clock. Nobody is on that road after about 5 at this time of year."

Donna got up to get the grappa bottle. "Ezio, that's terrible. Poor Annabella. She shouldn't be driving anymore."

"I know. I saw her on the highway to Reboli last week and she was weaving all over. She's a menace to everyone on the highway."

"Not to mention to herself."

"We've got to get her license taken away."

They realized that would be a problem. In the first place, she would resist. In the second, the Italian bureaucracy would take months, maybe years, to act.

"You don't know someone?" Donna asked.

"Not in that department."

They sat in silence.

"Well," Ezio said, "you know, something could always happen to her car."

"What's to happen? It's practically new. Nothing's going to go wrong."

Ezio thought some more. "Well, maybe nothing will happen unless someone makes it happen."

"Ezio! What are you talking about?"

"Oh, nothing."

Donna smiled. "Just don't tell me, OK?"

Nice drive in the country. Cold. Nice man. Wonder who he is. Should pay him.

February 4, 1975

Paolo thought Lucia would never go to bed, but finally he heard her gentle snoring and he went outside to wait. The moon was so bright he could see his watch.

11:20.

"He'd better come soon. I'm freezing my tail off."

Ten minutes later, Ezio did show up, turning the motor off on his truck as he glided in front of Paolo's house.

"Sorry. Donna was reading and she wouldn't go to bed."

"I brought a flashlight."

"I did, too."

"And a wrench."

"Me, too."

"OK, let's do it."

At this time of night there wasn't any traffic in Sant'Antonio, but as they stealthily walked against the bushes, they knew they didn't want to wake anyone. At the Fulcini's, the German shepherd growled and then barked loudly. A light went on in the second story and Paolo and Ezio leaned against a tree. Finally, the dog stopped.

As they rounded a corner, they could hear rustling in the bushes behind the Antonini's beehives. Paolo and Ezio froze. Then a disheveled boy and girl came out.

"*Buonasera, Professore!*" the boy said.

"*Buonasera,* Filippo," the startled Ezio said. "Aren't you out a little late?"

"Nah. Me and Amelia were just, um, talking. Aren't you out a little late?"

Amelia giggled.

Ezio stumbled. "My friend and I were just going for a late-night walk. See you tomorrow, OK? Better not be late. We have history first period."

Giggling, Filippo and Amelia disappeared into the bushes again.

"I don't like to call my pupils stupid," Ezio whispered to Paolo, "but that kid really should be home studying. He's been held back a year already."

"OK, we're here."

They knew Annabella's car wouldn't be locked. Nobody locked cars in Sant'Antonio. But it was parked just feet from her bedroom window.

"Shhhh," Paolo said.

Ezio got in and popped the hood.

Soon, two flashlights were aimed at the battery.

"Looks simple enough," Paolo said. Using his wrench, he removed the positive cable. Then Ezio used his wrench to remove the negative cable.

Suddenly a light went on in Annabella's bedroom.

"Shit!" Paolo said.

"Just stay quiet." They waited. And waited. Finally, the light went off.

"OK, you lift it out," Paolo said.

"Why me?"

"Because you're closer."

"Not because I'm stronger?"

"Of course not."

Ezio reached in and slowly lifted the battery from its case. "This thing weighs a ton."

"You know what?" Paolo said. "We should have driven over here. What are we going to do with this thing?"

"I don't know, but we better decide soon. I can't hold this much longer."

"Hide it in the bushes by that tree. Just leave it. She'll never find it."

"Maybe I can come back tomorrow and get it."

Paolo gently put the hood back in place, making a clicking sound. Again, the bedroom light went on. They waited again. Then the light went off.

"Well," Ezio said, wiping his hands, "that looks like the end of Annabella's driving."

"Thank goodness for all of us."

Wish I could sleep better. So much banging outside. Just an old lady. Sleep.

May 15, 1975

Having learned from the disaster last November when Leoni's ran out of flour, Flora Lenci always kept at least one extra bag on hand. She was pleased that her biscotti were particularly good tonight for the *briscola* group, crisp but not hard, tangy but not sweet.

"Love your biscotti," Rosa said as she took another.

The game itself had disintegrated, with Fausta Sanfilippo vociferously arguing with her partner, Viola Agnosto, over Viola's last play while Rosa and Flora gossiped about the supposed infidelity of a new neighbor down the street.

"You know," Flora said rather loudly, "I miss having Annabella here, but it's probably just as well. She really can't play anymore."

"I think she'll join us again soon," Fausta said. "I just stopped by her house. I knew she wasn't feeling well. She was lying on her bed. All her clothes on, just lying on her bed. But I think she's getting better."

"Fausta!" Rosa said. "Annabella's getting better? What are you talking about?"

Fausta put her cards down and placed her hands firmly on the table. "Well, that's just what I think. I mean Annabella has some bad days but she has good days, too. I see her almost every day, so I know. How often do you see her? Do you know anything?"

"Fausta…" Viola tried to get her to calm down.

"I'm serious," Fausta went on. "You women are always saying that there's something wrong with Annabella. Well, I don't think so. At least it's not as bad as you make it out to be. We all forget things sometimes. Just the other day I couldn't find my hairbrush. Looked all over. It was just where I left it but I didn't see it."

"It's not just forgetting, Fausta," Rosa said. "You know she acts, well, peculiar sometimes."

"Peculiar!" Fausta's voice rose. "What? So she goes for walks sometimes. She likes to get out."

"Fausta, Fausta," Rosa said. "She doesn't just go for walks. She doesn't know where she's going. I've had to take her home because she doesn't know where she is."

"And, you know," Viola said, "she, well, she doesn't take care of herself like she used to. Her hair, her dress. Even her shoes. Yesterday she had two different shoes on. And that song she keeps humming! Oh, my God!"

"And it's so hard to talk to her anymore," Flora said. "She just mumbles. I don't know what to say."

"It's like she's in her own little world," Viola said.

"Well, at least she's not driving anymore," Rosa said.

"Thank God," Flora said. "I was afraid to go out of the house when she was on the road."

"I still don't understand why that car won't start," Fausta said. "It's a perfectly good car. I told her to call a mechanic, but she won't."

"Fausta, you don't want her on the road, do you?" Flora asked.

"No, I guess not. I guess this is for the best. But I still wonder why that car won't start."

"Well," Rosa said. "Sometimes cars have their own minds. They just don't want to start anymore."

"Rosa," Flora said, "do you know something about that car not starting?"

Rosa's face grew red. "Me? Car not starting? What would I know? I don't know anything about cars."

"Hmmm," Viola said. "Seems kind of suspicious to me."

Fausta began to sob. "Oh, this is just so hard. I feel so bad for her. She doesn't know what's happening, the poor woman."

Flora put her hand on Fausta's arm. "Fausta, we all love Annabella. That's why we're so concerned. We know she's your best friend in the village."

"Sometimes," Fausta's voice cracked, "I think she's my only friend."

"No, no," the three other women said. "We're your friends. Really."

Fausta wiped her eyes.

"Fausta," Rosa said, "we just want you to realize what's happening with Annabella. Sometimes I think you don't want to know. But that isn't going to help things. When some people get old they get that way, they start acting strange, and we have to help them. Don't you realize that?"

Fausta blew her nose. "I don't know. This is just so hard."

Francesco. Miss Francesco. Where are you? You were just here. Where did you go?

June 13, 1975

As always, the Feast of St. Anthony, with its accompanying *festa*, was the biggest event of the year in Sant'Antonio. First there was the procession in which the statue of the patron saint was carried into the church. Then the Mass, which Father Sangretto again kept short. Then the pageant on the life of St. Anthony put on by the First Communicants, six girls and two boys this year. And then the feast in the church basement. Rosa brought her usual ravioli, and others bought mounds of various dishes that were quickly consumed by crowds who had come from great distances. Then Antonio played his concertina and little kids and a few elderly women danced.

The frivolity, however, did not extend to a long table in the corner. There, surrounded by her friends from Rosa's neighborhood, Annabella sat nervously, humming a song and tapping her fingers loudly on the table. The others didn't know what to do. Should they try to make conversation? Annabella didn't seem to understand what they were saying.

"Annabella, you're looking good today," Viola said.

Annabella stared blankly and continued humming.

"Annabella, do you know who I am?" Rosa asked. "Do you remember my name?"

Annabella continued humming.

Fausta put her arm around her. Until last year, they were both tall, strong women. Fausta was by far more outspoken, but Annabella could voice her opinions, too. Somehow, they had become good friends.

Now, everyone was shocked when Fausta and Annabella were seen together. Annabella seemed to have shrunk, with thin shoulders and hands and arms so fragile everyone was afraid to touch them.

Lacking any response, the villagers tried to make small talk among themselves, and focused on Dino, who had driven all the way from Florence.

"Remember, Dino," Paolo said, "when you were in high school and that girl kept wanting you to dance at the *festa*? What was her name again?"

"Benedetta Mendicino," Dino said. "She sure was a flirt. What happened to her?"

"She's studying law in Pisa," Lucia said pointedly.

"Oh. Guess you never know."

"Well, you had your chance, Dino."

Suddenly, Annabella began to sing. Loudly. The words didn't make sense, but it seemed to be an old nursery song. The dancers stopped abruptly and stared. Antonio put his concertina down. Only Annabella's crackling voice echoed through the hall.

Father Sangretto came over and put his hand on Annabella's shoulder. "It's all right, Annabella, it's all right."

Annabella smiled.

"Are you having fun tonight, Annabella?"

She smiled again.

"*Festa* is always fun, isn't it?" the priest said. "I'm glad you came. I've missed you at Mass, but I know sometimes you sleep in, and that's all right."

She hummed her song again. Father Sangretto moved away. "We need to pray very hard for her," he whispered to the others.

Fausta leaned close to Annabella. "Come," she said, gently lifting Annabella to her feet. "Let's go home. I think you're tired now. It's been such a long day."

Fausta, who was never known to cry, had tears running down her face.

The room remained silent after they left, but then one by one or in pairs, most people left, leaving only the villagers at the long table.

"This has happened so fast," Rosa said. "It was just last year that I started noticing things."

"Sometimes it happens fast," Sabina said. "I remember my mother. She was fine until she was eighty-five. Sharp as a tack. Remembered everything. Then suddenly she started forgetting. Didn't take her pills. Didn't wash up. Then she forgot meals. She died two years later."

"How old is Annabella?" Flora asked.

"Eighty-six," Rosa said. "Same age as me."

"Oh, I don't want to get old," said Flora, who was seventy-five. Viola, who was seventy-six, and Sabina, who was seventy-eight, agreed.

Nice party. But I don't know anybody anymore. Just want to stay home.

November 28, 1975

It was Viola's turn to host the *briscola* game, and her husband had retreated into the living room to watch a soccer game. But no one was in the mood to play cards. In the middle of the second game, Fausta threw down her cards and started to sob. Flora held her arm and everyone looked silently down at the table.

"Well," Viola said, "at least they found her in time. Who knows what would have happened if they didn't?"

"I was outside then," Flora said. "Five o'clock in the morning. The milkman had just put the bottles on the porch. It couldn't have been more than forty degrees."

Fausta sobbed harder.

"Poor Annabella," Rosa said.

Again, they recounted the events of the early morning. Father Sangretto's mother had gotten up early to go to the bathroom—for the fourth time that night, the women noted—and had seen something pink moving in the cemetery next to the church. She woke her son, who put on his shirt and pants and a jacket and went to investigate.

There, he found Annabella sitting on Francesco's marble grave, wearing only a nightgown. No shoes. She was singing a little song, but he didn't know what it was. He tried to get her to come with him, but she said she had to stay with her husband. Father Sangretto put his jacket around her shoulders and sat with her for a while until he could coax her to come to the rectory.

His mother made espresso and gave Annabella a warm bathrobe and socks to wear. They had her sit in a chair and they put on the television, but she wasn't interested. She kept singing the little song. Finally, the priest and his mother drove her home. The priest had to leave to say Mass, but Signora Sangretto stayed with Annabella until noon, made her some lunch and left because Annabella wanted to take a nap.

"Oh," Fausta said, "I don't want to hear this again. It's too terrible. I wish I had been there. But I was so tired. She seemed fine when I left her last night. I didn't think she'd wake up and go out." Her handkerchief was soaked with her tears.

"This is the way it happens," Flora said. "I remember my mother. First, it was just little things, like forgetting whether she took her pills. Oh, how many times she did that. I didn't know what to do, give her the pills even if she'd taken them? And then she wouldn't get dressed. All day! Friends would come over and there she'd be, in her nightgown. Then she started forgetting names. She knew who my sons were, but she couldn't remember their names. And then after a while she didn't even know them. And finally, she didn't even know who I was. Imagine. Her only daughter! That was so hard."

Flora began to cry and Rosa hugged her.

"The same with me," Viola said. "But it was my papa. Oh, it was so sad to see this big man, a farmer all his life. And then he became this little shrunken man, unable to do anything. We had to do everything, Mama and me, feed him, bathe him, change his diapers. And he'd get so upset because he couldn't get the words out. We prayed that he'd go, but he didn't. Not for four years, four years."

Then Viola burst into tears and Rosa and Flora hugged her.

"My Marco the same way," Rosa said. "I can't even talk about it." Tears fell on her white blouse. Viola and Flora put their arms around her and Fausta held her hands.

"*Allora*," Rosa said. "But I have my Antonio now."

Fausta wiped her eyes again. "It seems like only yesterday, but I guess it was about two years ago. Annabella and I would get out *The Divine Comedy* each night and we'd read a few pages. Annabella would explain everything to me, all the allusions, everything that Dante was referring to. I could never figure that out. I hardly went past eighth grade. But here she was, this wonderful, intelligent woman who had read so much. And she explained everything to me! Now look at her! Singing in her nightgown on Francesco's grave! In the middle of the night!"

Fausta's body trembled with sobs. Rosa put her arms around her and kissed the top of her head.

"It's all right, Fausta."

"This is just so hard for me, Rosa."

"I know, I know. Come, I'll walk you home."

Remember the song. Pretty song. Yes. About a butterfly.

February 15, 1976

Since Rosa kept a constant eye on Annabella's house across the street, she knew something was wrong when the kitchen blinds remained closed at noon.

"She always opens the blinds in the morning," Rosa told Antonio. "I'm going over there."

The door was not locked, of course, so Rosa went in, finding water at least an inch deep on the linoleum floor.

"*Santa Maria!*"

She slogged over to the sink and turned off the faucet. Then she smelled the burnt metal. The right burner on the stove was on, scorching a frying pan. She turned the burner off.

"*Santa Maria!* Annabella?"

No answer.

"Annabella, where are you? Annabella?"

Rosa went into the dining room, then the living room. "Annabella? Are you here?" She looked in the bathroom, and finally the bedroom.

"Annabella! What are you doing sitting on the floor?"

Her back to the wall, her pink nightgown rumpled around her knees, Annabella looked up with glazed eyes and began to sing.

Butterfly
Beautiful and white
Fly and fly
Never get tired

"Oh, Annabella, you remember that song from when we were little girls? What a lovely song."

Turn here
And turn there
And she rests upon a flower
And she rests upon a flower.

Tears flowed down Rosa's cheeks. "Oh, you know all the words. After all these years. Come, let's get up now."

Rosa put her hands under Annabella's arms, but she couldn't budge her. "Can you do it, Annabella? Can you try to get up now?"

Butterfly
Beautiful and white

"No, no. Let's try to get up now."

Fly and fly
Never get tired

"Oh, Annabella." Rosa couldn't stop the tears. "Stay there. I'll be right back."

Carefully sloshing through the kitchen, Rosa raced back across the street to her house. "Antonio! Antonio! Come! Come!"

Antonio ran behind Rosa to Annabella's house. Together, they lifted Annabella and let her sit on the bed.

"How are you, Annabella? Feeling a little better?" Rosa was out of breath.

Annabella traced the design of a flower on her bedspread.

Butterfly
Beautiful and white

"Oh, Annabella." Still sobbing, Rosa sat next to her and held her hand.

Then Fausta arrived. "I'm sorry. I overslept. I was here until 2 o'clock this morning. Dear Annabella. It's all right. It's all right."

Fausta sat on Annabella's other side and held her hand.

"I'll work in the kitchen," Antonio said.

It took a dozen large rag rugs to sop up the water on the floor.

Antonio carried them out in the backyard and hung some on the clothesline and spread the rest on chairs or the ground. Then he took a mop and wiped up the last of the water.

"Be careful when you come in here," he shouted to Rosa and Fausta. "The floor is still a little wet."

He tossed the scorched frying pan into the garbage and used some cleanser to wipe the stove clean. Then he returned to the bedroom.

"Feeling better, Annabella?"

And she rests upon a flower
And she rests upon a flower.

After a while, Rosa told Antonio he should go home. "There's soup on the stove, it should be stirred. We'll sit here with Annabella."

"She shouldn't be alone, should she?"

"No," Rosa and Fausta said.

Butterfly. Beautiful and white.

February 16, 1976

Rosa called Lucia first, then Donna, then Fausta, then Flora and Viola and Sabina. After she told them what had happened yesterday, they said they would be right over.

"Look," she said when they had all gathered around her dining room table. "We're her friends. We have to help her. She doesn't have anyone else."

"Are we sure there's no one else?" Sabina said. "No distant cousins or anyone?"

"No one," Fausta said. "Not a soul."

"Has she been to a doctor?" Viola asked.

"Doctor?" Fausta said. "I've been trying for years to get her to see a doctor. She just refuses. As far as I know she hasn't seen a doctor since she had that problem with her foot. And that was at least twenty-five years ago."

"What are we going to do?" Flora asked. "We have to do something! We can't let her go on like this." She began to sob.

"All right," Rosa said, "crying isn't going to solve the problem. Let's think."

They sat in silence, the only sound the tinkling of coffee cups.

"You know," Lucia said, "if this were America we wouldn't have to worry. They have places called nursing homes there."

"Nursing homes!" Rosa cried. "Do you know what those places are like? They're terrible. They're dirty. They're unsafe. People don't get fed. They lie in their own urine in their beds. The male nurses rape the women patients. They don't have locks on the doors and people wander out and get lost and die. I wouldn't send my worst enemy to one of those nursing homes in America."

The women sighed and shook their heads.

"How do you know all that, Rosa?" Donna asked.

"I know," Rosa declared. "I've read the papers. I've seen it on the news."

"I'm sure not all the nursing homes are like that," Donna said.

"Well, enough of them are," Rosa said. "Anyway, we don't have any nursing homes in Italy. We take care of our families."

"I did hear of one in Lucca," Flora ventured. "It's run by nuns. But I heard it's very expensive."

"Well," Rosa said, "we're not sending Annabella to a nursing home, even if it is run by nuns."

That ended that argument, but it didn't offer a solution to the problem. Rosa poured more coffee.

"I heard," Sabina said, "that there are women in Lucca who go into homes and take care of sick people. Annabella would have the money to pay someone, wouldn't she?"

"No, no!" Fausta cried. "We don't want a stranger going into her home. Annabella wouldn't like that at all."

"And who knows," Viola said, "they'll probably steal something."

"They do!" Rosa said. "I know of a woman who had a very expensive necklace and it was gone after her so-called helper was there. And they never found the helper or the necklace."

"And Annabella has such lovely things," Flora said.

"Where did you hear that, Rosa?" Donna asked.

"I don't know. I heard it somewhere."

More silence.

"Well," Donna finally said, "let me tell you what I think. Fausta, you've been doing so much for Annabella, going over there every day, cooking for her, doing everything."

"I don't mind," Fausta said. "Annabella has been good to me."

"But," Donna continued, "if you don't mind my saying this, I think you must be getting awfully tired. You know, you look tired sometimes."

"I do?"

"Just sometimes. So what do you think of this idea? There are seven of us. I know some of us are awfully busy..."

The women nodded, though in truth only Donna had real work to do, what with managing the Cielo and learning to cook gourmet meals.

"...but what if each of us spent one day a week taking care of

Annabella?"

"One day?" Flora asked.

"It's only one day a week," Donna said. "But it would mean spending the night, too, I think. We'd have to see how it goes."

The women thought about that.

"Of course, we have the *briscola* group on Tuesday nights, so some of us couldn't do Tuesdays," Viola said.

"I have my hair done every other Wednesday," Sabina said.

"Don't forget," Flora said, "we usually go to Lucca to shop on Fridays."

Fausta slammed her hand on the table. "All right! Enough! Enough excuses. Yes, I admit I get tired. I'm just an old lady. I don't have the strength I did when I was younger. But I think Donna has an excellent idea. Do we all care about Annabella or not?"

The women all knew that they did.

"Yes," Rosa said, "that's an excellent idea, Donna. Thank you. And Fausta, thank you for everything you've been doing for Annabella. Are we all agreed? All right?"

Rosa looked around the room. "All right?" she repeated.

"Yes," each of the women said.

Rosa got out a calendar. "All right. All we have to do is pick a day. It doesn't matter for me."

"I'll take Tuesdays," Sabina said.

"Mondays," Viola said.

"Thursdays," Flora said.

Rosa wrote the names on the calendar and soon the week was filled.

"One more thing," she said. "We should agree on what we're going to do."

Making meals, one said. Cleaning, another said. Shopping, another said. Helping Annabella wash. Fixing her hair.

"I'm sure we'll all find other things to do," Lucia said.

"And," Fausta said, "just staying with her. She just needs someone to sit with her. She's all alone." Fausta started to cry again.

"Poor Annabella," they all said.

The women got up and Rosa hugged Lucia and Donna hugged Fausta and everyone hugged one another. But when they looked out the kitchen window, they saw that Annabella's blinds were still closed.

"We have to go over there!" Rosa said.

They found Annabella rocking back and forth on her bed. She held a photograph of Francesco and was repeating something they couldn't understand.

"What is it, dear Annabella?" Fausta put her arms around her friend.

With vacant eyes, Annabella stared straight ahead. "Helpmehelpmehelpmehelpmehelpme..."

"Oh, Annabella," Rosa said. "Of course we're here to help you. All of us."

> *Butterfly*
> *Beautiful and white*
> *Fly and fly*
> *Never get tired*
> *Turn here*
> *And turn there*
> *And she rests upon a flower*
> *And she rests upon a flower.*
> *And she rests upon a flower.*
> *And she rests...*

Benvenuto!

Chapter One

It was one of those perfect Tuscan days that had now stretched into a perfect Tuscan evening, and they didn't want it to end. With temperatures hovering in the low seventies on this hazy late September night, they sat outside to savor drinks after Donna's sumptuous meal. A scattering of puffy clouds dotted the deep azure sky, and the patio offered an endless view of distant hilltop villages, occasional castles and rows of cypress trees. From this vantage point outside the hilltop farmhouse, Sant'Antonio looked like a tiny toy village down below.

"It doesn't get any better than this," Paolo said, lighting one of his rare cigars while ignoring the frowns of his wife.

"This is why we love living at the Cielo," Ezio said, putting down his grappa. "This is heaven."

There was little need to talk, and they didn't. Ezio and Donna had been friends with Paolo and Lucia for so long they could almost hear each other thinking.

"Ahhh," Lucia said, "there's the first star."

A long silence.

"Look," Donna said, "just a sliver of a moon."

More silence. Then: "Donna," Lucia said, "that *polleto cappesana* you made tonight was so good. How did you combine the sausages and the chicken breasts? It tasted just a little sweet, not too much, just a little."

"You have to get the right sausages. By now, Guido knows what I want."

"I can't believe you get along so well with that butcher. I'm always afraid to ask him anything."

"If you just smile sweetly, Guido Manconi is just a little puppy dog."

Paolo rolled his eyes, but Ezio smiled at his wife. "I never thought I'd marry a natural cook," he said, reaching over to hold Donna's hand.

"Hardly," Donna said. "Remember when you came to our house in Pietrasanta and all I could make was bean soup?"

"It was very good bean soup."

"Every day?"

"I didn't mind," Ezio said.

"I've come to enjoy cooking here, though," Donna said. "We've got so many things growing right outside. And I like to experiment. And of course Rosa has been my teacher."

"She's my teacher, too," Lucia said, "but I can't even make ravioli."

"You're coming along fine," Paolo said helpfully.

"Thanks," Lucia said, though her husband wasn't quite sure if she meant it.

"I just throw things together," Donna said. "I usually don't know what I'm doing."

That ended the talk about cooking, and the conversation turned to what everyone in the village was talking about. Mario Leoni and Anita Manconi were engaged.

"Well," Paolo said, "with everyone watching them, what else could they do?"

"Oh, Paolo," his wife said, "you're so cynical. I think it's sweet. It's about time Sant'Antonio had a little romance."

The talk then turned to what everyone was going to do the next week, since tomorrow was Sunday. Lucia planned to go to Lucca to shop on Tuesday, and Wednesday was her day to help Annabella. Donna was going to experiment with a few more recipes, and Friday was her day to help Annabella. Paolo said he hoped there would still be enough tourists to keep his *pasticceria* open in Reboli.

"And I'll be starting school again in a week so I've got to get some things done around here," Ezio said.

"My God," Lucia said. "School so soon?"

"Same time as always."

"That means summer will be over," she said. "I hate to think about that. It seems like summers get shorter every year."

"How many years have you been teaching now, Ezio?" Paolo asked.

"Well, I started in 1947, after the war, and it's 1976, so almost thirty years."

"My God," Paolo said. "You're an old man."

"Paolo," Ezio said, "you remember that you're only two years younger than I am."

"That's what I said. You're an old man."

Ezio poured another grappa for Paolo and himself and more wine for Donna and Lucia.

"Yeah," he said, "older but not any richer."

Again, more silence as they watched the stars appear, one by one.

"Ezio," Paolo said, "whatever happened to that idea about opening up the Cielo for tourists during the summer to make a little money?"

"I remember when you said that," Lucia said. "It was that Christmas in 1966 that Dino came home for Rosa and Antonio's wedding and we were all snowbound here."

"Well, obviously, we haven't done it," Ezio said.

"No," Donna said. "We haven't."

"Why not? It sounds like a good idea," Paolo said.

"Oh, lots of things," Ezio said. "We'd have to do a lot of work here to get rooms ready. I don't know whether I'd like strangers around. And it would mean Donna would have to cook more..."

"But she'd like that!" Lucia said.

Donna smiled.

"And, anyway," Ezio said, "how would we ever get tourists to come up here? I mean, it's a half-hour drive from the village and you know how bad that road is. And what would they do when they got here? There's nothing but a beautiful view."

"Exactly," Paolo said, waving his arm over the horizon. "A beautiful view. I bet a lot of people would come up here just to relax and enjoy the view. I mean, look out there. It's incredible!"

"It is, Ezio," Lucia said. "Look!"

"Yes, it is," Donna said.

Now outnumbered, Ezio thought of another reason. "But how the hell would anyone find out about us? I've heard of a few places near San Gemignano, but there aren't any around here that have tourists. We'd be the only one."

"Exactly," Paolo said. He stood up and dug the car keys out of his pocket. "The only great farmhouse with a spectacular view to welcome tourists from all over the world."

"Thanks for a lovely dinner," Lucia said as she kissed Donna.

"And, Ezio," Paolo said, "if you need help, you know where to find me."

Chapter Two

After twenty years of marriage, Ezio knew that when Donna remained silent, averted her eyes and hunched her shoulders, as she did now bending over the sink, she had something to talk about.

"OK," he said, wiping another dessert plate. "I know you want to talk about having tourists here."

She turned off the faucet. "Can we at least discuss it?"

"Sure."

They sat at the kitchen table, and she reached over and held his hand. "Ezio, please don't think we can't do this because of me."

"But, Donna, don't you see? It would mean so much more work for you. I'd be teaching, you'd be here, cooking, cleaning, running around after the whims of these, these foreigners. I just don't want to put you through that."

"Ezio, have you forgotten something? That I used to be a marble worker in Pietrasanta? That I lifted marble blocks better than any of the men? That I took care of my father all the while he was here until he died last year? After emptying bed pans for four years, I think I can handle rude tourists. I'm not a frail little schoolgirl, you know."

He squeezed her hand. "I know. And I wouldn't want you any other way."

"Ezio, I know I could handle this. And it would be fun to meet other people. Lord knows it's pretty quiet up here. I love that most of the time, but sometimes I think it would be nice to have other people around. So what are your other arguments?"

"Well, getting here. That road. You know how terrible it is. Paolo complains about it every time he comes here. We're used to it with the truck, but someone with a car, and these tourists would probably rent an expensive car, well, they'd find the axle broken before they even got here. The commune has been saying for years that they'll fix the last half-mile, but they never do."

"I know. It's terrible. Sometimes even I get mad about it. But don't you know someone in the commune who can fix it? How about Giorgio? Doesn't he owe you for tutoring his kid for three years?"

"I guess. Hadn't thought about Giorgio. I suppose he could get some of the other guys and they could do it on Sundays. They could get the material from the commune. It's not like the commune shouldn't fix it, right? It's their road."

"Right. And what else?"

"The rooms."

"What? We've got four very nice rooms upstairs. We've had guests before. Your partisan buddies from Florence. My girlfriend and her husband from Pietrasanta. Remember that time we were snowbound and we had all the rooms filled? We had such a great time. No one complained."

"I just think the bedrooms need some work before we can ask people to pay to stay in them."

Donna got up to pour more coffee. "What work? OK, the small one could use new paint. Maybe the others, too. There's a broken window on that one overlooking the valley. Those red drapes need cleaning. Nothing major."

"Well, maybe you don't think so, but what if we had guests from, say, England, and they were expecting some nice cozy inn with overstuffed chairs and flowered wallpaper and..."

"And tea and crumpets served at 2 o'clock? Ezio! No one expects an English bed and breakfast in the middle of Italy. The Cielo is a farmhouse on a hilltop in Tuscany. Ezio, listen to what I just said. The Cielo is a farmhouse on a hilltop in Tuscany. Doesn't just the sound of that make you want to stay here?"

"If I didn't see the cracks in the walls." He pointed to a large one just behind him.

"Ezio, the Cielo is four hundred years old. Of course there are cracks in the walls. That's how we can advertise it. A charming old farmhouse. Maybe historic?"

"I'm not sure just being old qualifies as being historic."

"Well, people can use their imaginations. They can imagine what it would have been like to live here in the 1600s."

"Donna, this was a stable in the 1600s. Cows and horses. I'm not sure if people want to stay in a place where there was a lot of cow shit."

"There isn't any more. I hardly ever smell it." She smiled.

Ezio looked startled. "You're kidding, right?"

"Ezio, you're a wonderful man, a devoted husband, a great lover, but you have absolutely no sense of humor. Yes, I was kidding."

"Sorry. I know. I'm much too serious."

"We'll work on it. Ezio, you have to admit the Cielo is quite beautiful now. Tonight, when we were sitting outside, I looked at the walls, how they glowed in the moonlight. And the view. Even Paolo said it's incredible."

"I know. It's a great place. I'll admit that. But there's still work to be done, and school starts in another week and then maybe I'll be tied up and..."

"And maybe you'll get sick and maybe the roof will cave in and maybe the house will be blown away and.... Come on, excuses, excuses."

Ezio grinned. "You can see right through me, can't you?"

"Always have. OK, what else?"

"Donna, what is there for people to do up here? I mean, young families aren't going to come. We don't have anything for kids. And there's certainly nothing in the village. They'd have to drive to Lucca."

"Which isn't that far away, you know."

"I know, but who would come? Old folks won't come. What are they to do except sit and watch the sun rise and look at the valley all day and then see the sun set?"

"Ezio, that's exactly the point. This is a place that has nothing but peace and solitude. I bet a lot of people look for that. A few hours ago we were all sitting on the patio with nothing to do but watch the sun set and the stars come out. That's why people would come!"

"Sit and watch the stars come out?"

"Yes. I can't think of anything I'd rather do on a vacation. If I had a job in, say, Florence or Rome or Paris or London and I really wanted to get away for a week or two, this is exactly the place where I would go. And I'm sure there are a lot of people like me. Think of all those people in other parts of Italy and even France, Germany, England, working, working, working. The last thing they want is to go to a place where they have to be doing something all the time.

Here, they could just do nothing. And not apologize for it. Just unwind."

"Donna, you know, sometimes I can't believe you."

"You'd think after twenty years you would."

He leaned across the table and kissed the top of her head.

"OK," she said. "Agreed?"

"Agreed."

Donna put the coffee cups in the sink. "OK. Tomorrow I'll call Paolo to see when he can come and help. Antonio, too. If we start now, and do a little each week, we'll be ready by next spring. And you can call Giorgio, OK?"

"OK. I'm tired already, Donna. Let's go to bed."

Chapter Three

As anyone could have predicted, work went slowly in and around the Cielo through the winter. First, there was the problem of getting the road repaired. While Giorgio was *molto grato* that Ezio had spent hours each week helping Little Giorgio with his mathematics and essay writing, he didn't know if he could get other workers in the commune to help him on Sundays.

"Mattias. He has to take his mother to the cemetery. Angelo. He has to stay home with his mother. She's getting worse. And Orsino. His wife won't let him out of the house on Sundays, except for church."

"But Giorgio," Ezio said, "it would only be about three Sunday afternoons. Four at the most. And I can help."

"And I'd have to get the gravel from the storage barn and they're not open on Sundays so I'd have to fill the truck on Fridays."

"But you can do that, right?"

"Yes. But then I'd have to get the lime and the asphalt concrete. And I'd have to get the grader from the garage."

"Right. So how is Little Giorgio doing in school now, Giorgio?"

Giorgio beamed. "Little Giorgio? He's doing so great! Does his homework so fast. Gets good marks on all his papers. I can't thank you enough, Ezio."

"Really? That's great to hear. He's a smart kid, Giorgio. You can be very proud of him. So when do you think you could start work on the road?"

Trapped, Giorgio stumbled. "Well, I guess, I guess we could start, um, maybe in two weeks?"

"Thank you, Giorgio. Donna and I really appreciate it."

And so, after many questions about Little Giorgio's progress in school, Giorgio rounded up his workers, delivered the gravel, lime and concrete and drove the grader to the site early on a Sunday afternoon. With Mattias, Angelo and Orsino working furiously so they could return to their homes, a new road was completed in three weeks. Donna and Ezio liked it so much that they took walks on it every night.

"How did you get Giorgio to get this done so fast, Ezio?" Donna asked as they paused to pick wildflowers that had survived the road building.

"Oh, just a few reminders. I'm sure he really wanted to do it."

Now that the Cielo was more accessible, work could begin on some of the bedrooms, and Paolo took charge, starting by painting the walls of the small bedroom at the rear. The problem was that the room was small and filled with a large bed with a canopy, a huge dresser, an armoire and an overstuffed chair. For reasons known only to him, Paolo declined to take Donna's advice to move at least some of the furniture out of the room.

"I can just paint around them. It'll be fine. I'll call you if I need you."

Since Paolo had chosen a brilliant orange to brighten the room, the paint spots on the top of the canopy, the side of the dresser and the back of the chair were not easily concealed.

"People aren't going to stay in the room very long," he told a dubious Donna. "They'll want to be outside."

"When it rains?"

"They can sit before the fireplace downstairs."

Through the cold winter months there were more projects, some of them unexpected. The shower drain in the only bathroom on the second floor clogged and had to be evacuated. Besides the broken window in the south bedroom, another one cracked when Paolo tried to open it. The frame on a door needed to be replaced. The fireplace backed up and Ezio climbed up on the roof and rescued a terrified raccoon.

In February, a fierce windstorm swept through the hills in the middle of the night, and in the morning, they found heavy branches knocked off the centuries-old kaki tree in front of the farmhouse. Worse, the branches crashed onto the roof, destroying seven tiles and letting rain gush down the walls of the east bedroom and into the kitchen.

Ezio and Paolo surveyed the damage as soon as it stopped raining.

"Can't put this off," Ezio said. "Looks like it's going to storm again."

"I've never fixed a tile roof," Paolo said.

"Neither have I. There's only one man around here who can take care of this."

But when Paolo asked Antonio to help, Rosa fretted that her husband was getting too old for heavy lifting.

"Antonio!" she cried, "you're ninety years old. You shouldn't be helping Paolo. You should be here watching the television."

"*Boh!* Rosa, you always say I'm a young ninety. Don't worry about it." He kissed his wife, put on his carpentry apron and walked up to the Cielo.

So, at the age of ninety and under threatening skies, Antonio was at the top of a none-too-sturdy ladder, with Paolo on an even flimsier ladder next to him and Ezio holding both on the ground. Fortunately, replacement tiles were found in the storage barn in the back.

"OK," Antonio said, "this is how you do this. You take this metal bar and you slide it under this broken tile, *comprendi*?"

"*Comprendo*," Paolo said.

"Now slide this other bar under this tile next to it. Now we lift off the broken tile. *Comprendi*?"

"*Sì.*"

"Now we put the new tile in its place."

Antonio struggled with this, but managed to angle it in.

"Now we do the same for this other broken tile."

Together, they replaced the seven tiles, but Paolo admitted that he was merely an observer. Slowly, Antonio edged down from the ladder, and the three of them admired the work.

"Well, they're brighter than the others, but no one will notice," Antonio said.

"Thank you, Antonio!" Both Ezio and Paolo hugged him. And then it started to rain again.

By St. Joseph's Day in March, the Cielo was ready. The rooms looked lovely with bucolic paintings decorating the newly painted walls and with freshly cleaned drapes on the windows and matching covers on the beds.

"Oh, one more thing," Ezio said. He took a small wooden plank and nailed a heavy stick behind it. On the plank, in bright red letters, he wrote "The Cielo" and pointed an arrow. Then he went down to the base of the hill and pounded it into the side of the road.

"All right," Ezio said. "Open the door. The tourists should be here any minute."

Chapter Four

After another delicious meal, this time *rosticciana,* Donna and Ezio and Paolo and Lucia remained at the table and tried not to hear the fierce winds of late March in the kaki tree outside.

"All right," Ezio said. "If we're going to open this summer, we'd better get busy. And frankly, I don't know where or how to begin."

Donna suggested that they publish a brochure, with some descriptions and colorful photos.

"We could take a photo of that little pool in the back," Ezio said.

Paolo laughed. "You call that a pool? The ducks can hardly get their feet wet!"

"Sure it's a pool," Ezio said. "And if we take the photo from a low angle, it will look huge."

"And maybe take it at midnight?" Paolo asked.

"Ezio, isn't that deceptive?" Donna asked.

"We're desperate, *cara.*"

"Photographs are never like how things really are," Lucia said, somewhat illogically.

Paolo knew a photographer in Reboli who would not be expensive. "He's a good guy. I think he owes me for something or other."

It was obvious who the designer for the brochure would be.

"Dino could do it in a minute," Lucia said. "I'll call him in Florence first thing tomorrow."

Ezio wrote a few sentences in a notebook. "OK, we can distribute the brochure around here, but how will anyone else know that we're open for business? I just wish there was some way we could shout this out to the world. If we could make a single phone call or something and everyone in the world would get the message."

"They're doing so much with technology now," Paolo said. "I bet someone right now is working on a way to do this."

"Well, it probably won't happen in our lifetimes," Lucia said.

"I'll make you a bet," Donna said. "By the year 2000 someone will have done it."

"And we'll only be in our seventies," Ezio said. "But that won't help us now."

As they moved to more comfortable chairs in front of the blazing fireplace to enjoy their tiramisu, Donna poured another round of coffee. From the expansive windows, they could see the evening haze developing in the distant hills and the remaining branches of the broken kaki tree waving just outside the front door.

"Ezio," Paolo said as he removed a stack of newspapers from a chair, "I don't know how you can read so much. It takes me all night just to get through *La Nazione.*"

It was true. Donna called Ezio a newspaper junkie. Whenever he went to Lucca, he picked up *La Repubblica* ("to find out what the left is doing today"), *La Gazetto dello Sport* ("to see how badly the Fiorentina are doing"), *Italia Oggi* ("for financial news"), *Corriere della Sera* ("because it's the best newspaper in Italy"), and the *International Herald Tribune* ("to find out what's going on in the rest of the world").

"I wish I could read English," Paolo said as he paged through the *International Herald Tribune*. "I just look at the pictures."

"You just look at the picture in *La Nazione,*" Lucia said.

"No, I don't. I read the articles. Some of them. Hey, look at this."

Paolo pointed to a small advertisement at the bottom of a back page. It showed a villa and he recognized the word "*Tuscano.*"

"Ezio, what does this say?"

Ezio needed only a minute to recognize that this was an ad for a villa in the south of Tuscany, near Montepulciano. It said it overlooked a peaceful valley and had four rooms available for rent.

"Ezio!" Donna, Paolo and Lucia cried almost together.

"What?"

"What?" Donna said. "Ezio, that could be us. We have four rooms and we overlook a peaceful valley. We should advertise in that paper."

Ezio had his doubts. Wouldn't it be false advertising to say just that? Didn't they have to also say that it was very difficult to get to and that there wasn't anything to do when people did get there?

"Ezio," Paolo said, "you don't have to say everything in an advertisement. Besides you can't afford a big ad."

"I may not be able to afford it as it is. The *Herald Tribune*. They're all over Europe. Their ads must be very expensive."

"Well, you won't find out unless you call them, right?" Donna said. "Remember what you've always said. You have to spend money to make it. And you just said the paper's all over Europe. Everyone reads it. France, Germany, Spain, England. That would be like making one phone call and letting everyone know about the Cielo."

Ezio looked at the ad again.

"All right. I'll call tomorrow."

Chapter Five

If Ezio and Donna had hoped for a quick response to the ad they placed in the *International Herald Tribune,* they were disappointed. The ad, just an inch high with tiny type, was published in the paper the second week of April, and each day Ezio found an excuse to go to Lucca after his school day to find a copy of the paper.

"Just want to make sure it's in," he told Donna every day.

"People may not want to plan their summers this early," Donna said.

"Always looking on the bright side." Ezio kissed his wife.

If the ad didn't produce any results, they hoped the brochure would help. Dino had prepared an exquisite one, using paintings of scenes instead of photographs.

"I didn't know we had that many cypress trees in back," Ezio said.

"We don't," Donna said.

On the cover was a single word in red letters, *"Benvenuto!"* which Ezio added to the sign at the bottom of the hill.

Ezio found a printer who would run off a thousand copies relatively cheaply, doing it after hours and wanting his money in cash. Ezio distributed them in shops in Pisa and Lucca. Still, there were no telephone calls or mail requests through May.

They had given themselves a deadline of June 15. If there weren't responses by then, they would forget about having any visitors this summer and instead plan their own vacation. Both Ezio and Donna had long wanted to spend a couple of weeks in Greece.

Delivering the brochure to a hardware store in Reboli, Ezio ran into David Richardson, an Englishman who had bought a run-down farmhouse, Le Stelle, on another hill four years ago.

"David! Good to see you again."

"Oh, hello. It's…. Sorry."

"Ezio."

"Ezio. Of course."

"Haven't seen you for a while."

"Well, you know, lots of work to do."

"Yeah," Ezio said, "when you own a house there's always a lot to do."

"Well, got to be going. Sheila's waiting for me in the car."

David fled the store, and the owner ran after him waving his bill. What a strange guy, Ezio thought. But it was not unusual.

The Richardsons had first visited Tuscany a dozen years ago on the advice of a friend, a pub owner in Liverpool. The friend had actually hidden out in the Cielo as a fugitive soldier during World War II and had loved the countryside ever since. "Go and spend some time around Lucca," he told David Richardson. "You're going to love it."

The Richardsons did, and they liked it so much that they began looking for property to buy. Some old houses were disreputable, others inaccessible. Then they found Le Stelle.

"The stars," Sheila Richardson said in her clipped British accent. "What a perfectly lovely name."

With a roof falling in, walls cracked and plumbing nonexistent, the farmhouse needed considerable work, but they were willing to tackle it. Two years later, they moved in.

They soon found other British expatriates in the area, forming a close-knit group that fancied they were in the tradition of Keats, the Shelleys, the Brownings and others who had abandoned damp England for sunny Italy.

Their Italian neighbors soon noticed, however, that the group was so insular that it was impenetrable. Stories bounced from village to village about how badly the Brits treated their Italian workmen, how they demanded special treatment in the shops, how they declined, politely, of course, any attempt to intermix with the Italians. Soon, every gathering of villagers invariably began with a question: What did the Brits do today?

Ever enterprising, the Italians quickly realized that there was something to gain from these new arrivals. Prices of old farmhouses, some of them almost inhabitable, soared, and a few clever villagers were known to have knocked down a wall or two to give a place a more ancient feeling.

"Aiutati che Dio ti aiuta," they reasoned. "Help yourself and God will help you."

Ezio remembered when he first met David Richardson. It was also at the hardware store, and David was having trouble understanding Italian *lire*.

"May I help?" Ezio asked.

"Can't seem to figure out the price of this faucet," David said.

Ezio told him the correct amount and held out his hand.

"I'm Ezio Maffini, by the way. My wife and I live in a place called the Cielo, up on a hill. I teach school in…"

David had already turned his back and went to the counter. Not a word of thanks.

"Oh, well," Ezio thought.

There were similar incidents over the years. Donna sometimes found herself in Manconi's or Leoni's alongside Sheila Richardson. Donna's ready smile was ignored.

"Oh, well," Donna thought.

Having placed the brochures on the counter, Ezio picked up the day's *International Herald Tribune* at the corner newsstand and drove back to the Cielo.

"Any phone calls?" He kissed his wife.

"Oh, yes. We've got a couple from Paris, two from Belgium and three from England. I had to turn some down."

"Really? Wow! Oh. Donna, you're kidding, right?"

"Ezio, what did I tell you about not having a sense of humor?"

"Sorry. OK, another day without a call."

"Right. I'll get the dinner on."

While Donna bustled at the stove, Ezio settled in his favorite chair next to the fireplace and opened the *Herald Tribune* to the page with the classified ads. It was there all right. But so was another.

"Donna! Come quick! Look at this!"

Next to the ad for the Cielo was another one, twice as big, with a photo and with bigger type.

"Do you desire peace and quiet? Choose our lovely farmhouse with four rooms overlooking an incredibly beautiful valley. The ultimate in Tuscan living: Le Stelle."

"Damn!" they both said.

Chapter Six

The Richardsons' advertisement for Le Stelle apparently received immediate results. Paolo reported to Ezio that he heard from a friend in Massarosa who heard it from a friend in Camaiore that cars were regularly seen going up and coming down the hill to the farmhouse. The visitors appeared to be foreigners, perhaps French or German or English. No one really knew because the visitors had little contact with nearby Italians and even sought out English or American restaurants to dine.

"Don't worry about it, Ezio," Paolo said. "People will start coming to the Cielo, too."

Not necessarily. There was one phone call, but the voice was so faint and the language so uncertain that Donna couldn't reply. There was a letter from a Belgian, but the writer wanted to be sure Ezio could provide free tickets to the Palio in Siena on August 16.

"I don't even know anyone in Siena," Ezio said. "And this guy obviously doesn't know that the price of tickets is out of this world."

In the middle of May they were visited by an odd-looking little man who wore a fedora and a mismatched suit. The man insisted on seeing every room in the farmhouse, toured the grounds to look at views from various perspectives, and asked many questions about rates, meals and neighbors. He took all this down in a little brown notebook, said *grazie*, and drove away in a battered old Fiat.

"What do you think that was about?" Donna asked.

"No idea. Unless it has something to do with the commune."

"You did get the permit to allow us to have tourists, didn't you?"

Ezio suddenly found that the faucet needed his attention. "Giorgio is a good friend."

"I'm not going to ask."

No one else called. Or wrote. Or visited. On June 14, Ezio called the travel agency in Lucca and booked passage for two to Greece, leaving the following week.

"We're going to have a great time," he said.

"Can't wait," Donna said. It was clear she would rather stay home.

On June 15, a letter arrived. The envelope was ivory colored with a Queen Elizabeth stamp. Engraved on the back were the initials of the sender, HM.

"HM?" Ezio wondered. "Do we know anyone with those initials? In England?"

Donna thought for a moment. "Not that I know of."

Ezio took out the letter, also in ivory-colored stationery, and looked at the signature on the back of the second page.

"Hortense McParpson?" Ezio said. "Does that sound familiar?"

"Hortense McParpson. Hortense McParpson. Vaguely familiar," Donna said. "Oh, my God, could it be? There's a Hortense McParpson who writes sleazy historical romance novels. I started one once about the sister of Marie Antoinette but it was so bad, I couldn't finish it. I think she lives in London. And her husband is some sort of royalty. She may even have a title, Lady or something, but she uses a pen name. But, my God, she must be eighty years old."

Ezio turned to the first page and began to read the elegant, fine blue-black script.

"*To Whom It May Concern,*

"*I am sending you this enquiry regarding the availability of your villa,*" he began.

"Villa? We have a villa?"

"Farmhouse. Villa. Whatever she wants to believe."

Ezio continued. "*I had intended to spend my time this summer at another villa in Tuscany that was also advertised in the* International Herald Tribune. *I will not even mention its name. When I telephoned the owner I realized at once that he was from England. Not only England, but from Liverpool! Imagine, someone who came from the same city as those vile Beatles! Pretending to operate a villa in Tuscany! Why would anyone stay at a villa in Tuscany run by an Englishman? An Englishman from Liverpool!*"

"Why indeed?" Ezio said. He was laughing so hard that he put the letter down to wipe his eyes.

"Read! Read!" Donna said.

"Because of that experience, I asked an agent in Lucca to visit your villa and to make certain that both it, and you, are satisfactory."

"So that's who that odd little man was," Donna said.

"She spied on us."

"Read some more."

"I intend to arrive on July 15 and leave on October 15. I will be coming from Florence where I will be completing my research on Eleonora di Toledo de Medici. I will need complete silence for my work and therefore will book all the rooms at your villa."

Ezio looked at Donna. "All the rooms?"

"For three months?"

Ezio could barely continue.

"I will take all my meals in my room. I do not partake of mushrooms, anchovies, spinach, swiss chard, leeks, arugula, red onions, broccoli or asparagus."

"Good grief," Donna said. "What can I make?"

Ezio continued: *"For cheese, I prefer sheep's cheese, what you call maremma pecorino. I abhor venison and wild boar. I do not care for Chianti wines. I prefer Cabernet Sauvignon. We will discuss the menu when I arrive."*

"Oh my," Donna said, "we'll have to order the cheese from Leoni's."

"I may have to go to Florence for the wine."

"Since this is during the heat of summer, I will need cross-ventilation. My bedding is to be washed every two days. The bathroom must be cleaned twice a day."

"Oh, my," Donna said.

"I will need complete silence. No loud talking, no sounds from the radio or the television. I will not permit any other visitors to your villa during my stay."

"So we won't be able to have Paolo and Lucia up here this summer," Donna said.

"We'll have to visit them."

"I want to make clear that I will be entirely occupied at my typewriter and I will not be disturbed!"

"She put an exclamation point after that," Ezio said.

"Oh my."

"*Finally, I will be accompanied by my driver, Giancarlo. He is to have separate accommodations in the next suite. Sincerely, Hortense McParpson.*"

"Suite?" Ezio said.

"The next suite?" Donna said. "Do you think Giancarlo is providing Hortense McParpson with material for her book?"

"It's called research. Oh, look, she added a postscript."

"*If I am completely satisfied with the accommodations and the meals are exceptional, I am prepared to pay you double your fee at the end of my stay.*"

"Oh, my God!" Donna shouted.

"Oh, there's a second postscript."

"*My representative from Lucca has assured me that you are indeed Italian and not, heaven forbid, British.*"

"Never fear, dearly beloved Hortense McParpson, we're as Italian as you can get," Ezio said. "Donna, can you believe it? Three months! All the rooms! Maybe even double our fee! This will provide us for all summer and next year, too!"

"If we can get through the summer."

Chapter Seven

Ezio was able to do some research about Hortense McParpson in authors' biographies and magazines in the school library. This was indeed a pen name, for she was officially Lady Alexandria, the fourth wife of a viscount who was notorious, it appeared, for his fondness for young girls. His exploits frequently made the tabloids.

The author herself appeared to live separately in a townhouse in Kensington Square. She had not begun her writing career until she was in her early sixties, but then turned out a best-selling novel almost biennially. Her subjects had all been obscure royalty from various European countries, and critics unanimously praised her thorough research if not her explicit details. All of her novels had been translated into foreign languages and one, about a cousin of Mary of Scotland, had been turned into a critically reviled but enormously popular film.

The dates for her birth varied. "She's either seventy-eight or eighty-two," he told Donna.

"I'm betting on eighty-two."

There was a dark photo in one of the books. It must have been taken years ago, for it showed a handsome woman of perhaps sixty, her skin flawless, her delicately coifed hair barely concealing a sparkling tiara. The woman was not smiling. That was a bad sign.

Word that a famous author from England was going to be staying in their midst for the summer quickly spread through Sant'Antonio. No one had heard of her before this, much less read any of her novels.

"What are we going to say to her?" Rosa asked Donna one day in Leoni's. "I can't think of a thing."

"Judging from her letter," Donna said, "I don't think you'll have an opportunity. It sounds like she's going to be in her room writing all the time. You'll probably never see her."

"But it would be a shame if she didn't see some of the countryside. We could take her to Lucca, to Pisa, to Barga, to the Garfagnana."

"We'll just have to wait and see."

What Ezio and Donna wanted to decide now was how to address this person who would be living with them for three months.

"I'll be damned," declared Ezio, the former member of the Resistance, "if I'm going to call her Your Ladyship."

"No, of course not," Donna said. "But we can't call her Mrs. McParpson because that's a pen name."

"And I suppose Alexandria would be too familiar. Hey, how about just Alex?"

"No."

"Maybe," Ezio said, "we could avoid it altogether and just mumble something."

"I don't think we could do that for three months," Donna said. "I guess we'll just have to wait and ask her. Or Giancarlo."

Because of the tone of Hortense McParpson's letter, both Ezio and Donna were nervous. They canceled their trip to Greece, of course, and in the first weeks of July Ezio washed down walls and floors throughout the Cielo. Donna went to Lucca to purchase new linens for all the beds in the guest rooms. They installed a supply of *maremma pecorino* in the refrigerator and of Cabernet Sauvignon in the coolest part of the house.

Since Hortense McParpson had not given a time for arrival, Donna and Ezio got up early on July 15. Donna cleaned the guest bathroom once more, dusted the shutters in each of the bedrooms and propped up the pillows on the beds. Ezio swept the patio and cleaned out chicken droppings from around the little pool. The chickens themselves, as usual, had the run of the place and seemed as nervous as their owners about the expected arrival.

After a fitful day of peering down the road and listening for a car horn, they were attempting to relax on the patio under a late afternoon sun when the telephone rang. Ezio ran to get it.

"They're coming!" Paolo cried. "They just stopped in front of Leoni's and asked directions."

"What did they say?" Ezio asked.

"I only saw the guy. He must have gotten lost on the way because he kept shouting, 'Where the hell is the Cielo? Where the hell is the Cielo?' A couple of us, Mario and me, tried to tell him, but he kept yelling. Finally, I said he should follow me. So I walked to the bottom of the hill and he drove behind and I pointed to the sign and he started up the hill. So he should be there any minute unless he makes another wrong turn."

"Doesn't sound like they're going to be too happy when they get there."

"Oh, Ezio, wait till you see their car!"

Ezio and Donna walked from the Cielo to the small parking lot at the end of the road that led from the village. And waited. And waited some more.

"He made a wrong turn, I know it," Ezio said.

"Well, if he ends up at the Muscellis, they'll tell him where we are."

"He's going to be even madder."

Finally, a brilliant red sports coupe turned the last bend to the Cielo.

"My God," Ezio said, "it's a Lamborghini!"

"Even I know that," Donna said. "I've never seen such a beautiful car."

"Paolo knows more about cars than I do, but I think that's an Espada 2."

It was hard to tell because two large suitcases covered the roof and another leaned out of the trunk. The car stopped within inches of Ezio's foot.

"*Benvenuto!*" Ezio shouted as the driver, dusting himself off with shaking hands, emerged.

The man, about thirty years old, wore a black suit, white shirt, narrow tie and a chauffeur's cap tilted at the back of his curly hair. He had a very thin mustache. Ignoring his hosts, he opened the rear door.

The photo Ezio had seen in the book in the library was obviously out of date. The author known as Hortense McParpson was short, less than five feet tall. Her face was a mass of wrinkles, her hair so thin it showed a pink scalp. She wore a paisley dress that fell to tiny feet encased in sturdy brown shoes. She opened an umbrella and then leaned on her driver's arm. She looked every minute of her eighty-two years.

"Benvenuto!" Ezio said again. Both driver and passenger ignored him.

Through thick sunglasses, Hortense McParpson inspected her surroundings. Gripping Giancarlo's arm, she hobbled up the stone pathway to the door, but then she stopped, took off her sunglasses and looked out at the valley. It was at its spectacular best, with a faint mist hovering over distant mountaintop villages and rows of cypress trees still glistening in the early evening sun.

She didn't say a word.

"We are so pleased you are here," Donna said. "Won't you join us inside?"

Instead, their guest walked from one side of the Cielo to the other to examine the various views. Her wrinkled face remained expressionless. Ezio grabbed Donna's hand.

"I think it's going to be a long summer."

Chapter Eight

It took seven trips for Ezio and Giancarlo to lug all the suitcases, trunks, bags and hatboxes from the car up to the second-floor rooms. Giancarlo was clearly irate about having this much work to do and stopped frequently to wipe his forehead and glare at Ezio.

Despite all of this activity, neither of the arrivals had spoken a word. The author busied herself unpacking a cosmetics case while Giancarlo arranged what looked like dozens of shoes neatly in a closet. Ezio and Donna stood by watching.

"Well," Donna said again, "we're so pleased you are here. But since it's so late, I imagine you want to retire. We'll see you tomorrow morning."

"There is one more thing," Ezio said. "Madam, we are just simple Italians. We aren't quite sure how to address you."

Hortense McParpson turned from her perfume bottles and looked up at her host. Her voice was deep and gravelly. "When I am writing a novel," she said imperiously in perfectly accented Italian, "I write it in the first person, and so I take on the character of the woman I am writing about. I enter into the body, no, the soul, of the character. I *become* that person. And so for the next three months here, I am Lady Eleonora di Toledo de Medici."

Ezio and Donna nodded and fled downstairs.

"Can you remember that?" he asked.

"I'm sure I won't," Donna said. "Are we going to go around all summer calling her Lady Eleonora di Toledo de Medici or was it Lady Eleonora de Medici di Toledo?"

"I hope not. She certainly is aloof. If I hadn't asked that question, I don't think she would have said a word."

"Maybe we should ask for payment in advance," Donna said as they got into bed. Both were exhausted and sleep came easily.

Donna had placed a tiny silver bell next to Eleonora's bed, but she didn't think it would ring so early.

She rolled over and poked her husband. "What time is it?"

Ezio picked up the clock on the bedside table. "6:20. Why?"

"She's ringing her bell already."

As they plunged into their clothes, Donna remarked, "You're right. I think this is going to be a long summer."

She hurriedly put together a tray of coffee, hard rolls, jelly and butter, but almost dropped the tray when she entered Eleonora's room. For a minute, she thought she had leaped back to another time, another place.

Eleonora stood against a wall, the early sunlight shining down on her tiny figure. She had donned a high-necked Renaissance gown of blue velvet over a long-sleeved golden tunic. A wig, parted in the middle and pulled back, covered her thin hair. A string of pearls wound around her neck. Her red lips were full, her cheeks rosy with rouge that did not disguise her wrinkles. She looked exactly like what she was, an eighty-two-year-old woman pretending to look like a twenty-year-old.

Giancarlo, now without his jacket and tie, sprawled in a chair in the corner, looking very tired.

"Madam…Eleonora…I…"

"My dear! I am Lady Eleonora di Toledo de Medici." Her voice, so harsh the day before, was now light and girlish. "Do you see?"

Improbably, she giggled as she unfurled a large rolled-up canvas and held it against the wall next to her. On it was a richly detailed portrait of a young woman dressed identically like her.

"How beautiful!" Donna said.

"Isn't it? I love that portrait. It was done by Alessandro Allori. Brilliant! I can just see Eleonora sitting for it, but I think she was trying to suppress a smile, don't you think? Look at how those lips seem to curl…"

"Yes…"

"And that lovely dress. I had mine made in Florence just exactly like it. Eleonora, you know, loved to have a good time. I imagine this was for a party she gave. Magnificent parties. Huge spreads of food, lively music. Sometimes she'd have little plays. And, you know, sometimes she gave naughty parties. Everyone in Florence knew about them. There was one game," this new Eleonora practically bubbled, "called 'schoolmaster' and the man would instruct the guests on, well, you know…"

Donna tried to focus. Was she in the second-floor bedroom of an old farmhouse near Lucca in 1977 or was she in a decadent palazzo in sixteenth-century Florence?

"…but, you know, her husband, Pietro, well, he was the crazy son of Cosimo the First. Medici, of course. Eleonora was the daughter of a Spanish duke. She was betrothed when she was only fifteen, and I don't think she ever really grew up. Pietro could have as many mistresses as he wanted, but when she had an affair with this tempestuous poet, Bernadino Antinori, well, he went insane. Now wasn't that a double standard?"

"Yes, of course."

"So he killed her! Strangled her in her bed! With a dog leash! Can you imagine?"

"A dog leash? Really?"

"Oh, this is such a marvelous story. I am enjoying writing it so much. And it's so juicy!" She glanced at Giancarlo, who looked away. Donna wondered if he wrote poetry.

Donna's head was spinning. "Eleonora, maybe your coffee is getting cold. I'll come back later, all right?"

"Of course. And what's your name, my dear?"

"Donna."

"What a lovely name. In Spain, you know, Donna was a title reserved for royalty!"

"Actually mine is an abbreviation of Madonna."

"Like the Virgin Mary?"

"Yes."

Eleonora was practically twittering. "Oh, I hope you're not like her!"

Donna rarely blushed, so she changed the subject. "And how, may I ask, should we address you?"

"Why, Eleonora is just fine, my dear!" She giggled again.

Back in the kitchen, Ezio was just settling down to his own cup of coffee.

"Ezio, you're never going to believe what's happening upstairs." Donna was still shaking her head.

As best as she could remember, because she had been in such

shock, Donna described Eleonora's gown, her makeup and her story of the real Eleonora.

"She really means it," Donna said, "when she says she becomes the character in her book. It does seem a bit extreme, don't you think?"

"Very strange."

"And Ezio, she's a completely different person than she was last night. I mean, she's even kind of nice in a pathetic sort of way. She's trying so hard to be this other person, as impossible as it sounds. And I don't even want to think about what's going on between her and Giancarlo."

"Very, very strange."

"It's like a time warp going up to her room. And she has so many names! Lady Alexandria, Hortense McParpson, Eleonora. She seems to have a personality to fit each one."

"I hope she doesn't want us to join in this make-believe," Ezio said. "I can't remember where I put my sword or my cape."

"Ezio! You made a little joke! I'm proud of you."

"Well, just a little one. We may need a sense of humor this summer."

Chapter Nine

An hour later, Donna was again in Eleonora's room. The author sat at the desk, still in her heavy dress although the July temperatures were beginning to soar. She was tapping away on an old typewriter, totally engrossed in her story. Discarded paper littered the floor. Giancarlo was nowhere to be seen.

"Ah, Donna," she said. "How nice of you to pick up the tray. As you can see I'm busy working already. It's such a fantastic story, I keep laughing as I write."

"Well, we're delighted that you have the atmosphere to work here. I know that's what you wanted. But I wonder if we could talk about menus. I'm perfectly willing to abide by your wishes."

Eleonora continued to type. "Oh, anything you'd like to make, my dear."

"But your letter said you did not eat certain things like mushrooms and anchovies and asparagus and red onions and...."

"Oh, my, did I write that? I eat everything, my dear. Just make whatever you'd like."

"And we have some of your favorite *maremma pecorino*, and Ezio somehow obtained a case of Cabernet Sauvignon."

Eleonora finished typing a sentence and turned to Donna. "Oh, my goodness. How kind of you! You didn't have to bother."

"But you wrote..."

"Did I? Oh, silly me. But thank you so much. Now, I really must be getting back to Eleonora's party. They're playing this wonderful game in which every guest pretends to be an animal. What fun! Do you want to hear about it?"

"Oh, I think I'll wait until the book comes out."

Eleonora was already typing as Donna went back downstairs.

"Glad you're back," Ezio said. "You should have seen Giancarlo. He ran to the car, got in, slammed the door and headed down the hill as if he were being chased. He has no idea how treacherous that road can be."

"Think you should drive down there to check?"

"Nah. I'll wait till Fernando calls and tells us Giancarlo has crashed into a tree."

"Fernando?"

"You know. Sant'Antonio's police force."

Ezio grabbed a hammer and went outside. The roof over the shed needed repair.

Donna looked in the refrigerator because she'd better start thinking about lunch. She found a couple of bottles of Marsala on a shelf and red peppers at the back of the stove. She knew immediately what she would make, and she opened a bag of flour and got out her rolling pin.

She finished an hour later and took off her apron and washed her hands. With time left before the final preparations, she took down the book she was reading and settled into her favorite chair near a window. She loved all of Guido Morselli's work but was especially engrossed in *Roma senza Papa*, in which the pope leaves the Vatican and lives a simple life on the outskirts of Rome.

"If only," she thought.

Then the telephone rang.

"Donna! You won't believe this!" Rosa was more breathless than usual.

"Calm down, Rosa."

"Donna, you should have seen this! That red car that came through yesterday and went up to the Cielo? Well, the guy was driving so fast through town that everybody jumped out of the way. Then the car stopped in front of Leoni's and that guy went in."

Rosa paused for breath. Donna waited.

"Well, he asked Mario for cigarettes. Not just any cigarette, but some brand Mario had never heard of. When Mario said he didn't have any, this guy..."

"His name's Giancarlo, Rosa," Donna said.

"This guy, Giancarlo, got so mad! He started yelling and pounding his fists on the counter. His face got all red. People thought he was going to kill Mario."

"Did you see this, Rosa?"

"No. Angelina told me. Anyway, people were starting to get afraid, so Marcello, that boy who works behind the counter, he went and got Fernando. So Fernando came and, well, you know Fernando, he's such a little guy, he threatened to arrest this Giancarlo, but Giancarlo just laughed and got in his car and drove away. Toward Lucca, we think."

"Oh my," Donna said. "I guess our guests aren't going to be too welcome in Sant'Antonio, are they?"

"Well, not the driver, at least. But tell me about your famous author, Donna. Have you talked to her? What is she wearing? How does she speak? Does she have an English accent? Well, I suppose she does, she's English. Have you talked to her about what she wants to eat? Will she be coming to the village? Can we meet her? Oh, you know how everyone would love to meet her, Donna."

Donna knew that if she told Rosa what Eleonora was wearing, how she talked, how she had taken on another personality, there would be no end to questions and Eleonora's story would be embellished every time it was told. Better not to say anything.

"Rosa, they got in late last night and she was working already early this morning so I really haven't had a chance to talk to her much."

"Well, we all want to see her, you know. Bring her down to the village, OK?"

"I'll see. But she really came here for peace and quiet in order to work, Rosa. Thanks for calling."

Donna had a hard time concentrating on *Roma senza Papa* after that. Certainly, the first foreign visitor to the Cielo was the most interesting person who had ever set foot in Sant'Antonio. She hoped their stay would be more peaceful as the summer went on.

Back in the kitchen, Donna got the pot boiling and the heavy pan sizzling. In a half hour, everything was ready and she arranged the plates on a wooden tray and covered it all with a linen cloth.

"May I interrupt you?" she asked as she entered Eleonora's room.

"It's all right, my dear. I couldn't think of the proper word for... well, you don't want to know. What have we here?" She removed the linen cloth and clapped her hands. "Oh, my!"

If Eleonora looked like the kind of woman who would peck at

her food, she certainly obliterated that image, almost smacking her lips as she savored the pasta.

"Oh, my dear! What are these? They're so tiny. They look like ravioli, but they're different, right?"

"It's agnolotti. It's kind of like ravioli, but the dough is folded over."

"And the sauce? What is that heavenly taste?"

"Oh, just a combination of chopped red peppers, onions, pancetta, bay leaves and thyme and Marsala."

"Donna, you're amazing!"

"Just something I threw together."

Chapter Ten

Despite the pleas of Rosa and other villagers, Donna declined to introduce them to the famous English author they had never heard of. For the most part, Eleonora remained in her room, clicking away on her typewriter. Some late afternoons she went out on the patio and read pages of her manuscript, her elaborate Renaissance gowns wilting in the sunshine.

And she had many gowns. A green brocade. A red silk. A deep blue velvet. And many more, all of them embroidered, elaborately designed and laden with jewels and pearls. Donna never knew what she would be wearing each day, and rushed down to give Ezio complete descriptions.

"You're kidding, right?" he would say.

"I'm not!"

"No wonder she had so many suitcases."

Eleonora never went down to the village, but she did make great progress in her writing. By the time July stretched into August and then into September, she had completed almost twenty chapters and was about to get to the juiciest part about the lovers' last encounter.

One o'clock was undoubtedly the highlight of her day. Then, Donna entered carrying a tray that, even after all these weeks, contained a new surprise. Eleonora invariably clapped her hands after removing the linen cloth. The *gamberi ubriachi?* "Fabulous!" The *crespelle alla Fiorentina?* "Incredible!" The *galleto al mattone?* "How on earth did you make this? It's Cornish hen, right? They don't serve Cornish hen like this in England, let me tell you!"

"Oh, just something I threw together," Donna would say, but she couldn't help smiling when she returned to the kitchen.

Meanwhile, Giancarlo sometimes lay out on the patio sunning himself in a skimpy bathing suit before dipping into the shallow pool. Almost every day, though, he took off in the Lamborghini in mid-morning and didn't return until late at night. Frequently, he and Eleonora would then engage in a loud, violent argument that Ezio and Donna tried unsuccessfully to ignore. This was followed by laughter and giggling and then quiet.

By now, everyone from villages near and far knew of Eleonora's presence, and a reporter from the newspaper in Lucca wanted to come over and interview her. Donna broached the idea to Eleonora, who would have none of it.

"Have you ever read a newspaper article that wasn't filled with errors?" She rearranged the string of pearls that fell over her drooping bosom and went back to her typing.

Ezio was surprised by one phone call he received.

"Ezio! My old friend!" The man had a distinctive English accent but Ezio didn't recognize the voice.

"It's David, old chap!"

"David?"

"David Richardson! You know, we have Le Stelle a couple of hills away from you."

"Oh, yes, David Richardson. How nice to hear from you." Ezio made a face at Donna, who was grinning nearby.

"Listen, old chap, we've heard that Hortense McParpson is staying at your place, doing a bit of writing."

"Yes, she's been here since the middle of July."

"Well, Sheila just loves her books. Just loves them! Read every one of them. I don't read much, but we saw the film. Loved it. We're big fans, big fans."

"I'm sure she'd appreciate that."

"Well, some of us Brits were talking the other night about how simply grand it would be if we could host a little party for Britain's most famous author. Nothing too fancy, you know, but I would think that after all these weeks in Italy, she would rather yearn to talk to some fellow Brits and have some good ol' food that she's used to, not all this pasta they serve over here. Righto?"

"I'm not sure about that, David."

"Well, would you mind, old chap, making the invitation? We would be so honored if she could accept. We would come and get her, of course, and bring her back to your place. Her driver could have the night off. Oh, and if you and your wife…"

"Donna."

"Oh, yes. If you and Donna would like to come, too, well that would be all right, I suppose."

"I'll give Eleonora the message."

"Eleonora?"

"Lady Eleonora di Toledo de Medici. That's her name."

"Really?"

"Yes."

"Well, we would certainly love to have Hortense...Eleonora over for a bit of a party."

"I'll tell her."

Donna was almost doubled over with laughter when Ezio hung up the phone.

"Should we tell the lady?" he asked.

"We can't very well censor her calls. I'll tell her."

But when Donna relayed the invitation, Eleonora's shrill, derisive laughter could be heard almost down to the village.

"A party with Brits? With Brits from Liverpool, for God's sake? With Brit food? Why on earth would I want to do that? I can't imagine anything more horrid. It sounds perfectly ghastly."

Ezio told David that Eleonora was very busy and didn't want to be interrupted.

There was one thing that eventually aroused Eleonora' curiosity, however. During the first week of the author's visit, Donna told her that she would not be at the Cielo on Fridays, and that Ezio would be serving the meals, which Donna would make in advance. At first, Eleonora thought nothing of it, but as she and Donna began to have longer chats, she began to wonder where her hostess was going one day a week. Finally, she asked.

"Donna, where do you go every Friday? To Lucca? Pisa?"

"No, I go to Annabella's."

"Oh. Where is that? I've never heard of a village near here with that name. Or is it a shop? I know, it's a dress shop."

This seemed unlikely, since Donna bought maybe three dresses a year.

"No, Annabella is my friend."

"How lovely! To spend a whole day with your friend."

"I'm just one of several friends who spend time with her. My day just happens to be Friday."

"So every Friday you spend the day with Annabella."

"Yes."

Reluctantly, Donna went on to describe the six other women who each spent a day with Annabella, and, finally, the reasons for their visits. Annabella, she said, was at a point where she didn't want to eat, had no control over her bodily functions and didn't know any of her friends anymore.

In seconds, a mask seemed to evaporate from Eleonora's face, revealing deep wrinkles. Her shoulders drooped, and she began to tremble. She was no longer a flighty twenty-year-old girl but a very fragile old woman.

"Oh, poor, poor Annabella."

"Yes, it's very sad."

"Oh, my," Eleonora kept repeating. "It's so kind of you to spend so much time with this poor lady, Donna. How are you related? Her niece, perhaps?"

"No, I'm not related."

"Not related. But the other women. How are they related?"

"No, none of us is related to Annabella. She's just our friend."

"Just your friend, and you spend all this time with her?"

Eleonora had read many books about relationships, about families, about filial devotion in her years of research for her novels. But she had never heard of anything like this.

"But couldn't Annabella go to another place to be cared for? In England we call them nursing homes."

"We take care of our own in Italy, Eleonora. And as I said, Annabella is our friend."

Eleonora crumpled in the chair, a tiny creature looking even smaller in her outsized costume. She looked out the window for a long time, and then reached out a withered hand. "Donna, may I ask you something?"

"Of course."

"Donna, I hesitate to ask this, but I wonder if perhaps sometime I might go with you to see Annabella. I promise I won't be in the way."

"Of course, Eleonora. Next Friday?"

Chapter Eleven

As Friday approached, Donna was amazed at Eleonora's transformation. At first, she still wore her Renaissance gowns but abandoned the wig, and sunlight played cruel havoc on her thin hair. Then she gave up wearing beaded slippers and donned her own very sturdy brown shoes. Two days later, she was in the paisley dress she wore on her arrival, with no makeup, no jewelry. Giancarlo, now very much present, hovered nearby, but she waved him away.

More astounding was the fact that she was not writing. Papers lay strewn on the floor, but the typewriter's black cover remained in place. Her eyes closed, Eleonora sat quietly in the corner chair, cheered only when Donna arrived with a *nodini di maiale* or a *pesce arrosto*.

"Oh, my dear, thank you so much. It's all so delicious, but I'm afraid I've lost my appetite and I won't be able to finish it all."

"Eat what you can, Eleonora."

"You haven't forgotten about Friday, have you, Donna? You'll still take me to see Annabella?" Her frail voice cracked.

"Of course, but, you know, Eleonora, I wonder why you want to see my friend. I mean, you don't know her at all."

Eleonora pushed the tray away and leaned back in her chair.

"Donna, let me tell you about my mother. I was an only child, and my mother doted on me so. She dressed me up in pretty dresses, she read to me, she took me to children's plays, she made me incredible butterscotch cookies. I can still taste them. She didn't want me to marry that terrible man, and of course she was right, I shouldn't have. When I finally left him and moved to Kensington Square, she came to live with me. Oh, Donna, we had such lovely years together. We never fought, never had the slightest disagreement. It was like we were sisters."

Eleonora paused to wipe her eyes with a lace handkerchief.

239

"And then I noticed that she started forgetting things. She'd repeat what she just said, she'd forget what she bought at the grocery store and go back and buy it again. Then she started doing some strange things, like wearing two dresses at a time. Or sometime she wouldn't put any dress on at all. One time she left the burner lit on the stove and her sleeve caught fire. Oh, I could tell you so many terrible stories. I kept her inside most of the time, but a few times, late at night, she got out and wandered the streets in her nightgown until some kind policeman brought her home. Finally, she wouldn't eat, she couldn't control her bodily functions. I was so worried, but the doctors couldn't do anything."

Eleonora wiped her eyes again.

"I just couldn't bear to see her like that. Donna, I was just sick. Eventually I knew I couldn't take care of her by myself, so I put her in a nursing home out in the country." She sighed.

"She died two months later."

"I'm so sorry," Donna said.

"But you know, Donna, the worst thing? I never, never once, went to see her in the nursing home. I just couldn't bear to see her that way. Everyone said, oh, she won't know who you are anyway. But even if she didn't know who I was, she would have known that someone who cared about her was nearby! I am so sure of that. But I didn't go, Donna, I didn't go. Not a single time."

"I'm so sorry."

"I've lived with this for forty years. I've tried to forget it all in my writing, but I never can. That's why I act so foolish. Dressing up in outlandish costumes. Putting on makeup to hide my wrinkles. I know I'm a foolish old lady, Donna. No one needs to tell me that."

"Eleonora, I don't think you're foolish. I think it's quite remarkable that you immerse yourself in your characters the way you do."

"It's just an escape, Donna, just an escape. I don't know how else to live with my guilt. If I pretend I'm someone else, then I'm not that horrid…"

Donna held Eleonora's shaking hand. "Eleonora, I'm sure you did the best you could."

"Not enough, Donna, not enough. Now do you see why I want to visit your Annabella?"

"Yes. I think so."

"I suppose I want to somehow say good-bye to my mother through Annabella. Silly, isn't it?"

"No, Eleonora, not silly at all."

"From what you've told me, Annabella and I are about the same age. The age when my mother died. And I could be Annabella, don't you know? I'm eighty-four years old. Oh, I know the books say I'm younger. Lies, lies. All lies."

Tears now flowed down her creased cheeks. "Donna, why is that God inflicts such things on some people and not on others? I just don't understand."

"I wouldn't presume to know why God does such things, Eleonora. If there is a God."

Eleonora ignored the last comment. "Well, I won't be a bother when we visit Annabella, Donna. I just want to meet her, and I'll say a few words, and then I'll go outside or somewhere else while you do what you have to do."

"That's fine."

"Friday, right?"

"Friday."

Chapter Twelve

Rosa had just finished making breakfast and was attempting to feed Annabella when Donna and Eleonora arrived. It had become the custom that the women who volunteered to help Annabella would change shifts after breakfast.

"There, there, just one more bite, my darling." Rosa tried to put a piece of bread soaked in milk into Annabella's mouth. "That's good. That's good. No, don't spit it out. That's good. Now swallow. No, just swallow, my dear. Look at me."

Rosa made a loud swallowing noise.

"*Bene! Bene!* All right, perhaps one more?"

But the next piece landed on the plate. "That's all right. You ate good, my dear."

But Rosa frowned and whispered to Donna. "It's true what they say. People at this stage forget how to eat."

Eleonora had stayed at the door, perhaps too shy, or maybe afraid, to enter until Rosa spied her.

"Oh my, you must be our famous author!" She rushed up and took Eleonora's hands. "Oh, we're so pleased you are here. Are you having a good summer? Donna tells me you've been writing so hard. The Cielo is so peaceful, isn't it? You know, that's where I was born, where I grew up. And Donna's cooking! Have you ever had any meals so magnificent?"

Rosa pecked the surprised author on the cheek.

"Thank you, Rosa," she said. "I've had a remarkable summer. I guess I've just been too busy to come to visit with all the people here. I'm so sorry."

Annabella began to clap her hands.

"Annabella!" Donna said. "You're clapping your hands again. You enjoy that, don't you?" Donna clapped her hands, too. "Look, we've brought a visitor today. This is Eleonora. El-eo-no-ra. Isn't that a nice name? Eleonora wanted to come to see you today. She wanted to meet you."

Annabella tried to focus on her visitor, but her eyes wandered.

Eleonora took her hand. "I'm so pleased to meet you." Her voice was hardly a whisper. "You're such a lovely lady."

Tears welling in her eyes, Eleonora smoothed Annabella's hair. "What beautiful hair you have. I wish I had your hair, Annabella."

Annabella smiled.

Donna put her arm around Eleonora. "Perhaps you'd like to sit with her for a while, Eleonora? Rosa has to leave and I'll do some cleaning."

And so two old women, both shattered in their own ways, sat silently on the couch in the living room, just holding hands. That was all Annabella needed. That was all Eleonora needed.

For lunch, Donna served fusilli, and Eleonora cut the tiny pieces into even smaller morsels and fed them to Annabella on a spoon.

"Lovely, lovely, my dear," Eleonora said after about an hour. "Oh, my, look, you've eaten it all."

Then they went back to sit on the couch. Annabella held Eleonora's hand and began to sing:

Butterfly
Beautiful and white
Fly and fly
Never get tired...

While Donna would stay overnight with Annabella, Ezio came to pick up Eleonora, who remained silent all the way back to the Cielo. Once in her room, she lay on the bed and stared at the timbered ceiling. And then she began to cry.

There were only three weeks remaining before Eleonora had to return to England, which meant only three Fridays. But Eleonora wanted to see Annabella more than that, and so four or five times a week Ezio or Donna drove her down to the village and Eleonora and Annabella would do what they always did, hold hands. Sometimes, Annabella would hum her little song as she leaned against her visitor. She was now refusing to eat.

"Donna," Eleonora told Donna on the way back to the Cielo

one day, "you don't know how much Annabella has meant to me. I know I can never forgive myself for what I did to my mother, but just being with Annabella has given me such…such…well, comfort. She's helped me somehow. I can never thank you enough, Donna."

"I'm glad you two have gotten along so well."

On October 14, the day before their departure, Donna and Ezio were the hosts and Eleonora and Giancarlo were the guests of honor at a gala dinner in the church hall. While Giancarlo stood sullenly in the background, Eleonora greeted each of the villagers, saying how much she enjoyed staying at the Cielo and regretting that she had not met them earlier. One little girl presented her with a bouquet of mums and a teenage girl confided that she would like to become an author "just like you" some day.

Father Sangretto, aware of the author's sexy novels, prayed at the beginning of the meal for books that would "uplift and celebrate the human spirit and not degrade God's creatures." Rosa, of course, brought ravioli, but for once, this was not the highlight of the meal. Somehow, in the kitchen off the dining room, Donna had made *nodino al tartufo* for the thirty or forty people, pouring white truffle wine sauce over the veal chops and then placing each on a bed of asparagus topped with shaved black truffles.

"*Eccellente! Magnifico! Splendido! Perfetto!*" The words spread throughout the room.

On the way home, Eleonora thanked Ezio and Donna for not inviting "those horrid people from Liverpool."

Chapter Thirteen

Unlike most of the summer, October 15 began as a gloomy overcast day with rain threatening from the west. After Giancarlo had grudgingly and noisily packed the car with all the suitcases and hatboxes, Eleonora took Donna aside.

"Donna, do you think I could see Annabella one more time?"

"Of course."

A half hour later, the two old women sat again on the worn couch of the living room. Half asleep, Annabella leaned her frail body against Eleonora, who smoothed her thinning hair.

"Oh, my dear. I am so grateful for getting to know you. You are such a lovely, lovely lady. I will never forget you. You will never know how much you have helped me. Thank you. Thank you. Oh, how do you say it? *Grazie!*"

For the first time in a long time, Annabella, still with her eyes closed, found the strength to smile. "*Grazie,*" she whispered.

Back at the Cielo as rain began to fall, Giancarlo made no secret of his displeasure for having to wait. Eleonora ignored his glares, and kissed Ezio and then Donna.

"Well, this is it, I guess," she said as she opened her umbrella. "I will write you, and please, please, tell me about Annabella. I know it won't be long now."

"Of course," Donna said.

"I know I can't repay you for how you have tolerated my childish actions, and especially for what you've done for me in the last weeks. I will never, ever, forget you."

"We will always remember you, too," Ezio said.

It was raining harder now, so Eleonora had to shout.

"What I will do," she said, "is tell everyone I know about the Cielo and your gracious hospitality. And your fabulous meals! Honestly, I will be spoiled forever. Through my books, I've gotten to know people in Germany and France and the United States, well, even Hollywood! I'm going to tell them all about the Cielo."

"Well, thank you!" Donna and Ezio said together.

Giancarlo opened the car door, but Eleonora turned around. "You'll find my check on the desk. Thank you for everything!"

The rain came down in torrents now. Giancarlo gunned the engine as Eleonora rolled down the car's window.

"There's one more thing," she shouted. "In my room you will find a big box filled with paper. Please burn it somewhere, won't you? I don't think the world needs a novel about Lady Eleonora di Toledo de Medici."

A month later, when Ezio was deep into the school year and Donna was still digging Renaissance beads out of the carpets, they received an ivory-colored envelope with a Queen Elizabeth stamp. Engraved on the back were the initials of the sender, HM.

My Dearest Donna and Ezio,

Forgive me for not writing sooner, but I have been so busy. This is the very first time I've had a chance to sit at my desk.

I want to thank you so much for letting me know that Annabella has finally found peace. I don't pray much, as you can imagine, but I will pray for her. What a truly beautiful woman! I think of her so often, and I sing her little song all the time. My condolences to everyone who knew her, especially you seven courageous women who took care of her in her final years. I will never forget your example.

In fact, your work inspired me to do a little of my own. I spend my afternoons now at the Resthaven Nursing Home just west of London. This is where my mother was. I don't do much, just a little reading if the patients are able to listen (not my silly novels, of course!), or I take them for short walks in the halls or I play recordings of old-time music hall performers for them. They seem grateful, and of course, I am honoured to be doing this.

Please accept my eternal gratitude.
Your loving friend,
Alexandria (Alex)

Ezio put the letter back in the envelope. "Well, I guess she's not Hortense or Eleonora any more."

"I'm going to miss them," Donna said. "But I think I like Alex best."

"Me, too. Are you surprised by what she's doing at the nursing home?"

"No. Not really. She needs to do this. It's partly guilt, I suppose, but I think she genuinely wants to help people."

"She certainly made this a summer we'll never forget. You know, with all that money she left us, we wouldn't have to take in any tourists next year."

"What? And miss out meeting some other extraordinary people? I can't wait!"

Cara, Caro

Chapter One

Her friends kept telling Rosa she had to go. It's too hot here, you have to get away. It's only for two weeks. It's not that far. You can call him every day. You need a vacation.

"But what will he eat?" Rosa asked.

"Eat?" Flora said. "Eat? Antonio can't manage to make his own meals for two weeks?"

"Who would wash his clothes?"

"He knows how to use the washing machine, Rosa," Viola said. "I've seen him."

"And cut his hair?"

"Rosa!" Sabina cried, "Stop making excuses! You have to join us. You haven't been to Lido di Camaiore in years. Come with us!"

Now that she thought about it, it had been eight years since she had gone on an August vacation to the sea with her friends.

In 1971, Antonio had fallen off a ladder and sprained his ankle. He was fine, but she didn't want to be away from him. Antonio himself wouldn't think of spending two weeks on a beach.

"That's crazy!" he said. "What would I do?"

"You could relax. You work so hard around here."

"*Boh!* I don't know how to relax. I need to keep busy. You go."

"No, I don't want to go without you."

In 1972, when Viola and Sabina and Flora were packing up, Rosa developed a cold and didn't want to risk making it any worse in the crowds of people at the beach. At least she said she had a cold.

In 1973, Antonio had a cold, or at least Rosa told her friends that he did.

The following year, Rosa and Antonio had taken a long-planned trip to Barcelona in June and Rosa said they didn't have any money left.

In 1975, the house needed a new roof and although Antonio did

251

much of the work, Rosa said she couldn't spend money on such a pleasure trip.

In 1976, well, she couldn't remember what reason she had.

Last year, Rosa said both she and Antonio had colds.

"Rosa!" Viola cried as she cornered Rosa in Mario Leoni's. "Now tell me straight. Flora and Sabina and I were talking. We think you don't want to go to Lido di Camaiore because you don't like us anymore. You always used to come with us, but in the last eight years you always found some excuse. So tell me straight. Is that the reason?"

Rosa put down the cans of tomatoes and packages of paper towels. "Viola, please. You know me better than that. How long have we been friends? Thirty years, forty years? We've gone through so much. All through the war. And look at how we all helped Annabella, bless her soul. It's just that something has always come up in August when we used to go."

"You sure?"

"*Santa Maria!* Yes, I'm sure."

"Positive?"

"*Santa Maria!*"

"All right, I'll tell Flora and Sabina. But nothing is going to come up this year, all right? It's only the beginning of July. There's time to make arrangements. Talk to Antonio, OK? Maybe he'd like to come along this time?"

"No, Antonio would never come."

Viola put her hand on Rosa's arm and her voice softened. "Well, then you come, Rosa. I know you hate to leave Antonio, but surely he'll be all right for two weeks. And Lucia can check on him. She's just across the street, she can practically look into your house, for goodness sakes."

"I'll think about it, Viola."

"All right. You do that. I'll call you tomorrow."

At home, Rosa broached the idea to her husband.

"Antonio, I was thinking that maybe, well, it's just a thought and I haven't made up my mind, but I was thinking that maybe, just maybe…"

"What is it, Rosa?"

"I was thinking that maybe I would go to Lido di Camaiore with my friends this year. Now I'm just thinking about it and I haven't made up my mind, but it would only be for two weeks and I'd make a lot of dishes and put them in the freezer for you, and Lucia is just across the street so if you need anything you could ask her and I could call you every day and…"

"Rosa! Go!"

"You wouldn't mind?"

"No, Rosa."

"You'll be all right here alone?"

"Yes, Rosa."

"You won't get too lonely?"

"Well, I'd miss you, but it's only for two weeks, you know. I'll be fine. I've got lots of things to do. I want to make another bookcase, and some more birdhouses, and there's the garden. I can't leave the garden for two weeks, Rosa."

"Are you sure?"

"Yes, Rosa."

"Well, all right. I'll think about it some more."

Rosa didn't want to talk about it with Antonio, but she wondered if she was getting too old for this sort of thing. Packing, driving two hours to the beach, getting settled in the hotel, then doing not much else except lying on the beach for days among hundreds and hundreds of others who wanted to escape August's dreadful heat. Occasionally, she would go into the warm water for a brief swim.

She was almost ninety now, and the others were younger. Viola was seventy-nine, Sabina was eighty-one and Flora was seventy-eight.

"Well," she thought, "maybe just one more time."

She knew she liked going to the beach. She liked being with her friends. Sometimes she met people from all over Italy and they told such interesting stories, which she could repeat when she returned to Sant'Antonio. It was just a time to relax, and she knew that she always came home somehow feeling better.

But then there was Antonio. He was ninety-two now. He still did his carpentry work like a man twenty years younger. He thought nothing of walking two or three miles, even up to the Cielo. His appetite was good, and he devoured her meals.

Still, he had never given up smoking, and his cough seemed to be getting worse. That was the only thing they argued about.

"Antonio, you know it's bad for you," she would always say.

"Not so bad."

"Yes, it is. The doctors have said so."

"What do doctors know?"

"Well, they've seen people die from smoking."

"Who?"

"Well, I'm sure there have been a lot."

"Look at Lupa," Antonio said. "He's ninety-seven now. Smokes a pack a day. Strong as an ox."

"Well, look at your son," Rosa said. "Ezio gave up smoking years ago and hasn't started again. Ever. Look at how strong and healthy he is."

"*Boh!* My son can do what he wants."

"*Santa Maria!*"

Rosa would throw up her hands and walk away. There was no arguing with him. Stubborn as always. *Ostinato!* He'd find out. And then she'd be a widow.

After the same argument this time, she went back and sat down next to her husband, who was in his favorite armchair reading the newspaper and smoking a cigarette.

"You'll be all right?" She grabbed hold of his hand.

"Yes, Rosa."

Chapter Two

Rosa hadn't even finished packing when she heard Flora beeping the car horn outside. As the youngest of the four, Flora was selected to drive, although she was certainly not the best. Fernando, who made up Sant'Antonio's entire police force, had warned her three times in the last four months that she had to stay on her side of the road.

Beep!

"Oh, they can wait," Rosa told Antonio, who was assembling boards to build another bookcase that they didn't need. "Are you sure, Antonio, that you don't mind if I go? I can still stay home. I didn't pay my money yet. It wouldn't bother me. In fact, I could go to Lucca one day and get those dishes I was telling you about and I could..."

"Rosa, go!"

Rosa put her one-piece blue-and-white striped bathing suit on top of her clothes. She had worn the garment for almost thirty years, and was quite proud of the fact that she had let out the waist section only twice. It may have been entirely out of fashion, but why should she buy another when she wore it for only two weeks a year?

Beep!

"Well," she said as she closed the suitcase, "you know I have plenty of meals in the refrigerator and the freezer. You can put the ravioli into the boiling water right from the freezer. The turkey slices should be eaten this week. For vegetables, there are plenty in the back."

"Rosa, go!"

"And if it gets too hot in here, you can use that big fan, but be careful to turn it off at night, OK?"

"Rosa..."

"And be sure to go over to Lucia's if you need anything. Paolo can help you."

"Rosa..."

"And don't walk to the Cielo in this heat, OK? Call Ezio and Donna and they can come get you if you need to go there."

"Rosa..."

"Have I forgotten anything?"

"Rosa! Go!"

"OK, I'm going."

"Have a great time."

"All right."

"Don't think about me."

"I'll call you every day."

"Don't worry if I don't answer. It just means I'm outside."

"Then I'll call Lucia."

"Rosa, go!"

BEEP!

As Rosa embraced her husband, he suddenly began to cough, a rasping, hacking cough that left him momentarily red-faced and breathless.

"Antonio!" She grabbed his arm. "Are you all right? *Santa Maria!*"

"I'm fine. Just swallowed the wrong way. I'm fine. Go, Rosa, go, they're waiting for you."

"You're sure? Drink some water."

Antonio went to the sink and obeyed.

"Feel better now?"

"Yes, sure. Go, Rosa."

"All right."

BEEP! BEEP!

She stood on her tiptoes and hugged him extra long and kissed him hard on both cheeks. "I'll go now, Antonio, but I'll call you when we get there."

"No need to, Rosa, it's only two hours."

"You never know how long it will take to get into the hotel. I'll call you, all right? And I left the hotel number on the refrigerator if you want to call."

"All right."

Rosa picked up her small suitcase and went to the door. Then she turned around and ran back into Antonio's arms.

"I love you so much, Antonio! *Caro!*"

"*Cara!* And I love you, too, Rosa. Now go. Have a good time."

After she had gotten into the car, Rosa waved to Antonio. She wondered why he put the lace curtains back in place and suddenly sat down. But then Sabina began talking about the latest news to grip the village, that Mario Leoni and Anita Manconi had set the wedding date for just before Christmas.

"Flora! Watch the road!" Viola suddenly shouted as the car skidded along in a rut just beyond the pavement.

"I am, I am!" Flora shouted back. "Why do they make these curves the way they do?"

"Be careful!" Viola cried. "We're going to be dead before we get there."

"Do you want us to be quiet?" Sabina asked, knowing that it would be impossible for the four women not to tell stories all the way to Lido di Camaiore. They did try, though, to keep their conversations brief and subdued.

Except for Rosa, who barely said a word all the way to the hotel.

"Rosa!" Sabina cried, then lowered her voice to a whisper. "You've hardly said anything all the way. We're going to have fun, Rosa! Really!"

"Aren't you glad you came along?" Viola said. "Look, see how the sky is getting brighter? Can't you just smell the sea air?"

Rosa smiled a little and looked out the window.

"We're going to have fun, Rosa!" Sabina said.

"Don't worry so much, Rosa," Viola said.

"Antonio will be just fine," Flora said.

Rosa continued to smile and looked out the window.

The hotel was the same one where Flora, Viola and Sabina had stayed for the last five years, since it gave a small discount to returning customers. Only a block from the beach, it featured an extravagant breakfast that lasted the women all day. At night, they split a dinner three ways, and if it weren't for the trinkets they bought from the ubiquitous gift shops, they would have returned home with extra *lire* in their purses.

After arguing about who was going to sleep in the double bed and who would suffer the two cots in the room, the women began unpacking. Except for Rosa, who had returned to the lobby to make a phone call.

Ring.

"Why doesn't he answer?"

Ring. Ring. Ring.

"Maybe he's outside."

Ring. Ring. Ring. Ring. Ring.

"Maybe I should call Lucia."

Ring. Ring. Ring. Ring. Ring. Ring. Ring.

Then she heard the receiver being picked up. *"Pronto!"*

"Antonio! Where have you been? I was worried sick! Are you all right?"

"Rosa, I'm fine. I was out in the back sawing some boards."

"You sound out of breath. Are you sure you're fine?"

"Yes, Rosa. I had to run to get the phone, remember?"

"OK. Have you eaten yet?"

"Rosa, it's 11:15. I'm not hungry yet."

"Remember, there's turkey in the refrigerator. And provolone."

"Yes, Rosa."

"And pick some green beans and zucchini from the back. You can fry the zucchini bottoms."

"Yes, Rosa."

"And after that…"

"Rosa, have a good time."

Rosa had never known Antonio to hang up on anyone. "He must be sick. He probably had to sit down. Maybe I should go back."

Chapter Three

After a desultory dinner in which her friends tried to make small talk among themselves and generally ignore Rosa's silence, all four went up to their room.

"Aren't you going to call Giovanni?" Rosa asked Viola.

"Giovanni? Why should I call Giovanni? He's all right."

"And I'm not calling Bernardo," Sabina said. "I think he was glad to see me go."

"And I'm on vacation," Flora said. "I'm not going to even think about what's going on in Sant'Antonio."

And with that, they all went to bed.

Rosa was the first one up the next morning. She went out on the balcony and stretched out on a deck chair as the seagulls sometimes flew so close she could hear their wings flapping. She looked down as the first beachcombers, mostly elderly because young people had not recovered from the night before and made their way to the sea, lunch buckets in hand. She tried to see glimpses of Pietrasanta, to the north, or Viareggio, to the south, but the sun had not yet burned off the morning mist.

As she always did when she went to Lido di Camaiore, she thought about her past. What a life she had had in almost ninety years. Growing up in the Cielo, alone on the hilltop except for her parents. Taking care of her father in his final days. Living a single life, happily, she thought, because she didn't know any other. Then meeting Marco, who was so kind and gentle and loving. What a wonderful marriage they had, despite the terrible things that happened during the war and afterwards. And then taking care of Marco in the years when he slowly slipped back into childhood and needed constant attention. She didn't mind. Then, after his death, living alone again. And then Antonio. How could she be so lucky to have found two men so similar, and yet each different, who would love and take care of her?

She knew she must be hard to live with. She was bossy. She gossiped too much and said things she shouldn't. She was impatient. And Lord knows she wasn't pretty. Never had been, and her eyes seemed to grow smaller and her Italian nose bigger as she grew older.

Why did Marco and Antonio put up with her? Even marry her? She henpecked both of them so much.

It must be my cooking, she decided.

And then she thought of Antonio. It was 7:30, and he would have been outside for an hour weeding the garden. He did that every morning although he found few weeds. She wondered if his coffee was all right. Maybe she should call him.

"Rosa!" Viola wore a bright red beach robe over a brilliant orange bathing suit. "What are you doing out here all alone? Come inside! They're serving breakfast. We want to get there before it's all gone."

Flora and Sabina were close behind. "Rosa! Come to breakfast!"

Rosa found her beach robe, a flowery thing she couldn't believe she bought, and followed her friends to the breakfast room on the top floor of the hotel. As Flora, Sabina and Viola loaded their plates with sausages, ham slices, fruit, muffins and toast, with glasses of fruit juice in their other hands, Rosa chose a single bagel and coffee.

"I'm not hungry," she said. "We had such a big meal last night."

Her friends frowned and began to demolish their breakfasts.

"You're going to be hungry before tonight," Flora said.

"I can buy a snack," Rosa said.

With wide-brimmed straw hats to shield their faces, and with light robes covering their bathing suits, they made their way down to the beach.

"Look at all the people here already," Viola said. "I thought we would be first."

"Get that place over there before it's taken," Sabina ordered.

They found a corner far from the water. They had not come to swim, and they wanted to avoid the crowds near the sea. Some foolhardy youngsters were already in the dank waters, ignoring the cries of their mother to return to shore. Teenagers crowded the soft drink stands playing loud music on portable radios.

"Isn't this fun?" Flora said. "Look at all the people. Isn't it good to get away from Sant'Antonio for a while?"

Rosa looked at her as if she had two heads. She had brought a book along, Natalia Ginsburg's *All Our Yesterdays*. She had read it twice before, but she identified so well with the characters as they suffered through the war. Before Antonio, she had never been much of a reader, but he introduced her to some fine Italian writers and they often spent their evenings just reading, side by side.

Bathed in suntan oil, the women settled on their beach chairs, trying to ignore the children's shouts and the occasional seagull dropping. Flora, Sabina and Viola even fell asleep, with Sabina's snoring causing nearby sunbathers to giggle.

Rosa put down her book and stared into the hazy distance for a long while, but when Flora moved, Rosa interrupted the silence.

"Flora, what would you do if something happened to Lanzo?"

Flora struggled awake, and had to ask Rosa to repeat the question.

"Lanzo?" Flora said. "What are you talking about? Why should something happen to Lanzo?"

"Well, nothing, of course. But what would you do if something did happen? Have you thought about it?"

Flora took off her hat so she could see Rosa better. "Oh, I don't know. I guess I'll think about it if it happens. But Lanzo is as strong as an ox. I'm sure I'll go before he does."

Awakened by the conversation, Sabina and Viola wanted to take part.

"I know what I'd do if something happened to Bernardo," Sabina said. "I'd go live with Magdelena in Lucca. I know she would love to have me, even if her bastard of a husband doesn't."

"And I'd go stay with my sister in Pisa," Viola said. "I think we would get along, maybe not right away. But nothing is going to happen to Giovanni."

Rosa sat up. "But wouldn't you miss your husbands? You've all been married for so long, forty, fifty years, longer than Antonio and I have been married. How could you live without them?"

"I don't know, I just would," Viola said.

"I don't want to think about it," Sabina said.

"It's not going to happen," Flora said.

The three women settled back on their beach chairs. Then Sabina sat up again. "I know one thing. If Bernardo gets sick, I hope he gets better right away. I know I'm supposed to be a loving wife and take care of him, but I really hate being a nursemaid. Remember how I took care of my mother for two years? I hated every minute of it. The feeding, the bathing, the bedpans. Oh, my God, the bedpans! And if Bernardo has to go, I hope he goes quick."

"Don't you think he'd take care of you if you got sick?" Rosa asked.

"Well, yes. He's good like that. I'm not. I'm just not."

Flora and Viola nodded. "I wouldn't want to take care of Lanzo very long," Flora said. "He can be so demanding. I'd be running in there every minute."

Viola agreed. "When Giovanni broke his leg and he was laid up for three weeks, I thought I'd go crazy. I don't know how you took care of Marco all those years, Rosa. You're a saint, a living saint."

"I loved Marco!" Rosa said.

"Well, I guess I love Giovanni, too. You don't think about those things. All I'm saying is that I hope I don't have to take care of him for a long time. I don't think I could do it."

"And yet," Rosa pointed out, "we all took care of Annabella when she got sick."

"That was different," Sabina said. "It was only for one day a week for each of us. And anyway, Annabella was our friend."

Somehow, Rosa didn't understand this logic, but it seemed perfectly acceptable to the others. She couldn't understand why her friends wouldn't want to take care of their husbands.

"But, Rosa," Flora said, "what about you? What would you do if something happened to Antonio?"

Rosa sat up and looked off into the distance where two little boys were playing with a ball. "I couldn't go on. I wouldn't want to live anymore," she said quietly.

"Rosa!" all three of her friends said together.

"What do you mean?" Sabina asked.

"How can you say that?" Flora asked.

"Are you saying you'd do something to yourself? That's a sin, Rosa!" Viola said.

Rosa leaned back in her chair. "I just mean that I couldn't live without Antonio. I couldn't."

Her friends shook their heads. Rosa had obviously been out in the sun too long. They didn't want to talk about this anymore.

Rosa picked up her book, but the words were all blurry. It must be the sunlight that was causing her eyes to tear, she thought.

The women left the beach at 6 o'clock, wanting to avoid the rush in the dining room. But in the hotel lobby, the manager stopped Rosa.

"Signora Tomaselli?"

"Yes?"

"A neighbor of yours has been trying to reach you all afternoon. Lucia Sporenza. But then she left a message. Here."

Rosa opened the folded note.

"Rosa, come home quick. We're taking Antonio to the hospital in Lucca."

Chapter Four

It was fortunate that no *carabinieri* were on the highway. Flora drove at her most erratic, trying to pass every car on the road. Seated in the front, Rosa closed her eyes and prayed the rosary. In the back, Sabina and Viola held each other's hands. Sabina dared to look out the window, but Viola kept her other hand over her eyes.

"Be careful! Not so fast! We're going to get killed!" Sabina shouted every other minute.

"We have to get there!" Flora shouted over her shoulder.

Eventually, they reached Lucca's outskirts. Rosa only knew that the Hospital Campo di Marte was outside Lucca's walls and somewhere near the Stadium. Flora pulled up onto a sidewalk and kept the motor running while Sabina ran into a tobacco shop. She returned, reciting directions over and over, which Flora tried to follow. There were many wrong turns, cries of *Santa Maria!*, tears and angry declarations, but they finally arrived on Via Teodoro Borgognoni and found the sign to the hospital.

Flora dropped Rosa and the others off at the main door while she tried to find a parking space.

"My husband! Where is my husband!" Rosa cried to the first person she saw, who turned out to be the wife of a Russian patient and didn't know what she was talking about. But then Ezio and Donna came out of the waiting room.

"Rosa!" Ezio said, hugging his stepmother.

"Where's Antonio?" Rosa cried. "What have they done with him?"

"Papa is very sick," Ezio said. There were tears in his eyes. "They've got him in the intensive care unit."

"But what happened? I was just with him yesterday and he seemed fine."

Ezio and Donna tried to explain that Antonio had pains in his

264

chest and called Lucia. He said he was weak and was sweating. Lucia called Ezio and Donna, and they took him to the hospital right away.

"But I want to see him!" Rosa said.

A doctor appeared out of nowhere and gently took her arm. "Signora Tomaselli. Please come with me." He led her to a tiny room crammed with nightclothes, bottles and bedding.

"Where is he? Where is he?" Rosa demanded. "I want to see him!"

She tried to open the door but the doctor held her back.

"Signora Tomaselli, your husband is in very serious condition. In a case like this, it is important that the person get immediate treatment. We don't know how long your husband had been suffering before he called Signora Sporenza. It appears that he waited a while."

"Stubborn! Stubborn! *Ostinato!* I knew it!"

"Signora Tomaselli, please be aware that your husband is in a serious condition. Very serious. But we are doing everything we can."

"I need to see him! Now!"

"Come with me, Signora, but please remember that your husband is in very critical condition."

Antonio was in the farthest bed, the one closest to the window. A nurse was adjusting an oxygen tube. He lay still, his hands folded on his chest. His eyes were closed. His face was ashen. Rosa put her hand on his.

"Oh, Antonio!"

Ezio wiped his father's forehead. "He's been sweating a lot."

"Signora Tomaselli," the doctor said, "we need your permission to perform surgery."

A nurse held out a clipboard with a paper on it.

"Surgery? You're going to cut him open? God in heaven!" With all the tears in her eyes, she couldn't see the paper.

"Signora Tomaselli, it appears that the artery in your husband's neck is blocked. We will make a cut in his groin..."

"In his groin? For a problem in his neck? God in heaven!"

"It's what they have to do, Rosa," Ezio said.

"Please, Signora Tomaselli," the doctor said. "I won't give you all the details. But we must do this right away. It should have been done within ninety minutes of his heart attack, and it's more than that now."

Rosa grabbed hold of his arm. "Doctor! A heart attack! He's not going to die, is he? Doctor, please! Tell me!"

"We're doing everything we can, Signora Tomaselli."

Nurses and aides gently lifted Antonio onto a cart, and Rosa tried to follow it through the automatic doors, but they closed behind him and she fell into Ezio's arms.

"It's all right, Rosa. Antonio will be fine. He has a good doctor."

"How do you know that, Ezio? How do you know that? You don't know that."

Of course, Ezio did not know anything about the doctor. He led Rosa to the waiting room where Donna, Flora, Sabina and Viola were attempting to read magazines that were months old. The clock said 1:15 a.m.

They sat for a while, all six of them, fidgeting, not talking. Sabina went to a vending machine and bought coffee. They couldn't drink it.

The clock said 1:40.

"There's something wrong with the clock!" Rosa shouted to a man mopping the floor. He looked at the clock and shook his head.

Donna suggested that they go into the café and get some soup or a sandwich or something.

"But what if the doctor comes when we're waiting?" Rosa asked. "We should stay right here."

"He'll find us," Ezio said. "We have to do something, Rosa. It's too hard here. Besides, I'm hungry."

They returned just as the doctor came through the swinging doors. His mask was pushed to the top of his head and he looked very tired.

"Doctor! My husband is going to be all right? I can take him home now? Or maybe tomorrow? I can take care of him. Really. I can."

The doctor lifted Rosa's hands from his arms and put his own arm around her.

"Signora Tomaselli, I think this was a very difficult operation for your husband. He's very tired. As I said, it would have been better if we had done it right away. Right now, we can only hope for the best. He's sleeping now, and that's the best thing."

"I can't take him home tomorrow?"

"No, Signora, I'm afraid not. He needs the care we can give him here."

Rosa's eyes pleaded with the doctor. "May I see him, doctor? May I just see him?"

"For a few minutes, Signora. Just you and Antonio's son. We need to administer some…we need to take care of him."

Antonio was now in the recovery room. The only other patient was an ancient woman who was moaning in the corner bed.

Antonio seemed to be sleeping peacefully, but Rosa didn't like the oxygen mask over his mouth or the tubes running out of his arm. She couldn't speak and held Ezio's hand. Then, without a chair, she knelt by the bed.

"Antonio, please. Don't leave me. Please."

Chapter Five

For the next three days, after Antonio was brought to a semi-private room, Rosa did not leave her husband's side. She washed up in his bathroom, she nibbled at the food he was brought and she slept on a cot a kind nurse provided. Ezio visited every day, and stayed as long as he could, but he had to return to the Cielo to help his wife each evening.

For much of the time, Antonio remained motionless. He was still connected to an oxygen tube and multiple machines that Rosa didn't understand. She did know, though, that a monitor behind his bed kept track of his heartbeat and she couldn't take her eyes off it. Every time there was the slightest variation she panicked and often called a nurse who assured her that everything was normal.

Antonio's eyes were closed, and he seemed at times to be sleeping normally. At other times he became restless, and Rosa massaged his arms and forehead. This quieted him for a while.

The nurse told her that it would be good if he heard her voice, so she began to tell him long stories about her childhood and about people in the village, some of which were entirely made up. Mostly, she told him how much she loved him and how much she cared for him and how she couldn't wait for him to come home.

She never mentioned that maybe that wouldn't happen.

But at night, staring at the monitor behind his bed, she thought about it.

It was on the fourth day, while she was trying to read a soccer article to her husband from *La Gazzetto dello Sport*, that she looked up and saw his eyes start to flutter. She dropped the paper and stood over him. Maybe she just imagined it. No, he really was opening his eyes. Slowly. She held his hand.

"Antonio, I'm here."

His eyes closed again, then opened.

"I'm here, my love. *Caro* Antonio."

She gripped his hand and, for the first time, she sensed something in return.

"Antonio, Antonio…"

His mouth quivered, as if he were trying to say something.

"Nurse!" she cried. "Nurse!"

A nurse came running. This was the one Rosa had come to know as Florina, a sturdy woman who grew up on a farm near Barga.

"My husband! Antonio is waking up! Can't you see?"

Florina checked all the tubes and instruments, then leaned down to talk into his ear. "Signor Maffini? Signor Maffini? Can you hear me?"

Antonio's eyes blinked and his mouth twitched.

"Signor Maffini? Your wife is here. See if you can hear her."

Rosa bent down to Antonio's other ear. "Oh, Antonio, can you hear me? I've been so worried. Are you feeling a little better, maybe just a little? I love you so much, Antonio. *Caro, Caro, Caro.* Are you hungry? I can get…"

"Maybe," Florina said, "you had better give him a chance to say something."

Rosa could feel her husband's hand grip hers. And for the first time since she arrived at the hospital, she let her tears flow freely. Florina put her hefty arm around her.

Antonio seemed to look at his wife, but his eyes were clouded and she couldn't tell. But she did know what he said. "*Cara* Rosa."

"Oh my darling." She leaned down and kissed his damp forehead. "You're going to be all right. I know you're going to be all right."

Antonio closed his eyes again. The monitor behind him showed a steady heartbeat. His hand grew softer in hers.

"I think he's going to sleep again for a while," Florina said. "Why don't you go home for a while, Signora Tomaselli. You look like you need some rest."

"No, no, I'm all right." Rosa smiled and sat next to her husband. "I just want to stay here."

And she did just that. For four more days. Each day, Antonio would rouse a little, mumble something that Rosa took to be "*Cara* Rosa," and then go back to sleep. On the fifth day, having been in his room for more than a week, she felt a desperate need to wash her hair and take a bath, so when Ezio agreed to sit by his father and Donna offered to drive her from Lucca to Sant'Antonio, she went home.

She found her home spotless.

"Ezio and I came down and straightened things out," Donna said. She didn't mention finding the stale sandwich and half-empty wine glass on the counter, the dirty dishes in the sink, the chair knocked over in the living room or the rumpled carpet in the hall. She and Ezio figured out that Antonio had the attack while sitting in his favorite chair and then crawled to the telephone in the kitchen. The receiver had been off the hook.

"Thank you, Donna. You've been too good to me." She kissed her.

The shower felt good, but it was even better to get her hair washed. She would look nice for Antonio when she returned to the hospital. When she had put on a new dress and dried her hair, she found that Donna had warmed up some bean soup and made a sandwich of ham and provolone.

They tried to talk about other things. The upcoming wedding of Mario Leoni and Anita Manconi. Father Sangretto's mother acting even more strange. Rosa even laughed a little.

And then Rosa said, "Donna, what would you do if something happened to Ezio? I mean, I don't think anything is going to happen, he's only fifty-five..."

"Fifty-six."

"A young man. But you know there are accidents..."

"Rosa, as you know Ezio and I are very practical people. We've talked about this. Several times."

"You've talked about it? God in heaven!"

"Well, you know, death is inevitable. It's something we all have to deal with."

Rosa had trouble imagining Donna and Ezio talking about death. They were too young!

"So, Donna, what did you decide? I'm just curious."

"Well, we decided that if something happened to me, Ezio would take care of the tourist business at the Cielo and eventually retire from teaching and maybe do some writing."

"And you?"

"If Ezio died, I couldn't leave the Cielo. We're so busy now with tourists every summer. But I'd have to get a handyman or someone to help with the hard work."

Rosa hesitated. "Donna, do you think...do you think you could ever marry again?"

"Ezio and I have talked about that, too. We both said that we would want each other to be happy. And so if we found someone we really liked and wanted to spend our lives with, yes, we would marry again. I guess we gave each other permission to do so."

"I see."

Rosa got up and cleared the table. How strange. Ezio and Donna had actually talked about death. She and Antonio never had. And her friends certainly talked differently about their husbands.

"Donna," she said, "if something happened to Antonio I don't think I could go on living."

"Oh, Rosa, you'd find a way."

"No. I don't think so."

Washing dishes, Rosa suddenly stopped and leaned into the sink. Donna put her arm around her.

"It's going to be a long time before he gets better, isn't it, Donna?"

"Yes." Donna also didn't tell her that the doctor had told Ezio it was unlikely that Antonio would recover.

Rosa was just drying her plate when the phone rang.

"Who could that be? If it's Flora or Sabina or Viola, tell them I don't have time to talk now. I need to get back to Antonio. Donna? Donna? Who's on the phone?"

Donna put the receiver back. "It was Ezio, Rosa." Her voice was so soft Rosa could hardly hear it. "Rosa, Ezio says we should go back to the hospital right away."

Chapter Six

The trip from Sant'Antonio to Lucca took little more than twenty minutes, and Donna was making it in even less time, but to Rosa it seemed like hours.

"I shouldn't have gone, I shouldn't have left him, I should have stayed at the hospital," she kept saying. "See what happens. When I went to Lido di Camaiore he had the heart attack, when I left the hospital, something happens and he gets worse. Maybe he's dead. Oh, my God!"

Donna gripped the wheel and drove even faster. "Ezio didn't say what was happening, Rosa. He just told us to come. We'll find out soon enough. And anyway, it has nothing to do with whether you were there or not. He's got fine doctors and nurses, and Ezio is right there."

Rosa flew through the hospital doors as soon as Donna left her off, and ran up to his room. Only to find that he wasn't there.

"Signor Maffini has been taken to the intensive care unit," a kindly nurse said.

"Oh, my God!"

She found Ezio outside the room and she clutched his arm. "What's going on? What's going on?"

Ezio put his hands on her shoulders. "Papa had trouble breathing and then his heartbeat went all over the place, so they brought him here. They can take care of him better here."

He didn't tell her all the other reasons.

"Can't I go in now?"

"The doctors said we should wait here."

So they waited. The chairs outside the unit were hard, the seats covered in green plastic that stuck to anyone sitting there in this heat. Both Ezio and Rosa decided to stand, leaning against the wall or trying to look through a tiny window to see what was going on

272

in the room.

At last a doctor came out, a man so young Rosa couldn't believe he was taking care of her husband.

"Signora Tomaselli, Signor Maffini, I'm afraid...that is...I'm afraid Signor Maffini is nearing, that is, close to..."

"Doctor, may we go in now?" Ezio said.

"Yes. Of course."

Rosa hardly recognized her husband. He was just so...small. He seemed to have shrunk in the hours since she last saw him. There were no tubes or oxygen violating his little body now. But he was still breathing, very slowly and with great difficulty.

It was Ezio who couldn't keep control now. His shoulders shook and tears flowed freely. Rosa put her arm around him, but she leaned forward to her husband.

"Antonio? Antonio," she whispered, "can you hear me?"

There was no recognition.

"Antonio. It's me. Rosa. Can you hear me?"

Antonio's eyes fluttered but did not open. His lips quivered.

"Antonio, please. Can you say something?"

Rosa leaned close. It was only a soft sound, but there was no mistaking what he said.

"*Cara* Rosa."

"*Caro* Antonio." She kissed his lips.

In less than a minute, his body relaxed. Ezio cried even harder and Rosa held him close. "Don't cry, Ezio. Your papa is at peace now."

She put her hand on Antonio's forehead and kissed his eyes, his nose, his lips.

Much later, when she looked back on the days following Antonio's death, she could hardly remember anything. She remembered the nurse, kindly Florina, pulling a sheet over Antonio's face. She remembered Ezio falling into Donna's arms in the waiting room. She remembered going back to her empty house.

And Flora and Sabina and Viola reciting the rosary over and over as Antonio lay in his little casket in the living room. And Lucia bringing over some very bad ravioli but some excellent cannoli. And Mario Leoni bringing a spread of bread and cheese and Anita Manconi a huge plate of prosciutto. And Ezio sobbing.

The Mass. The shocked looks from her friends when they saw that she refused to wear black but instead chose the red dress she had worn at her wedding to Antonio. The cassock that was too small for Little Dino who had come from Florence to be a very tall altar boy. Father Sangretto's awkward sermon, thanking Antonio for making the *presepio*, but also including something about how everyone should attend Mass every Sunday because "we know not the day nor the hour."

And the burial in the little cemetery next to the church. Before she married Antonio, Rosa had thought that she would be buried next to Marco because there was only one space. But she chose to have her two husbands together.

"They would have liked each other. Now they can be together for all eternity," she said. "I hope they don't talk about me."

Her friends couldn't understand. They did not see Rosa cry or break down. Her face was an impenetrable mask, and they tried vainly to see behind it.

"She's in shock, poor thing," Viola said.

"She just doesn't want us to see how terrible she feels," Sabina said.

"It will hit her," Flora said, "and we need to be there with her then."

But as the weeks and months went by, Rosa went about her business, quietly and firmly. On Mondays, she washed clothes and hung them out to dry. On Wednesdays, she bought her groceries at Leoni's and her meat at Manconi's and cooked little meals for herself. On Fridays, she dusted every inch of her furniture and vacuumed the carpets. She went to Mass on Sundays, arriving early and staying later and never talking to anyone.

Early each morning, when she knew no one else would be there, she went to the cemetery and prayed, first at Marco's grave and then at Antonio's.

Then she went home and locked the door.

Otherwise, she did not leave her house. She never played cards with her friends anymore. She rarely answered the telephone, and always told visitors she was busy. The only person she allowed in was Ezio. He looked so much like his father, tall, with curly black hair tinged with white. Black eyes. A bright shiny smile that lit up a rugged face. Broad shoulders and not an ounce of body fat.

They talked for hours about Antonio. Ezio told Rosa about how his father worked so hard in the woodworking shop in Florence and how they both grieved when Ezio's mother died. Rosa told stories about Antonio making so many birdhouses and bookcases that every house in Sant'Antonio had one or the other, sometimes both.

They laughed, they cried.

"He was a good man, your papa," Rosa said.

"Yes."

One day, Rosa brought up another subject. "Ezio, when I was talking to Donna once, she said you and she had discussed what you would do if one of you passed away."

"Yes, we did."

"Ezio, I don't know how long I can live without Antonio. Maybe I'm going crazy, but I think he's still here. I sit and try to watch the television and I think he's right next to me. I try to read a book and talk about it with him. I make meals for the two of us and then throw it all away."

"Rosa..."

"The other day I thought I heard him sawing boards in the back and I ran out there but it was only kids playing. In the morning, before I get up, I can hear him making breakfast in the kitchen. I can even smell the eggs."

"Rosa..."

"I take out his clothes from the closet and wash them and hang them back up. The worst part is at night. I lie in bed thinking of him. And I cry and cry. I hug that old flannel shirt that he wore all the time. Remember that?"

"There were rips all over."

"I cry so much, Ezio. All day. All night. I can barely get through a day. People said it would get better but it's not getting better. What's the point of going on?"

"Rosa, Rosa. You've gone through this before, you know. When Marco died."

"That was different. Yes, I loved Marco as much as I loved your papa, but I was seventy-three when he died. Now I'm almost ninety years old. I'm going to be dead soon anyway. Why can't I just die now?"

"Rosa…"

"I don't mean I'd take my own life. How would I do it, for heaven's sake? I don't have any pills. I wouldn't want to run in front of a car. How would that poor driver feel? And I couldn't drown myself in that little creek they call a river. I can barely get my feet wet in it. No. But you know, Ezio, sometimes I have these pains in my chest…"

"Rosa! Have you told a doctor?"

"A doctor? What would a doctor do? Give me some pills? I don't want any pills."

"Rosa, please see a doctor."

"Ezio, people die of broken hearts, you know."

"Rosa…"

"They do! I've read about it. Someone is so sad, they just die. Have a heart attack, I guess."

"Rosa…"

Chapter Seven

Although it was 3:30 in the morning, and it was still dark on this cold October day, Flora could not wait any longer. She left the side of her snoring husband, went into the kitchen and dialed the number she knew by heart.

After many rings, she heard a gravelly voice. *"Pronto!"*

"Sabina, it's Flora. I figured it out."

"Flora why are you calling at this hour? What have you figured out? Couldn't it wait until tomorrow?"

"No, it can't wait. I figured it out."

"Flora, make sense."

"It's Rosa. I figured out what's going on."

"God in heaven! Tell me, Flora, or go back to bed."

"Sabina, remember when we were at Lido di Camaiore?"

"Of course."

"And we stayed only one day?"

"And that bastard hotel wouldn't give us our money back."

"Well, remember how we were talking at the beach?"

"We talked about a lot of things."

"No, I mean with Rosa. And Rosa asked us what we would do if our husbands died."

"I remember."

"And we all said we'd go live with a son or a daughter or something."

"Yes."

"But Rosa said she couldn't go on if Antonio died."

"So?"

"Sabina, *stupida!* Don't you see? Antonio died last August. Rosa has never been the same since. She's going to kill herself!"

"No! She wouldn't! She's Catholic!"

"Sabina, what does that have to do with it? Lots of people kill themselves."

"Who?"

"Well, I don't know, but I imagine a lot of people do. You read about it in the paper all the time."

"Flora, I don't believe you."

The call was interrupted by a voice in the background and Flora heard Sabina say, "It's just Flora with some crazy idea. Go back to bed, Bernardo."

"Sabina, are you there?"

"I'm here."

"Well, listen. We have to talk about this. Call Viola. And come over to my house at 8 o'clock. We have to talk about this. We're Rosa's friends, for God's sake."

At 7:55 a.m., Sabina and Viola sat down at Flora's kitchen table. Flora had made coffee and there was some crusty bread.

"What are we going to do?" Flora asked. "We have to do something!"

Her friends nodded. "But what? She's so proud. She won't let us do anything for her."

"Well, we'll just have to insist," Sabina said. "We'll tell her we love her and we don't want anything to happen to her."

"And whatever she wants us to do, we'll do it," Viola added.

"All right then," Flora said. "Let's go."

It didn't take them long to get to Rosa's house. It was just a few streets away from Flora's. The shades were pulled. There was no answer when Sabina knocked.

"Rosa? Rosa! Are you in there?"

"Knock again," Viola said. No answer.

Flora went to the kitchen window and rapped on it. "Rosa? Your friends are here. We would like to talk to you! Are you all right?"

No answer.

"The door's locked," Sabina said. "I tried. There must be some other way."

They circled the house, and Viola remembered then that Rosa kept a spare key under the mat on the back porch in case she ever locked herself out. It was quickly found, and they let themselves in.

The kitchen was neat and clean, all the dishes put away. Two sets of her good dinner plates were set on the dining room table, as if Rosa was expecting a single guest. The television set was on in the living room, and a children's puppet show blared.

Rosa was seated in her favorite chair, next to Antonio's. Her head was bowed, she had a faint smile on her lips and she hugged a ragged flannel shirt.

"Rosa!" Viola cried.

Flora touched Rosa on the shoulder.

"Oh, my God!" Sabina whispered.

They made the sign of the cross.

Florence

God's Babies

Chapter One

If she had been wearing her white habit, Anna thought, someone might have given her a better seat on the train. Instead, in a gray dress that was two sizes too big, she was wedged between a large man who smelled of sweat and garlic and a young mother holding a baby. Fortunately, the man got off at Castiglione and she was able to slide over to the window for the remainder of the trip to Florence.

She put her wicker satchel under the seat and only then could she gaze out at the distant hills and ponder what she had done.

After more twenty-eight years in a cloistered convent, Anna had left. Forever. Yesterday she was a nun, today she was not. Released from her vows. Out into a world she knew hardly anything about.

She was both excited and terrified. And alone.

When she had arrived at the train station near the Abbey of Santa Margarita di Cortona, it was like entering a new world, one that seemed harsher and crueller than she remembered. People talked louder. Women wore more makeup and shorter dresses. Teenagers went around holding radios that blared a strange kind of music. The air even smelled different. How was she going to fit in?

As the train rumbled past vineyards, through valleys and tiny villages, she took out her rosary beads and prayed. It was, after all, about 10:45 a.m. and she always said the rosary at this time.

But, she thought, I don't have to now. I'm not a nun anymore. She smoothed out her dress and adjusted its white cuffs, grateful that she could leave her white woolen habit behind when the cooks at the abbey gave her undergarments, a dress, stockings and thick shoes. She tightened the scarf around her shaved head, wondering if anyone thought it odd that she wore a scarf in mid-August.

Although she was miles from the abbey, she knew that a part of her was still there. She wondered what the other nuns were doing now. Well, of course, they would be saying the rosary. Little Sister

Brunetta, always fumbling with her beads and trying so hard to concentrate. Ancient Sister Pelegrina, who now needed two canes and couldn't kneel anymore. Enormous Sister Susetta, who, everyone thought, required two habits to be stitched together.

As Anna remembered the rows of nuns in the chapel, she also remembered the empty places. Sister Fabiola, who left more than a year ago, Sister Uliva, eight months ago, Sister Maddelena, five months ago, Sister Tecla and Sister Jemma, who left together four months ago, and, in the last three months, a half dozen more. And now she was one of them.

There were ninety-one nuns in the abbey when she entered in 1948. Now, in 1976, there were only twenty-seven.

She was suddenly aware that the baby next to her was trying to grab her rosary beads. She dangled them in front of the little girl, who cooed and laughed.

"You have a beautiful baby, such lovely golden hair," Anna told the mother. "What's her name?"

"*Grazie*. It's Carmella." The mother was no more than seventeen. She had bright red hair, tied in little braids, and a very short red dress.

"Carmella," Anna whispered. "Carmella…Carlotta…"

Anna thought of the dream she'd been having in recent weeks. It always started the same way. She was in a corner in something like an attic, and she was holding a baby, a girl with curly golden hair just like this one. She was getting the baby to laugh by making silly faces. The baby seemed to be sick, but she giggled loudly. Then Anna played peek-a-boo with a blanket and the baby practically went into hysterics.

And then a woman took the baby away.

Then she saw the baby in a box, although it might have been only a dresser drawer. The baby looked as if she was sleeping. Anna put a doll next to the baby. Then Anna cried and so did the woman holding her hand.

It was at this point that Anna always woke up.

It wasn't as if she didn't recognize the place. She knew it was when she was ten years old, and the baby was her little sister, Carlotta. They were trapped with her mother and her sisters and brothers in a farmhouse in the hills during the German occupation of their village during World War II.

Carlotta was very sick, and Anna was the only one who could make her laugh. But then Carlotta died.

But why was she having the dream now, more than thirty years later? And did that have anything to do with her decision to leave the convent?

Carlotta...Carmella, she thought. What pretty names.

"I don't suppose, I mean, would you mind if I held your baby for a minute?" Anna asked the mother.

"Sure, go ahead." The mother seemed relieved to hand the baby over.

Anna gently took the baby in her arms, kissed her on the forehead and held her close. She could feel the warmth of the baby's body under her pink dress and she could smell her talcum powder.

"She's so beautiful," Anna whispered. She made a funny face, and the baby smiled. She put the edge of her scarf over her face and played peek-a-boo, and the baby laughed so loud she hiccupped.

"You seem to have a natural touch with babies," the mother said. "You must have been a mother yourself."

"Me? No, no. I never have."

"But I wish I had," she whispered to herself.

Chapter Two

Anna was still playing with Carmella when the train stopped at Vernio.

"I love this little town," the baby's mother said, digging into a big cloth bag decorated with sunflowers. "They have a fantastic chestnut festival every year. I go with all my friends. We have a blast."

"A blast?" Anna thought. What could that mean?

"By the way," the mother said, "my name is Pina." She held out her hand, which had a rose tattoo on the middle finger but no wedding band.

"And mine is Sister...I mean my name is Anna."

"You said Sister."

"Well, until yesterday, I was a nun. I lived in the Abbey of Santa Margarita di Cortona. But I've left the order."

"Really? That's fantastic! You gave up being a nun?"

"Yes." Anna didn't know if she wanted to continue this conversation, but, with little Carmella on her lap, she felt obliged. And maybe it would be good to talk to someone, anyone, about how she felt.

"I think that's so fascinating," Pina said. "I have an aunt who was a nun for twenty years, but then she left. Everyone was so surprised. I mean, she's old, forty, I think."

"Forty?"

"Oh, sorry, I didn't mean that forty is old. I mean...well, I don't know what I mean. Forgive me."

"It's all right. I'm forty-two myself."

"Really? You don't look old."

"*Grazie.*"

In the awkward silence that followed, Anna again tried to make Carmella laugh, but the baby was tired and, finding Anna's arms warm and comfortable, closed her eyes and fell asleep.

"May I…may I ask you why you became a nun?" Pina unwrapped a stick of gum and popped it in her mouth.

"Certainly."

But first, Anna had to think about it herself.

She remembered the exact day she decided, a terribly hot August day just like today. It was three years after the war and she was fourteen years old. Almost everyone in the village of Sant'Antonio remained inside, hiding from the relentless sun. Upstairs, Anna's mother and father were in their stifling bedroom, and her mother was attempting to calm her husband. Pietro had returned from the war broken in both mind and body, and kept yelling and screaming.

"They're coming! They're coming! Get down!" he kept shouting. He pushed his wife to the floor.

"No, no, Pietro. No one's here. It's all right." She took him by the arm and led him to the bed.

"Nonononono…"

"It's all right, Pietro. It's all right."

Anna covered her ears.

Downstairs, Anna's brothers, Roberto and Adolfo, were engaged in one of their frequent loud wrestling matches, one of them pounding the other before the other got on top.

"Be quiet!" her mother kept shouting from upstairs. "Your father needs his rest!"

"We're being quiet," one or the other yelled back. "We're just playing."

The brothers continued to wrestle.

Across the hall, Anna's sister Lucia lay on her bed, hugging her boyfriend Paolo and giggling. Paolo had become a frequent visitor, sometimes staying late into the night before Anna's mother told him to go home.

"Mama," Lucia would say, "we were just talking. Paolo was telling me stories about Dino."

Dino, Anna knew, was the father of Little Dino, who was born just after Dino was killed in a firefight outside the farmhouse where the family had been trapped during the war. Paolo had been his best friend.

That left Anna to care for four-year-old Dino. He wasn't much trouble, mostly wanting to sit at a table and draw pictures, but he had to be watched all the time, and she felt overwhelmed. She couldn't leave him. She couldn't play with her friends. In fact, she didn't have any friends.

Her father's screams, her brothers' yelling, the strange noises from Lucia's bedroom, taking care of Little Dino. Every day, the same thing. It was driving her crazy. She had to get away, find some quiet.

It was then that she thought about what a visiting priest, Father Filippo Filici, had said in a sermon last Sunday. It was the feast of Saint Clare of Assisi and he described this wonderful woman who left her family and became one of the most important saints in heaven.

Anna made up her mind right then. She didn't want to be an important saint in heaven. She only wanted to get away, to find some peace and quiet. After all, she didn't mind going to church. She rather liked looking at all the paintings and statues and listening to the organ music. She even liked to say the rosary sometimes. She would become a nun. One of those nuns who never left the convent.

Next to her, she felt Pina tugging at her arm. "I'm sorry," Pina said, "you were going to tell me…"

Anna hugged Carmella closer, remembering another baby long ago. "Yes. Well. I guess there were a lot of reasons. It just seemed like the right thing to do. At the time."

"Would you do it again?"

"I don't know. I'm a different person now. Anyway, I've left."

She leaned down and kissed the baby in her arms.

Chapter Three

Pina had taken out a small radio and held it to her ear, humming along to music that Anna couldn't comprehend. With Carmella still sleeping peacefully in her arms, Anna gazed out the window at the changing landscape as the train approached Florence.

Was she having second thoughts? She could always get the train back to the abbey after she got off in Florence. Mother Superior had been very kind. Of course, she had said Anna could come back to visit, not to rejoin the order.

Maybe she should have thought about it more. Mother Superior said she thought it was a rather impulsive move, but the idea had been born more than a year ago and just seemed to grow. Anna had begun to realize that she had become too comfortable, too complacent. Yes, even too safe. Every day, the same schedule. Rising at 4 o'clock and going to the chapel for Lauds.

Praise the Lord.
Praise the Lord from the heavens;
Praise Him in the heights above.
Praise Him, all His angels;
Praise Him, all His heavenly hosts.

She had actually come to love the morning ritual. It made her feel a part of the Lord's kingdom, where she belonged.

And then private adoration of the Holy Eucharist, followed by Mass. There had been a succession of priests over the years, most of them very old, and Father Bernardo, who had come three years ago, could barely get through the service because he coughed so much. But she loved the Consecration and Communion, and truly believed that Our Lord entered her body.

That's why she was glad to stay after Mass, to pray silently for the poor, the starving people of Africa and India, for an end to war and suffering. She knew her prayers would be heard.

The rest of the day was scheduled to the minute, something she always liked, even as a young postulant. Prayer, work, meals, more work, more prayer. Even the work was enjoyable, with the nuns lined up in the huge kitchen making communion wafers that were sold to churches throughout the region. Two would pour wheat flour into huge pots of water to get the right consistency, then others rolled the dough out into very thin sheets. When the sheets were dry, two nuns would take a hot iron and press down, cutting the dough into tiny circles, each imprinted with the Greek symbol for Christ.

As always, the nuns remained silent during this whole process, truly believing that what they were handling would no longer be bread when the priest said, "This is the body of Christ" at the consecration of the Mass. The tiny wafers would actually be transformed into the body of Our Savior.

If she missed anything about convent life, Anna thought, it was the making of the altar breads.

At night, the nuns had an hour of "recreation," and indeed a few of the younger ones played table tennis, but most knit or sewed. Anna liked to read books from the selection the governing sisters had reviewed. There was no television set, but a radio could be turned to classical music.

At 7:30 p.m., the nuns gathered in the chapel again for nightly prayers and the rosary, and at 8:30, everyone went to the long dormitory on the top floor of the abbey. By 9 o'clock everyone was asleep.

For years, Anna's sleep was undisturbed. It was only in the last months that little Carlotta had appeared in her dreams.

Pina had put down the radio, but made no attempt to lift Carmella from Anna's arms.

"Anna," she said, "what was your name in the convent?"

"It was Sister Santa Anna della Croce."

"Saint Anna of the Cross. That's nice."

Anna smiled. She wondered how long she would identify herself with the name.

"Anna," Pina said, "can I ask you something? Are you angry that you spent all those years in the convent?"

"Angry? Why on earth should I be angry?"

"My aunt is angry. Oh, my, is she angry. She says she wasted years and years of her life and she should have left long ago. In fact, she says she never should have become a nun. You should hear her. Every time she comes over, that's all she talks about. My mother tells her to shut up, but she just goes on and on. And she hates wearing a wig. It is rather ghastly, sort of a mousy brown. I wouldn't be caught dead in a wig."

Anna smoothed Carmella's curls. "I'm sure your aunt has her reasons for being angry. Everyone has her own reasons for entering and everyone has her own reasons for leaving. I'm not angry. On the contrary, I thank God for the time I spent at the abbey. I became closer to Him, and I'll always feel that way."

"Then why did you leave? This doesn't make sense to me. My aunt says there are hundreds and hundreds of nuns leaving. Something to do with Vatican II, but I'm not even sure what that is. I think I was just a baby when it happened."

"Yes, Vatican II changed a lot of things in the Catholic Church. It was, well, this big meeting of cardinals, and basically they said we should be more open about what we do. A lot of nuns, including me, went into the convent in the old days to escape from something, and they found refuge there. Now, some of them want something more. They want to contribute, to help people."

"Like you?"

"Yes, like me."

Anna pulled down the window blind to shield Carmella's eyes.

"Sometimes it doesn't make sense to me either, Pina. The best way I can explain it is that I came to realize that perhaps God wants me to do something else with my life now. I have given Him almost three decades of my love, and now maybe I should give my love to someone else."

"I knew it!" Pina shrieked, and Carmella stirred on Anna's lap. "You have a boyfriend in Florence!"

"What? No! My goodness, no. How could I have a boyfriend in Florence, or anywhere else for that matter? How could I ever have met such a person?"

"Then who would you give your love to?"

Anna hugged Carmella closer to her bosom. "I don't know.

Lately, I've been having a dream about my little baby sister, who died in the war. I loved her so much. Maybe I'd like to give my love to God's babies."

"God's babies?"

"Babies that don't have mothers. Maybe I could act like their mother."

Chapter Four

As the train neared the station in Florence, Pina put her radio in her cloth bag and took Carmella back from Anna. She kissed the baby on the top of her head.

"So," she said, "if you don't have a boyfriend in Florence, why are you going there?"

"I could have gone back to my village, but there are only about two hundred people there so I know I couldn't find employment. I still have a sister there. My parents are buried there. And my little sister, though she's buried up on a hilltop where she died."

"Oh, how sad."

"All these years, I wasn't permitted to write letters. When my parents died, I just sent my sister prayer cards. But when I decided to leave, Mother Superior gave me permission to write to my sister. I told her I wanted to go to Florence, and she told me that's where my brothers, Roberto and Adolfo, are. Also my sister's son, Dino, is there. He was Little Dino when I took care of him, but I imagine he's a big tall man now."

"Think they can find you a job?"

Anna pulled her satchel from under her seat. "I hope so, Pina, I hope so. I'm praying so hard. I'll be honest with you. I'm frightened."

Pina put her hand on Anna's arm. "I think you will, Anna. Oh, do you know how to find your brothers?"

Anna had never been in Florence. "My sister sent me their addresses and she said she wrote to them that I was coming. I thought I'd just ask someone for directions."

"I can help. I've lived here forever. Where do your brothers live?"

Anna took out a slip of paper from her purse. "Adolfo and his wife, her name is Mila, live in Piazza Santa Croce."

"Oh, I know where that is. My friends and me go there all the time. One of my friends has a fantastic apartment and we have great parties. I'll walk you part way."

As soon as she stepped down from the train, Anna stopped short. So many people rushing by. So much noise. She felt like climbing back up the stairs, but she grabbed Pina's arm.

"I'm here, Anna," Pina said. "Just follow me."

Anna obeyed, careful not to lose track of Pina's bright red hair and Carmella's smile over her shoulder.

Away from the station, the crowds were only marginally thinner. They crossed through Piazza di Santa Maria Novella, and Anna recognized the church from a photo album in the abbey. It was not as pretty as she had imagined. They turned on Via dei Fossi.

"We'll walk down to Lungarno Corsini," Pina shouted. "It will be quieter there."

When they got to the avenue lining the Arno, Anna stopped to catch her breath. At mid-day, the palaces along the north side of the river glowed in the sunlight. She had never seen anything so beautiful.

"Come along, Anna," Pina said. "I have to hurry because Carmella is getting hungry and wants to be fed. I don't want to feed her here."

They hurried along, with Anna keeping an eye on the green waters of the Arno and looking to the other side.

"What's that church?" she asked.

"Santa Spirito. There's a little piazza just in front and a lot of mothers go there. Sometimes I do."

"Do you go to Mass there, too?"

"Mass? No, I don't go to Mass. My friends don't, either. Hardly anyone does. Just old ladies."

At Ponte Santa Trinita, Pina stopped. "Well, here's where I have to cross the river. I live on that side of the Arno. It's called Oltrarno. It's cheaper living over there. Now you just follow this avenue. You'll go past the Ponte Vecchio…"

"I've seen photographs of that, the bridge with the shops."

"Just keep walking and walking. After you pass the National Library…it's a huge building on your left, you can't miss it…turn left and go about two blocks. You'll be in Piazza Santa Croce, and you can ask someone for the right number."

Anna kissed Pina on both cheeks and then Carmella on the forehead. "*Grazie*, Pina. I don't know how to thank you."

"It's been lovely to meet you, Anna. I hope you find some of God's babies."

"I do, too. Good-bye, little Carmella."

Anna followed Pina's directions, afraid to look on either side, afraid to inspect shop windows, afraid to look anyone in the eye. She soon found herself in the piazza in front of the immense Basilica of Santa Croce. The entire Abbey of Santa Margarita di Cortona could fit inside it. There were people coming out of shops and battalions of tourists heading for the basilica. She knew, from the photo books at the abbey, that such legendary figures as Michelangelo were buried there. Michelangelo!

Anna felt like she was fourteen years old and had just arrived from Sant'Antonio, and then realized that wasn't far from the truth.

Chapter Five

Anna had gone up to three people in the piazza, two women and a man, but each time she became flustered asking where to find Piazza Santa Croce, 49. Finally, she whispered a prayer and strode up to a man selling souvenirs in front of the basilica.

"Number 49?" he said. "Right over there. Two doors down from the purple door."

"*Grazie.*"

Anna found the bell next to the door and pushed it. Again. And again.

"Oh, dear. Maybe they're still at work. It's not even 5 o'clock."

Then she heard a woman's voice. "Yes? Who's there?"

"Mila?"

"Yes."

"Mila, it's Anna. I mean Sister Anna. I mean Anna."

"Oh, Anna, of course. Come right up."

After going up and down stairs at the abbey for twenty-eight years, Anna found the two flights to Adolfo and Mila's apartment easy.

"Anna!" Mila was standing in the doorway, an apron over a shirt and jeans.

"Mila! You're so…so young!"

"I sure don't feel young. We had so much to do at work today."

Anna was used to the big white kitchen at the abbey. This one had bright orange walls with blue window frames and a dark green linoleum floor. It was welcoming and cheerful. A man got up from the kitchen table and approached her. He was about forty years old, with thick black hair and glasses. He wore a blue plaid work shirt and tan pants. His face and hands were ruddy, as if he had been working outside.

"Adolfo?"

"Yes, Anna, it's me. Been a long time, hasn't it?"

"Oh my, you were twelve years old when I entered the convent."

"And now I'm forty. Can you believe it?"

"Adolfo!" The brother and sister embraced, slowly and awkwardly, trying to let the years slip by.

"I can't believe it," she said. "You're, well, you're almost as old as I am."

"Anna, I was almost as old as you were when you left, and I'm almost as old as you are now. Right?"

Anna laughed. "I guess you're right. Forgive me. I've been away from the world so long, I guess I've lost my sense of time."

Adolfo held her in his arms. "You'll get used to it. Lots of things have happened since you left, not all of them good. Maybe it was just as well that you were in the convent."

Mila interrupted. "Well, let's talk about that later. I just called Roberto and Dino. They're coming over as soon as they can. Sit down, Anna. You must be exhausted. Would you like to take your scarf off?"

Anna tightened her scarf around her head. "No, no, that's all right. You see…I…well, you know that I just left the convent and we wore those wimples all the time."

Mila and Adolfo suddenly realized that Anna's head was shaved. "It's all right, Anna," Mila said. "Your hair will grow back soon enough. My hair grows so fast I have it cut every two weeks."

As Mila prepared coffee and cookies, Anna sat across from Adolfo at the kitchen table. She told them about her train trip from the abbey, about Pina and her red hair and dress and about little Carmella. Her eyes moistened then.

"Such a beautiful baby," she said. "I think I miss little Carmella already."

"Adolfo and I always wanted to have a baby," Mila said. "We just never got around to it. But that's all right. We have each other." She stood behind Adolfo's chair and hugged his shoulders.

Anna looked at the clock on the wall. "I still can't believe I'm here. Yesterday at this time, I was…well, let's see…I would have been having dinner with the other nuns. I remember. We had some sort of stew."

"Well, we're not having stew tonight," Mila said. "I've made pasta and chicken cacciatore. My mother's recipe."

"Oh, my," Anna said. She couldn't take her eyes off Adolfo. "How have you been, Adolfo? Have you been well? You look, well, kind of sad."

"Anna, I'm fine. I used to work in the basement of the National Library, restoring books. It was very damp there and I think it got into my lungs. And then, of course, there was the flood…"

"I heard about that. And the library was the hardest hit, wasn't it?"

"Terrible. Well, after a couple of years, after I helped restore more books than I could count, I decided to join Roberto in his business."

"You joined Roberto? Doing what?"

Adolfo explained that after the flood Roberto became part of an organization that helped poor people repair their homes, even build new ones. It was unofficially called *Gli Angeli della Casa*.

"Angels of the home," Anna said. "How lovely."

"Most of the homes have been rebuilt, but there are still a few to do. We also try to find people jobs, buy cars, just help them in general," Adolfo said. "We work with a priest who has a soup kitchen near the basilica."

"That's amazing. Or as my new friend Pina would say, that's fantastic. How satisfying that must be."

"It's better than cleaning pages in old books," Adolfo said.

"And you, Mila, what do you do?"

"I've been working at the Casa del Popolo for years, long before the flood. We find clothing and furniture for poor people. Only a couple of us get paid, the others are all volunteers."

Thinking about what Adolfo and Mila were doing and about the years she'd spent in solitude at the abbey, Anna didn't hear the doorbell.

Chapter Six

"They're here!" Mila shouted.

A minute later, a man who looked like a slightly older version of Adolfo bounded through the door followed by a tall younger man with a shock of blond hair and big ears.

"Oh, my heavens," Anna cried. "Roberto! And is this Little Dino? It can't be."

"It's Roberto," Roberto said, "but don't call this guy Little Dino anymore. He's likely to punch you."

"Roberto! Dino!" Anna hugged them both. "Dino, you were only four years old when I left. And now you're…"

"Thirty, auntie."

For the next hour, questions were asked, sentences were started and not completed, one voice overlapped another as a sister, her brothers and a nephew tried to recount what had happened over the years. There was the story of Dino's mother, Lucia, Anna's sister, and how she married Paolo and still lived in Sant'Antonio. There was Roberto's boisterous life in Florence, something he didn't want to discuss. There was the feud between Roberto and Adolfo over Mila, which the brothers both claimed was peacefully resolved. And there was the flood that changed their lives, especially Dino's.

There was also Roberto's new life, in which he managed the organization fixing houses for the poor.

"And Adolfo is with you," Anna said. "That's so wonderful. And you two are getting along now?"

Roberto punched his brother. "Of course!"

Anna hesitated, then asked Roberto if he had gotten married.

Roberto's face reddened. "Well…um…no, but I've had a few girlfriends."

"A few!" Mila said. "I can't even count them anymore. But this one is serious, Anna, don't let him fool you. Her name's Rosanna.

She's beautiful, she's smart, and she makes Roberto behave."

Roberto smiled.

"Roberto and Rosanna," Anna said. "Now I'll be able to go to the wedding."

"Which may be soon!" Mila said as she started to bring plates to the table.

Roberto smiled again.

"Aunt Anna," Dino said, "I actually remember when you were taking care of me."

"You were so busy drawing, I don't think I did much."

"But I remember one time, I had drawn some flowers or something, and you looked at it and you said, 'Dino, that's really beautiful.' I still remember that, Anna."

"I guess I don't remember, but I'm sure your drawing was exceptional." She held Dino's hand.

After the long meal, which Anna said was the best she had had in years, there was time for a long phone conversation with Lucia in Sant'Antonio. It was mostly one-sided, with Lucia asking her sister many questions but not waiting for answers. Anna promised to visit soon.

Then they settled into the living room. Mila brought out old photograph albums, and Adolfo even turned the television off.

"You know," Anna said, looking at Roberto and Adolfo as they sat side by side on the couch, "when I thought of you in the convent, the most important thing I remembered was when we were trapped in the farmhouse..."

"The Cielo," Adolfo said.

"And you went down to the village even though we weren't supposed to leave the Cielo."

Roberto smiled, remembering. "Well, Carlotta was sick and we had to get her medicine."

"And we almost got killed by the SS," Adolfo said. "Thanks, Roberto." He punched his brother in the arm.

"But it didn't do any good," Roberto said. "Carlotta died anyway."

"But you tried!" Anna said. "You risked your lives to help our baby sister. And you were only..."

"I was twelve," Roberto said.

"And I was eight," Adolfo said.

"And you did everything I told you to do," Roberto said.

"You were always so boisterous," Anna remembered. "Always wrestling and getting into trouble. I never thought I'd see you all again. And you know what? I never realized how much I missed you until now."

"We missed you, too, Anna," Adolfo said.

How true this was could not be determined. Anna, after all, had not been a part of the family for almost three decades. Adolfo and Roberto and especially Dino were so young when she left they didn't remember much about her. But they were family, and for Italians, there was nothing more to say.

"*Chi si volta, e chi si gira, sempre a casa va finire,*" Adolfo said. "No matter where you go or turn, you will always end up at home."

Everyone nodded.

Finally, Roberto asked the questions everyone had wanted to ask all night.

"So, Anna. Why did you leave the convent and what do you plan to do now?"

Anna adjusted her scarf, which had become loose through the evening. "I'm not sure. I left the convent because I felt I should be doing more with my life. I was too comfortable, too safe there. Yes, I'm frightened about what will happen next. When I saw all the crowds here...well, I was scared. But I'm still determined to give myself to God in another way. And after hearing about the wonderful things all of you are doing, I know I want to do something like that, too. Here in Florence, I hope. As I told my little friend on the train, I have given my love to God for many years and now I want to give it somewhere else."

Roberto and Adolfo thought there might be a place at the *Gli Angeli della Casa,* but they weren't sure. Mila said she would inquire at the Casa del Popolo.

"I wonder," Anna said, "and I know this may sound like a silly idea, but I kept having dreams about little Carlotta, and when I held that baby, Carmella, on the train, well...I wonder if there were some place where I could take care of babies. Do you think?"

"Babies?" Roberto said.

There was only a minute of silence.

"Father Lorenzo!" Dino shouted.

"Of course!" the others cried.

Dino explained that a priest at the Basilica of Santa Croce ran a soup kitchen, but he wanted to expand it with a nursery because young mothers who had to work had no place to put their babies. He already had the upper floor of the soup kitchen painted, and beds and cribs installed.

"He hasn't been able to start," Dino said, "because he can't find anyone who would be willing to manage the place, to spend days with crying babies."

"I would!" Anna said. "I would in a minute."

"Hold on!" Dino went to the kitchen and came back with the phone in his hands.

"Father Lorenzo wonders if you could start tomorrow."

"Oh, my heavens," Anna cried. "Of course I can start tomorrow. Oh, my. This is going to be...what did Pina call it?...fantastic!"

"You know," Dino said, "he's even got a name for the nursery. *Figli di dio*. God's Babies."

Two for One

Chapter One

It had become so bad that Mila hated the thought of visiting her mother every Sunday afternoon, but she knew she'd need a good excuse if she did not.

Every Sunday, there was the same old harangue over the same old issue. Sometimes, her mother would pile on thick layers of guilt.

"Mila," she would say, sobbing into her lacy handkerchief, "I'm getting old. I'm in my sixties. I don't know how long I have. You remember your father died suddenly, and he was only fifty-eight. Do you want me to go to my grave like this? So lonely?"

Or she would make comparisons.

"Yesterday I saw old Evangelista Ferari out in the piazza in front of Santa Spirito. I never liked that woman, and here she was, hugging her two little grandchildren and giving them chocolate gelato. I could tell she was just showing them off for me. How do you think that made me feel?"

Sometimes, she invoked the saints.

"Why," she asked Mila one day, "don't you pray to Saint Elizabeth?"

"Saint Elizabeth?" Mila asked. "Why should I pray to Saint Elizabeth?"

"Because she was barren, too. And then she had a baby in her old age. Saint John the Baptist. He baptized Jesus!"

"And he was beheaded," Mila said. "Do I want a child who will be beheaded?"

Angelina Torticelli had no answer to that.

As Mila and Adolfo prepared to visit her mother on this November day, Mila tried to think of another excuse not to go, but she had run out of them. Last week, she feigned a cold. The week before, she said the car needed work. The week before that, it was raining too hard.

"All right," she told Adolfo as she wrapped up a plate of salami

307

and cheese. "I'm ready. Let's go."

"You sure?"

"As ready as I'll ever be."

They could have walked from Piazza Santa Croce to Piazza Santa Spirito on the other side of the Arno, but clouds hung low and it looked as it would storm any minute. Ever since 1966, twelve years ago, when the Arno overflowed and devastated the city, all Florentines looked to the sky and prayed whenever it rained in November.

Both Mila and Adolfo cast a wary eye on the river as they drove along its banks.

"It looks higher today," Adolfo said. "Say a prayer."

"If I prayed, I would." Mila gazed at the ravaging river.

They passed the foreboding National Library, its face grim in the darkness.

"I'm glad you're not working at the library anymore, Adolfo," Mila said. "That was a terrible job to begin with, and it was worse after the flood."

"I'm sure they'll still be restoring books years from now."

"Well, I'm glad you left," Mila said. "I think all those chemicals were affecting your health. And it's better working with your brother rebuilding houses, isn't it?"

"Roberto and I get along. It's a good job."

"That's all you're going to say?"

"You know me, Mila. I take things as they come."

Mila put her hand on her husband's knee. "I wish you could be happy sometimes, Adolfo," she said softly.

Adolfo looked far into the distance. "I wish so, too, Mila."

If the Florentine weather was bleak, it was even gloomier inside Angelina Torticelli's apartment. For reasons only she understood, she kept the place in almost utter darkness, illuminated only by votive candles in front of statues of the Blessed Virgin, Saint Joseph, Saint Anthony and, yes, Saint Elizabeth.

"If I open the blinds when the sun comes out, the carpets will get faded," she reasoned, ignoring the fact that the pattern in the carpets had long disappeared. "If I open them when it's cloudy, then I have to look at how gloomy it is outside."

"*Ciao*, Mama," Mila said as she began turning on lights in every room.

"*Ciao,* Mama." Adolfo kissed his mother-in-law on both cheeks.

Since Mila was her only child, Angelina Torticelli treated Adolfo as her beloved son, ordering him to sit—"*Sedere! Sedere!*"—as soon as he got in the door. The drive was long, he must be tired, here, watch some television. To her mind, Adolfo could not do anything wrong. Much to her consternation, he did chores around the house.

"Mila," she would tell her daughter, "why do you let him wash the dishes? He must be tired after working all day, building all those houses."

She conveniently forgot that her daughter worked all day at the Casa del Popolo.

Angelina managed to get through the Sunday meal—pasta, chicken cacciatore, vegetables, pears, cheeses—with only a few hints about the painful subject. Mila ignored them.

As Mila cleared away the dishes, her mother suddenly put her hand to her chest.

"Oh!" she whispered.

"Mama, what is it?"

"Oh, it's nothing. Sometimes I get these pains in my heart. They go away. Usually."

"Take a little wine, Mama," Adolfo said.

"Oh, thank you, son. You are so good to your mama. See, Mila, see how good Adolfo is to me?"

Mila and Adolfo noticed that Angelina's hands were quite steady and that her face was not flushed.

"Oh!" Angelina said again.

"Are you all right, Mama?"

"I'll be fine, Adolfo. Don't worry about it. The pains, I've noticed they come more often now. But it's nothing. Don't worry."

"Mama..."

"It's just that, you know, I don't know how long I have. And when I see Evangelista Ferari out in the piazza with her grandchildren, I wonder why God didn't bless me with a little grandchild of my own, and then..."

Mila picked up her handbag from the chair. "Come on, Adolfo, let's go home."

"You're going? You're going home?" her mother cried. "You can't go yet. We haven't had the *dolci* yet. Come, sit. We'll just talk while Adolfo watches the television. Come, sit."

"Not today, Mama. We've got to get home. Adolfo has to…And I have to…Anyway, we have to go home."

"Oh, Mila." Angelina Torticelli's handkerchief was now very wet.

"Good-bye, Mama."

Adolfo kissed his mother-in-law on the cheeks. "Bye-Bye, Mama. Thank you for dinner. Delicious as always."

As they always did when they returned from the Sunday visit, Mila and Adolfo remained mostly quiet on the drive home.

"Sometimes she just gets to me," Mila said. "Putting on that dying act again. It's not going to work. Never has."

"Sometimes I feel sorry for her."

"Well, don't. We've got our lives, and she's not going to make us feel guilty, right?"

"Right."

They were almost back at the Piazza Santa Croce when Mila said, "Adolfo, I wish you'd tell me how you feel about this."

"What's there to tell? It's my fault. I have to live with it."

Chapter Two

Mila and Adolfo were married in 1960. She was only twenty, and Adolfo was twenty-four, and they should have been happy. But the marriage started off dreadfully. Just before the ceremony, Adolfo had a terrible fight with his brother Roberto, who was also in love with Mila. Roberto fell into the Arno, and, for reasons he couldn't explain even to himself, Adolfo did not jump in to help save him.

Guilt-ridden and estranged for years from his brother, Adolfo went into long periods of depression, becoming withdrawn and morose. Nothing Mila could say or do could get him out of it.

"Adolfo, please," she would say. "I want to help you. Can we talk about it? Please?"

Adolfo would smile a little, hold her hand, and go back to lie on the bed.

Then there were times when he would come out of it. Not completely, but enough so that Mila didn't worry as much. Oddly, they wouldn't talk about Adolfo's "bad times" then.

During those early years they lived with Mila's mother. Mila's father had just died, and Angelina Torticelli whimpered that she didn't like being alone. Since the newlyweds couldn't afford their own place anyway, they moved into the old library Mila's father had used and converted it into a bedroom.

Angelina worried about Adolfo, too. When he was withdrawn, she blamed Mila for his troubles.

"What did you do to this poor boy?" she asked her daughter. "He looks terrible. He needs to eat more."

When Adolfo felt better, Angelina kissed him on both cheeks.

"Ah, Adolfo, what a sweet boy. Why aren't you always like this?"

As the months went by, Angelina began to drop hints about wanting a grandchild, and then became more direct.

"Mila," she would say, "don't you think it's about time you started having a family?"

"Not yet, Mama."

"Not yet? But when? When, Mila?"

"Not yet, Mama. I'm only twenty-one years old."

"Twenty-one? Girls have babies when they're sixteen, seventeen!"

"Mama, you were almost thirty when you had me!"

"Yes, but my parents were dead. I couldn't give my mother a grandchild. You can!"

After a year, Angelina became more insistent.

"Mila, is something wrong? Don't you think you should be pregnant by now?"

"No, Mama."

"But why not?"

"Mama, I'm only twenty-three. And I've got a job. Casa del Popolo is very busy now, and I'm tired when I get home. I couldn't do the job if I was pregnant and I couldn't take care of a baby."

"But, Mila, you could quit your job."

"And how would you live? You know you depend on the money we pay for rent."

Angelina knew she would struggle if she didn't have the little rent money every month. But a few months later, the rent money was no longer an issue. Angelina's brother Gregorio, a ne'er-do-well who gambled incessantly, died, leaving Angelina a small but comfortable inheritance. Angelina mourned briefly, then promptly went to the bank.

"I'll miss Gregorio," Angelina said. "I never saw him much, though."

Freed from the need to pay Angelina rent, Mila and Adolfo began looking for their own apartment. Angelina then went into mild hysterics over being "abandoned by my own daughter." Mila and Adolfo continued looking.

They needed to find a place closer to their work, they said, and the area around Piazza Santa Croce was almost equidistant from the National Library and Casa del Popolo. It was also about as far from Mila's mother in Piazza Santa Spirito as they could get and still find something affordable.

"When will you come to see me?" Mila's mother asked. "You'll never come! I'll never see you again!"

"Mama," Mila said, "we'll come every Sunday afternoon."

She regretted the words as soon as she said them.

They found an apartment on the second floor of an old palazzo right on the piazza. It had a kitchen that also served as a living room, a bedroom and a miniscule bathroom. As small as it was, it strained their budgets, and on some nights they skipped dinner entirely.

But the view—if they leaned far out of the kitchen window—was stupendous. The massive Basilica of Santa Croce dominated the piazza, and on many days, lines of foreign visitors chattered away as they waited to march past the tombs of Michelangelo, Galileo, Ghiberti and Rossini, plus a fake tomb for Dante. Then they would buy postcards in the gift shop to prove to their relatives back home they were actually there.

On sunny days the place was also filled with the sounds of children playing soccer, shoppers arguing with merchants, neighbors gossiping. One night as they watched the children, Mila said, "Adolfo, what do you think about having a baby? It wouldn't be for Mama, it would be for us. Wouldn't you like a little boy or girl?"

Adolfo was in one of his "good" moods. "Do you think so? A little Mila?"

"Or Adolfo?"

The more he thought about it, the more Adolfo liked the idea, and he was getting tired of the men in the library talking about their kids and teasing him about not having any.

So, for more than a year, they tried, even when Adolfo was otherwise withdrawn. Mila made the mistake of telling her mother what they were doing, and Angelina went straight to the church to begin a novena to Saint Jude.

"He's the saint of desperate causes," she explained, ignoring Mila's grimace.

Saint Jude did not respond, so Angelina resorted to remedies endorsed by generations of Italian women before her. "Mila, do you eat red meat? No? Then you should. Mila, do you eat chocolate? No? Then you should. Mila, do you eat fish and vegetables? Yes? *Santa Maria*, you will have a baby!"

But fish and vegetables were not the answer, and even Mila and

Adolfo eventually became worried.

"Maybe we should see a doctor, Adolfo?" Mila said one day. "Would you mind? Maybe there's something they can do."

"I don't know, Mila. I don't like to discuss these things with other people. Let's just keep trying."

She let the idea rest.

After another year without success, she brought it up again. "Adolfo, I really think we should talk to somebody about this."

"I don't know. Maybe we should just keep trying."

"Adolfo? Please?"

Through friends who had a similar problem, they found a doctor who would examine them and conduct a few tests. There were days of waiting, and then the doctor asked them to come back.

"Mila," he said, "I'm pleased to report that there's nothing wrong with you. You could get pregnant any time."

Mila and Adolfo beamed.

"But Adolfo," he continued, "I'm afraid you have a very low sperm count. That's why you haven't been able to have a child. I'm sorry."

Chapter Three

If Adolfo had suffered from depression before their visit to the doctor, he was even more withdrawn and dejected afterwards. At the library, he stayed in one corner of the table where workers were restoring ancient manuscripts. He rarely spoke, and barely listened to the conversations. When they talked about their children, he went outside and smoked a cigarette.

When he came home, he silently ate some of the meal Mila had prepared and pushed the rest of it away. Then he went into the bedroom, lay down and buried his face in the pillow.

Mila became even more frantic.

"Adolfo, please!"

She wanted Adolfo to return to the doctor for more tests and perhaps even treatment. The doctor had said that his infertility might have been caused by stress. She certainly understood that. Or maybe by his cigarette habit. She had nagged him about that for years.

"Adolfo, maybe they can do something about this. There have been so many advances. I've read in the newspaper about them. They can do things now! Please!"

Adolfo refused to go. "I can't have kids. I know that. You know that. Let's not talk about it, OK?"

Mila threw herself into her work at Casa del Popolo, which had become more and more important as poor immigrants and others moved into the Santa Croce area. They needed clothing, food and shelter, and she reached out to many people to help. The job, at least, made her feel good.

She did not, of course, tell her mother the results of the tests. Angelina wouldn't understand about sperm counts and Mila had no intention of discussing them with her. Besides, it wouldn't occur to Angelina that Adolfo was the cause of the problem. It had to be Mila.

And so every Sunday Mila and Adolfo drove over to Angelina's, where they ate the identical meal of pasta and chicken cacciatore and endured the questions and complaints of a woman who longed for a grandchild.

Adolfo lightened up, but only a little, in October 1964 when his nephew, Dino Sporenza, arrived in Florence to study art and stayed in a room in the basement of the palazzo. Dino reminded Adolfo of himself when he was a boy in the village of Sant'Antonio, free and without any worries. He remembered how his brother, Roberto, four years older, got him into trouble. Sometimes he wished he could see his brother again.

Two months later, Adolfo's mother died in Sant'Antonio and he and Mila went home for the funeral. They returned to Florence right after the Mass. "I don't want to answer any questions," he said. Others thought he was referring to his estrangement from Roberto, but Adolfo, who couldn't stop thinking about his infertility, believed they would ask him why he didn't have any children.

In October 1966, things had gotten to the point where Mila knew she couldn't go on like this. Her friend Nicola at Casa del Popolo told her she had to leave Adolfo.

"Mila," Nicola said, "you come to work all tired and droopy, you get mad at the people who come for help, you just aren't yourself anymore. It's because of Adolfo, isn't it?"

"Yes. No. Yes."

"Then you have to leave him. You can manage. You can find a little room near here. Or you could go back and live with your mother..."

"Never! I could never go back to live there."

"Then find a room near here. I bet Father Lorenzo could find one for you."

Mila said she'd think about it.

A month later, on November 4, 1966, Florence was changed forever when the Arno erupted over its banks and flooded much of the city. The area around Santa Croce was among the worst affected, and Adolfo and Mila couldn't even leave their second-floor apartment for days. They were without telephone service, and so didn't know that Angelina had barely survived in her own flooded apartment in the Santa Spirito district.

In the months, even years, that followed, both Adolfo and Mila were too concerned about other things to worry about their personal problems. The demands on the Casa del Popolo multiplied, and when Mila returned home late at night she was exhausted. The National Library was faced with the enormous task of restoring and repairing thousands and thousands of manuscripts and books. In a different way, Adolfo crept home tired and wasted.

If anything good came as a result of the flood, it was Dino's efforts to finally get Adolfo and Roberto grudgingly back together. Reluctant at first, the brothers gradually restored some of the relationship they shared as boys. When Roberto asked Adolfo to join him in his business repairing flood-damaged homes, Adolfo agreed.

"Now I won't have to listen to those guys at the library talking about their kids," he told Mila.

And so, life gradually became more pleasant. Mila and Adolfo were content in their jobs. They enjoyed life on Piazza Santa Croce. They suffered through Sundays with Mila's mother, but her nagging didn't bother them anymore.

But they still did not have a child.

Chapter Four

It was on a Sunday night in 1978 when Adolfo's sister Anna called. They talked a little about her work at the *Figli di dio,* and how she loved taking care of babies there. But it was clear that Anna wanted to talk to Mila, and he didn't understand why she took the phone into the bedroom so that he could hear only brief parts of what was said.

"Really! Really! Oh my!…Do you think so?…I don't know, Anna, I just don't know…Well, I guess I could see…tomorrow? OK, tomorrow."

"What was that all about?" Adolfo asked when Mila returned to the kitchen. "Why did Anna call?"

"Oh, well, ah, Anna just wanted to tell me something. It, was, ah, nothing."

Mila busied herself washing dishes that had already been washed.

"Nothing?"

"Nothing important."

Adolfo went back to reading *La Gazzetta dello Sport.*

On Monday, Mila explained to her co-workers at Casa del Popolo that she had to run an errand and would be back in, maybe, an hour. She crossed Via Ghibellina and was soon at the oak door on Borgo Allegri.

The nursery *Figli di dio* had been established by Father Lorenzo only two years ago, and he had hired Anna Sporenza to manage it. Just out of the convent, she had poured herself into caring for almost thirty babies while their mothers worked, loving every one of them no matter how much they cried or soiled their diapers or threw up on her clean white blouses.

Anna was trying to get one of her charges, little Angela, to have "just one more sip, just one more sip, please," when Mila arrived.

"Ah, Mila." She kissed her sister-in-law. "You won't believe what happened."

As they sat at Anna's desk in the middle of the nursery, the sounds of coos and cries all around them, Anna told Mila how Father Lorenzo had brought a new baby to the nursery last week. Unlike all the others, this baby was an orphan. Her parents had been killed in a terrible accident in the Apennine Mountains. The baby, five months old, somehow survived and was brought to her mother's sister in Florence.

"The sister didn't want the baby!" Anna cried. "Can you believe it?"

"I can't imagine not wanting a baby," Mila said quietly.

"Do you want to see little Clara?"

Anna led Mila to the last row of baby cribs. Clara was wide awake, her bright blue eyes looking at something on the ceiling. Her curly yellow hair lay in ringlets around her face. And then she smiled.

"Oh, my God!" Mila whispered.

"Mila," Anna said, "I know you and Adolfo have been trying for years to have a baby. Sometimes God doesn't open every door, but then sometimes He opens a very special one."

"What do you mean?"

"Little Clara will be put up for adoption."

"Oh, my God."

"As I said, the sister doesn't want little Clara. Doesn't want to ever see her again. I guess she's got a half dozen children of her own and can't stand to take care of a baby again."

Anna lifted little Clara and placed her in Mila's arms. Mila could feel tears welling in her eyes.

"Come, sit down," Anna said. "Get to know Clara a little."

While Anna made the rounds of the other baby cribs, Mila sat in a rocking chair and held Clara to her breast, then in her arms. She began making faces. Clara laughed. She tickled Clara gently under her chin. Clara laughed harder. She made funny noises. Clara went into hysterics.

Then Mila began to sing a lullaby she remembered from her own childhood.

Stella stellina
la notte si avvicina:
la fiamma traballa,
la mucca é nella stalla.
La pecora e l'agnello,
la vacca col vitello,
la chioccia coi pulcini,
la gatta coi gattini;
e tutti fan la nanna
nel cuore della mamma!

Star, little star
The night is approaching:
The flame is tottering,
The cow is in the cowshed.
The sheep and the lamb,
The cow with the calf.
The hen with its chicks.
The cat with its kittens;
And all are sleeping
In the mother's heart!

In a minute, Clara was asleep, nestling against Mila's breast. Mila couldn't take her eyes off the sleeping infant.

There was no need for Anna to ask the question when she returned, but Mila answered it anyway.

"If it were up to me, I'd take Clara home right now. But I have to talk to Adolfo. I don't think he's going to like the idea of adopting a child."

"Adoption is not as common in Italy as in other countries," Anna said, "but now there are laws to make it easier, and also to protect the baby's rights. I'm sure there will be a long court process, and you'll have to prove that you're worthy and that you can take care of Clara, but, really, I think it could happen. Where else would Clara go? What would become of her?"

"What would become of her?" Mila repeated.

"Well, talk it over with Adolfo. I know, my brother can be very stubborn at times, but bring him to see Clara. I'll start checking on the process of adoption. I have to admit I'm not all that familiar with it myself."

"Tomorrow? Can I bring Adolfo tomorrow?"

Anna took the sleeping baby from Mila's arms. "Of course. But, Mila, there's one more thing. You see, it wasn't only Clara who survived the accident. She has a brother, Leonardo. He's seven years old. The mother's sister won't have anything to do with him, either. Father Lorenzo couldn't bring the boy here, so he's staying with one of the women who come to the soup kitchen, Caterina Rossi, for now. She has a little boy of her own."

"So you're saying that if we adopted Clara, we would have to adopt Leonardo, too?"

"Well, we couldn't separate them, could we?"

Chapter Five

"Adopt? Adopt? You want us to adopt someone else's child?"

Mila had known that Adolfo would not take the suggestion easily.

"But, Adolfo, she's so beautiful. Lovely curly hair. Such bright eyes. And the sweetest smile you ever saw."

"Someone else's child?"

"Yes, but…"

"How could I take care of someone else's child? Every time I'd look at her I'd think that she wasn't mine. And she wasn't mine because I can't have kids!"

Adolfo turned to look out the window.

"But, Adolfo, maybe you'd forget about that. Maybe you'd just see this lovely child and watch her grow up. And, Adolfo, she would love you, I know she would. And I think you need that, right?"

"I need something…"

"Can you just go to see her, Adolfo? Please. Will you come with me to see her tomorrow?"

Throughout all their years of trying to have a baby of their own, adoption had never occurred to Adolfo. If Mila thought about it at all, she quickly dismissed the idea because of the tangle of Italian laws they would have to break through. They didn't know of any other couple that had adopted a child, and rarely read about it in the newspapers.

But now here was a baby, just a few blocks away, who could be theirs and theirs alone.

Mila did not, would not, could not, bring up the existence of Leonardo. Adopting a baby girl was one thing; adopting a seven-year-old boy was another. She'd have to tell Adolfo eventually, but not yet.

"Adolfo, can we go see little Clara tomorrow?"

Adolfo paced the room, and for a long time stared out the window at children playing in the piazza.

"All right."

The next day, Anna was waiting for them at the door of the *Figli di dio.* She kissed Mila and slapped her brother gently on the cheek.

"Adolfo! You never come to visit. How long has it been, two weeks? We need to get together. With Roberto, OK?"

"OK, Anna. You're still the bossy one, aren't you?" He kissed his sister.

"Well," Anna said, "let's go back. When I checked a few minutes ago Clara was still sleeping. These babies. Sleep, sleep, sleep. Or else eat, eat, eat. Or else—well, you know what happens then."

Clara was doing something else at that moment. She was lying in her crib, staring at the ceiling and giggling. Loudly.

"Clara!" Anna cooed. "What are you laughing at? What's so funny?"

Clara giggled some more, and soon Anna and Mila were also laughing. Adolfo, fearing that he would show any emotion, stood back, trying to look at the other babies but eventually looking down at little Clara as well.

And then he started laughing, too. That prompted Mila to put her arms around him, and Anna to put her arms around the both of them, and the three of them held on to the crib and laughed and smiled.

"You like her, don't you, Adolfo?" Mila said.

Adolfo wiped tears from his eyes.

"She's just…she's just…she's just so little!"

"Yes, now," Anna said. "But just wait. She'll grow up so fast you won't know it. Here, do you want to hold her?"

Adolfo hesitated. "I don't know. I don't know how to hold babies."

"Well, time to learn."

Adolfo couldn't remember the last time he held a baby. He imagined it was more than forty years ago, and the baby was Carlotta, his little sister.

"Remember Carlotta, Anna?" he asked. "This baby looks sort of like her. Curly hair and all."

"I remember," Anna said quietly. Carlotta had died during the war.

Anna placed little Clara in Adolfo's arms, which seemed to grow stiff. Instinctively, Clara snuggled closer and reached her little hand up to his mouth.

"She wants me to say something, I think," Adolfo said.

"Well, say something!" Mila said.

"Ah, hi! Hi, baby!"

Clara put her finger in Adolfo's mouth. "Is that OK? Will I spread some germs?"

"It's fine," Anna said. "Let her do what she wants."

Adolfo began to walk with the baby in his arms. Soon, he was actually humming, and Clara smiled. Then he tickled the baby under her chin, making her laugh even harder. Adolfo laughed, too.

"He likes her!" Mila whispered to Anna.

"Praise be to God."

For more than an hour, Adolfo and Mila took turns holding the tiny baby. They grinned at each other every time she smiled.

When they left to return to their jobs, he to help Robert's carpentry business and she to the Casa del Popolo, they held hands until they got to the corner. In front of the milling tourists on this steamy August afternoon, Adolfo kissed his wife.

"I love you, Mila."

At the kitchen table that night, they began to make plans. Adolfo didn't even question the idea of adoption now. It was something they were going to do. They made a list of expenses they would have now and as Clara grew up. They tried to figure out where she would sleep.

"We're going to have to get a bigger place," Mila said.

"I can get more work from Roberto."

"Maybe my mother can help," Mila said. It was the first time that they thought about Angelina and what her reaction would be.

"She'll go crazy!" Adolfo said. "Can you imagine her fussing with the baby? We'll never get a chance to hold Clara."

"Let's not tell her until the papers are all signed and we get Clara."

"Agreed."

That brought up the subject of the legal process, which might take months, years.

"Clara will be five years old before we get her!" Adolfo cried.

"Let's take one step at a time. But I can't believe we're doing this. What made you change your mind?"

"I don't know. Maybe it was seeing kids playing in the piazza all these years. Maybe Clara reminds me of Carlotta. Or maybe…"

"What?"

"Maybe I just want to be a father."

"Oh, Adolfo. But, you know, there's one more thing we need to talk about."

Chapter Six

Angelina could not believe that Mila and Adolfo were not coming for Sunday dinner.

"But why, why? I bought this fresh chicken at the market yesterday. I made the pasta last night. I made biscotti, the chocolate kind that Adolfo likes. Why aren't you coming?"

Mila explained that she and Adolfo had an appointment, and held the phone away from her ear.

"Appointment! What kind of appointment? On a Sunday? Who keeps appointments on a Sunday?"

"It's the only day we could do it, Mama."

"But what's going to happen to the chicken? I bought it fresh at the market yesterday. And the pasta?"

"You'll think of something, Mama."

Since all his other days were occupied at the soup kitchen, Father Lorenzo could take Mila and Adolfo to meet little Leonardo only on a Sunday. Mila didn't want to risk postponing it because Adolfo had finally agreed to meet the boy.

"A boy?" he had said. "A seven-year-old boy? Why didn't you tell me about him? What am I supposed to do with a seven-year-old boy?"

Mila didn't have a good answer. She hadn't known how Adolfo would react to the very idea of adopting a child. She hadn't known how he'd react to adopting a baby. And now she certainly didn't know how he would react to adopting a seven-year-old boy.

"I just wanted to take this one step at a time," she said finally.

They met Father Lorenzo at the soup kitchen and made their way to Caterina Rossi's apartment. It was a sunny afternoon and, as always, children were playing in Piazza Santa Croce. Mila noticed two young boys running up and down and darting in and out of the shopping stalls.

326

"Look, Adolfo," she said, "aren't they cute?"

"Looks like one of them is going to get hurt, he's running so fast."

"They're the Scamponi boys," Father Lorenzo said. "Angelo and Nicolo. Angelo is twelve and Nicolo is eight. Good boys. Angelo is always trying to get Nicolo into trouble."

"That was just like me and Roberto," Adolfo said.

Before ringing the bell at Caterina's apartment building, Father Lorenzo took Mila and Adolfo to a quiet place under an awning.

"I have to tell you something," he said. "Clara is too little to remember her parents, so she's fine at the *Figli di dio,* and Anna loves her to death. But Leonardo is seven years old. He remembers his parents very well. Caterina says that he has nightmares. He apparently doesn't remember the crash at all, but when he woke up in the hospital he kept crying for his mama."

"The poor kid," Mila said. "Not his papa?"

"No. That's strange, isn't it? He's gotten sort of used to Caterina, and he is starting to play with her little Pietro. But he seems to be terrified of men. Caterina said she overheard him tell Pietro that his dad drank a lot. That may be the reason why their car crashed into the truck in the Apennine Mountains."

"Oh, the poor little kid," Mila said.

"It gets worse. Caterina said the boy had bruises and scars on his back and backside. Even with her poor eyesight, she knew something was wrong, but when she asked him about it he just said 'Papa' and started crying. She says he has nightmares and he starts crying 'No, No, No!'"

"Oh my God," Mila said.

"Now, whenever he sees a man, the postman, the delivery man, he becomes very agitated. He seems to be afraid of every man he sees."

"Not you?" Adolfo asked.

"He doesn't seem to mind me so much, maybe because I'm wearing this brown robe and he knows I'm a priest and so it's as if I'm not really a man."

"Great," Adolfo said. "He's going to be afraid of me. Mila, do you really want to go in there?"

Even Mila hesitated. "Father, do you think we should? We don't want to upset the boy."

Father Lorenzo put one hand on Mila's arm and the other on Adolfo's arm. "Look. Leonardo can't avoid men forever. If he gets upset, well, we don't have to stay long."

He rang the bell to the apartment, and they climbed three flights of stairs to get to Caterina's rooms. The kitchen was simple and spotless, with only a table, chairs and a couch on the worn linoleum floor. Pietro's books and a toy gun were in a corner.

Caterina looked very tired. "I haven't gotten much sleep lately. Leonardo's been having so many nightmares. I love the boy, but I don't know how long I can keep him."

"How's he doing now, Caterina?" Father Lorenzo asked.

"I think a little better. He still has nightmares. He doesn't eat hardly at all. He misses Clara, keeps asking me where she is. I tell him she's in a place for babies and that someday maybe he and Clara will be together again. He's very worried about that." Caterina wiped her forehead. "I'll get him. He's in the bedroom with Pietro."

Pietro emerged first, a sturdy little boy about eight years old. He ran over and hugged Father Lorenzo.

"Ah, Pietro, my boy. You grow a foot every time I see you." He hoisted the boy in the air.

At first, they didn't notice the scrawny boy in the doorway. He was smaller than Pietro, and Pietro's borrowed shirt hung on him. While Clara had yellow curly hair and fair skin, Leonardo had black curly hair and a dark complexion.

"We think maybe Leonardo had another dad," Father Lorenzo told Mila. "We don't know."

Mila quietly went up to Leonardo and knelt in front of him. His eyes were downcast and his mouth was quivering.

"Hello." She held out her hand. "My name is Mila. Can you tell me your name?"

The boy put his hands over his eyes. "Leo…Leo…Leonardo," he whispered.

"Leonardo. What a lovely name. Do you know who Leonardo da Vinci was?"

Leonardo shook his head.

"Well, Leonardo da Vinci was a very famous artist. A very important artist. Do you like to draw and paint?"

Leonardo nodded his head.

"That's wonderful! Maybe someday you can show me some of your drawings? I'd like that."

Leonardo looked down at the floor but nodded his head.

"I like to draw," Mila said, "but I'm not very good at it. My husband, though, is very good. That's him over there."

Adolfo had stayed in a corner, trying to hide behind Father Lorenzo, but now he came out. Leonardo looked at him and buried his face in Mila's blouse.

"No! No! No!"

She held him close. "Oh, no, Leonardo. Don't be afraid. Adolfo won't hurt you. He loves children. And, you know, we already met Clara. You have a beautiful little sister, Leonardo."

They could hear Leonardo sniffling into Mila's blouse.

"Wouldn't it be nice if you and Clara could live together again?"

She could feel a slight nod against her breast. Adolfo hadn't moved, afraid of Leonardo's reaction.

"Well," Mila said, "I think that's all for today. Would you like us to come back to visit you again?"

Again, a slight nod.

"That's wonderful! We will. Maybe next Sunday?"

Mila began to get up, and Leonardo wiped his nose on her sleeve. Caterina took the boy's hand. "Come, Leonardo, why don't you and Pietro go back to whatever you were playing in the bedroom."

Pietro bounded off. Leonardo looked over his shoulder at Adolfo. He didn't smile, but he had stopped crying.

Chapter Seven

As Mila and Adolfo walked across Piazza Santa Croce with Father Lorenzo, they decided what they would do. Every Sunday afternoon, the three of them would visit Leonardo and maybe he would eventually grow to know, perhaps even like, Adolfo.

"I think it would be better if I tagged along for a while," Father Lorenzo said. "He knows me so you can't be all bad, Adolfo. I'm sorry I can only do this on Sunday afternoons."

Mila's mother, of course, went into hysterics when she found out.

"What is so important on Sunday afternoons that you can't come to see me?" she screamed. "I can't believe you're doing this to me! I'm an old lady. And my heart…"

"Your heart is just fine. The doctor always says so."

"But what are you doing on Sunday afternoons? Can I come along?"

"No, Mama, no."

Mila and Adolfo established a routine. On Tuesday and Thursday afternoons, they went to the *Figli di dio* and took care of Clara while Anna looked after the other babies. They learned how to give her a bottle, how to introduce her to spoonfuls of cereal and how to give her a bath. Even Adolfo learned how to change her.

He was incredulous the first time. "Me?"

"Yes, you," Mila said. "You have to learn sometime."

Clara obliged by having the messiest diaper she had ever had.

"Yuck! Look at this!" Adolfo cried. "It's terrible! It's all over the place!"

"Well, take some of these wet paper napkins and wipe her off. No, no, all over. That's right. Now take a damp cloth and wipe her down. Now dry her. Use the powder. Now put this new diaper on."

"What do I do with this dirty one?"

"There's a can over there."

When Clara was finally dressed again, she rewarded Adolfo with a huge smile and a giggle. He lifted her onto his chest, where she promptly threw up all over his clean flannel shirt.

On Sunday afternoons, Father Lorenzo accompanied Mila and Adolfo to Caterina's. Leonardo was usually in the bedroom playing with Pietro and followed Pietro only reluctantly out to meet the guests. Father Lorenzo would greet the boys and make little jokes and sometimes got Pietro, at least, to sing a song. Leonardo would stand against the wall, his eyes downcast, his fingers fidgeting.

Slowly, Leonardo warmed to Adolfo. He didn't seem to mind when Mila and Adolfo took him to the piazza for a gelato, although he held Mila's hand but not Adolfo's. He allowed Adolfo to play a little soccer with him and Pietro and Father Lorenzo in the piazza, though he never kicked the ball to him.

After a couple of months there was a breakthrough when Adolfo slipped on the cobblestones and Leonardo ran to him. "Are you hurt?"

"No, not at all," Adolfo said. Leonardo reached out his hand to help him up.

After that, Father Lorenzo said he didn't feel a need to come on Sunday afternoons anymore, but he did arrange to meet with Mila and Adolfo the following Wednesday.

"I think it's time we talked about adoption."

He had books and papers spread out on his desk when the couple arrived.

"You know," he said, "you're sort of pioneers. Not a lot of people are adopting children in Italy yet. Probably because they can't get through all these books and laws."

He explained that, as in other countries in Europe, adoption had generally been used by childless persons who wanted someone to inherit their estates. The minimum age for persons to adopt was fifty.

But in 1967, he said, Italy passed a law that opened up the modern concept of adoption for children up to the age of eight and reducing the age of people who wanted to adopt to thirty-five.

"Leonardo is seven," the priest said, "so we should start this process because it's going to take a long time."

"How long?" Mila asked.

"Maybe years."

Adolfo groaned.

Father Lorenzo sifted through the papers, complaining how complex the law was. He finally found a summary, and explained that adoption was under the control of the *tribunale per il minorenni,* the juvenile court. A prosecutor investigates the child's condition and reports to the court whether the child is adoptable.

"Well, Clara and Leonardo are, that's certain," Mila said.

"Then," the priest said, "a social service agency will investigate you to make sure you will be good parents. They have 120 days to do that."

Mila held Adolfo's hand.

"If you get the OK, then you'll have to wait for a year for the court to decide. Or longer."

Adolfo groaned again.

The priest put the papers down. "As I said, it's going to take a while. But, listen, I know some people. The prosecutor is a good friend of mine. He's in the film group I'm in. I think he can speed things up. And I know just the social service agency. They've been very helpful to the soup kitchen, and I've helped them. And the judge? Well, he's one of our biggest benefactors. I'll talk to him."

Adolfo hugged his wife.

"Yes, it will take a year at least."

"And in the meantime?" Adolfo said. "What's going to happen to Clara and Leonardo? Clara can't stay at the *Figli di dio* much longer, and Caterina is exhausted from taking care of Leonardo."

"Let me work on this," Father Lorenzo said. "I think we can pull a few strings and they can live with you."

Chapter Eight

It took a little rearranging of furniture after Father Lorenzo's happy phone call three weeks later, but Mila and Adolfo couldn't wait for the children to arrive. Leonardo would sleep on a cot in the kitchen and Clara's crib would be in a corner of their bedroom. Both Mila and Adolfo knew they would have to start looking for a bigger place very soon.

On a Sunday afternoon, Anna carried Clara from the *Figli di dio*, and Caterina, Pietro and Father Lorenzo brought Leonardo. It was the first time since the fatal accident that Leonardo had seen his sister, and he didn't know quite what to do until Anna placed the baby in his arms. After a few minutes, Clara smiled at her brother, and he started tickling her. Soon, they both giggled.

"Well," Father Lorenzo said, "I don't think you need me here anymore. I'll be in touch when I hear something. I have a feeling it will be soon."

"We'll be leaving, too," Caterina said. "Say good-bye to Leonardo, Pietro. He can come over to play anytime."

The little boys shyly hugged each other.

Mila and Adolfo and Clara and Leonardo sat on the freshly scrubbed linoleum floor, parents and children making awkward attempts to get to know one another. Leonardo sat next to Adolfo, and every once in a while their hands brushed.

Now eight months old, Clara was crawling all over the place, and soon Leonardo followed her around the room.

"Come on, Clara," he cried. "Faster! Faster!"

They fell into a heap in the corner.

"I have an idea," Mila said. "Let's go see Mama!"

"Really? Are you sure?" Adolfo asked.

Except for occasional brief visits on a Wednesday or Friday, Mila and Adolfo hadn't seen Angelina for weeks. She called almost daily, wondering what was preventing their Sunday afternoon dinners. Mila mostly mumbled or changed the subject. Angelina was sure she would never see her daughter and son-in-law again, and spent much of her days crying in her big chair or praying in the church.

On the drive from Piazza Santa Croce to Piazza Santa Spirito, Adolfo pointed out the boats and ducks on the Arno and told Leonardo that he would take him boating someday.

"I want to go NOW!" Leonardo shouted.

Mila held Clara when Angelina opened the door, with Adolfo trailing behind, holding Leonardo's hand.

"Oh, my God!" Angelina cried. "It's you! But what's this?"

"Here, Mama. Here's your new granddaughter."

"What?...But...How?...When?...Mila!!!"

If Mila responded, Angelina didn't hear because Clara was nestling into her neck.

"Oh, my goodness. When did you have her? You couldn't have! She's too big. Mila, this isn't your baby. Whose baby is this?"

"She's mine, or rather ours, Mama. And look, here's your new grandson."

Leonardo clung to Adolfo's pants, wary of this old lady with a mess of tangled hair and a frumpy apron.

"My grandson? Oh my goodness! *Santa Maria!* Oh!"

With a little push from Adolfo, Leonardo put out his hand and Angelina took it.

"Oh, my goodness!"

Angelina had never even heard of anyone adopting, and at first wondered if these were her "real" grandchildren. It took hours of explaining. But that evening, after the hastily cooked pasta and chicken cacciatore, and with gelato—three scoops for Leonardo—for dessert, she settled back in her plush chair, the crocheted doily behind her head. She held Clara in her arms as Leonardo sprawled at her feet looking at a book with gory pictures of saints.

"Now I know what you were doing all those Sunday afternoons," Angelina said. "I couldn't imagine. And now, look at this. Two grandchildren! Tomorrow I'm going to church. I'm going to thank Saint Elizabeth. I knew she'd answer my prayers."

Something More

Chapter One

Father Lorenzo knew he was running late, but he couldn't help it. Where were the beans? How could the *cucina popolare* serve bean soup tonight without beans? But where were they?

Not in the barrels, where the beans were supposed to be. Not in the cupboards that lined the long kitchen. Not in the bins in the storage room. Nowhere. And on an Easter Sunday morning, there was no place in Florence where he could find some.

"Well, we're just going to have Tuscan bean soup without the beans," he thought. "We'll just put in more tomatoes and bread, and a lot more spices. Oh boy, look at the time. I've got to go. It seems like I'm always late for the *Scoppio del Carro*. Odd. It's not like Dino to forget to fill the barrels. That's what he does every Saturday. Not like Dino at all."

Father Lorenzo, who had celebrated an early Mass, rushed out the door and crossed the piazza in front of the Basilica of Santa Croce. The crowds grew thicker as he sprinted down Borgo dei Greci into the Piazza della Signore. He passed the statue of Hercules, glanced at the gigantic copy of Michelangelo's David, and zigzagged north to the Duomo. He was out of breath.

"I'm getting too old for this. I'm going to be forty-eight in September."

As always on this Easter Sunday, he was to meet his friends in front of Ghiberti's Gates of Paradise doors on the Baptistry next to the Duomo. As he pushed his way through the crowd outside the cathedral, he saw that Fabrizio, Flavio and Giuseppe from his documentary film group were already here. Salvatore and Bernardo from his cooking group were nearby. And Father Fortunato from a retreat in the mountains two years ago.

Almost everyone was already here, in the place they thought was the best to watch the festivities.

"*Buongiorno*, Father!" Fabrizio could barely be heard above the milling throng. "Wondered when you'd come. We've been here for hours."

"There was a problem with the beans in the soup kitchen. Who are we missing?"

"I saw Antonio over by the Campanile a while ago," Flavio shouted. "Then I lost him."

"And Dino? Where's Dino?"

"Dino Sporenza? Haven't seen him, Father," Salvatore said.

As Father Lorenzo began to scan the crowd, knowing that Dino was taller than almost anyone else, Giuseppe started jumping up and down. Less than five feet tall, he couldn't see anything.

"*Boh!* This is crazy," he yelled. "There's a bigger crowd every year. They should move this somewhere else."

"Where?" Father Lorenzo said. "*Scoppio del Carro* has been going on right here in front of the Duomo for more than five hundred years."

"I hear something!" Fabrizio shouted. "They must be coming."

"Damn!" Giuseppe said. "Sorry, Father. But I can't see!"

"Here," Fabrizio said, boosting his cousin onto Flavio's back. "Look over his shoulders."

"Hey!" Flavio shouted. "Now I can't see!"

Giuseppe dug his knees into Flavio's shoulders. "I'll tell you all about it. Look! They're coming!"

If tradition and folklore can be believed, *Scoppio del Carro*, literally "Explosion of the Cart," had its origins in the year 1099. During the First Crusade, a member of the prominent Pazzi family led more than two thousand Florentines to take control of Jerusalem. As a reward, he was given three chips of stone from the Holy Sepulcher where Jesus was supposed to have been buried, and these were eventually brought to the Chiesa degli Santi Apostoli in Florence.

Every year, the chips were used as flints to light the Easter fire, and over the years, and centuries, the ceremony became more and more elaborate. A cart was built to carry the fire to homes of the wealthy. The cart itself grew in size until it was thirty feet high and oddly resembled a Chinese pagoda. At some point, probably because of the Italians' love of spectacle, someone thought to load it with fireworks that would burst forth into the air when the cart was lit.

Then, with even more ingenuity, someone decided to have the fire lit in the Duomo after the Gloria of the Easter Mass. Using the flints from the Holy Sepulcher, a deacon would light a fuse and put it into a *columbina*, a little rocket shaped like a dove reminiscent of the Holy Spirit. The rocket then shot down a wire from the Duomo's choir loft to the cart in the piazza outside, and the cart exploded in a twenty-minute extravaganza of fireworks. Miraculously, the cart was never seriously damaged.

Since every Italian spectacle has to have a meaning, Florentines say that a successful fireworks display will guarantee a good harvest.

But before all that there was the pageantry, and Father Lorenzo and his friends had arrived just in time. First, there were flag throwers, clad in medieval costumes, who performed in front of the Duomo, hurling their flags thirty, forty feet in the air and magnificently catching every one of them. Then there was the parade with men and women also dressed in historic costumes, the drummers almost drowning out the peals from the Campanile bells. And then the cart was brought in.

"Here they come!" Giuseppe shouted.

"Who?" With Giuseppe on his shoulders, Flavio couldn't see. "Who's coming?"

"The oxen towing the cart. The white oxen, Flavio. Just like every year. Flowers on their heads. Banners around their bellies."

The cart loomed into view, and the crowd, once boisterous, stood back in awe. This was the moment.

"Look!" Giuseppe shouted again. "The *columbina* is coming!"

Out of a window in the Duomo, a small silver metal dove slid down the wire, above the heads of the spectators and right into the cart. Immediately, fireworks shot out of the cart and into the air.

"Get back!" Father Lorenzo yelled. "We don't want anyone hurt."

For their own safety, the Florentines knew they had to stand clear of the booming rockets that sent out so many clouds of black smoke, then red, that people covered their faces with handkerchiefs. Finally, the smoke subsided.

"Another great *Scoppio del Carro*," Fabrizio said.

"It gets better every year," Father Fortunato said. "What are you looking for, Lorenzo?"

"I don't know why Dino didn't show up. He's always here."

"Maybe he overslept," Giuseppe said.

"Not like him," Father Lorenzo said. "Unless he was with Bruno and Rico last night."

Chapter Two

Francesca had been worried about not seeing Dino in the past week, but now she became frantic after the call from Father Lorenzo. He hadn't seen Dino since Tuesday, and here it was Sunday. He hadn't been at the Holy Thursday Mass or the Good Friday service, in which he always led the procession carrying the cross. He hadn't been at *Scoppio del Carro*. Worst, Father Lorenzo said he hadn't filled the bean supply for the soup. It wasn't like him. Something must have happened and she had to find out.

Sofia was the last person Francesca wanted to talk to, but she didn't have a choice. Sofia had been going with Dino for so long, she must know something.

She pulled out the notebook she had received from her mother as a high school graduation present. Running her hand over the Florentine design on the cover, she said a little prayer and hoped that her mother had at last found peace.

Sofia's number was on one of the last pages.

"Hello? Sofia, it's me, Francesca. No, please don't hang up."

"Francesca? Why are you calling me?"

"I just wondered if you'd seen Dino lately. Nobody seems to know where he is."

"Why do you want to know?"

"Because I'm worried. Wouldn't you be worried?"

"Francesca, I haven't seen him for two months. I don't know where he is."

"Sofia, I'm so worried."

"Dino can take care of himself. I really don't care where he is."

"Sofia…"

"Really. I don't care. I don't care at all."

"Sofia, don't hang up." Francesca's voice always rose when she was nervous. "Please. Look, can we talk about this?"

"What do we have to talk about?"

"Well, Dino's been our friend for so long, and I just think we should talk about things and maybe something has happened to him and maybe we can figure something out, and..."

"What's there to figure out? Dino is a stupid ass."

"Sofia!"

"It's true!"

"Sofia!"

"Look, if you want to meet, all right. But I don't think I know anything. Where do you want to meet?"

Francesca explained that Dino liked to go to an *osteria* near the Ponte Vecchio, *il Cinghiale*. Maybe someone there would know something.

"All right, I'll meet you there in an hour," Sofia said.

Francesca had never been in *il Cinghiale* before, and found that it was exactly the kind of place one would expect named after a boar. Rough wooden walls, somewhat obscene posters, loud music. Men and women in plaid shirts and jeans drinking beer. It seemed like everyone was smoking, and a thick purple haze hung over the room. The patrons, about her own age, were continuing their celebration of the *Scoppio del Carro*. Francesca was too shy to ask anyone about Dino and found a battered wooden table in a corner. She didn't have to wait long, recognizing Sofia through the haze.

"Well, I'm here, Francesca. What do you want to talk about?"

No one would ever say that Sofia was anything less than blunt. Perhaps she was hardened by her tough upbringing in Calabria. Perhaps she learned more about life in her first job in Florence, as a life model at the Academia di Belle Arti. Perhaps it was in her current work, employed by a court to get teenage delinquents off the streets.

Her life had been much different than Francesca's, who grew up as the only child of a working mother in Lucca. Here in Florence, she earned a meager wage as a seamstress in a dress factory. For reasons they couldn't explain, neither Francesca nor Sofia had married, and now, in 1978, Sofia was thirty-eight, Francesca the same age as Dino, thirty-two.

"Thank you for coming, Sofia. I really feel that we need to talk." Francesca made room on the wooden bench.

"Well?"

"Sofia, I know we haven't been friends. I guess I was jealous when I found out that Dino was seeing you. Dino and I had been so close in high school in Lucca, and when he moved to Florence we sort of lost touch until I came here to help after the flood."

"Well," Sofia said, "how do you think I felt when you showed up here? After Dino had been seeing me for so long, he suddenly became interested in you again."

"I didn't mean it to happen, Sofia. It just did. But really, we're just friends now. Sure, we go out to dinner every few weeks, but we just talk about the old times in Lucca when we both studied art. Dino always wanted me to continue, but I just don't have the talent. Really, Sofia, Dino and I are just friends, that's all."

"You know," Sofia said, "Dino isn't the only guy I go out with. There's Enrico. There's Filippo. There's Stefano."

She drew her finger on names that had been scratched on the wooden table.

"But," Sofia said, "I have to say that I don't care about any of the others like I do Dino. But I don't know how long we can go on like this. My God, it's been fourteen years!"

Francesca put her hand on Sofia's arm. "I know he's in love with you, Francesca, always has been."

"Well, I wish he'd tell me that."

"It's true. I can tell by the way he talks about you."

"What does he say?"

"He thinks you're so kind, so loving, so generous, besides being so beautiful."

Sofia looked off into the distance. "I've always wondered what he thinks of me, if he thought I was just another one of those *terrone* from the South. I know what you people in the North think."

"I don't! I don't, Sofia! And I know that Dino doesn't either."

"Well, everybody else in Florence does. I can't tell you how many times I've been called lazy or dirty, that I'm immoral, that I must be connected with the mob. Just because my skin is a little dark…"

"Sofia, I know a lot of people here have that attitude. It's terrible. But, really, Dino doesn't have a prejudiced bone in his body. I know that for a fact."

"I guess we've never really talked about it, Dino and me. I just thought…"

"Well, Sofia, don't think. You need to talk to him about this. You need to hear it from him what he thinks."

"How am I going to talk to him? I don't even know where he is."

"That's what I'm worried about," Francesca said. "Dino hasn't been seen for five days. That's not like him. When you saw him the last time, did he say anything about going somewhere or anything?"

Sofia thought a bit. "No. Nothing. We had a pleasant evening. We saw a movie. He always wants to go to movies, and I haven't told him that I hate them. *Superman*. Stupid, but I guess he liked it. Christopher Reeve was good."

"And afterwards? I don't mean to pry, but…"

"Afterwards? I thought we would go to my place, like we sometimes do. But, no, he said he wanted to see Rico and Bruno. Just like that. He didn't even walk me home. He wanted to see Rico and Bruno! Well, I hope he's happy with Rico and Bruno!"

Suddenly Sofia's eyes filled with tears, and Francesca put her arm around her. Francesca wasn't surprised that Dino wanted to go off with Rico and Bruno. This had been happening more and more lately, and that's why she was worried. Every time she had dinner with Dino lately, he mentioned them, how they were his new good friends, how they led such exciting lives. He didn't go into detail about what made their lives exciting, and she wondered.

She didn't understand why Dino wanted to be with them. Here he was, the most stable man she knew, kind and gentle, a regular volunteer at Father Lorenzo's soup kitchen, working with his uncles on projects to provide homes for the poor. But ever since he got involved with Rico and Bruno, she noticed that he stayed out late and that he drank too much. His uncle Adolfo said that Dino sometimes showed up late for work and one time didn't show up at all.

"He's changed, Sofia. I don't know why, but he's changed. And now I'm afraid something's happened to him. Did you really mean it when you said you didn't care?"

Sofia wiped her eyes. "No. No. I still care. I just wish to hell he'd never met Bruno and Rico!"

Chapter Three

By any measure, these should have been Dino Sporenza's best years. He had a satisfying job at *Gli Angeli della Casa*, the agency run by his uncles Roberto and Adolfo to help the poor in Florence find good housing. Never afraid to negotiate, he had learned which companies would provide quality lumber, which painters were the most reliable, which carpenters were the most careful. It was satisfying work, and he liked it.

He had moved into a nice, if small, apartment on the third floor of an apartment building off Piazza Santa Spirito in the Oltrarno district. He could walk to work along the Arno, but he had also purchased a relatively new Fiat, his first car after years of riding a Ducati motorbike. Early some mornings, before going to work, he drove up in the hills above Florence and painted. He liked to think he had shown promise as a student at the Academia di Belle Arti.

At thirty-two, he was still unmarried, which was not unusual for Italian men. He knew several men at work and some volunteers who were even older, still living at home and still dating the same woman over many years. At least he wasn't living at home.

He was serious, though, about sultry Sofia from Calabria, with her dark hair and flashing eyes. They went out almost every week and almost always to films. He thought she liked them and he never told her he didn't. Often, he would spend the night in her little apartment near Santa Maria Novella. They made terrific love together, and he wished he could get up the courage to tell her how much he loved her. But she seemed to think he was like other people from the North, prejudiced against people from the South, and he didn't know how to convince her otherwise. Some day, they would have to talk about all this. Maybe he'd ask her to marry him someday. He wasn't ready yet.

There was a time when he thought he was serious about Francesca, his girlfriend in high school who now lived in Florence. But over the years, they both realized that no matter how ardent they had been as teenagers, they were and would remain only good friends.

In his mid-twenties, he had bulked out and was no longer "skinny like a string bean," as his mother often said. His flat hair had developed a curl, covering up his protruding ears. He was aware that some young women even found him attractive.

In the last few years he had established a weekly routine. On Sunday afternoons, he went to Adolfo and Mila's to play with their children, Leonardo and Clara. Leonardo was eight now, and he had learned to kick a soccer ball to Dino and Adolfo in the Piazza Santa Croce. Little Clara was learning to walk and Dino often brought her a small toy.

On Monday nights, he did his laundry, a tedious task in his small sink, and wondered when Florence would ever get places with washing machines for people to use. He'd heard they were already available in Rome.

Tuesday nights were his favorites. He left work early to volunteer at Father Lorenzo's *cucina popolare*, something he'd been doing for so many years that he knew every one of the patrons. He joked and laughed with them, knew all of their troubles and sometimes slipped a few *lire* into their purses or pockets. After the dishes had been washed and the floors scrubbed, he and Father Lorenzo got out their guitars and played songs from the Beatles era. They joked that they would never improve.

On Wednesday nights, he visited his old friend Tomasso Nozzoli, who was the benefactor of *Gli Angeli della Casa*. Dino had found a job for Tomasso's son Massimo at the agency, nothing complicated, just a matter of sorting used pieces of lumber. The three of them worked jigsaw puzzles and played checkers. Massimo, injured so long ago in a violent soccer match, seemed to be making a little progress.

On Thursdays, Dino sometimes took Francesca to dinner. On Fridays, he almost always went out with Sofia, usually to a movie. Otherwise, he stayed home and read. He had become fascinated with American politics, reading biographies of President Kennedy, Robert Kennedy, the Rev. Martin Luther King Jr., and descriptions of the civil rights movement.

On Saturday mornings, he returned to Father Lorenzo's soup

kitchen to replenish supplies of beans, bread and spices for the week. Twice a month on Saturdays, he drove to his home town, Sant'Antonio, almost two hours away. His mother wanted him to visit every week, but that was too much even for a devoted son. Lately, she had been pointing out that he was still single.

"Dino," she would say, "isn't it about time you settled down? Marry one of those girls, Sofia, Francesca, that you go out with. I like Francesca a lot. Sofia, well, I guess she's all right, too."

"Lucia," his papa would say, "you're only saying that because you want some grandkids."

"No, Paolo, that's not true. Well, maybe partly true. Anyway, Dino is thirty-two years old. It's time. He's not Little Dino anymore. That was a long time ago."

Dino gritted his teeth.

The best part of each visit was driving with his parents up the hill to the Cielo to have dinner with Ezio and Donna. They arrived at the farmhouse early enough so that Dino could watch, and sometimes even help, Donna with the preparation of what Donna called *la cucina povera*, good Tuscan food. If he ever had time, Dino thought he'd like to take a course in Italian cooking.

It was a good life. He had good health. He had no worries. Except for his mother's nagging, he had no complaints.

But it was, well, routine. For more than a year, he felt there must be something else for him to do, and he didn't know what it was. He remembered the best time of his life, after the flood when he was so involved in helping the victims that he hardly slept. He would never forget the look on the face of an old woman when he rescued her from her home. And then, how she laughed and smiled when he brought her a puppy to replace the one that had drowned.

Father Lorenzo said he had grown up during the flood. Perhaps he did. That was an exciting time, a fulfilling time. Now, life sometimes seemed boring.

Maybe he should get married to Sofia. That would be good. She might be too old to have kids, but that was all right, no matter what his mother thought. Yes, he was going to ask Sofia to marry him. Soon.

Walking home from Tomasso's on a cool October night, Dino passed an *osteria* near Ponte Vecchio that seemed to be frequented by

Florentines about his own age, not college students and certainly not tourists. He had passed it many times before, but was always reluctant to enter because of the smoke and noise.

"*Il Cinghiale*. What the hell. It's early. Might as well stop and have a drink and get warm."

There were only a few lights along the walls, but through the heavy smoke that permeated the room he could make out posters on the walls. The place was crowded, but he found an old wooden table next to one where two men were obviously enjoying their beer. They were about his age, but more muscular. One had long hair and a mustache; he had an obscene word tattooed on his wrist. The other was completely bald with the same tattoo on the back of his head. Their faces and arms were tanned, as if they'd recently been on vacation on a warm beach.

They were talking so loudly, Dino could hear their conversation even above the din.

"And then, you know what she did?" The man whispered the rest, and the other man whooped.

"You must have been pretty drunk," he said.

"Hell, I don't remember."

"Hey, remember that girl on Corfu? The one who wouldn't stop talking?"

Dino ordered a beer and tried not to listen. Their talk was soon drowned out by the jukebox playing I Nomadi's *Dio è morto*.

"God Is Dead," Dino thought. "Seems like a good song for this place. Think I'll have another beer."

"Hey, man!" one of the men at the next table shouted over the music. "Want to join us?"

"Me?"

"Sure. Come on over."

They made room for him on the wooden bench.

"I'm Bruno," said the man with the long hair and mustache.

"And I'm Rico," said the bald-headed man.

"I'm Dino."

Two hours and a half dozen beers later—he had stopped counting—Dino walked woozily home. "What great guys," he thought. "They don't care about anything. Free as a bird. They go all over the world on vacations. What a life. But they also seemed so interested in me. Where I was from, what I did, who my friends were. And they wouldn't let me pay my bill. What great guys. Gonna see them again Thursday night."

Dino was late for work the next morning and had to endure the jokes from Roberto and Adolfo about his red eyes.

Chapter Four

Two months later, Dino had added another element to his weekly routine. On Mondays after he did his laundry and on Wednesdays after he visited Tomasso and Massimo, he stopped at *il Cinghiale*. Bruno and Rico were always at the same table.

"Hey, Dino! Over here! Come join us!"

With barely a greeting, they always had stories about their latest exploits, about the trips they'd taken and the gambling places they frequented, but mostly about women. Dino couldn't keep them straight. Bianca. Margherita. Giulina. Renata. Nunciata. They all sounded the same, whether blond or dark-haired, sultry or delicate. Every one of them conquered by Bruno. Or Rico. Or both.

Dino thought about his nights with Sofia. He wished they were more exciting.

For a while, they talked incessantly about their two-week stay in Dubrovnik, which Dino had never heard of.

"It's in Croatia," Bruno said.

"Terrific beaches," Rico said.

They went on about their winnings at the roulette tables in the casinos. How the Croatian beer was so much better than the Italian. How they never went to bed until 4 a.m., always accompanied, of course.

Dino was impressed. "Just you two went?"

Bruno and Rico exchanged glances. "Oh, we had a friend. Nice guy. You should come with us sometime, Dino."

Except for a disastrous summer trip to Pietrasanta with other students from the Academia and a few summer vacations with his parents in Viareggio, Dino had not gone anywhere. He hadn't even been to Rome.

One night, Bruno dug a plastic bag out of his jeans, along with some thin white paper. Dino knew immediately what it was. He had smoked pot only once in his life, fourteen years ago when he went on that vacation to Pietrasanta. He remembered how sick he had become.

"Here, Dino," Bruno said. "Have one."

Dino shook his head. "No, that's all right. But thanks."

"Come on, Dino," Rico said. "What are you afraid of?"

"Nothing. I'm not afraid of anything. I just don't want any, that's all. Thanks anyway."

Bruno put his hand on Dino's arm. "Come on, Dino. Have some fun! You afraid of having some fun?"

Rico and Bruno both stared at him. Dino shook his head again.

"Come on, Dino. Loosen up, will you?"

Dino looked around the room to see if anyone was watching, and then reached across the table and took what Bruno offered. And then another. The next morning, he couldn't remember what anyone said that night or how he got home. He couldn't remember paying the bill, but when he looked in his wallet the next morning, he found that it was empty. Late for work, and with a splitting headache, he kept his cap down over his eyes so Roberto and Adolfo wouldn't see his eyes.

In February, his new friends talked about going to Barcelona for the big carnival before Lent.

"We going to be staying in the Santa district," Bruno said. "There'll be parades and costumes and floats and everyone wears masks. There's nothing like it."

"And the Catalan food!" Rico added. "Incredible! Want to come with us?"

"No. No. No, I can't."

"Can't, can't, can't. You never want to do anything that's fun."

"Yes, I do."

"That's all right. We have another friend who wants to go."

When they returned two weeks later, they couldn't stop talking about Gracia and Marcella and Paloma and so many others Dino couldn't keep track.

"Just you two guys?"

"No," Rico said. "Another guy came with us. What was his name again?"

"Bernardo or something like that."

Dino started tuning the conversations out.

In the weeks that followed, Dino found that he was picking up the check more and more often when he was with Bruno and Rico. Then he was paying all the time, especially after rounds of smoking. He didn't mind. He'd never had friends like that.

In early March, Dino's new friends were excited about going on a three-week cruise to the Greek islands after Easter.

"Oh, man, I can't wait," Bruno said.

"Remember the gallons of ouzo we drank last time?" Rico said.

"And the food! Not even in Paris is there food like that!"

Rico grabbed Dino's shoulder. "Hey, Dino, have you ever been with a Greek girl?"

Dino stumbled for an answer. "No, but I'm dating a girl from Calabria."

Immediately, he regretted what he had said.

"Calabria!" Rico and Bruno shouted. Everyone in the *osteria* looked over at their table. "Calabria!"

"Well," Dino muttered, "I mean, um…"

Bruno laughed so hard he knocked over the three bottles of beer in front of him.

"Why," he asked, "would a man from the North date a girl from the South? That's impossible!"

Dino was red-faced and defensive. "She…she…she's very nice, and I…"

Bruno put his arm around Dino. "It's OK, it's OK. You can date whoever you want."

Bruno and Rico both snickered.

"Hey," Rico suddenly said, "want to come to Greece with us?"

"What?" Dino said. "What are you talking about?"

"Why don't you come with us? We'll take you. We'll pay for everything!"

"How would you do that?"

Rico and Bruno looked at each other.

"Oh," Bruno said, "we've got the money. Really."

"What are you thinking?" Dino said. "I can't go. I can't get away from work. I've got a job, you know."

"Dino, Dino, Dino." Rico said. "Can't do this, can't do that. When are you going to stop saying you can't do something? Come on. Loosen up, will you? Have some fun in your life. How old are you anyway?"

"Thirty-two."

"Thirty-two!" Bruno said. "Half your life is over. And when was the last time you had some fun? Tell me."

"Well..."

"You can't tell me because you never have, right?"

"No! That's not true! I have fun. I enjoy things. I play music. I paint. I have friends."

"Dino, listen to me," Rico said. "Why the hell are you always such a tightass? Think about it. You are."

Dino couldn't respond.

"Look," Bruno said, "think about coming on the cruise with us. Will you think about it?"

Dino needed to get out of *il Cinghiale* fast. "OK, I'll think about it. See you Wednesday."

In the cool night air, blessedly free of cigarette smoke, Dino walked slowly across the Ponte Vecchio.

"They're right, I guess. I am a tightass. Always have been. In Sant'Antonio. Here in Florence. Sometimes I think I should have stayed in the village. I'll always be the boy from Sant'Antonio. And I'm thirty-two years old. When am I going to feel free?"

Dino paused on the bridge and stared down into the Arno's murky waters. He thought about the next weeks at work. It was a slow time. Roberto and Adolfo could fill out the orders, find the wholesalers, schedule the work. Father Lorenzo could get somebody else to help at the soup kitchen. Sofia and Francesca would be upset, but they'd get over it. Tomasso and Massimo wouldn't like it. Well, Massimo would miss him.

"No!" The lone beggar on the bridge was startled awake by Dino's outburst. "No! I can't think about it. I can't go to Greece!"

He dug some change out of his pocket and tossed it to the beggar.

"But why would they ask me to go with them? What do they want from me? And where do they get the money to do all this? They don't seem to have jobs. They don't seem rich. I just don't understand."

Chapter Five

Dino had talked a little about Bruno and Rico with Roberto and Adolfo, and also with Sofia and Francesca, but he could tell that the women didn't want to hear much about two guys he had met in a bar. He had not, however, mentioned them to Father Lorenzo, fearful that the priest would find some moral reason for him to avoid his new friends. It was time to do that.

He found Father Lorenzo in the kitchen of the *cucina popolare*, still washing dishes as midnight approached.

"Ah, Dino. Good to see you. Tony had to leave because his mother is sick and Renata had to study for an examination tomorrow, so I guess I'm the chief cook and bottle washer here tonight. And Lord knows, with Holy Week and all, I've got a few other things to do."

"Let me help."

As Dino wiped the dishes and stacked them in the cupboards, he told Father Lorenzo about meeting these two men in an *osteria*, how they seemed so free and took expensive vacations and dated all sorts of women. He did not get into details or talk about pot.

"And they're so interested in me, Father. They seem to really care about me."

"So you're fascinated by these guys, right?" the priest said.

"Well, sure, wouldn't you be?"

"I imagine anyone would be. But how much do you know about them? Where do they get the money for all this?"

"That's what I don't know, Father. And that's why I wonder about them. I don't know what they do for work, or even if they have jobs. I guess I don't know much about them at all."

"Do you know their full names?" the priest asked.

Dino had to admit that he didn't.

"You've known them for six months and you don't know their names?"

354

Father Lorenzo had a way of looking over his glasses that clearly indicated his disapproval of something.

"I guess it never came up," Dino confessed.

Father Lorenzo put the last big pots away and took off his tattered apron. The sleeves of his brown robe were sopping wet.

"Well, Dino, I might know something. I've heard some talk lately about two guys who apparently came to Florence from Milan last year, but nobody knows for sure where they're from. Anyway, they go into bars and meet up with other guys who, well, let's say they look naïve and gullible."

"Like me, I suppose," Dino said.

"I'm just saying," the priest said. "They get to know the guy and buy him drinks and even get him to smoke some pot. Sometimes there is stronger stuff."

Father Lorenzo looked over his glasses at Dino, who looked away.

"They seem very interested in the guy and ask a lot of questions about his background and his family and where he works. And the guy thinks they're great and that he has new friends, which he probably never had."

Dino picked up a towel and began to polish the counter.

"Well, then, after they've had a lot of drinks and smoked a lot of pot, the two guys let the new guy pay the bills. It gets to the point where he pays most if not all of the bills."

Dino polished faster.

"And then the guys invite the new guy on trips. The only problem is that when the trip is finished and it's time to pay the bills, they suddenly have no money, so the new guy pays."

"Really?"

"These guys are conning the new guy. They're not just freeloaders, they're con artists."

Dino was now polishing the same spot over and over.

"Dino, have you seen that young guy Beppe, who's been coming here lately?"

"The one who looks like he just came off the farm?"

"That's him. Well, Beppe said that he was in an *osteria* one night a few months ago and two men invited him to their table and bought him a lot of beers and told him about the exciting life they led. They invited him to come back the next night, and he did, and the night after that and many nights after that. Beppe told them that his mother had just died and he received an inheritance. They seemed very interested in that. Beppe doesn't have any friends in Florence, so he was glad to have someone to talk to, and they seemed to like him."

"Sounds familiar," Dino said.

"Well, about six weeks ago, the guys asked him to go with them to Spain. This was for the carnivals before Lent. They said he would have such a great time. And he did. Met a lot of women, ate wonderful food in Barcelona. But when the trip ended, the guys said they didn't have any money, said they lost their wallets or something, so Beppe had to pay. There went his inheritance."

"Father, did Beppe know the names of these two guys?"

"I don't think…yes, I do. One was Nuncio, the other was Pino."

"Oh," Dino said, "I guess those are two other guys."

"I remember one other thing Beppe said about them. He said one had an obscene word tattooed on his wrist, and the other had it on the back of his head."

Dino threw down the towel. "Damn! Didn't Beppe go to the *carabinieri*?"

"What could the *carabinieri* do? The guys hadn't broken any laws. Now Beppe doesn't have any money so he comes to the soup kitchen every night."

"So are there other cases like this?"

"I've heard about two or three. They took one guy to Paris, and the guy paid, of course. The two guys always have different names and nobody seems to know much about them. They hang out in different places. I don't know that much about psychology, but I imagine they're just doing it for the thrill of it all. Besides getting a lot of free beer and trips."

"Haven't any of the victims confronted the guys later, asked for the money back or maybe even beaten them up?"

"Not that I know of."

"Maybe it's about time somebody did."

Father Lorenzo looked over his glasses again. "Be careful, Dino, these guys are tough."

"I'll be careful."

As Dino ran out the door, Father Lorenzo called to him. "The bean supply is running low, Dino."

"I know. I'll fill it Saturday."

"OK. I'll see you at the *Scoppio del Carro* Sunday."

Chapter Six

Since it was his turn to volunteer, Dino returned to the *cucina popolare* the next night. He avoided Father Lorenzo, but waited until Beppe had finished eating to talk to him. Beppe sat alone in a dark corner. He looked even younger than Dino remembered, and completely forlorn.

"Hi, Beppe. I don't think we've met. I'm Dino. Dino Sporenza." Beppe shook his hand. "I volunteer here on Tuesday nights. I'd like to talk to you about something. I think we may have something in common."

Beppe made room at the table, and Dino told him his whole story about Bruno and Rico. Beppe's eyes grew wider with every detail, knowing that, except for a few details, his own story was exactly the same.

Beppe then told Dino his story. "I met them at an osteria called *il Falco*, over near the Duomo. Most every Tuesday and Thursday nights. It was the same thing. I thought they were my friends. So I started picking up the bills. And then I paid for that damn trip to Spain. They said they lost their wallets. All the money I got from my mother. My papa is going to kill me if he finds out, so I can't go home. And pretty soon I'm not going to be able to pay the rent on that little room I have."

Beppe put his head in his arms on the table and his shoulders started to shake. Dino reached over.

"Don't you have a job?"

"I quit it when I went to Spain. I thought I could find something else, but I haven't. I didn't like it anyway, sorting pictures in a photographic studio."

Dino thought for a minute, and decided to ask Roberto and Adolfo to hire Beppe as the new apartment inspector for *Gli Angeli della Casa*.

358

"Pretty sad, right?" Dino said. "We both were taken in by these two con artists."

"They seemed like good guys." Beppe was practically sniffling now. "They told such great stories. And they seemed to really like me."

"Yeah, well, it was all a game. I heard they were from Milan. They probably go all over Italy playing the same game. I was with them on Monday and Wednesday, you were with them on Tuesday and Thursday. I wonder who they fleeced on the other nights."

The soup kitchen was virtually empty now. Father Lorenzo stacked the last dishes and prepared to leave. Beppe was busy moving a single bean, left over from his soup, around the table with a knife.

"Guess there's nothing we can do," he said.

"You don't think so?"

"What? What can we do? They conned us, Dino, but they didn't do anything illegal. We were just fools and they knew it."

"You think that's right?"

"Hell no."

"Well, why don't we do something? We can't let them get away with this, Beppe. Who knows what *osteria* they're in right now, conning some innocent guy who thinks they just want to be his friend."

"What can we do?"

"Listen. They're going to be in *il Cinghiale* tomorrow night. They'll be expecting me. They think I'm still thinking about going to Greece with them. Let's pay them a visit."

"And do what?"

"We'll figure it out."

"Both of us?"

"Of course! Come with me?"

"Hell yes."

The smoke was heavy as always in *il Cinghiale* the next night, but Dino and Beppe quickly found Bruno and Rico, also known as Nuncio and Pino, at their regular table. Dino came right to the point.

"You bastards!"

"Dino!" Rico shouted. "You came back! And you brought, what's your name again?"

"Beppe."

"Right. Sit down. Have a beer. We were just talking about what fun we're going to have in Greece."

"You bastards!" Dino rarely raised his voice, but he liked the sound of it. "You go around conning innocent guys and fleecing them of all their money. You did it to Beppe, but you're not going to do it to me!"

"Dino, Dino, Dino," Bruno said. "Settle down. Don't get so excited. We invited you to Greece, sure, but you don't have to go if you don't want to, or if you're afraid. You're afraid, right? Little Dino, always afraid to have fun!"

"And you bastards had Beppe pay all your bills in Spain."

"Beppe didn't have to go to Spain with us," Rico said. "We just thought he'd like to have some fun. Listen, we're nice guys."

"Then why did you force me to pay for the trip?" Beppe shouted.

"We're sorry about that," Rico said. "But we didn't force you, Beppe. We just couldn't find our wallets that morning when we were leaving. You know what, Bruno? I bet that girl took them. What the hell was her name? Delora?"

"No, Delphia," Bruno said.

"No, Destina," Rico said.

"That's right, Destina. She took our wallets."

"Stop that, you bastards." Dino couldn't think of anything stronger to say.

"Sit down, Dino. You, too, Beppe. We'll buy you both a beer. You'll feel better."

"We're not sitting down, you bastards!"

Dino suddenly realized that everyone in the *osteria* was looking at him. "Come outside!"

He had no idea why he said that, except that he'd heard it a lot in movies, and he had to get out of there.

Bruno and Rico stood up, and Dino and Beppe pushed them out into the cool March night. Since this was the Wednesday of Holy Week, to be followed by Holy Thursday, Good Friday, Holy Saturday and finally Easter Sunday, the streets of Florence were filled with tourists and college students on vacation. An inebriated crowd followed them up the street to the Ponte Vecchio.

Trying to push Rico, Dino knocked him down. Rico got up, his arms flailing.

"Hey," Rico cried, "you want to fight, let's fight!"

He punched Dino in the stomach, then hit him in the jaw. "You call me a bastard? Let's see if you call me a bastard now!"

Dino felt blood coming out of his mouth, but instinctively struck back, missing Rico's face by an inch. Rico, who was not as tall but much stronger, grabbed Dino's arms and pushed him to the ground. He wrapped his big hands around Dino's throat.

Beppe ran toward them. "No!" he yelled. "Let him alone!"

Bruno was on Beppe's heels. He grabbed him by the shirt, spun him around and slugged him in the jaw so hard, Beppe fell to the ground.

A few feet away, Dino struggled loose and tried to beat Rico on the chest. Rico grabbed Dino's arm with one hand and struck him in the jaw with the other. That's when the real fight started. Rico slugged Dino around the face and chest. Blood splattered from Dino's nose all over Rico's shirt. Dino was sure something in his chest broke, and blood was now pouring out of his mouth.

"Hit him! Hit him again!" the crowd shouted.

Summoning strength he never knew he had, Dino punched Rico in the stomach, sending him rolling down the embankment to the Arno. Dino rolled after him. His shirt was torn and he could feel his wallet fall out of his pants. He had no time to retrieve it, but grabbed Rico and hit him in the face.

"Bastard, you fucking bastard!" Dino could barely get the words out. He had never used such language before in his life.

"Call me a bastard, you fucker!" Rico grabbed Dino by the arm and turned him over so that his face was buried in the cobblestones. Rico grabbed a big rock and started pummeling Dino's head, shoulders and back. They were perilously close to the surging waters of the Arno.

The crowd had enough. "Call the *carabinieri,*" someone yelled.

Seeing what was happening, Beppe broke free of Bruno and tried to run to Dino's aid. But Bruno tripped him, knocked him down, sat on his back and began to beat his head and arms.

Dino was now motionless. Beppe was curled up nearby.

It was then that the *carabinieri* arrived. Whistles blowing, they cleared their way through the crowd to the battle scene.

"Stop!"

The police pulled Bruno and Rico from their victims. Both Dino and Beppe lay unconscious.

Chapter Seven

It was not until the Monday after Easter that Beppe gained a measure of consciousness. Through swollen eyes, he could make out a room painted all in white and machines and tubes near his bed. Then he saw a kindly looking woman with white hair and glasses standing near his bed. For a minute, he thought it might be his mother. Her voice was soft and comforting.

"Hello," she said. "We've been wondering when you'd wake up."

It was not his mother.

"The *carabinieri* told us you were in a bit of a fistfight. Looks like more than that to me."

Beppe realized that his left arm was in a sling tied to a cord from the ceiling. He hurt all over, especially in the back of his head. He had a fierce headache.

"Can you tell me your name? You didn't have any identification when they brought you in."

The words, at first, could not come out. Then, finally, "Beppe. Beppe Martoli."

"I'm glad to know you, Beppe Martoli. My name is Mariana. I'll be your nurse today."

Beppe tried to smile.

Well, Beppe Martoli, do you always go to bars without any identification?"

"Left...it...home."

"You left it at home. I see. Well, we haven't been able to notify anyone because we didn't know your name or anything. Do you want us to notify your family?"

"No...no." He'd be in enough trouble when his father found out about the inheritance. Better not add a fight to that.

"All right. If that's what you want. How do you feel now? Where do you hurt the most?"

"All over."

Mariana smoothed the pillow under his head and pulled the sheet up to his chest. "I know, I know. It's going to take a while. You had a terrible concussion and your arm is broken and you've got bruises all over. But you're young. You'll get better. I'm glad you've awakened."

She checked the monitors and adjusted the tube in his arm. "Just try to sleep for now."

Mariana was almost out the door when she turned and went back to the bed. "Beppe, do you know anything about the man they brought in with you? He didn't have any identification either. What is this world coming to? People go to bars and don't have any money or identification? How can they expect to pay their bills? Anyway, do you know the man's name?"

"Dino. Dino Sporenza."

"Dino Sporenza." She wrote it down on a piece of paper.

"Is he all right? Where is he?"

"He's across the hall."

Beppe repeated the question. "Is he all right?"

Mariana adjusted his pillows again. "Try to get some rest now, OK?"

When Mariana crossed the hall to Dino's room she found, as always, two nuns from the convent of Santa Baudolino kneeling and saying the rosary very softly. For the last three days, there had been a procession of nuns praying at Dino's bedside. The chaplain of the hospital had given him the Last Rites as soon as he had been brought in.

Dino didn't know any of this. His head was encased in a thick bandage. His arms were outstretched in casts. His face was covered in cuts and bruises. His right leg was suspended from a pulley. Tubes led from various machines to his chest, neck and arms. There was no sheet, and a breeze from the open window cooled his blue and white gown.

Mariana fussed with the tubes and recorded the data from the monitors. She pulled the bottom of his gown down to cover his thighs. Then she sighed, smiled at the nuns and went into her office to make some phone calls.

There were three Sporenzas in the Florence phone directory.

Besides Dino, it listed an Adolfo and a Roberto. No one answered.

"Well, they're probably working. I'll try again tonight."

Mariana couldn't reach Roberto that night, but a frantic Mila answered the phone at Adolfo's.

"He is? Oh my God! We've been worried sick! Oh my God! How bad! Oh my God! We'll be right over."

Adolfo and Mila found Roberto at his favorite *osteria* and were at the hospital in twenty-eight minutes, good time considering the Florentine traffic and the distance. Mariana was again checking the monitors and the nuns were still praying when they tiptoed into the room, Mila and Adolfo holding hands, Roberto right behind. Mila immediately began to cry, Adolfo held her tightly and Roberto turned away.

"I'm glad you came," Mariana said. "Sometimes, in cases like this, the patient somehow seems to know when family is here."

"Oh my God," Mila murmured. "I can't bear to look."

"Is he…is he…is he going to be all right?" Adolfo's voice was raspy. "He's going to get better, right?"

"We're doing everything we can," Mariana said.

Mila began to cry harder, and both Adolfo and Roberto could barely hold back tears.

"Why don't you sit here," Mariana said. "It's a bit crowded, but I'm sure the good sisters will be leaving soon."

The nuns understood the hint, gathered up their black robes and rosaries and crept out.

In the hour that followed, Adolfo, Mila and Roberto tried to talk to Dino, but didn't know what to say. They mainly sat stiffly on the hard chairs, watching if he made any move. He did not.

"Oh," Mila suddenly cried. "We need to call his parents. Why didn't we do that right away?"

"Because we weren't thinking," Adolfo said. "I'll go."

"And we need to call Anna," Mila said. "She's probably still at the nursery."

"And Father Lorenzo," Roberto said.

While Adolfo and Mila went to find a phone, Roberto stayed behind. He drew his chair up to the bed and put his hand gently on Dino's side.

"Don't die, Dino," he whispered. "Remember how you saved my

life? When I was so messed up, drinking and getting in fights and not eating? It was you. If you didn't help me, if you didn't make me, I wouldn't have helped myself. I wouldn't have gotten better. I wouldn't have made friends again with Adolfo. I wouldn't have a girlfriend. Get better, Dino. Please. I'd do anything to get you better."

If Dino heard, he did not respond.

Chapter Eight

Lucia and Paolo rushed over from Sant'Antonio right after Adolfo called, Lucia unaccountably bearing cookies she had in her cupboard. As soon as she saw Dino, she knew he wouldn't be eating cookies, or anything else, for a long time. If ever.

Predictably, she became hysterical when she saw her son, and Paolo had to take her from the room. He tried to comfort her but couldn't find any words.

"Oh, my baby, my baby," was all she could say.

They took turns with Adolfo and Mila and Roberto in Dino's room, but by midnight, and with Dino showing no change, Mariana shooed them all out.

"Go home, get some sleep. We'll call if there are any changes."

"You're sure you'll call? We'll be staying with my brother Adolfo," Lucia said.

"Yes, I'll call."

"You have the number?"

"Yes, I have the number. Please, go home now. You need the rest."

If the hospital hadn't limited visiting times to two hours with a limit of two persons at a time, Dino's room would have been crowded all the time in the next days. Lucia and Paolo arrived early and had to wait until the nurse let them into Dino's room. Mila and Adolfo followed, and sat quietly by Dino's bed for the allotted fifteen minutes. Then it was Roberto's turn. He was going to bring his girlfriend, but feared that this would be so upsetting she might not want anything to do with him.

As the days wore on, other visitors arrived. Anna prayed the rosary. Ezio and Donna drove over from Sant'Antonio several times a week. Father Lorenzo visited every day. Even he lost his composure when he first saw Dino and went across the hall to visit Beppe. Beppe

367

himself was making good progress, and Mariana was talking about sending him home in a week or so.

Francesca visited as often as she could and got in the habit of going over to see Beppe, too.

Sofia came daily and stayed the longest.

"Can you hear me, Dino? Please. Can you hear me?"

Then, as word spread, Tomasso came alone to visit. It would be too traumatic for Massimo to see Dino in this condition. And there were others. The regulars from the soup kitchen, fellow employees and clients of *Gli Angeli della Casa*, even his former professors from the Academia di Belle Arti.

"You'd think he was the pope, with all these visitors," Mariana said as she shooed a couple from the soup kitchen out of his room at the close of the day's visiting hours.

With little variance, one day followed another. Mariana, or whoever was the nurse of the day, checked on Dino every forty-five minutes or so. They recorded the monitors, checked all the tubes, changed dressings, and talked to Dino as if he could hear.

"How are you today, Dino?" Mariana said. "It's a wonderful day outside. The trees are starting to bud. Maybe you'll be able to see them soon."

"Your Mama and Papa were here again last night," another said. "And your uncles Roberto and Adolfo and Adolfo's wife, Mila. Oh and your aunt Anna. She's quite a character, isn't she? I love the way she tells little jokes. Can you hear them?"

"Father Lorenzo was here," a third said. "He said to tell you he wants to start playing guitar again with you real soon. I didn't know you play guitar. I bet you're very good. Maybe you can play for us sometime."

"And your friend Beppe?" a fourth said. "He's getting out tomorrow. You're going to want to see him again, aren't you?"

On the tenth day, Father Lorenzo happened to be in the room when he thought Dino said something. He ran out to get Lucia and Paolo, who were keeping their customary vigil.

"I'm not sure what he said, but he said something," the priest said.

They gathered around the bed, hoping for another sign.

His eyes were still closed, but Dino began to mumble something.

"I think he's saying something like 'Sofia,'" Paolo said.

Dino said it again.

"Yes," Father Lorenzo said. "That's it."

They listened more.

Through swollen lips, the word came out again. "Sofia."

"He's calling his girlfriend," Paolo said.

"That girl from Calabria," Lucia said.

"I'll call her," Father Lorenzo said. "I know where she works."

In less than an hour, Sofia was standing at the bedside, holding Dino's hand.

"Can you hear me, Dino? It's me, Sofia. Can you say my name?" She leaned down to whisper in his ear.

Dino's eyes remained closed, his body still.

The next day, Father Lorenzo was again in the room when Dino opened his eyes, just a little. The priest rushed to the waiting room, and, defying hospital rules, Lucia, Paolo, Mila, Adolfo, Roberto and Anna all trooped in. What with all the tubes and monitors, Mariana had to restrain Lucia from hugging her son.

"Dino, my baby," Lucia cried. "Can you hear me? Talk to me. Say something."

"Keep it down, Lucia," Paolo said. "Let the boy wake up first."

Dino opened his eyes wider. He seemed to take in everyone standing around his bed, and Lucia thought he smiled.

Mariana looked at the crowded room. "Maybe you better all stand back. Give him some air. He's going to make it."

Chapter Nine

With so many things to be repaired—head, chest, arms, legs, internal organs, the list went on and on—Dino was in the hospital for fifty-three days. He desperately wanted to leave, but then there was another complication, another test, another exam, and he was forced to stay. Finally, Mariana came in smiling late in May, with the good news. He could leave the hospital, but only under the condition that he return for therapy three times a week.

During the last weeks, there had been much discussion about where he would go upon his release. Lucia, of course, insisted that she bring him back to Sant'Antonio.

"I'll make you everything you like to eat, pasta, chicken cacciatore, veal parmigiana, lasagna, everything. Paolo will bring you gelato from the shop. You'll be strong in no time."

"But, Mama," Dino pointed out, "I have to go for therapy at the hospital three times a week. How can I do that if I'm in Sant'Antonio?"

Lucia couldn't find a solution to that problem.

With two small children and only two bedrooms, Adolfo and Mila didn't have room. Roberto had only one room and, according to Mila, "the place is so messy you wouldn't want to stay there." Anna had only a small room, little more than a closet, behind the nursery.

"Well, Dino," Father Lorenzo said, "there's a room next to mine at Santa Croce that's been empty for years, ever since Brother Andrea was sent off to Urbino to take care of elderly priests. It's not big, but it has a bed and a desk. We can bring some chairs in and a table."

"And a place for my guitar?" Dino asked.

"Yes!" Father Lorenzo shouted. "Yes! We'll play so loud all the other priests will complain."

Lucia didn't like the idea of not taking Dino home with her, but at least he would be in safe hands with a priest.

"We'll take good care of him, Lucia," Father Lorenzo said. "We'll see that he eats well, not just in the soup kitchen, but regular meals, too. And we'll have a driver take him to therapy three times a week. He'll be good as new before you know it."

With only his clothes, some books and his guitar, Dino didn't take long to move in. He was still using one crutch, so climbing the marble stairs was a slow process. Gradually, he regained his strength, crediting much of it to his therapy, good food, and restful sleep in a place that was so quiet even the mice seemed to whisper.

Father Lorenzo checked on him daily, but wanted to let Dino have as much freedom as possible. It was too soon for Dino to resume volunteering in the *cucina popolare*; he could not stand up behind the serving tables very long.

Lucia and Paolo drove over a couple of times a week, Lucia bringing plates and cartons of food because "you can't eat in a soup kitchen." Adolfo, Mila, Roberto, Anna, along with Ezio and Donna and Tomasso, were also frequent visitors. They all remarked about how much better he looked since the last time they saw him, which might have been only yesterday.

His right leg still hurt when he walked, he still had throbbing headaches, and the pains in his chest worsened when he coughed. The doctors and therapists said he was doing just fine, to have more patience.

Sofia came at least three evenings a week. They walked around the piazza until he tired, then sat in the courtyard. Sometimes she read to him. They avoided any serious conversations.

In June, Francesca, flushed and unusually animated, arrived with surprising news.

"Dino, guess what? I'm going to be married! And guess who? Beppe!"

"Beppe?"

"Yes, Beppe. I started visiting him in the hospital. Remember, he was just across the hall from you, and we hit it off. Well, when he got out, we started going on dates. Just dinners, movies, things like that. He's very funny, Dino, did you know that?"

Dino could not have guessed that.

"And he's kind and generous and he really loves me. And you

know what? I love him, too."

"But, Francesca, isn't he…?

"A lot younger than me? Not really. Only nine years. And Beppe doesn't mind, at least he says he doesn't. And I want to have babies, Dino. My time is running short, but the doctors say there's still time. And Beppe wants to have kids, too. And thanks to you we can afford it because he's got the job at *Gli Angeli della Casa*. Thanks for talking to Adolfo and Roberto about him."

She was out of breath.

"I know there's something more out of life, Dino. For me, it's Beppe and a flock of kids."

Dino couldn't imagine Beppe as a father, but then he wondered how he would be as a father.

"And I've met his papa, he's such a sweet old gentleman. He kissed my hand! He came from the village just to meet me, and he said he likes me very much. Oh, Dino, I'm so happy!"

"And I'm happy for you, too, Francesca. Give me a kiss."

Francesca kissed him on the cheek. "I wish you'd tell Sofia how much you care for her, Dino. You're a great guy. You deserve to be happy."

Francesca practically bounced out into the street.

Chapter Ten

Now that it was June, the sun soaked the piazza almost every day, and for exercise, Dino walked all around its perimeter, just once the first few days, then twice and then three times. That usually tired him out so much he had to sit on the cobblestones and watch the tourists lining up to enter the basilica, the residents shopping at the outdoor stands and the children running and playing.

He still had some pains, especially in the morning, but the therapy helped, and he began to work part time at *Gli Angeli della Casa*. On Tuesday nights, he even resumed volunteering at the soup kitchen.

He liked to sit across from the old palazzo where he had lived when he was a student at the Academia. He wondered if someone lived in his old damp basement room now, since it was so badly ruined in the flood. He wondered who lived in Adolfo and Mila's second-floor apartment, where he took refuge during the flood and which they had vacated when they adopted Leonardo and Clara.

And he wondered who lived in the ground-floor apartment with the purple door. The door was freshly painted, so new people must have moved in after Signora Alonzo died seven or eight years ago.

He learned the answer one day when a boy about ten years old emerged with a large black dog that lumbered more than walked.

"Hello," Dino said. "Do you live in that apartment?"

The boy had been warned about talking to strange men, but this one had a crutch, so he must be harmless.

"Yes."

"Have you lived there long?"

"I think I was six, no seven. Why?"

The dog was now sniffing Dino's feet. "Oh, I just knew the lady who lived there before. She was a very nice lady."

"She was my Nonna. She died and went to heaven."

"I heard that she died. I'm sorry."

"My papa says she almost died in the flood, but some guy saved her. We don't know who that was. Just some guy who lived around here."

The dog was fascinated with Dino's crutch and was licking it. Dino reached down to pet it, and the dog licked his hand.

"Your dog is very friendly."

"She's very old. She's *ancient!* She's thirteen!"

"She seems to get around OK."

"That's because I feed her good and take her for walks. You know what? She's my favorite thing in the world!"

"What's her name?"

"Jambalaya. We tried to give her another name but she wouldn't answer. Isn't that a silly name? Who would give a dog a name like that?"

"They must have had a reason."

Dino stroked behind the dog's ears, and the dog licked his hand again.

"Jambalaya is a pretty name," Dino told the boy. "Take care of her, will you?"

"I will!"

That night, taking a break while washing dishes at the soup kitchen, Dino told Father Lorenzo that he had seen Jambalaya again.

"Oh, yes," the priest said, "I see her every once in a while in the piazza. She's starting to show her age, though. I'm glad Signora Alonzo's son took her after she died."

"Remember when Sofia named all of Elvis' puppies after Presley songs? 'Hound Dog'?

Father Lorenzo laughed. "And 'Shake' and 'Rattle' and 'Roll'?"

Dino laughed, too. "And 'Jambalaya.' It's a good thing Elvis didn't have more puppies or we'd have run out of names."

They were both lost in thoughts.

"That was a time, Dino, wasn't it?"

"The best time of my life."

"I've told you this before. It's because you were helping the poor, Signora Alonzo and the others. You felt more alive than you had ever been. You knew you were doing something good, you were helping people."

"Adolfo said I was a hero when I carried Signora Alonzo out of her apartment. I didn't feel like a hero."

"You were, Dino. You were."

"It was a good time. I wish I could feel that way again."

Father Lorenzo looked over his glasses. "So when are you going to ask Sofia to marry you?"

"Been wondering when you'd ask me that. Soon, I think. We have a lot of things to clear up first. But you know, Father, I'm so restless, I don't know if marriage is the answer. I mean I can see myself ten years from now, married to Sofia, still working at *Gli Angeli della Casa*, volunteering here, going home to Sant'Antonio twice a month. The same life. I'm afraid I'm still going to be restless.'

"Wanting something more out of life?"

"Yes."

"Let's go out in the courtyard, Dino. It's cooler out there."

Florence's hot summer day had yielded to a mild evening, and Father Lorenzo and Dino settled on stone benches under an apple tree. The priest stretched his legs. "Remember that time, Dino, in 1974, when I went on a vacation in Rimini?"

"Sure. You needed it. We were all worried about you. You were acting, well, pretty strange. I thought you were off your rocker."

"Thanks for your honesty. But you're right. I was going through a bad time. Father Alphonsus said I was worn out after the flood, but the flood was in 1966, so there had to be more reasons than that. I thought I wanted something more."

"Did you find it?"

Father Lorenzo had never told anyone except his Father Superior about what happened in Rimini. But he knew he could trust Dino.

So the story came out. How the priest had met a beautiful woman, Victoria, at an event for his mother in Siena. How he went to Rimini purposely to see her. How they spent glorious days on the beach and their nights at quiet dinners and even dancing. How he became so infatuated with her that he even thought of leaving the priesthood. And how he finally came to his senses and realized that the priesthood was his calling, specifically to help the poor at Santa Croce.

The story took almost an hour to tell. Dino wanted to ask questions from time to time but remained silent, his eyes getting bigger with every new revelation.

"So, that's the story, Dino. Do you have any comments or questions?"

Dino hesitated. "Well, my first is that I can't imagine you dancing."

Father Lorenzo laughed. "Hey, even Victoria said I wasn't half bad."

Dino seemed to be engrossed in a black-and-white shrike that had perched in the apple tree. Its sharp calls muted the sounds of car horns on a nearby street.

"I still don't understand, Father, why you left this beautiful woman to return to run a soup kitchen. That doesn't seem to make sense. I mean, you weren't even that old then."

"Thanks. I was forty-three."

"See."

"Well, Dino, it took a couple of incidents to make me realize that I'm needed here. Nothing big. Just an old man on crutches and a young mother with a little boy. Both of them seemed so desperate and no one cared. I guess I knew then that someone had to care, and it was going to be me. And I knew that I really wanted to come back here. That's all."

Dino had to think about that for a while.

"But, Dino," the priest continued, "what I'm trying to say is that in Victoria I thought I had found the 'something more' in my life. You thought you had when you met Bruno and Rico. For different reasons, they weren't the answer. Sometimes, we may not have to look far for the 'something more.'"

"Where would that be?"

"I don't know, Dino. Think about it."

Chapter Eleven

His best—although only—blue jacket. Button-down light blue shirt. Tan pants. Scarlet tie with diagonal white stripes. Dino combed his newly cut hair, picked up the bottle of Chianti Classico and the bouquet of red roses and patted his pocket for the twelfth time. The little box was still there.

He checked his watch again. He did not want to be late for this dinner at Sofia's.

Her apartment near Santa Maria Novella was not in Florence's best neighborhood, but she had splashed bright colors all around and hidden the deformities on the walls. He could smell her Calabrian specialty, *macherroni alla pastora,* ground pork with ricotta, even before he reached her fourth-floor door.

"Mmmm. Smells good." He kissed her before she had a chance to wipe her hands.

"Just a little thing I whipped up. It'll be ready in a minute."

Their talk over dinner was about small things. Her day helping juveniles in the court system ("Frederico has been brought in five times, and he's only fifteen years old!"), his morning at *Gli Angeli della Casa* and his afternoon walking the perimeter of Piazza Santa Croce ("It's been a week since I've used my crutch and I don't miss it at all."), the weather ("It's awfully cold for September."), news from Father Lorenzo ("He's heard Bruno and Rico are still in jail and may not go to trial for assault for another three months. Well, that's the Italian court system. Such a shame!").

After another Calabrian specialty, stuffed figs, they settled on her bright orange couch. Dino cleared his throat. He had to get this out right away. "Sofia, I want to ask you...I mean, would you be willing...I've been thinking and..."

Sofia put her fingers on his mouth. "Wait, Dino. I'm pretty sure I know what you're going to ask, but we need to talk about some things first, right?"

"Sure."

"We've been dating for, what, fourteen years now. I mean, that's an awfully long time. If I had any relatives, which I don't, they'd be asking me why I'm not married."

"Mine are asking," Dino said.

"It doesn't seem that long. We've had a lot of fun, you're a great lover, we've had some wonderful meals and we've seen countless films, even though I've hated them."

"You hate movies? Why haven't you told me?"

"I don't know. You like them, so why should I complain?"

"Well, now I feel bad."

"Don't. We were together. That's all that mattered. But anyway, we've never—ever—talked about how different we are."

"Sofia, we are not!"

"Dino, I don't have to remind you that you're from the North and I'm from the South. There's been a division for centuries, ever since the South was under the Kingdom of the Two Sicilies. It's like Italy is two different countries. Everybody knows that. The North is rich, the South is poor. OK, that's an oversimplification, but it's basically true. There's industry in the North, poor farming in the South. The people in the North call the people in Calabria, Campania, Naples and Sicily and all the other regions dirty, uneducated, shiftless. They say we all belong to the Mafia or the *Camorra*. They look down on us. We're not as good as they are. They think they're so elite! The Renaissance and all that shit. They call us *terrone!* You know, that's like white people in the United States calling African Americans 'nigger.'"

Dino shuddered. He remembered an old woman in his village, a woman who had been a Fascist during the war, using the term when he told her he was dating Sofia.

"But Sofia..."

"Let me go on. I need to say this. Ever since I came to Florence, I've felt it. I can see people grimace when they see me, even cross the street so they don't get near. I can tell how clerks in the stores don't want to touch my hands. Do you know that in my job, I'm only assigned kids from the South who get in trouble? No kids from the North! How do you think I feel?"

"Sofia..."

She was crying now, and he clumsily handed her his handkerchief.

"You know all this as well as I do, Dino. Yet you've never wanted to talk about it. We're different, you and I, Dino."

"No! No! I don't believe that. I've never—ever—thought of you as being different. Yes, your skin is darker than mine, but I like it that way. No, I love it that way."

"Wouldn't you want me to be as fair as Francesca?"

"No! I like you the way that you are."

"Say that again."

"Sofia, I like you the way you are. OK, you're different from a lot of girls I've known. And I love you for it. You're so strong. You know what you want and you go out and get it. I suppose that's because of your childhood, your mother dying in childbirth, your father murdered. I can't imagine the courage you had to leave your village and go to Naples and then to Rome and then Siena and then here. And you were only seventeen! And I thought moving from my village to Florence was such a big deal."

"I had to do it."

"You could have stayed where you were…"

"What? And marry Bernardo or Luciano and have fifteen kids?"

"I'm glad you came here. I'm glad we met. I'm glad we could work together at the soup kitchen. I'm glad we were with each other during the flood."

"That was thirteen years ago."

"I know. I can't believe it."

"But, Dino, don't you have a little prejudice against people from the South?"

"Sofia, I came from a village where there were no Southerners. I didn't even know about them. How could I have prejudice against people I didn't even know? I know you, and when I'm with you I never feel like, well, I'm from the North and you're from the South. You're you. I'm me. That's all that matters."

"You make it sound so simple."

"And that's why, Sofia, I want you to marry me. To marry me now. We love each other, right?"

"Yes."

"Well, then, let's do it."

Chapter Twelve

Soon after Sofia moved into Dino's apartment, she and Dino were married by Father Lorenzo on November 4, 1979, in the Rinuccini Chapel in Santa Croce. They deliberately chose the anniversary of the 1966 flood; they wanted to declare their love as a statement of defiance and endurance.

It was a small wedding. "I'm thirty-nine years old, for God's sake," Sofia said. She wore a simple beige dress that she made herself.

Lucia, of course, wept through the entire ceremony, happy that Dino was finally getting married but sad that she would probably not have grandchildren. Paolo looked on proudly, and Adolfo, Mila and Anna smiled and laughed. Roberto brought his girlfriend, who remarked how lovely the ceremony was and wouldn't he like to do that, too?

Near the front of the chapel, Francesca and Beppe held hands. They had been married for five months and Francesca proudly wore a light blue maternity dress.

Ezio and Donna came from the village, but all of the other neighbors there said they were too old to travel in this weather and sent little presents they found at Leoni's.

The obvious place for the wedding dinner was the *cucina popolare*, and all the regular guests turned out in force. They sang suggestive songs as the bride and groom entered. Donna's menu followed the traditional Tuscan bean soup with exquisite chicken breasts covered with mushrooms, artichokes, garlic and tomatoes. Mila made the customary confetti for every guest, candied almonds tied in lace.

At their age, and since they'd been together for so long, they didn't call their trip to Venice a honeymoon. It was just a getaway. Neither of them had been there before, so they enjoyed the gondola rides, the Doge's Palace, the Bridge of Sighs, the Murano glass factories. Even on these cold November nights they tried to find a secluded table in

Piazza San Marco, far enough to avoid the ubiquitous violinists.

"Chilly?" Dino helped button Sofia's jacket and tightened his arm around her.

"I don't mind. Are you happy?"

"Oh, God, yes. Delirious."

"I am, too." She rubbed his hands.

Their coffee was cold by the time they got around to drinking it, and they watched the last remaining pigeons scouring the plaza for crumbs.

"You know, Dino, I think about the years ahead of us and wonder what we'll be doing. Do you think we'll still be pretty much the same? I mean, we've had the same lives for so long, you working at *Gli Angeli della Casa*, me at the juvenile court. It's not very likely I'm going to have children, so there will just be the two of us. I guess that's all right, but…"

"But?"

"I don't know, Dino. For years now, I've been wondering if there's not something more out of life. If there's more I could be doing. I mean, my job is satisfying, and God knows it takes a lot out of me, but I just wonder about this."

"You, too?"

"Is that the way you feel, too?"

"Sofia, if you only knew. I mean, why do you think I got so involved with Bruno and Rico, the bastards. I thought it was exciting to know them, and I guess I was sort of living vicariously off them. But it was fascinating. I hadn't felt that way since, well, since the flood. In a totally different way, of course. But I felt, if you'll excuse the expression, alive again."

"I wish I could feel that way."

"I wish I could feel that way again."

After four days, they reluctantly packed their bags and took the train back to Florence. A week later, they drove to Sant'Antonio, where Lucia and Paolo wanted to host a post-wedding reception. Dino didn't know many people in the village anymore, so the guests consisted only of Ezio and Donna. Donna supplied the dinner of veal scaloppini with morel mushrooms.

As they sipped their grappa before the fireplace, Ezio and Paolo argued about soccer, Donna told Lucia about new recipes she had found, and Dino and Sofia tended to the logs. It would soon be Christmas, Paolo remarked, and the talk got around to who was going to cook what.

"Sofia," Lucia asked, "how do you people celebrate Christmas?"

Dino rolled his eyes, but Sofia answered quietly. "Well, Lucia, we people celebrate it the same you do. We have the same meals, the same decorations. Oh, some people may have a more elaborate *presepio* on the mantel, but that's mostly in Naples."

"Oh, Sofia," Lucia said, "you should see the lovely *presepio* we have here in the church here. Rosa's husband Antonio made it about eight years ago. It has the figures of the Baby Jesus and Mary and Joseph, but then it also has all the people of the village and all the houses and the little river and..."

"It really is something to see," Paolo said.

"I've seen it," Dino said. "It's beautiful. We'll have to come back here for Christmas."

"I'd like that," Sofia said.

Lucia wasn't finished. "But I always thought that things were different down there in the South. You know, different customs, different foods, different clothes."

"I'm afraid, Lucia," Sofia said, "we wear the same clothes that you do, only we don't pay as much as they do in Florence."

"Mama," Dino said, "the South isn't in Africa or some other country, though maybe it seems like it to people in the North."

"He's right, Lucia," Ezio said. "It's terrible the way some of us in the North think about Southerners. These stereotypes have existed for so long, we just seem to accept them. And nobody seems to want to do anything about them. Not even talk about them. I'm sure it's hard for you, Sofia."

"I've learned to accept a lot of things," Sofia said.

"You shouldn't have to accept things," Donna said. "These things shouldn't happen in the first place."

"No, but what are we going to do about it?" Sofia asked.

No one had an answer. The conversation turned to something else, but when Dino and Sofia left the next day, Lucia kissed her new daughter-in-law on both cheeks. "I'm glad you're in our family," she said. "I like you very much."

"I like you, too, Lucia."

On the drive back to Florence the next day, Sofia commented, "Well, that was an interesting little conversation with your mother last night."

"My mother means well, but she just doesn't know how to say things sometimes. I mean, 'you people'?"

"Do you think she's actually prejudiced against people from the South?"

"I think she just hasn't had any exposure to them."

"It didn't affect you."

"Not at all. I love my Southern wife!" He squeezed her hand.

"And I love my Northern husband!" She leaned over and kissed him on the cheek.

They drove silently past Pistola and Prato. As they neared Florence, Sofia suddenly had an idea.

"Dino, remember how that conversation ended last night? When Ezio and Donna brought some sense to it? And you just said that your mother hasn't had any exposure to people from the South."

"Yes. So?"

"Well, like Ezio said, people don't want to talk about these things. Wouldn't it be great if people from the North and South could talk to each other and see that there really aren't many differences? I don't mean big conventions, I mean just little groups. Maybe if people talked together they would understand. Isn't that the real problem? People don't communicate?"

Dino unconsciously slowed down. "Sofia, you may have something there. I remember reading about the United States after the civil rights revolution. Small groups were formed. All kinds of groups with different names. Cherishing Our Differences, Learning About Diversity, Let's Talk Together and so forth. OK, some of the names were pretty bad, but it was the same principle. Whites and blacks would just meet in living rooms and talk about things."

"Did it do any good?"

"Maybe not at first, but over time, I think it had an effect. It just showed that people are pretty much the same, no matter the color of their skin. This book I was reading said that it showed that people could do things on their own and not expect governments to. It said that you can't legislate how people think, but if people understood one another better, maybe there would be change."

With car horns blaring behind him, Dino resumed the normal speed.

"Dino," Sofia said, "do you think we could start something? You and me?"

Dino almost drove off the road. "Really? Hey, why not? Why not try at least? I think other people would be interested. I think a lot of people are just tired of having this go on for so long."

"Who? Who would we invite?"

"Well, Father Lorenzo, for one."

"Adolfo and Mila. Anna. Roberto and his girlfriend. And all of them would know other people."

"And people from *Gli Angeli della Casa*."

"People from the soup kitchen," he said.

"I know some judges and lawyers," she said. "And friends from Calabria. And Naples. And Sicily."

"Sofia, this is going to be exciting!"

They were almost on the outskirts of Florence. "Dino, aren't we being naïve? Really. If this was going to work, wouldn't people have done it before? I mean, can just a few people really do anything about something as big as this?"

"I don't know, but at least we can try."

"At least it will give us something to do, something good to do. Maybe the something more?"

Chapter Thirteen

Two weeks later, Dino and Sofia organized their first meeting. "I think we should keep it small this time," Dino said, "just a half dozen people from the North and the same from the South. Then everybody has a chance to talk. If this turns out well, we can ask other people."

To represent the North, Dino selected Father Lorenzo, Adolfo and Mila and Francesca and Beppe.

To represent the South, Sofia chose Anita, a secretary in the juvenile court where Sofia worked and who came from Naples; Michele, a lawyer from Campania; Antonio, who, like Sofia, had come to Florence from Calabria; Claudia, a cleaning woman at the Duomo who came from Palermo; and Maria, who lived across the hall in Sofia's old apartment and had come from Syracuse in Sicily.

"She's very outspoken," Sofia warned. "She says what she thinks. Don't be surprised."

"That's exactly what we want," Dino said.

They thought the people from the North might be on the defensive, so they wanted the meeting place to be somewhere neutral. Dino chose the back room of a *trattoria* near the Duomo that advertised "authentic Neapolitan pizza."

Promptly at 8 p.m., everyone had gathered. After the introductions, there was some small talk about the weather on this cold December night, the new gift shop down the street, the latest gossip about the prime minister.

When they sat down at the long table, Sofia ordered the two groups to intermix. Francesca and Beppe, who had been holding hands, didn't like the idea but managed to rejoin hands behind Anita's back.

After that, the waiter arrived to take their orders, and Maria raised her voice.

"You know, Dino, just because pizza originated in Naples and we're from the South doesn't mean that we all like it," she declared.

Red-faced, Dino said, "I...uh...I just thought this was an easy menu and we could just pick something and get on with the discussion."

"You weren't stereotyping us?" Maria asked. "That's typical for someone from the North."

"No! I didn't mean that at all."

"Well," she said, "I don't happen to like pizza. I think I'll just have a beer."

Sofia broke the silence that followed. "Maria, I agreed with Dino. Just a simple menu. No stereotyping intended."

More silence as everyone else at the table studiously looked over their menus.

After the waiter had taken their orders and left, Father Lorenzo attempted to get the discussion going.

"I'm very glad Dino and Sofia got us together," he said. "You know, I work with many people from the North and the South, have for many years, and it's always been disturbing for me to see the divide that somehow exists between the two sides."

"And you think that us talking will help that?" Michele, the lawyer, asked. He had brought his briefcase and took out a notepad and pen. "This has been going on for centuries."

"That's exactly why," Dino said, "we thought we should discuss this. Why should it go on for more centuries?"

"I agree," Anita said. "I work in the court system, and I see examples of stereotyping every day. A kid from the South gets in trouble and comes in, the judge throws him in jail. A kid from the North comes in, the judge gets him a lawyer."

"But I'm never the lawyer, it's always someone from the North," Michele said. "There's nothing we can do. The judges aren't violating any laws. But everyone knows how they feel. I graduated from the University of Naples! Isn't my degree every bit as important as one from the University of Milan or the University of Florence? I ask you!"

"I'm so sorry, Michele," Mila said. "I never knew these things were happening. That's terrible."

Others nodded. There was considerable small talk again, as

everyone obviously wanted to avoid the reason they were there. But when the waiter arrived with the pizzas, Dino knew they had to get at the subject, as delicate as it was.

"Well," he said, "while we're eating, Sofia and I had this idea. What if we asked those of you from the South to identify a word or a phrase that's associated with someone from the North, and vice versa."

"Isn't that going to make everyone uncomfortable?" Adolfo asked.

"I don't think we're here to make people comfortable," Sofia said. "I think we should get things out in the open and then go from there. OK, I'll start. When I think of someone from the North, this is the first thing that comes to mind: 'Elite.'"

"Right," Maria said, looking at Dino, "and the first thing I think of is, 'they think they know everything.'"

"Takes my job," Michele said.

"Pushes in front of me," Antonio said.

"Thinks I can't read or write," Anita said.

"Thinks I'm invisible," Claudia said.

"OK," Dino said, "all very good. We're glad to know that. Now people from the North about people from the South. I'll start. 'Lazy.'"

"Why the hell do you say that?" Maria demanded. "Do you know how hard I work? Do you know…"

"Maria," Sofia said, "these are stereotypes, they're not personal."

"Sounds personal to me," Maria said.

"OK, anyone else from the North?" Dino asked.

"Well," Mila said, "they always say people from the South are connected to the mob."

Maria was about to say something, but Sofia shook her head.

"I know this isn't true," Adolfo said, "but I've heard Northerners call Southerners dirty."

"But…" Maria started.

"But I know it isn't true!" Adolfo said.

Sofia tried to move on. "Francesca and Beppe, do you have anything to say?"

Francesca and Beppe had apparently been lost in their own

thoughts and didn't hear a word of the conversation. "Oh," Francesca said, "I just think it's great that we all got together like this." Beppe nodded.

"All right," Dino said, taking another slice of pizza. "let's try something else. Let's go around the room and people from the South say a word that they think is good about the North, and then we'll do the same. Sofia?"

"Renaissance," she said.

"Industry," Anita said.

"Wealth," Michele said.

"Fashion," Claudia said.

"Beautiful landscapes," Antonio said.

"Great food," Maria said.

"And now people from the North about the South," Dino said. "I'll start. Beautiful landscapes."

"The Greek heritage," Father Lorenzo said.

"Excellent food," Mila said.

"Friendly people," Adolfo said.

"The Isle of Capri!" Francesca cried. "Beppe and I dream of going there."

Dino attempted to summarize. "Well, you can see there are some things that are the same on both lists. So both North and South have a lot of things in common and a lot to be proud of."

Father Lorenzo raised his hand. "I think we all know the stereotypes, and it's terrible that they have existed for so long. But I just want to point this out. When you folks from the South look at us from the North—Dino and Mila and Adolfo and Francesca and Beppe and even me—do you think any of us are prejudiced against any of you?"

Even Maria shook her head.

"And," the priest continued, "may I ask Dino and Mila and Adolfo and Francesca and Beppe this? Do any of you hold any prejudice against Sofia and Michele and Anita and Claudia and Antonio and Maria?"

"No, no, no."

"Well, you see," Dino said, "that's why we got together. I know we haven't discussed much tonight, but at least we've gotten to know each other a little bit."

"And that's a start," Sofia said.

For two more hours the conversations continued, sometimes everyone talking at once, sometimes two or three people talking together. At times the talk got loud and at times there was considerable laughter. At one point, Maria sang a Sicilian folk song and everyone clapped. When it came time to pay the check, the waiter came in with an announcement. "We are so glad you came here to discuss this tonight. There is no charge."

Of course, everyone was pleased with that, and everyone asked when the next meeting would be.

"Maybe in three or four weeks," Dino said. "We've got your phone numbers. We'll call you."

Dino and Sofia were the last to leave and found themselves following Michele and Maria and Mila and Adolfo, who were having a very Italian, very animated conversation. They could hear only a smattering.

"Have you ever eaten at…?"

"I love that place, especially the…"

"And it's next to…"

"Yes! I go there all the time for their…"

"Do you go there, too? I always go on…"

Dino nudged Sofia. "I think they've made friends."

Sofia put her arm around her husband. "And I think we've made a start."

"A beginning. Let's see how this will develop."

Sant'Antonio

A New Year

Since they were ending not only a year but also a decade, Donna outdid herself for her New Year's Eve dinner on December 31, 1979. Seafood *crostata* to start, then white bean and prosciutto soup. Then risotto with pumpkin and porcini mushrooms. Then chicken with chestnuts. And finally, poached pear in chocolate sauce. Ezio, meanwhile, kept replacing bottles of *Brunello di Montalcino* until finally everyone collapsed in front of the roaring fireplace.

The party consisted only of Donna and Ezio and their friends Lucia and Paolo. They had celebrated every New Year's Eve together since the 1960s, and, as they always did, they dressed up, at least as much as anyone in Sant'Antonio ever dressed up. Ezio and Paolo wore sport jackets and ties, Lucia the dark green gown that she had worn for the last six years and Donna a dark blue pantsuit that she bought last year.

"Let the dishes wait," Donna said as she put leftover risotto in the refrigerator. "We'll do them tomorrow. Next year!"

"Magnificent meal as always, Donna," Paolo said. He took out one of the Cuban cigars he had been saving for the occasion, and this time, Lucia didn't mind. It was, after all, New Year's Eve.

"Someday," Lucia said, "I'm going to come up here and watch you make a meal. I haven't so far because, well, I know I could never be a tenth as good as you."

"Yes, you would," Paolo said. "You'd be a tenth. At least."

For a long time, the only sounds were the crackling logs in the fireplace, and flickering flames bounced shadows off the white walls and beamed ceiling of the otherwise darkened room. Beyond the casement windows, a half moon, surrounded by myriads of stars, lit the night sky above a distant castle.

"Another perfect night at the Cielo," Ezio said, pouring *frangelico* for Donna and Lucia and grappa for Paolo and himself.

They watched as the logs burned down and Ezio stacked another supply. He asked if anyone wanted to listen to some music, but no one did.

"I can't say," Ezio said as he settled back into his well-worn blue chair, "that I'm going to miss the '70s. All this tension in Italy. The fights between the right and left. The bombings."

"Aldo Moro was killed on May 9, 1978," Lucia said. "I remember the date because it was your birthday, Paolo."

"They've never figured out who was responsible for Moro's murder," Ezio said. "Sure, the Red Brigades kidnapped him, but there are all these conspiracy theories."

"Too bad," Donna said. "He was a good prime minister."

"Twice," Ezio said.

"Forget about Italy," Lucia said. "What happened in the rest of the world in the '70's?"

They thought. For a long time.

"Wasn't it in 1970," Paolo said, "that the United States attempted to land another crew on the moon but they couldn't?"

"Apollo 13," Ezio said.

"And then," Paolo laughed, "NASA called it a 'successful failure.' That was a nice way to put it."

Ezio took a sip of his grappa. "But the Soviets landed another unmanned spacecraft on the moon later in the year."

"I don't understand," Donna said, "why anyone would want to go to the moon in the first place. I mean, my God, all that money! Why don't they take care of the poor people in their own countries?"

"Well," Lucia said, "I doubt if Italy will ever try to send someone to the moon. Why go to the moon when you can go to Tuscany?"

No one could disagree with that.

"Didn't anything else notable happen in the '70s?" Donna asked. "It all seems like a blur."

"I remember something," Lucia said. "The first test-tube baby. In England. Her name was Louise Brown. In 1978. Now why can I remember that? Honestly, I have such weird facts tucked in my brain."

"The Vatican got all upset," Paolo said.

"Well, the Vatican gets upset about a lot of things," Donna said. "It won't allow contraception either. Not to mention abortion. Not to mention divorce."

"And yet," Ezio said, "both abortion and divorce laws were passed during the '70s in Italy. So much for Italy being a Catholic country. Well, that's a whole other discussion. OK, what was something not controversial that happened?"

After a long delay, Paolo shouted, "I know! Elvis Presley died!"

"On August 16, 1977!" Lucia cried. "Now how did I remember

that? I'm amazing. I should go on one of those quiz shows and earn us a lot of money."

"And the cause?" Paolo asked his wife.

"Drugs."

"Very good!"

No one could think of anything else eventful that had happened.

"Well," Donna said, "I think when historians look back on the '70s, they'll say it saw the rise of the women's movement. Thank God!"

"Yes, and if it wasn't for women, Italy wouldn't have those divorce and abortion laws," Lucia said.

Ezio and Paolo found that they had nothing to add.

"Allora," Lucia said.

"There," Paolo said, "she's done it again. I swear my wife is becoming more like Rosa every day. She's nosy just like Rosa..."

"I am not..."

"Yes, you are. And now you're starting to talk like her."

"Poor Rosa," Donna said.

"She died the way she wanted to," Ezio said. "Quietly, gently. And now she's with papa."

"And Marco," Lucia said. "I miss her and Antonio so much. You just don't know."

Even Ezio and Paolo took out their handkerchiefs.

"That's one thing we'll always remember the '70s for," Paolo said. "Rosa. Antonio. Annabella. All gone."

"And Fausta!" Lucia said. "Don't forget Fausta. The poor thing. She must have been dead for days last March before Fernando found the key to her house and went in. She died like she lived, all alone. I feel so bad. I should have made more of an effort to be nice to her."

"We all should have, but everyone still remembered how she sided with the Fascists during the war," Ezio said. "Thirty years later, Italians don't forget."

"Or forgive," Donna said.

"Allora," Lucia said, and Paolo smiled.

Ezio replenished the *frangelico* and grappa. He put another log on the fire.

"You know," Lucia said, "I was thinking the other day. I'm the last member of *Il Gruppo di Cielo* still in Sant'Antonio. Everyone else is dead. Oh, my brothers Roberto and Adolfo and my sister Anna were in the group, too, but they're all in Florence now. It's just me here."

"*Il Gruppo di Cielo*," Donna said. "I haven't thought about that for a while. I don't know how all you people from the village stayed trapped here in the Cielo during the war and managed to keep your sanity. For three months! I mean, I find a reason to go down to the village or to Lucca almost every day."

"I was so young," Lucia said, "only sixteen. I hardly knew there was a war going on, and I didn't care. I was only interested in that handsome young army deserter who came to our door."

"Dino was my best friend, I still think about him," Paolo said. "And if he hadn't been killed, and if you didn't have Little Dino, then we would never have gotten together and gotten married, right?"

"Right."

It was the first time Ezio and Donna ever saw Lucia and Paolo hold hands.

Lucia sighed. "*Allora*. The old generation is dying out. I feel so old myself."

Paolo crumbled the last of his cigar in an ashtray. "And a new one is coming in. You know, every night when I go for my walk around the village..."

"I don't let him smoke cigars in the house," Lucia said.

"...and on my walks around Sant'Antonio I'm amazed at the changes. I mean, have you seen how the commune has given us sidewalks? And street signs? We didn't even have street names a year ago and now we've got signs!"

In the last year, new members had been elected to the village's governing body, and they took a more active role than any of their predecessors. They began by naming the few streets in the village. The one leading to the church was now Via Chiesa di Sant'Antonio. The street next to Paolo and Lucia's house was designated as Via Giacomo Matteotti, for a former Socialist leader, and the main highway through the town was Via XX Settembre, for the final event in Italian unification in 1870.

"And they've put signs at both ends of the village telling drivers to slow down," Paolo said.

"Not that the drivers do," Lucia said. "They drive through the village like the devil is in the backseat. I swear somebody's going to get killed. Just last week I saw a little girl almost get hit. She ran back just in time. And the driver just kept going! *Santa Maria!*"

In addition, Paolo reported, he heard there were plans for a playground next to the little river, with swing sets and seesaws, and a soccer field was going to be made for kids behind the church.

"I'm telling you," he said, "I've never seen so many kids in Sant'Antonio."

He started ticking them off. Bernadetta Miniotti and her three children had moved from Camaiore into the old Pini farmhouse at the end of town. Bernadetta was a large woman with brilliant red hair and a ruddy complexion. Her children, Manfredo, who was twelve, Manuela, who was ten, and Mandina, who was seven, looked exactly like her.

"They seem like awfully nice kids," Donna said. "I've seen them in Leoni's and they're very polite."

"I know they're all working hard in school," Ezio said.

"Bernadetta won't talk about it," Lucia said, "but I heard that her husband left her for a slut in Livorno," Lucia said. "That's why she got the divorce. Imagine, a divorced woman in Sant'Antonio!"

"Where did you hear that, Lucia?" Donna asked.

"I don't know. Someone told me."

"And then," Paolo said, "there's this new family from Algeria in the old Maroni house. Algeria! Mohammed Issiakhem and his wife and four kids. They seem pleasant enough, but I have a hard time understanding what he's saying sometimes."

"I've talked to him in French," Ezio said. "Nice guy. He said they moved here because they wanted to be as far from Algeria as possible. He said he and his wife wanted to be equal and that wasn't possible there."

"I love those scarves she wears," Lucia said. "What are they called again?"

"*Hijab*," Donna said.

"Their kids are struggling in school, but that's just the language problem," Ezio said. "They'll be fine."

"The kids are so beautiful, dark skin, black eyes," Lucia said. "Imagine! A family from Algeria in little Sant'Antonio."

"Just like the rest of us," Donna said. "Imagine."

"And then," Paolo continued, "there's the Marincola family from Calabria. Three kids. They've really fixed up Annabella's house. Nobody's lived in it for two years."

"Annabella would have a nervous breakdown if she saw what had happened to her beautiful house when it was empty," Lucia said. "I heard the pipes broke and flooded the basement. I wonder what she would have thought about a family from Calabria in her house. I'm sure she wouldn't have minded. Imagine, a family from Calabria in Sant'Antonio. Well, Dino's wife is from Calabria and she's very nice. I like her a lot. Very much. Yes."

"Let's see," Paolo said, counting on his fingers, "that's a total of fifteen people, parents and kids. I figure the new ones raise our population to 215. That's pretty amazing, don't you think?"

"It's a population explosion!" Ezio said.

"Maybe the word has gotten around that Sant'Antonio is a good place to live," Donna said. "Even Calabria. Even Algeria."

"But you realize," Donna said, "that all these new kids weren't born here. We haven't had a baby born in Sant'Antonio since, well, since…I don't know when."

"I can't think," Paolo said.

But they thought. And thought.

"My God," Lucia said, "it was Dino! I had Dino in 1945, and he's thirty-four now. There hasn't been a baby born in Sant'Antonio in thirty-four years!"

No one could think of any other baby during that time.

"Well," Lucia said, "it's going to be up to Mario and Anita."

"Not too much pressure," Paolo said.

With every single resident of Sant'Antonio looking on, Mario Leoni, who now owned his grandfather's *bottega*, and Anita Manconi, who now ran the butcher shop next door, were married last Christmas. Every woman in the village was now looking for any signs that Anita might have an offspring.

"Maybe they'll have a baby next year," Lucia said. "I'll let you know when I know."

"I'm sure you will," Paolo said.

To change the subject, he remembered two other newcomers to the village.

"Oh, I forgot. There's more," he said. "The two guys who moved into Fausta's house. Stefano somebody and Gino somebody. They keep to themselves and nobody seems to know anything about them."

"I know Stefano Frazzetta," Ezio said. "He teaches at my school. Great guy. The kids love him. And Gino Rubino is a travel agent in Lucca. They've been together for years."

"Fine with me," Lucia said. "I'm just glad they're restoring Fausta's house. It was so beautiful when the Contessa lived there alone, beautiful woodwork and paneling and bookcases and everything. Fausta kind of let it fall apart."

"Look," Paolo said, "we've got a divorced woman and her kids, we've got a family from Algeria, we've got a family from Calabria, and we've got two homosexual men. I would say that Sant'Antonio has become, what do they call it, a melting pot. Yes, a melting pot."

"*Allora.* Sant'Antonio is changing," Lucia said.

"As far as I can tell," Donna said, "people do get along here pretty well. They stick to themselves, and they don't care what other people do. But when someone's in trouble or needs help, they're quick to come to their aid."

"Don't be too quick to canonize, Donna," Ezio said. "All these newcomers have had problems, probably more than we'll ever know. Kids making fun of other kids because of the color of their skin or the way they talk. I've seen it in my classroom and had to talk to the kids. I know some of the new mothers have said older women won't talk to them. And Stefano said he's heard snickering behind his back. It's going to take a long while. A long while."

"Remember," Paolo said, "when Father Sangretto had Antonio build the *presepio*?..."

"So beautiful," Lucia said.

"...and when everyone looked at the big nativity scene that didn't show only Mary and Joseph and the Baby Jesus but all our houses, too? And people? And everyone seemed so proud of Sant'Antonio and they seemed to get along pretty well after that. I think that still happens. Maybe more at Christmastime, when he puts the *presepio* out again, but I think that feeling lasts through the year, more or less."

"It would be nice if we felt that way all year," Donna said.

The others nodded, and the conversation turned to Father Sangretto, who had not looked well since his ailing mother moved to her daughter's house near Pisa. Lucia said she heard Father Sangretto was going to retire next year.

"And then we'll get another priest," Paolo said.

"More changes," Lucia said. "*Allora*."

Only embers remained in the fireplace now and the big room was almost totally dark. Donna lit a few candles here and there, and Ezio poured more drinks. With midnight approaching, the four friends went through the annual ritual of announcing their new year's resolutions.

"Well," Lucia said, "I'm resolving to do the same things as I do every year. I'm going to go on a diet. That will last a week. I'm going to try to make better ravioli. I'm not going to call Dino so often. Sometimes Sofia answers and it's kind of awkward."

"Good," Paolo said. "And you're not going to nag your husband anymore."

"And I'm not going to nag my husband so much."

Her husband raised his hand. "And I'm going to buy a motorcycle."

"You say that every year, Paolo," Ezio said.

"I know, but this time I'm going to do it. I know a guy in Lucca who will sell me one. Cheap. Really. I'm going to."

He didn't look at his wife, and she rolled her eyes.

"I'm going to make some new dishes for my guests," Donna said. "I've got some new books and there are things I want to try. I was getting tired of making the same things for them all the time."

"I'm sure they loved everything you made, Donna," Lucia said.

"And I'm sure," Ezio said, "that we're both enjoying not having guests for a few months."

Ever since Donna and Ezio had opened the Cielo to guests three years ago, they had had a steady stream of visitors each summer. Some stayed a week, some two, some as long as a month. They came from Germany, France, Belgium, even the United States and Canada, but especially from England.

"We're still getting people who say the place was recommended by Alexandria," Donna said.

"That ditzy writer?" Paolo said. "I thought her name was Hortense. Or Eleonora."

"No, Alexandria, though she likes to be called Alex," Donna said.

"I got a Christmas card from her just a few weeks ago."

There was still a little *frangelico* and grappa, and Ezio emptied the bottles.

"Well," he said, "I'm going to do something that I've thought about for a long time. I haven't written anything since my memoir of the war, *A Time to Remember*. But I think I'm going to try fiction for a change. I think I could make a good story about *Il Gruppo di Cielo*, a group of people trapped in a farmhouse like this during the war."

"That's a great idea, Ezio!" Paolo said.

"Most of the people are dead, as Lucia said, so I'll just have to make things up. And maybe Lucia could tell me a few things."

"Will there be a handsome young partisan who is leading a *banda*?" Donna asked.

"Me?" Ezio said.

"Of course."

"Well then," Paolo said, "there should be a handsome young member of the *banda*."

"You?" Lucia asked.

"Of course," Paolo said.

"And then," Ezio said, "maybe in another book I could write about things after the war, something based on how Donna and I met in Pietrasanta. And there could be other stories based on other people who have lived in Sant'Antonio. Sant'Antonio is such a special place. I just want other people to know about it."

Suddenly, everyone was shouting suggestions on what Ezio should include in his novels about Sant'Antonio. They were finally interrupted by the cracks of fireworks down in the valley. Donna and Ezio and Lucia and Paolo went to the window to watch the red, white, green and blue shooting stars and candles, rockets and fountains take their turns lighting the midnight sky.

They raised their glasses.

"It's a new year!"

CPSIA information can be obtained at www.ICGtesting.com
Printed in the USA
LVOW06s1819091113

360673LV00002B/435/P